Neanderthal Marries Human

A Smarter Romance

By PENNY REID

Caped Publishing

Made in the United States of America

First Edition: June 24, 2014

PRINT EDITION

ISBN-13: 978-0-9892810-7-2

DEDICATION

Do you love Janie and Quinn?

If so, this book is dedicated to you.

fist bump

high five

bottom pat

… too far?

Part 1: Setting the Trap

CHAPTER 1

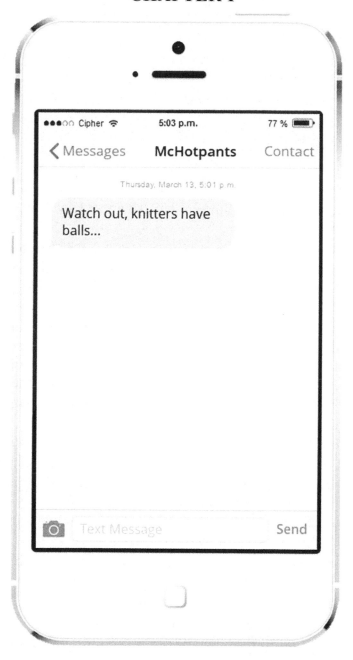

Janie

"YOU HAVE BLACK Rod and Silver Stick?"

"Yes."

"And Black Rod, what is his role again?"

"He summons the House of Commons—Parliament, you know—to the House of Lords."

"But they shut the door in his face? The Commons?"

"Yes."

"And he has to knock again?"

"Yes."

I wrinkled my nose at this news. Ceremony, pomp, and circumstance were as baffling in their allure as Kim Kardashian's fame. Neither made sense.

When Quinn had announced last week that we were traveling to London, one of my first actions was to look up a knitting group in the city. I found Stitch London, a group open to all who lived in the area or passed through it.

They rotated their meeting location all over the city and assembled several times a week; sometimes meeting at a wine bar in Covent Garden, sometimes knitting in a pub, and sometimes—like this fine Thursday evening—congregating during the dinner hour at a restaurant in Spitalfields Market, just east of the City of London.

Super double bonus: they didn't care that I wasn't knitting.

My eyes lowered to the yellow scarf in Bridgett's hands—Bridgett was a fast knitter—then to the cavernous expanse of Spitalfields Market behind her. Vendors that usually crowded the market had left about an hour ago, leaving an echoing and lonely void behind.

I frowned, fascinated. "But, then they open the door, right?—to let Black Rod in?"

"Yes," Bridget responded.

"And they can't actually keep him out, can they?"

She nodded, the skin around her eyes crinkled. Judging by the lines surrounding her eyes and mouth, her face appeared to be in its natural state while smiling.

"Yes. Quite. Commons has no authority to bar the man from their chamber. Merely, they can question his presence. In closing the doors, they are flexing their ceremonial muscle. It's a reminder to the Lords and Monarchy that the Commons does not bow to their whims." Bridgett grinned in a small way that bespoke her delight; then she chuckled. "It's all rather silly, isn't it? When one talks about it to a foreigner, it seems so silly. But then, I suppose, all traditions sound silly when explained or discussed."

I nodded at this truth. It was a good thought, worth remembering, worthy of further contemplation. I tucked it away as a data point to be mulled over later.

Bridgett's daughter, Ellen, smiled at me over her crochet work. "Don't you have any oddities of government in the United States, or—as I like to call them—the wayward colonies?"

"Other than being completely ineffective and self-serving? Not that I know of."

"Maybe if you installed a Black Rod and Silver Stick to slam the door in the face of the Senate you might find that your government miraculously improves in competency."

"It's worth a thought," I said.

Bridgett gifted her daughter a wry smile; she turned her eyes back to her scarf while she continued to speak on the subject. "Truly, I believe these traditions—as silly as they might sound—have real merit. Tradition builds confidence and gives people a sense of security, safety. If you know what to expect, you become part of the process, even if it's in a passive way. Rites of passage are essential, and traditions endure because they have value. I think your generation under values the importance of traditions lest anything be sacred."

Halfway through her mini pronouncement I began to nod. Her words, again, made a lot of sense; before I could fully process their implications I discerned a buzzing sound to my left, felt the vibration against my leg, and fought against my initial desire to audibly growl.

It was my cell phone.

Someone was calling me.

Thor!

Here I was, sitting with approximately seventeen to twenty-three lovely ladies—I didn't know the precise number as several ladies had come and gone over the last two hours, and I hadn't yet recounted—enjoying our discussion on the opening ceremonies of Parliament. Suddenly, a conversation absconder, likely halfway around the world, was interrupting my pleasant yet bewilderingly informative interaction.

I offered Ellen and Bridgett a remorseful glance. "I'm sorry. It's my phone. Someone is calling me."

Bridgett shrugged, entirely unperturbed by the interruption. "It's quite all right, my dear. Go see to your business."

I reached for my bag, still displeased at being interrupted despite Bridgett's lack of indignation. I contemplated our discussion about Black Rod as I rummaged for my phone. If I'd been asked two hours ago, I would have said that enduring or supporting an action or behavior simply because it had always been done, without thought to its utility or necessity, seemed completely illogical.

This distinction, I recognized, was the line between progress and tradition.

I pulled the blasted device from my satchel and stood from my chair. Steven's name flashed on the screen. If my phone hadn't been set to silent, I also would have been listening to *It's Raining Men,* which was Steven's personalized ringtone. I didn't the wherewithal—or, honestly, the desire—to navigate the phone's settings to change it.

Regardless of my warm feelings for Steven, my acrimonious aversion to answering the cell phone every time it rang was hardcoded in my DNA—much like my love for Cosplay or my ambivalence for reality television.

I swiped my thumb across the screen while I walked to the entrance of the restaurant. I might be saddled with the blasted device, but that didn't mean I wanted to be *that person* who talks on her cell phone while within earshot of her companions.

"Hello?" I tried not to sound too grousey, and yes, I failed.

"Hey, Janie! Where are you? Is Mr. Sullivan with you?"

"No. I'm at a knitting group. He's not with me."

"Oh, I thought you two—wait, you knit? How did I not know that you knit?"

"I don't knit."

"But you just said—"

"Steven, is there a reason you're calling?" I glanced at one of my guards, Jacob, and gave him a tight smile then took several steps into Spitalfields Market proper; my four-inch heels echoed on the cement. "Because this is definitely a conversation we can have at some point later and in person." Impatience was building a treehouse in my chest out of rusty nails and splintery, arsenic-treated wood.

"Oh, sorry, Toots. I keep forgetting about your IPS—irritable phone syndrome. I'll try to keep it short, but I really must talk to you, so you'll just have to put up with me for a moment longer. Are you and The Boss having fun with the Britons? Have you attended a tea party yet? Raised a ruckus or the roof? Met the Queen? Run naked through Trafalgar Square? I hope the answer is no regarding Trafalgar Square, as I'd like for us to make the attempt together."

I couldn't help but smile at Steven's teasing. "When you arrive tomorrow I'll be sure to fill you in on all the very fascinating times we've had in London over the past two days, and don't call me Toots."

The truth was I'd barely seen Quinn in the last two days. The original plan was to fly over early, before Steven and the team arrived, to have some time to ourselves before meeting with a large potential corporate client. Grinsham Banking and Credit Systems was the corporate client, and they were a big deal and big news. Quinn's private client meetings were supposed to take less than two hours of his day; however, they'd ended up filling his mornings, afternoons, and evenings.

My feelings on my present state of Quinn-less-ness were a bit muddled; especially since—per Quinn's crazytown insistence—I had to take three guards with me everywhere.

At best, I was disappointed. At worst, I was rabid with resentment. I hadn't decided yet which sentiment more accurately described my mindset because my brain kept pendulating between the two.

"Good, good. I'm looking forward to it. They're about to start the pre-boarding process for my flight." His huff was audible through the line. "This will be the first time I've traveled on a commercial flight in two years. I forgot how much I hate the airside terminal, those weird neck pillows, and...people."

"Steven, you're flying first class. Do you know what percentage of the population ever flies first class? Less than six percent. Even Prince William flies coach."

"You just made that up. Don't think you can fool me. Seventy two percent of statistics are made up on the spot."

I tried not to laugh. "You know I never make up statistics, and I think you can suffer through flying first class even if it means you have to be around people."

"I'll do my best." He sniffed, sighed then sighed again. "The Boss must be rubbing off on me. His disdain for the human race might be contagious."

A faint echo of footsteps resonated from over my right shoulder. I half turned toward the sound, searched the darkened expanse. Jacob must've heard it too because he crossed to where I stood and placed his hand on my upper arm.

"Ms. Morris, do you mind moving back inside the restaurant?"

I nodded at Jacob and turned toward the entrance to Cluckingham Palace, the chicken curry establishment where my new knitting acquaintances were gathered. "I have to go now, Steven."

"Fine. That's fine. I'll find you tomorrow, though, and we'll scope out how long it will take us to sprint across Trafalgar Square."

I rolled my eyes even as I grinned. "Goodbye, Steven."

"Goodbye, Toots." He ended the call with a kissy sound.

Jacob had released my arm but he stilled hovered. The footsteps were closer now, and for some inexplicable reason, I shivered.

Then, I saw him.

I couldn't be certain as he was still approximately forty yards away, but his blue eyes seemed to glitter and flash when our gazes met; at least my toes, ears, heart, and internal organs thought so. His steps, as usual, weren't hurried; but his movements were swift, adroit, and marked by a careless confidence and grace that straddled the line between self-possession and arrogance.

Twisting pleasure pain followed by shortness of breath held me in place—my expected companions every time Quinn initially came into view. I watched him as he crossed to me.

Even after our five months of dating, I always felt a little helpless and flustered by his presence—especially at first—as though I'd been blindfolded and spun in a circle then subsequently told I needed to write a eulogy for Dr. Seuss in iambic pentameter.

I noted that his pace slowed as he neared and that his eyes were snagged on my shoes. I was quite proud of them to be honest. They were red satin with an oversized matching bow at the toe. The heel was severely spiked. But since they were slightly platform, the four-inch heel was really only three inches, max. I'd just acquired them earlier in the afternoon from a remarkable shoe store in the fashionable alleyway behind Liberty of London.

The purchase had cheered and warmed me at the time. Now, under the level and pointed heat of his gaze, I was nearly burning up.

He stopped some two yards from where I stood and slowly tucked his hands into his pockets. His eyes were still pointed at my feet when he said, "Nice shoes."

I let that statement and the delicious timbre of his voice dance between my head and heart; then predictably, it settled between my hipbones in the vicinity of my ovaries. If my body were a map, the area currently suffering prolonged side effects was just south of my uterus and north of my thighs.

So, my vagina.

Hence, my helplessness.

Before Quinn, my vagina and I were acquainted but not really friends. It seemed like a bother mostly, a mystery, always underperforming or causing me pain. I reflected that my troubles were likely user error; but I wasn't certain how to operate it. Admittedly, I'd never successfully navigated the labyrinth known as the labia, never mind the confounding clitoris.

However, since Quinn, I'd become willingly powerless against all of its parts (not to mention his parts).

"Thank you." I watched as his languid perusal began at my ankles and climbed to my legs, thighs, and upward. Aside from my shoes, I was wearing the outfit he'd picked out for me earlier that morning. He'd left it on the edge of the bed along with black lingerie accompanied by a note that simply stated *Wear me*.

The little black dress with white polka dots was much tighter and shorter than I was accustomed to wearing. But he'd never explicitly requested that I wear anything before. In fact, all of my clothes seemed to irritate him, my underwear especially. Therefore, as it was no bother to me, I dressed as requested.

Finally, his eyes met mine. Judging by the ferocity of his gaze, I'd made the right decision to wear the outfit he'd prescribed. My chest dually tightened and expanded. The sensation was discombobulating, and his eyes, so blue, had arrested my breath and brains.

"Your eyes are blue." I said.

He blinked once, his mouth hooked subtly to one side, and he leisurely strolled three steps closer to me. "Yes. That is true."

"I have brown eyes." I said; the words fell from my mouth like chunks of unmasticated food—clumsily and with the inattention that accompanies being mesmerized and brainless.

Quinn bit his top lip and glanced over my shoulder at Jacob. I knew he was fighting a smile. This was how he frequently reacted to my strange blurts of nonsense.

"We're going out." Quinn was now addressing Jacob. "Bring the car."

"Yes, Mr. Sullivan." The guard's curt reply was soon followed by the sound of his retreating footsteps. I noted that only Jacob was departing; this left us with my other two guards, not counting any that might be trailing Quinn.

Not for the first time since we'd arrived in London, my confusion at the need for such a breadth of security snagged my attention. However, my disgruntlement at being saddled with a nuisance of men (where *nuisance* is the collective noun) dressed in nicely tailored suits dispersed the longer I gazed at Quinn.

I watched as he scanned the cavernous space, his gaze lingering for a brief moment on two distinct spots over my left shoulder. His eyes seemed to be a source of light and were more than visible in the dimly lit expanse. They were the exact color of glacial ice—as filmed by National Geographic in their very informative IMAX film on the retreating solid formations of the Antarctic.

"Why is Dan here? Where's Pete?" he asked me, his attention still over my shoulder.

I blinked twice, pulled from my recollections of the Antarctic as related to Quinn's eyes, and glanced behind me. I attempted and failed to find Dan (or Pete) in the shadows.

"Is Dan here? Where is he? I don't see him." I squinted and asked the echoing vastness. "Are you here, Dan the security man?"

Quinn's hands were suddenly at my waist, and I started, jumped at the unexpected contact, and turned back to him. He was in my space. I didn't hate that he moved silently or that he had a habit of suddenly appearing where before I was alone. But I hadn't yet been able to acclimate to it.

He gazed down at me. I gazed up at him. A soft sigh—at his nearness, his warmth, the smell of his lovely cologne, the small whisper of a smile hovering in his eyes—passed between my lips.

Then, in his quiet way that always disarmed me, he said, "I missed you today."

I sighed again, this time because his sweet words chased the breath out of me. I grinned like a content cat—which didn't make any sense, because no other animals but humans smile in order to demonstrate pleasure.

I pressed my lips together to keep from relating this as a fact.

Quinn's gaze narrowed on mine. He must've perceived that I was suppressing a tangent, because he said, "Say it."

"What?"

He lifted his eyebrows, dipped his chin, and issued me a very effective glare that said, *You know what.*

I shook my head. "It's nothing."

"Tell me."

"It's completely unnecessary information."

"I want to know." He dropped his voice nearly an octave and held me against him as though to emphasize his point.

This only served to make me more deliciously agitated. "Quinn..." I whispered. I didn't know why I whispered.

"Janie, everything you say is fascinating." He whispered too.

"No, it's not. And the fact that you think I'll believe that you believe that I'll believe a statement so patently false is somewhat concerning to me."

He took a moment to sort through the tangled web of my words before he responded. "I'm not really sure what that means. However, the fact that you think I'd say something patently false *to you* is very concerning *to me.*"

We held each other's eyes, a showdown of manufactured guilt. He won.

"Fine. You want to know? I was just thinking that I was smiling like a contented cat, which troubled me as an analogy because no animals other than humans smile as a demonstration of pleasure. Some people think animals do, especially cats and dogs, but those people are mistaken. The mouth curve is incidental. Cats purr to demonstrate pleasure, and dogs wag their tails."

"How do we know for sure that purring is the only way cats demonstrate pleasure?"

"The two studies I reviewed on animal behavior didn't definitively rule out other outward signs of pleasure. Rather, they noted that the only reliable demonstration—specifically, for a cat—was purring."

"People do more than smile to show happiness and contentment. It seems to me that cats, dogs, and other animals likely display other outward manifestations as well." He shrugged. As usual when we conversed about such things—some tangent of my trivial knowledge—he appeared to be genuinely interested and engaged.

I loved this about him. No one had ever done this with me before, engagement on the random topics. He always asked questions, tried to relate it back to a different concept, make the small fact seem large and important.

I nodded at his excellent point, because it was an excellent point. "You are absolutely correct. I admit that one major flaw of both the studies was that they only sought to discover whether animals smile to denote happiness or pleasure. Once they ruled smiling out, they provided very little in the way of additional information. Maybe I should contact one of the authors and ask if there were any outward displays shared between species in the entire animal kingdom."

"Maybe we should document all your outward demonstrations of pleasure first."

I frowned at him, opened my mouth to ask what the scientific value would be, then snapped it shut when I noted the subtle simmer in his usually icicle eyes.

I didn't have to wait for the blush that stained my cheeks. All these months later and I was still embarrassed by his ability to fluster me.

Actually, embarrassed wasn't the right word.

I used to get embarrassed. Now I just felt hyperconscious of him, of his reactions, the tilt of his head, the subtle lift of his lips.

Like right now, how his expression abruptly became impossibly soft and cherishing as it moved over my flushed skin as though I was some great treasure or new discovery. It disconcerted and thrilled me, and I was becoming addicted to it. Logically, I couldn't fathom that his response could possibly last. No one could sustain this level of interest in my eccentricities forever. At some point, I was going to bore or irritate the hell out of him.

Nor could my hyperawareness of all things Quinn last. Eventually this—what we shared, the intensity—would have to fade.

Therefore, I blurted, "Do you think this will ever stop?"

"What's that?"

"Do you think I'll ever be able to look at you without losing all my wits?"

His smile intensified; the softness sharpened. "I hope not."

"You like me witless?"

"Let's just say it evens the playing field a little."

I frowned at that. Now that I had something to focus on and think about, my head settled more squarely on my shoulders. "You can't be suggesting that you're witless."

He gave me a silent smile in response then a quick kiss, or what I imagined he meant to be a quick kiss. No sooner had his lips left mine did he grunt disapprovingly and fasten his mouth on mine once again. Then he really kissed me.

As usual—when we *really* kissed—I lost track of my surroundings, the operation of my limbs, and the functionality of my vocal chords. I may have started to climb him.

After an indeterminate period, Quinn set me away, though his hands gripped my upper arms a bit too tightly.

Of course, I felt immediately bereft without him, his body against mine. I opened my eyes and found him glaring at me, his jaw tight. This was not unusual, especially after a kiss in public. I had to wonder at the saneness of his perpetual, self-imposed frustration.

However, at present—and of particular note—a perceivable undercurrent of something else flashed behind his eyes, something that startled me. Yes, he usually glared at me and/or parts of me for several seconds after separating us from our public displays of affection. This time he looked like he wanted to speak but was holding himself in check. His lips were pressed together in a tight line. He swallowed twice.

The light sound of my somewhat labored breathing was interrupted by a burst of laughter from the restaurant. His eyes flickered to the sound, and I could tell he was looking without seeing. I recognized that he was lost in his thoughts, and they appeared to be of the stormy sort.

"Quinn?"

"We need to leave. Dan will grab your things." His attention moved back to me as he spoke, and I was surprised to find his expression guarded. Not giving me any time to respond, he released one of my arms, turned, and used the other to pull me after him toward the exit.

"Wait!" I glanced over my shoulder, saw Dan and my other guard emerge from the shadows, and gave him a small wave. "I'd like to say goodbye to the knitting group, and I need my jacket."

"He'll get your jacket. I made reservations and we have…" I heard him clear his throat before he continued, "…things to discuss."

"We're going out?" I blinked at his back; usually, after post-public-kiss-frustration, we would go back to his apartment—or, since we were in London, the hotel room—and attack each other for several delicious hours.

"Yes."

"In public?"

He hesitated before responding, yet his steps never faltered. My legs were long. His were longer. I was forced to move in double time to keep pace.

"More or less." He said.

"More or less?"

"Yes. It's a place where the public goes."

I grimaced at his back. "This is you being purposefully vague."

He stopped suddenly and spun around. I tripped on my own feet and Muppet flailed into his arms—which he'd opened to embrace me, as though he knew my movements would be markedly ungraceful.

No sooner had I lifted my chin to chastise him for his sudden stoppage than Quinn brushed his lips against mine, his hands smoothing down my form-fitting dress of his choosing until they rested on my backside. I may have made a small noise resembling a whimper when his fingers dug into my bottom.

"Sometimes…" Quinn whispered against my lips, his voice both painfully seductive and sweetly teasing, "…it's fun to be surprised."

CHAPTER 2

I WAS SURPRISED.

I'd expected Sir McHotpants Von Grabby Hands as soon as the limo door was closed. However, what I got instead was Sir McCoolpants Von No Touchy.

One minute into the car ride and I deduced that he had plans for our evening that didn't include limo groping. I surmised this fact when he didn't make an attempt at getting me naked.

Actually, he sat apart from me on the bench and faced the window, giving me the back of his head. His hand rested between us, his arm stiff and straight during most of the very short ride to our destination.

I hadn't yet grown accustomed to riding in limos; I didn't know if I ever would. It felt extravagant and elitist. Taxis would do just as well, or even better, public transportation. The Tube would certainly have been a more fuel-efficient method of transportation.

But I tolerated the limo because it meant alone time with Quinn. Alone time with Quinn was precious. Therefore, I kept glancing between him and the surrounding streets, waiting for him to make a move and not hiding my confusion.

Mansell Street became Shorter Street, and when the car stopped, I knew where we were.

"The Tower of London?" I bounced a little in my seat. "We're going to the Tower of London?"

A big black bird swooped upward from the stone wall in the prolonged dusk of late spring. My eyes followed its path as it circled above the imposing structure. The bird was a raven.

This was impossibly exciting and explained why I'd been cajoled by my guards into going everywhere in London other than the Tower. Along with the British Museum and the Globe Theater, the Tower was on my list of must-see places during our visit.

I glanced back to Quinn as the limo slowed then stopped, and found him watching me. His face was an impassive mask, but this didn't bother me. I knew him well enough now to know that impassive-mask-face was his baseline. What bothered me was how the usual mischief in his eyes had been replaced with an air of guarded distraction.

"Are you okay?" I covered his hand with mine, wanting the physical contact. This was an action on my part that would have been remarkable six months ago as I'd never been one to seek or give physical touches as comfort. But with Quinn, touching and being touched felt as natural and essential as breathing or reading comic books.

"Yeah. Fine. You?" His eyes searched mine, but they were cagey and distant.

I frowned at him for a moment before speaking my thoughts. "I feel like there is something wrong—with you—and you don't want to tell me, or you're waiting to tell me. Is it work? Does it have something to do with why I have three guards with me everywhere I go?"

"Why do you think there's anything wrong?"

"Because you're McCoolpants Von No Touchy since we entered the limo."

One of his eyebrows arched, his cool expression wavering.

"What's this? A new nickname?"

"I hope not. But it's the most efficient way I can think of to describe how strangely you're behaving."

"What's strange?"

"You haven't made any attempt to take off my clothes. In fact, you haven't even reached under my skirt. Based on historical data, this behavior is strange."

He gave me his slow, sexy grin—made even more potent by our semi-touching closeness. "It was a short ride."

I shrugged. "That's never stopped you before."

"This is good news." His voice was barely contained mirth.

"What is good news?"

"I now have your expectations calibrated to expect sex every time we ride in a limo."

I blinked at him with wide eyes, considered the veracity of this assertion then nodded at the accuracy of his statement. "You're right. Although, more accurately, it's not sex that I expect. I expect groping at a minimum and an orgasm at a maximum."

"Just one?"

"No need for me to be greedy, although it's always nice when you exceed my expectations."

"You know how I love to exceed your expectations."

"The feeling is mutual."

We smiled at each other for a beat, all of the earlier distracted aloofness evaporated from his eyes and expression. We shared such a lovely moment of silent staring that my mind cleared, I stopped thinking, and all I felt was warm and loved.

The sound of a siren in the distance brought me back to the present. I shook myself, blinked at him. "Wait, what are we talking about?"

His smile grew. "How you've come to expect, at a minimum, groping in the limo."

"Yes, right. Those are my expectations. Congratulations. Very nicely done."

"Thank you." He tipped his head in acknowledgement of my praise. I had the distinct impression that he would have bowed had we been standing. In truth, I had a sudden desire to applaud.

The door to the limo opened, pulling our attention from each other and to the chilly spring evening. Quinn exited first then held his hand out for me.

Sure enough, Dan stood just outside and handed Quinn my jacket, which Quinn immediately placed on my shoulders. He was always doing this kind of stuff—holding my coat while I shrugged it on, helping me take it off, holding doors, pulling out chairs—and it had taken me some time to get used to.

Sometimes it felt nice, and sometimes it felt antiquated and annoying. I couldn't entirely explain why, not even to myself, but his stringent display of gentlemanly manners made me feel like a hypocrite, which then pissed me off.

When, in western civilization, women were the weaker sex, when they needed protection, the *ladies first* rule of etiquette made sense. It was an acknowledgement of our place; by placing us first, it was really the patriarchal society's way of telling women they were fragile and incapable, and that men, through good manners, recognized our feebleness of abilities and were displaying honor by allowing us to precede them.

It's polite to hold the door for a child or the elderly. It's good manners to give up your seat on public transportation to someone who is physically disabled. It's honorable to assist those in need.

Weakest first.

By allowing Quinn to hold my doors and take my hand and help me in and out of my jacket, wasn't I passively admitting that I was weaker in the relationship? Wasn't I ceding power every time he displayed chivalrous deportment?

But, dammit, I liked it most of the time. I liked it so much that I let him do it, and I'd never talked to him about my cognitive dissonance on the subject. Hence my constant self-directed irritation and feeling like a hypocrite.

Ruminations running rampant were interrupted by a very pleasing female voice.

"Hello, and welcome to the Tower. You must be the Sullivan party." The owner of the voice was a very cheerful looking woman in her mid to late fifties. She was dressed in a black and red tour guide costume, complete with a funny looking hat and a red appliqué crown at the chest. Her eyes were a bright blue, and she wore her brown hair pulled away from her face.

We'd walked all the way to the entrance, me tucked under Quinn's arm and against his chest while I stewed in my feminist guilt. But her voice and expression were so pleasant, I immediately forgot about the inner turmoil.

Quinn nodded to her and I reached out my hand. Her engaging smile made me smile as she gave me a firm shake. "I'm Emma," she said. "Pleased to meet you both. Is this your first time with us?"

"Yes," Quinn said.

I added, "I'm Janie; it's lovely to meet you, and I'm really looking forward to seeing the ancient torture device room as well as where Anne Boleyn was executed."

Her smile widened and she released my hand. "That's excellent. You know, however, that most of the executions did not take place within the Tower itself."

I nodded, licking my lips as a precursor to my enthusiasm. "Yes. Historians agree that there were only seven deaths at the Tower itself, and only for those who might incite a riot if executed publicly. The majority of the executions took place on Tower Hill."

Emma giggled at my recitation, and I liked her even more. "You'll pardon me, but most young ladies are more interested in seeing the Jewel House than the torture device room."

"Ah, I'd forgotten that the Crown Jewels are also here." It definitely had slipped my mind. I wasn't opposed to seeing the Jewel House, but it wasn't the highest on my list of priorities.

Quinn fit his hand in mine and gave it a squeeze as he addressed our guide. "I trust all the preparations have been made?"

Emma responded, "Of course, sir, just as you instructed."

I only half listened to this interaction as I was distracted by the remains of the Lion Tower drawbridge pit.

Emma turned toward the Tower, called over her shoulder, and waved us forward. "Let's get out of the cold. It looks a bit like rain, doesn't it? Come on. We've a lot to see and only a few hours to see it."

***

QUINN WASN'T IRRITATED, and he wasn't upset. However, all of his earlier aloof detachment was back, and I was trying not to notice.

Presently we were in the Jewel house standing on a people mover that wasn't currently moving. During the day, Emma had explained earlier, tourists would stand on the conveyor belt and gaze at the glittering jewels within the thick glass cases.

They'd added the people movers for a few reasons, not the least of which was to encourage people to keep moving rather than crowd around a single case.

I wasn't sure, but my attempts to draw Quinn out with facts

about the different towers, who built them and when, appeared to be falling on deaf ears. As a last ditch effort, I'd pointed out that the Beauchamp Tower marked the first large scale use of brick as a building material in Britain since the Romans departed in the fifth century.

He'd only nodded.

I stood in front of the third jewel case and stared into it unseeingly. Part of the problem might have been that it was so completely full of shiny objects that my mind had difficulty focusing on just one.

"What do you think?"

I pulled my gaze away from the case and found him watching me. "What do I think?"

"Yeah. See anything you like?" He tilted his head toward the glass.

I lifted a single eyebrow at his ridiculous question and at the fact that he was finally speaking. We'd been through half the tour already and he'd barely uttered a word. Now, here we were in the Jewel House—an afterthought as far as I was concerned—and he was suddenly interested in our surroundings.

I shrugged. "Not really. It all looks scratchy and heavy."

"Nothing?"

I glanced back at the case. Within it was an ornate crown laden with multi-carat diamonds and an obscenely large amethyst at the center. A giant sapphire was at the top surrounded by four equilateral triangles of white gold and diamonds.

It was too much. It was like covering a perfectly good cake with a hundred pounds of frosting.

I twisted my mouth to the side and wrinkled my nose. "You know the diamond trade encourages exploitation in Africa—of the people and their resources—and it fuels much of the heinous crimes against humanity on that continent."

I slipped my eyes to the side to gauge his reaction to my calmly spoken tirade and I found him grinning.

"I've heard that before." He threaded his fingers through mine and tugged me to the next case. I followed and glanced at my watch. I wasn't sure how much longer we had for the tour, but we hadn't yet made it to the ancient torture devices room. This made me feel a little antsy.

"What about this case?" Again he indicated his head toward the case, but his eyes were on me.

I studied the contents at his insistence and recognized a crown inset with the famous Koh-i-Noor diamond from India. "That diamond is over one hundred carats," Quinn commented. "It was presented to Queen Victoria by the British colonial governor-general at the time. Some people believe it was basically stolen from India and should be returned to atone for the Brits' past poor behavior."

"Do you think it should be returned?"

I turned back to Quinn and found him looking interested for the first time since we'd started the tour. I considered the question for a long moment, glanced at the ceiling as I quickly debated the merits and ramifications of both positions.

"I don't know if I can give you a simple yes or no to that question. Restitution is not a rare concept, but it's not always—or even frequently—applied in cases where, I think, it would be obvious to do so. In this specific example, the Koh-i-Noor diamond has become part of world history and British history especially. On the other hand, history tells us that it was stolen from India. Then again, that was almost two hundred years ago. The fact that we'd still be debating ownership says more about the perceived value of an object and less about the actual wrong committed."

"Then let me rephrase the question." He shifted a step closer to me. "Do you think offering an item of great value would do any good in atoning for past wrongs?"

I studied him for a beat before responding. "Sometimes an apology is enough, especially if it's heartfelt."

"But not always."

"No. Not always," I allowed, but then I was gripped with an urge to clarify. "Between countries, a heartfelt apology is usually not enough. Between corporations and employees, more than an apology is typically necessary. But between individuals, especially people who love each other, restitution feels like a dirty word."

He nodded slowly, his eyes moving over my features as though memorizing them. As usual, I lost myself a little under the luxury of his gaze, and tangentially my brain told me that his eyes were more beautiful and precious to me than a hundred-carat flawless diamond could ever be.

"Let's look at the last case." His words brought me back to the present and I followed where he led.

To my surprise, the last case was full of rings. This struck me as more than a little odd as the others contained crowns, scepters, and giant gemstones.

I smiled a little as I took in all the rings. Some were quite old, I could tell right away, as the metalwork was heavy and thick and perfectly imperfect. But all the inset gems were flawless; they shone as though new or just polished.

"Oh, they're lovely!" I leaned against the rail and toward the box to garner a better look. Almost immediately, a gold ring with a red stone caught my eye and I gasped a little. I lifted my hand to point at it and had to catch myself before I actually touched the outside of the case. "Look at that one."

Quinn wrapped his arm around my waist and leaned beside me. "Which one?"

"The oval one—the garnet—with the thick rose gold band." Foil work held the gemstone in place, which likely dated the piece to pre-Victorian. In truth, they were all lovely. I noted that only one or two of the twenty or so rings were diamonds. The rest were emerald, sapphire or tanzanite, ruby, or garnet.

Quinn offered a non-committal "hmm."

My eyes were drawn back to the red stone ring, and I marveled at the rose gold band, how it was sturdy and thick but detailed with delicate scrollwork.

"I don't know as much as I'd like about antique jewelry, but—if I had to guess—that one looks to be Georgian or maybe older. Do you think that's a ruby or a garnet? I'm thinking it's a garnet and not paste jewelry. Rubies from that time were usually more fuchsia than red. True red rubies were exceptionally rare, especially the size and cut of that one—faceted like a diamond rather than smooth and polished. Wow...."

"Wow?"

I nodded, my eyes still on the ring. "Yeah. Wow. Think about all the history behind that single item. I wonder who the original owner was. It's just...if rings could talk."

I felt rather than saw his smile, and I answered it with a shy one of my own. "Seriously, if that ring could talk, I wonder what it could tell us about its life." I turned my face to his and found I was correct about the curve of his mouth. "Maybe even intrigue—a ring like that must've been present during more than one important discussion. Maybe the owner even wore it while planning someone's torture and murder."

"Or maybe it was locked away in a dowry box for hundreds of years, just recently discovered, and placed here on special exhibition."

I frowned at the thought, glanced back at the case, and sighed. "You're a killjoy."

He rubbed my back. "Fine, you're right. It was worn to plot murders and the overthrowing of governments."

"That's right." I nodded once. "No one could forget about such a ring let alone lock it away for hundreds of years. You have an overactive imagination, but with boring ideas."

This last statement earned me a laugh, and I found it infectious. Quinn laughed so rarely even though I considered him a funny guy. He liked to tell me jokes deadpan without giving me any warning; I often didn't know it was a joke until the punch line.

As an example, one morning over coffee while he was reading the newspaper and without looking up, we had the following interaction:

Quinn: "The Chicago sewer department called for you."

Me: "Oh, really? What about?"

Quinn: "They said they're tired of taking your shit."

It took me about seven seconds to realize and understand the joke.

Usually my resulting laugh would garner a smile from him. If I laughed so hard I snorted, he'd usually chuckle. But very rarely did he laugh out loud; maybe once or twice a week if I were lucky.

Therefore, when he did, I always felt a heated supernova explosion of a star formation in my chest and abdomen.

Quinn's hand stilled on my hip and squeezed. "Come on. We should get going."

I gave the ring one last glance then allowed Quinn to guide me from the non-moving people mover. We sauntered to where Emma was standing at attention in a room full of what appeared to be solid gold serving dishes.

"What do you think of our treasures, Janie?" She asked me with a smile.

"They are…numerous." I finally settled on the word *numerous,* because it felt like the most accurate description for the treasures as a whole.

Her smile widened at my response and she turned her attention to Quinn. "I'm afraid you've received a call, Sir. Your cell phone won't have reception down here, so if you'll follow George," she motioned to a gentleman in a business suit standing just inside a doorway marked *Staff Only*; "He'll take you to the Tower office."

I barely got a glance of George before Quinn gave me a quick kiss on my cheek and whispered against my ear, "I'll catch up with you." Then he left me standing with Emma in the middle of the room as he rushed through the open door. I didn't have even one second to object and my body gave a surprised flinch when it shut with a *thud.*

Emma nudged my elbow to draw my attention away from where he'd departed and I blinked down at her softly smiling face.

"Come dear, I'll show you the ancient torture devices room you've been asking about." She sounded apologetic.

I dutifully followed Emma, though my heart sunk a little as I reflected on the past days in London. Certainly, I was a solitary creature, but I'd seen Quinn less since we'd arrived in the UK than I usually did in Chicago.

I wished that Quinn had told me before we left that I'd be

spending most of my time without him. If I'd known what to expect, calibrated my expectations as we often referred to it, I might have asked one of my friends to come along to share the new sights and experiences.

Discovering a new place was one of the few exceptions to my preference for solitude. It's always nice to have someone with which to compare notes and thoughts, point out items of interest, and discuss the day. I made a mental note to create a survey; I would require him to complete it prior to future business trips if I were invited to attend.

I could score the survey, assigning a point value to each of his answers to determine whether to accompany him and, furthermore, whether to bring a companion.

I began making a list of the questions that would comprise the survey, and this seemed to lighten my mood. Though the fog of melancholy hadn't abated entirely, not even when we arrived at the torture room, I was feeling less despondent about my current state of aloneness now that I had an actionable plan.

"I'll go find your man." Emma waved me toward the room. "You have a peek inside, and feel free to touch the instruments. Just be careful, as they are quite old and, you know, were used for torture."

"Thanks, Emma." My previously sunk heart gave a little leap when I entered the room and I beheld the wonder of the gruesome devices.

I forced myself to take my time to study each of the implements with detailed scrutiny. I wasn't a sadist or a masochist, but I felt a certain amount of both reverence and repugnance for them. They were, in essence, devices of influence, the muscle with which a great deal of power was flexed. They were each terrible and beautiful—a product of early engineering and disturbed minds.

I recognize an instrument called The Scavenger's Daughter, which compressed a person into a ball and was known to have crushed bones as it was tightened—a truly awful way to die.

I noted the manacles, giant iron handcuffs, affixed along one of the walls. Prisoners were hung from their wrists, suspended in the air. I suppressed a little shiver down my spine as I imagined myself so completely vulnerable. It was a disorienting, dizzying sensation.

Peripherally, I was aware of footsteps approaching and turned toward the door just as Quinn and Emma entered.

"Having fun?" Emma's cheerful tone felt jarring given the surroundings.

However, I was having fun, so I said, "Yes. This is all quite incredible."

Quinn gave me a once over with his assessing gaze. I was disappointed to find him again stone faced and aloof.

Regardless, I affixed a half smile on my face and lifted my eyebrows in question. "Everything okay?"

He nodded once, his eyes darting around the room; he seemed to be cataloguing each detail with his typical rapid efficiency.

I motioned to the manacles behind me. "Being hung in manacles was like being crucified. It actually kills a person by collapsing their lungs. The lungs can't inflate properly against the weight of the suspended human body."

I saw Quinn's jaw tick. His voice was devoid of inflection when he said, "That sounds awful."

"It was." I nodded.

"Not at all romantic."

"No." I frowned at his comment. "Of course it's not romantic. It's death by crucifixion and suffocation. Nothing remotely romantic about that."

He closed his eyes, inhaled through his nose then sighed. "You're killing me here, Janie."

A wooden apparatus just behind Quinn caught my attention and distracted my thoughts. It had been previously overlooked in my slow perusal of the space, and I sucked in a startled breath. "That's a rack!"

Quinn glanced over his shoulder then away, back to the room. "Yep." His response was distracted, a little sarcastic, and maybe a touch frustrated.

I walked past him, crossed to it with swift steps and reached out, catching myself before I touched it. I glanced at our guide. "Can

I?"

Emma nodded, looking every inch British politeness. "Yes, of course. Take your time. I'll return at half past to collect you."

Faintly, I registered her steps retreating from the room and out the door. My attention was focused on the cruel apparatus in front of me.

A rack.

A real rack.

It didn't look like a replica.

"The rack was developed for use in England in the thirteenth century by the Duke of Exeter, who was the Constable of the Tower. They used to call it Duke of Exeter's Daughter. Why they called torture devices *daughter* never made much sense to me. But the first documented use of the rack was by the Greeks in ancient times."

"Hmm," was Quinn's reply. I couldn't tell if he was listening, but it didn't really matter.

I was seized with a sudden inspiration.

"Quick, Quinn, tie me up." I shifted from one foot to the other, trying to figure out how to mount it.

"What?"

"Tie me up—tie me to the rack. I want to see what it's like." I finally decided to sit on the edge first then navigate toward the center.

"You want me to tie you to the rack?"

"Just for a minute." I tested my weight then awkwardly lifted my legs to assume a prone position. My feet dangled over the end of the table. I was a bit too tall but I'd get the general effect. "Here, tie my hands." Voluntarily, I stretched my arms over my head.

"Are you serious?" Quinn was suddenly by my side looking perplexed, but he was used to my quirks by now, so he picked up a length of rope attached to the table and studied it as if determining the best way to knot it. I thought it interesting that he'd opted for the rope rather than the very antiquated leather straps with buckles. He glanced between the door, the rack, and me.

The rope appeared to be newer than the rest of the implement, likely hemp—not quite historically accurate—but the original rope had likely turned to dust over the last seven hundred years.

"That'll do fine." I offered him my wrists then turned my attention to my feet. "Do my feet too. This is so cool! And take a picture. I want to send it to the knitting group."

Quinn hesitated, his expression a mixture of surprise and uncertainty. Then, abruptly, he set to work. Apparently, he was an efficient and thorough knot tier, as he swiftly finished my wrists then moved to my feet. He still looked distracted, on edge, but now focused on tying me up. I wriggled my fingers to test his knot. The rope bit unpleasantly into my skin where my arms were bound to each corner of the device.

It seemed that Quinn Sullivan didn't mess around with knots.

I didn't care that my legs were spread in an unladylike way— especially true considering that my short skirt had to be hiked higher to accomplish the aforementioned spreading. I was too absorbed in the fact that I was actually bound to a real-life rack!

"Hey—do you think this is the same one that they tied Guy Fawkes to? Although, it's only *rumored* that they used the rack on him. He must have been pretty short. See how my legs are too long? I wonder how tall he was. Did you know that humans are getting taller? In fact, since the industrial revolution, we're growing by an average of just under a half inch every generation."

I continued relating miscellaneous facts to Quinn as he completed his task. I was so absorbed in the gushing well of information spewing forth that I didn't really notice that his hand was tracing circles around my inner ankle until I felt a shiver race up my leg.

"...they thought it was...they...they..." I trembled at the contact, blinked, and pulled Quinn into focus—really looked at him— rather than at the facts tumbling inside my brain.

Quinn was standing next to me at my calf, his hip leaning against the wooden table, his face wearing one of his barely there smiles. His eyes, which had been notably distracted virtually all evening up to this moment, suddenly felt piercing and heated.

He looked diabolical.

"Quinn?"

"I like this. We should get one of these." His fingers moved up the inside of my leg causing me to jerk on reflex, but to no avail. I was bound and restrained…with rope.

He laughed lightly—a perverse chuckle considering my state of helplessness.

I lifted my eyebrows and managed a breathless laugh in response. "Ha…ha ha…ha." I swallowed as his fingertips slid behind my knee and caressed the sensitive spot. "You can untie me now."

His barely there smile spread until it became a thoroughly devilish grin. "Well, now, not so fast…." He narrowed his eyes as though he were in deep thought.

I was not smiling. "Quinn."

"Shhh…." He shook his head slowly, shuffled his feet until his hip was adjacent to my knee. Before I could reprimand him for shushing me, his hand behind my leg moved to the inside of my thigh and under my skirt with a feathery touch. I sucked in a sharp breath. Electric sparks followed the path of his fingers and my heart skipped two beats.

"You know, I had tonight all planned out: take you on the private tour, marvel at the Crown Jewels, candlelit dinner next to the Thames…."

"Quinn, you sound like a monologuing supervillain."

He ignored my attempt at humor. "But you've presented me with…." Quinn's eyes traveled down the length of my body to where his hand was still moving on my leg. "You've presented me with a very unique opportunity." He said this last part almost to himself and sounded every inch the monologuing supervillain. His grin was brazenly sinister.

I knew this man and I knew that look. I fought against a shudder and a moan. The fogginess, the delicious murkiness of arousal had blanketed my usually sporadic thoughts with a suddenness of force. I felt at once calm and frenzied.

This is what he did to me.

"Quinn…." this time I whispered his name because I couldn't

manage anything else.

"What am I going to do to you?" He murmured softly—so softly that I almost didn't hear his words—his touch growing bolder, inching higher. I gasped when he traced the line of my thigh-high stockings with his fingers. He laughed again, a dark, mischievous, ominous chuckle. His eyes moved back to mine and I saw true enjoyment, happiness there. He'd shed every ounce of his previous distraction, his air of practiced aloofness, and devoured me with his gaze.

We stared at each other for a long moment; my lips parted and my face flushed with pleasure and tense expectation. The villainous glint in his eyes gradually ebbed, leaving him with a dreamy expression as though he were lost in the sight of me.

I'd caught him staring at me this way a few times. Sometimes it was after we'd made love, and I'd write it off as the high of post-coital endorphin euphoria. But sometimes he'd wear it while I carried on unchecked about the difference between hemotoxins and neurotoxins, or why goats are superior to sheep, like he'd done earlier at Spitalfields Market.

It was during these times that his gaze felt most unsettling because I hadn't done anything to earn such a worshipful expression.

The sight slightly sobered me and, despite how much I wanted him to continue teasing me with his hands, I knew we only had a few more minutes. It would be much better to re-create the scenario tonight in our hotel room instead of inside the Tower of London on an antique instrument of terror.

"Janie." He said my name suddenly, and I noted his face had lost a bit of the dreamy quality; it'd been replaced with a measure of solemnity. "I have to ask you something."

"Okay." I breathed, tried to ignore the fact that his hand was still up my skirt, resting on the inside of my thigh. "But can you untie me first?"

Again, he gave me the slow headshake. "Not until you answer my question."

"O-kay." I gripped my hands into fists. My fingers were tingling with the first signs of poor circulation. "But you know..." I cleared my throat, hoping the action would also clear away some of my arousal fog. "I'll tell you the truth, whatever you ask. You don't have to put me on the rack."

His mouth hooked to the side for the briefest of seconds before all trace of a smile disappeared. "It's not that kind of question."

I frowned, because his voice sounded almost sad. I searched his eyes for clues. I found none.

"Quinn." I said his name a third time now, feeling a measure of concern. "Ask me anything."

"I love you," he said, surprising me. His eyes lost their focus as though he were talking to himself. "I remember the precise moment I realized I wasn't going to be able to walk away from you, that you were it for me."

I thought back over our relationship as I studied his face, trying to pinpoint the moment I realized I was in love with him. Before I could begin to collate my findings, he interrupted my thoughts.

"It was that Sunday I first showed you the apartment, before all the business with your sister and Seamus. We had that picnic, and I fell asleep. Later, when I woke up, my head was in your lap. I realized you hadn't moved at all, maybe for an hour. You just let me sleep...."

"You'd earned it after the way I'd annihilated you in Frisbee." My back was starting to cramp, and I shifted in a fruitless effort to find a more comfortable position.

He continued as though I hadn't spoken. "You asked me what creatures I would create if I had magical sperm." Quinn's eyes lit with the recollection, and his smile was as sudden as it was breathtaking; he squeezed my thigh. "Then you offered yourself as my personal snake-haired Medusa, a magical sperm repository."

Quinn's gaze found and refocused on mine through the memory. I ignored the discomfort of my wrists and back in favor of returning his infectious smile. I'd never heard him speak this way before about us. Yes, over the course of our relationship, he'd reminisced about his family, told me funny stories. But never about us.

"I was serious, you know." I chimed in earnestly, because I had been serious. "I wanted to know. You still haven't told me."

Quinn responded with equivalent earnestness. "I didn't answer because I didn't know what to say."

I scrunched my nose, shook my head just barely as my movements were impinged by my position. "That's when you fell in love with me?"

He nodded, shifted on his feet, and I noted that the hand not on my leg was in his pants pocket. In fact, I realized that it had been in his pants pocket since he'd secured me to the rack.

"But, we'd only known each other, like, three weeks, and we hadn't even technically been on a date yet."

"I knew." His answer was quiet and certain. My heart leapt and, strangely, my eyes stung.

"Was it the Greek mythology reference or the sperm reference?" I pressed even as my attention moved between his hidden hand and his face as it loomed over me.

"It was you, Janie." His voice was soft, maybe the closest he'd ever come to sweet-talking. "You and your Medusa hair and your honey colored eyes. It was your questions, your intelligence, and your insatiable curiosity. It was your goodness and sweetness, your honesty and trust."

Peripherally I noted that he'd withdrawn his hand from his pocket and he held something within it, but his words held me mesmerized and—despite my curiosity—I couldn't look away from his gaze. My back was now seizing, my hands were numb, but I didn't care. I wanted to remember this moment.

"And, if I'm going to be completely honest..." Quinn gathered a deep breath, lightly caressed my inner thigh, his knuckles brushing against the bare skin above my stockings. "...it was the thought of using you, your body, as my own personal magical sperm repository for the rest of our lives."

My eyes widened and I choked on air as his face cracked with a slow, sexy grin of epic proportions.

The villain.

"Quinn!" My face flamed and I moved my legs restlessly as much as I was able given my current state. All at once I was beyond ready to be released from my bondage.

"Janie Morris…" His voice was steady, measured—but I wasn't listening.

"I didn't say that…I mean…." I tried to move my hands and winced when pain shot down my arm. I was completely ridiculous, and I should have known better than to willingly allow Quinn to tie me to a rack. Even worse, I'd suggested it! Of course he was going to tease me or torture me at the first opportunity.

"…will you make me the happiest man in the world…"

Still struggling, and pointedly ignoring him, I glanced at my wrists as my continued chastisement burst forth. "I did say it, but I said it as a hypothetical. Now please untie me!"

"…and do me the honor of becoming my wife?"

"You are…! I…wait…what?" My indignation morphed into stunned confusion. I glanced at the object in his hand—an open black velvet box with the red ruby ring I'd admired earlier winking back at me—and blackness colored my vision.

"Oh, my God." My eyes widened on the ring then moved to his face.

I didn't faint, but I seriously considered faking it.

I didn't know what to freak out about first, so I ordered the issues in terms of most pressing and/or potentially illegal.

"Quinn, that's the ring from downstairs!" I hissed in a loud whisper because I was afraid of the answer. "Did you steal that ring?"

CHAPTER 3

HIS EXPRESSION MORPHED from serious to seriously incredulous. "What? No! No, I did not steal this ring!"

My forehead wrinkled and I frowned at him then whispering louder. "Well, what am I supposed to think? One minute I see an antique ring in the Jewel House, and the next minute you're holding it while I'm tied to a rack."

"Getting tied to the rack was your idea."

My eyes flickered to his then back to the box. I wondered if I looked as panicked as I felt. "I know that, but I didn't think that you'd use the opportunity to try to give me a stolen ring!"

"It's not stolen! It's your engagement ring."

My breath left me with a sudden whoosh.

Engagement ring.

He'd knocked the wind from my lungs.

I wasn't expecting this. In fact, this may have been the very last thing I'd been expecting—just after Quinn telling me he was a woman and that he had aspirations of reprising Barbra Streisand's role in *Hello Dolly* on Broadway.

"Janie."

I heard my name and refocused my panicked eyes on his.

This was too soon—way too soon. This was a mistake. Even if the ring wasn't stolen, he was making a mistake and, when he realized the mistake, we would be over. There is only one way to become unengaged just like there is only one way to become unmarried.

"Untie me."

"Not until you answer my question."

"Quinn…."

"Janie, I know what you're going to do as soon as I untie you. You'll run out of here. I'd planned to get you drunk first so you wouldn't be mobile, but tied up is better."

"Why better?"

"Because we can talk about this, sober, and you can't avoid me by feigning gastrointestinal distress."

"My hands hurt."

Concern cast a shadow across his features. His eyes flickered to where my wrists were tied then back to mine. Reluctantly, he offered, "I'll untie you if you promise to talk this through." His eyes zeroed in on mine to show me he meant business, and his face was as serious as I'd ever seen it. "You have to promise, no avoiding."

I nodded, my voice strained as I agreed. "I promise—no avoiding. We'll talk it through."

Quinn glared at me for a moment as though assessing my honesty then removed his hand from my thigh. I felt the loss of it like a physical blow and wished I'd been paying more attention to how his hand felt on my body so I'd be able to recall it effortlessly, at will.

He plucked the ring from the velvet then stuffed the box back in his pocket. I had to crane my neck to follow his movements and didn't miss the fact that he placed the ruby on my left-hand ring finger before he moved to untie me.

It was a very Quinn thing to do. The ring was now in my possession, and as they say—whoever they are; I would have to look that up—possession is nine-tenths of the law.

Releasing the knots took less time than securing them, and I rubbed my wrists when he moved to the ropes at my ankles, my hands coming to life. The hemp left marks, not cutting or real injury. The lines encircled my wrists like a brand. I glanced at my hands and caught a glimpse of the brilliant red gemstone that made my finger feel heavy and foreign. I stared at it and felt a surge of possessiveness.

I wanted it. I wanted that ring. It was the most exquisite piece of jewelry I'd ever seen, including the crown jewels I'd just ogled.

Independent of becoming engaged, the ring was stunning and beautiful and exactly what I would have chosen for myself if the entirety of the world's designer jewelry were mine to peruse.

And it was mine.

Very clever of him to give me something my heart didn't know it wanted in exchange for a promise. I would have a hard time taking it off. Then again, very clever was typical Quinn.

When he finished, keeping one hand on me the entire time, he reached for my arm and pulled me upright. Blood rushed from my head and he allowed a few short seconds before tugging me to my feet. Unsurprisingly, my legs were unsteady.

I was still looking at the ring on my finger, my breaths deep and ragged as I struggled with a war of emotions and desires.

"What are you thinking?" he asked.

One of his hands was gripping my waist and he slipped the other between mine, his fingers curling around my palm so that he was cradling my left hand.

I pressed my lips together then lifted my eyes to his. His face was carefully blank, but watchful.

I felt so many things, looking at him, standing so close. I felt fearful in a way that I thought I'd left behind.

But, though I was a cornucopia of feelings, I wasn't able to actually manage a complete thought.

"Quinn…." I swallowed. My chest ached. "I wasn't expecting…I wasn't expecting this."

"I know."

"We haven't even talked about it, discussed it as a possibility."

"No time like the present." His hand slipped from my waist to my lower back, pressed me against him, my left hand beneath his jacket, over his heart.

"We've only been together five months."

"I know." He sighed like it was irrelevant.

"Do you honestly think that's enough time to make an accurate and valid judgment about the viability of a person as your *wife*?"

"With you, yes, it's more than enough. Too much."

"That's completely illogical. In five months, we've barely scratched the surface. We can't possibly know enough about each other in order to make a decision like this. This is the tattoo of life decisions."

"Tattoo of life decisions?"

"Yes. Tattoo. Marriage is the forever and permanent branding of one person to another. Sure, you can get it removed—but it's expensive, it's a process, and you're never the same after. You're scarred. It's always a part of you, visible or not. You get a tattoo with the intention of a life-long commitment. You have to defend its existence and take ownership of it in front of others for the rest of your life regardless of how it sags or droops or changes shape and color—because it will! It will change and fade, and not in an aesthetically pleasing way."

The side of his mouth lifted as I spoke and his eyes danced between mine. "Let's get matching tattoos."

I yanked my hand from his and pushed against his chest. He didn't budge.

"No." I shook my head. "This isn't the kind of decision you make after knowing someone for five months—five amazing, lovely, wonderful, perfect, beyond sexually gratifying months. This is the kind of decision you make after two point four years— at the least. When the spark has faded, when you've been through at least two flu seasons, several holidays—with relatives—and holiday travel, seven to ten misunderstandings, and maybe one surgery."

"What does the flu have to do with this?"

"Are you a grumpy sick person? Do you prefer me to hover or give you space? I don't know! We haven't done that."

"Janie...."

"There have been no hard times, Quinn! We've proven very little other than we're compatible in times of feast, but we know nothing about times of famine."

"Janie...."

"I won't be able to repeat the words *in sickness and in health* because I honestly have no idea."

Quinn opened his mouth to respond but we were interrupted by the practiced sound of throat clearing.

"Mr. Sullivan, if you and Janie are ready...." Our tour guide's voice sounded from over my shoulder. I closed my eyes for a long moment, my hands fisting in the lapels of his jacket.

Three seconds ticked by before he responded. "Of course."

He covered my fists, encouraging me to release him, but kept hold of one of my hands, turning me toward the door and pulling me after him. I glanced at the floor then up to his profile, hoping to find some indication of his thoughts, but was disappointed.

As ever, he was cucumber cool and appeared entirely unruffled.

Not like someone who has just been refused or accepted a proposal of marriage; more like someone who glides through life in charge of everyone and taking his superiority for granted.

As soon as we were through the door, his hand moved to the base of my spine, a possessive touch, and steered me down the stone hall after our guide. She glanced over her shoulder, her smile small and sincere, and pointed out items of interest.

This time I wasn't listening. I was too preoccupied with all that was unsettled, how I would convince Quinn that this was lunacy, yet still not jeopardize our chances to be together for as long as possible.

If I really gave the matter some thought, I supposed—if we could get past his proposal without too much damage inflicted—we likely had another four years before he irrevocably tired of me and my eccentricities.

I was okay with that. I felt like four years was about my expiration date. Four flu seasons, holiday cycles, and yearly vacations. Really, there were only four destinations worth a vacation: beach, glacier, desert, and mountains. Bonus if we could pair them with a visit to the wine country or a world heritage site.

The first two years would likely be stellar. The last two would become increasingly strained until, finally, he grew cold and aloof all the time. He would make excuses to work late, avoid discussing future plans until—finally—I would suggest we split.

It would be the look of relief that I was most dreading—that moment when he would nod his agreement. It would be the first real emotion he would show during the last months of our future three-year and seven-month relationship, and it would be the last.

After that, I would move out, spend more time at the library, and invest in a truly excellent vibrator. He would resume his Wendall/Slamp lifestyle. Maybe we could part as friends. Maybe he'd put up with quarterly lunches or at least an annual check-in dinner.

We would have to take turns paying for the dinner, and I wouldn't have to put up with him ordering for me anymore.

I was in the middle of making a mental note to look for investment properties now in neighborhoods that might likely improve in value over the next few years when I felt Quinn's warm breath next to my ear.

"Stop it." He whispered, sending a sudden shiver along my spine.

I blinked. We were approaching a staircase—narrow and medieval appearing—and Quinn had wrapped his arm around my waist, pressing my side to his.

"Stop what?"

"Stop having an entire discussion without me."

I stiffened and his hand squeezed.

"One at a time, and please be sure to hold on to the rail. These stairs are very steep." Emma called over her shoulder and demonstrated the appropriate technique for descending the spiraled steps.

"Are you going to be okay in those shoes?" Quinn separated from me, holding my hand and bringing me to a stop.

I nodded, my voice shakier than I'd like. "Yeah. I'll be fine."

I wasn't concerned about the stairs. I was concerned about what came after the stairs.

He narrowed his eyes at my tone but allowed me to precede him. I noted that he stayed close the entire way down. When we arrived at the bottom, he reassumed his position—arm around my waist—and kissed my neck.

I was handed my jacket and we were escorted to the wharf. A tent—large for two people—had been placed on wooden planks overlooking the Thames, likely to protect us from intermittent rain. Three of the sides were enclosed and the fourth was open, the Tower Bridge immediately to our left and London Bridge some distance to our right—lit and casting both shadow and illumination on the expansive river below.

Within the tent was a table, elegantly set for two. My eyes drifted over the white linens, the fine china, the crystal goblets, the silver cutlery, and the low candles. Small circular lanterns hung from the ceiling casting the inside with a warm, amber glow. A leather upholstered, heavily cushioned bench—like a tall, deep-set sofa—was positioned facing the opening, and a plethora of pillows, wool blankets, and furs were arranged along the sides and back.

And, of course, three bottles of champagne were cooling in three different standing silver buckets set to one side.

"Come. Sit." Quinn slipped his hand from my waist and caressed it down my arm until our fingers entwined. He pulled me after him to the bench, not releasing my hand even as we sat. He placed it instead on his thigh and held it there as magical—and up to this point, invisible—waiters appeared. They poured the champagne, revealed food, unfolded napkins on our laps, and offered pillows for comfort.

The wool blankets turned out to be cashmere.

Of course. Of course they were cashmere.

I knew they were cashmere because of all the yarn fondling I'd been required to do on knit nights.

I felt like a queen, really and truly pampered, and utterly swept off my feet.

Through all this, I stared at the Thames biting the inside of my lip and trying my best to refrain from continuing my one-sided internal conversation. Instead, I thought about all the submarines that had purportedly navigated the river during World War II.

Quinn's touch roused me from the question under consideration—the current depth of the river Thames—and I turned my face to his. He'd lifted my left hand from his lap and was touching the circle of gold on my fourth finger, his gaze was affixed to the spot.

I briefly glanced around the tent. Our magical serving staff disappeared as quickly and quietly as they'd appeared and we were left with at least the illusion of completely privacy.

"I'm glad you like the ring."

My eyes darted back to his. I became a little lost in his man-handsomeness, noting again that he would make a horribly ugly female if he'd ever decided to dress in drag. The cut of his jaw was too strong, the angles of his cheeks too sharp, his nose decidedly masculine and Romanesque.

I pressed my lips together and swallowed once before responding. "I do. I do like it. More accurately, I love it." My gaze flickered to the ring on my finger then back to him. "It's disconcerting to feel so possessive of a material thing."

His mouth hitched to the side and his eyes moved between mine. "Then keep it and wear it." His expression changed, and he looked both grave and vulnerable. "Marry me, Janie."

I half blinked to hide the wince of pain inflicted by the intense sincerity of his words, and their impossibility.

He didn't give me a chance to respond. "You said I make you fearless. Then don't be afraid. Trust me."

"I do trust you, and I'm not...I'm not *precisely* afraid. It's more that I want us to be smart about this."

"You want to overthink it." He didn't sound annoyed. Rather, he sounded like he was opening a negotiation.

"No. I want to do it right."

"Then let's do it right." Quinn turned so that he was facing me, his torso angled toward mine, his arm resting on the table, his other hand on my leg. It was his you've-got-my-full-attention posturing. "What will it take for you to become my wife?"

I took a deep breath, glanced around the tent, noted that champagne had been poured. I reached for it, not precisely stalling, and took two large swallows.

I was bolstered by the bubbly when I spoke. "Well, first of all, I think we should wait two point four years."

"No. What else?"

"Quinn...you asked me what it would take."

"I'm not waiting two point four years. On the issue of time, of waiting, I will not negotiate."

"Fine. Then how much time are we talking about? When do you

propose we get married?"

"On Tuesday."

"You mean the day after we get back to Chicago?"

He nodded.

My mouth fell open and my eyes bulged. "What? We can't—no! And, besides, that's the night my knitting group meets. You know that."

He plucked his champagne from the table, appearing not at all perturbed, and shrugged. "What's your counter offer?"

"Split the difference, one point two years."

"Nope. I'm not willing to delay any longer than two weeks." He shook his head. "Final offer."

I narrowed my eyes at him. "Or else what?"

"Or else we get married next week, in Chicago."

"I won't do it—absolutely not. You...you behave as though I have no choice."

Quinn grimaced, sipped his champagne, considered me over the rim, and said, "One month."

"Three."

"Deal." He returned his glass to the table, grabbed my right hand, and shook it. "We good?"

I shook my head. "No." Then I blurted the first idea that popped into my head. "I want a big wedding."

His brow pulled low and the negotiation mask slipped, his features plainly betraying his surprise. "You want a big wedding?"

I nodded. "Yes. I want a really big wedding."

"I wouldn't have guessed that about you. In fact, I would have thought you'd want something really small and simple." He sounded and looked suspicious.

"Usually I would, but since I only have three months to manufacture two point four years of normal relationship stress, the wedding will have to be quite big and complicated, with seating charts and video montages. We'll have a fireworks display and a band and a DJ and little favor bags for all the guests."

"Favor bags?" He looked alarmed. Actually, he looked horrified.

"Yes. And you'll be in charge of them as well as the programs and invitations. And you'll have to find a groom's cake. And we'll have family members in our wedding party."

His eyes, a little dazed, drifted to the Thames.

I continued multi-tasking by ticking off superfluous wedding appurtenances on my fingers while holding my champagne glass. "Then there are flowers, photographers, framed pictures of our grandparents and parents on their wedding day, centerpieces, a choreographed first dance, toasts, the tuxes and the bridesmaids' dresses, my dress, my veil, my shoes, my bridal lingerie...."

Quinn's gaze abruptly met mine, heated and intense, but I forged on.

"And we're going to do all the extra stuff too, like a wedding scavenger hunt, a chocolate fondue fountain, flying doves, air balloon rides, maybe a pony for the kids, a guest book, and a signed picture frame of our engagement picture."

He held his hands up then gripped my arms, cutting me off. "Janie, this is ridiculous. You don't want this, I don't want this— why would we do this to ourselves?"

"Because you won't wait the two point four years necessary to test the strength of our relationship, to allow us to say our wedding vows with honesty and knowledge that yes, we will stick together for better or worse. This wedding—planning this wedding—is going to be a nightmare. It's going to be years of worse and sickness rolled into three months, and we're going to make every single decision together. You will taste hors d'oeuvres and be required to give an opinion on steak or chicken."

I gulped the rest of my champagne, braced myself for his refusal, and readied my counter strategy.

Really, he was right. This was not me. When I thought about my wedding—specifically and at this moment, my theoretical wedding to Quinn—I thought about taking a lunch break to run down to the courthouse. Then, on the following Tuesday, celebrate with hot dogs, potato chips, and lemon drops during knit night.

But this wasn't about the wedding; the wedding didn't really matter. I never understood the preoccupation with the wedding day, all that planning and focus and money. It was like preparing for childbirth with no thought to the fact that, after labor, you would have a new person to take care of.

The wedding was just one day.

This was about the care and feeding of the marriage, building a lasting foundation, bonding over shared suffering, and the thousands of days that would follow.

If he refused the rigors of wedding planning, my second suggested marathon of madness was going to be dropping us off on a deserted island for one month without food, water, or shelter. In fact, as I reflected on it, I was glad that I'd launched the ridiculous wedding idea as my first volley because when Quinn rejected it, the island might actually happen. It sounded like fun. I'd always wanted to take a foraging class, and a spearfishing naked Quinn was also a bonus.

"Okay."

I blinked at him, startled out of my spearfishing-naked-Quinn daydream, and found him glaring at me. He looked...determined.

"Okay?"

He nodded once, taking my empty champagne glass out of my hand and setting it on the table.

"Yes. Fine. I'll do it."

I could feel my eyebrows pull together. I was shocked. "You'll do it?" I croaked.

"Yes. I'll do it. But, after it's over, no more tests. No more fake problems or hoops to jump through—and no backing out either, no matter what. In return, you will promise me that once we get married, no waiting for the other shoe to drop." He lifted his eyebrows meaningfully, reminding me of a conversation we'd had months ago, before we started dating, when he happened upon me at Smith's Take-away and Grocery, and I'd explained the history behind the idiom *waiting for the other shoe to drop.*

I tore my bottom lip through my teeth as I thought about this promise and what it would mean. I would be giving up all the safety that comes with testing a hypothesis before taking a plunge.

"I know you love me." His abrupt statement was said with conviction.

At his words, unexpected though they were, my mind calmed. I looked at him—really looked at him—and saw the set of his jaw, the resolve in his gaze.

I nodded, agreed softly. "Yes. I love you."

He lifted a hand and threaded his fingers through my medusa hair, gently grabbing a fistful as though to hold me in place.

"I love you." His words were released on a breath, like the admission cost him. "I will do anything to prove that to you...."

"You don't need to prove...."

"Let me finish. I will do anything to prove that to you. I will do anything to prove that what we have is worth a battle. What we have is worth a war. But I don't want to spend any more of our time together fighting about hypotheticals. We haven't done that since Vegas and Jem. It's a waste of time."

I pressed my lips together and nodded my understanding.

"No more steps backward. No more wasting time. You need us to prove that we can make it through a crisis. I understand that. I do." He shifted closer, loosening his grip on my hair, his fingers moving to my neck. "In fact, I even agree with you."

He gave me a small smile, which I couldn't help but return, and pulled me forward so that our foreheads touched.

"You agree with me?"

"Yes, but only because I know you need tangible proof. You struggle with what-ifs, and until we've had our trial by fire, you'll worry." He pulled away so that our eyes connected as he said, "I don't want you to worry. I want you to know."

My eyes stung and I reflexively swallowed.

"But, once you know, that's got to be it." His voice held an edge of warning.

I nodded. "Okay."

He hesitated for a moment, his eyes growing wide. "Okay?"

"Yes." I couldn't help my smile, nor could I stop two fat tears from rolling down my cheeks. "Yes, Quinn Sullivan, I will marry you. I will become your wife."

He stared at me for a moment, his blue eyes filling with the wonder and softness that usually concerned me, but in the current situation made me feel like I was flying.

Then I felt the impulse to add and clarify, just in case there was any question, "This also means that you'll be my husband. We'll be married... to each other."

His face split with one of his rarely used and extremely dazzling wide smiles.

It took my breath away.

Then he literally took my breath away when he grabbed me and kissed me.

I was on his lap, the hem of my dress nowhere near appropriate levels of modesty. His mouth was fierce, hungry, and I felt both his relief and possessiveness in his kisses. They were deep, adamant, greedy. Likewise, his hands were all over me, or at least felt that way. One was on my upper thigh then in my hair, then pressing firmly against the center of my back, then flexing on my bottom under my dress. I got the impression he wanted to touch me everywhere at once.

I was being thoroughly and unequivocally claimed.

The less than subtle insistence of his fingers gripping and tugging my underwear alerted me to the precariousness of our situation and current surroundings.

I pulled my mouth from his and moved my head to the side, tucked against his neck. My breathing was understandably heavy when I gasped, "Quinn."

He answered my gasp with a growl, kissing then biting my neck, his fingers still hooked in my panties. "Take these off."

"Wait, wait, wait-"

"Take them off or I'll rip them off."

"Guh." Was my response, because the arousal fog was back, and I was losing my grip on caring about my surroundings. I was entering the territory of only caring about getting his pants off.

The last thing that happened before I was pulled under, beyond caring or shame, and engaging in a scandalously explicit semi-public display of affection, was my underwear being torn in two by the very happy, very domineering, and very soon to be my husband, Quinn Sullivan.

Part 2: The Engagement

CHAPTER 4

Quinn

I WANTED TO touch her, but I didn't want to wake her up. Not yet.

Without premeditation, I reached for and carefully pulled her left hand away from her body. She was holding it close and tucked under her chin.

The clock on the side of the bed told me it was just before 5:30 a.m. Heavy curtains blocked most of the pale, early sunlight, but the beginning of a gray morning still filtered in, filling the room of our suite just enough to make everything visible. I had a meeting at 9:00 a.m. and needed to get up and moving if the day's schedule was going to proceed as planned.

Instead, I continued to stare at her.

Janie is cute when she sleeps. More accurately, she is fucking adorable.

I've studied her enough to memorize her face. Her eyelashes and eyebrows are a shade darker than her hair, and they flutter just before she wakes up. Every so often, she scrunches her nose as if the light freckles on her pale skin tickle her while she sleeps.

She is a quiet sleeper; even her breathing is silent. The first time we slept together, in Vegas, she was so motionless and quiet that I'd checked her neck for a pulse.

Her hair is a mess. She says it's like curling snakes. I agree. They reach out in every direction. I've been pulled out of sleep more than once by a mouthful of her hair, and I've come around to her way of thinking, that her hair has a mind of its own.

She once told me that there were four independent, sentient beings in our relationship: her, me, her hair, and my eyes.

I reluctantly moved my attention from her face to her left hand, now held in mine. I rubbed the skin around the gold and ruby ring with my thumb. The band was thick, substantial, and the ruby was huge.

Elizabeth was right about the ring. It was perfect.

Seeing it on Janie's finger and feeling the weight of it there was tremendously satisfying. Giving the woman you're going to marry an outrageously expensive ring to mark her as your own was genius. Women probably thought they were the winners of tradition in this scenario. They were wrong.

Men were the winners, because the prize wasn't the ring. The prize was the woman.

The engagement hadn't gone according to my original plan. It went better.

Every guy is nervous when he proposes to his girl. If he isn't nervous then he's a fool, or he's not in love.

Proposing is like giving someone your dick and a sharp knife, then waiting to see what they do next.

So, yeah, I was nervous.

The original plan called for getting her drunk before proposing. This wasn't ideal, but I'd been prepared to do what was necessary to secure a yes.

I was trying to be romantic, and she kept bringing the conversation back to beheadings, suffering, and patricide. No one wants to give a girl his dick and a sharp knife, especially not when she keeps talking about torture.

She was frustrating. She was driving me crazy. She was ruining my plans.

The first glimmer of hope came when she saw the ring among the Crown Jewels. She pointed it out to me. Of the rings, it was also the one I liked the best.

Then, the medieval device room, the rack, and tying her up….

God bless Janie's insatiable curiosity.

Yeah, yeah—I know. I'm not a good guy. I try to be, for her. I want to be worthy of her brain and heart. I want to deserve her trust and admiration.

But I'm still selfish, especially about Janie. I'd like to say I'm working on it. I'm not. Not really. But she doesn't seem to mind, so I'm just going to go with it.

After all, she's wearing my ring, right?

I approve wholeheartedly of expensive jewelry. In fact, the bigger the better. If I could have gotten away with it, I would have given her a 24-karat gold necklace that read *Property of Quinn Sullivan.*

But I didn't think she'd go for that.

I also don't think of her that way—as property—but I do think of her as belonging to me, because I belong to her.

I belong to her, and I am completely screwed, because I want her ownership. I want her to use me. I want to give her everything. I wouldn't have a problem getting a tattoo that reads *Property of Janie Sullivan.*

I smiled, blinking once as I thought about the realization. But my devotion was an affirmation more than an epiphany.

She wouldn't want me to do that. She wouldn't want me to get a tattoo about her. Sometimes her selflessness was exasperating, but it was also fucking adorable.

Janie stirred and I loosened my grip on her hand. She immediately tucked it back under her chin. Her legs straightened, stretched under the covers. She snuggled into the pillow.

She shifted to her side and back; the covers slipped and exposed one of her perfect breasts. I held my breath and tugged the covers even lower to expose the hidden twin. She settled again, her lips slightly parted. I watched her bare chest rise and fall with her silent breath, and stifled a groan.

She was no longer fucking adorable. She was now sexy as fuck.

I gritted my teeth, reached down, and gripped the morning stiffness between my legs, glanced at the ring on her finger.

After last night's events—ripping off her underwear, inadvertent and frantic tent-sex, her embarrassment during dinner, making out in the limo, then making love in the shower before collapsing on the bed—my first instinct this morning was to wake her up with my mouth between her legs.

I studied her and recognized signs of fatigue. I'd kept her up late, and we'd been very active. She needed time to recuperate. We had a meeting today with a corporate client. She needed her rest. I knew she didn't like having to take three guards with her everywhere she went. It was wearing her down, but we were far from my base of operations, so I considered it necessary.

My influence in Europe is limited, unlike how it is in the States. The presence of three guards might be overkill. I don't care. I need her safe. If I can't be with her every minute of the day, it gives me peace of mind that she is well protected.

She is mine to protect, and I will do the right thing: I will let her sleep.

I closed my eyes to augment my resolve. If I kept looking at her, thinking about her, smelling her, then I'd likely ignore my newly found conscience and have her for breakfast.

Moving silently, I got up, dressed, and grabbed my gym bag. I gave her a kiss on her cheek before I left.

Kissing her was a mistake.

I was still hard when I left the room. I needed to stop thinking about her lying naked in our bed. If I kept thinking about her, and how she had excitedly told me about Roman stone work and hundred-carat diamonds while tied to the rack, I wouldn't make it to the elevator.

So I thought about restitution. I asked her about restitution last night because I wanted to see what she would say.

Something Janie and I have in common is that we both look at the world and see black and white, right and wrong, good and bad.

I look at myself and see black. I see wrong, bad. When I look at her, I see white. I see right, good.

Shades of gray are for idiots, assholes, and cowards, and politicians (which, again, idiots, assholes, and cowards).

She isn't perfect. No one is perfect. But she never knowingly hurts people. I do. Or, more accurately, I used to.

I need to believe in restitution. I have to believe in penance. I don't have a choice. If I don't believe, then I am screwed. My brother is dead because of me; my parents blame me; I blame myself.

Getting revenge didn't help.

Janie helped.

Maybe restitution would help.

I'm not a saint, and I don't think I'll ever get there, but Janie deserves better than a sinner.

***

THE GYM WAS empty when I arrived. I checked the closets, cabinets, exits, and perimeter before setting up the high frequency audio pulse (what my company had patented under the nickname *the Bug Smasher*). I set it for fifteen seconds, left, closed the door behind me, and gave the pulse adequate time to disable any listening or video devices within the room.

Thirty seconds later, I re-entered the gym, packed up the Bug Smasher, claimed the best treadmill of the three, and hooked my headset to my ear before setting my pace. I set the machine to a ten-minute warm-up. Then I called Dan.

His phone rang five times before he picked up.

"Someone better be dead or horny."

"Good morning, Dan."

"You're seriously calling me at five-fucking-fifty in the morning?"

I glanced at my watch. "Sorry, are you on vacation?"

"Wait, are you on the treadmill? Jesus, Mary, and Joseph— please don't tell me you left Janie to go run on a treadmill? What happened to your dick, Quinn? Did they confiscate it at customs? I can't think of another straight man who would leave all that a-"

"You didn't give me a report yesterday." I thought about the previous day, remembered that Dan took Pete's place guarding Janie last night. "Anything I should know? Why'd you replace Pete?"

"Oh, that. We thought some guy was tailing her. Pete called it in. I replaced him so he could follow up. Turns out the guy was a nobody, some banker. Thought she was pretty, wanted to ask her out for a drink."

"Did he approach her?"

"No. Pete interceded and took him for a walk. I think you're driving her crazy with all the guards."

"I know. But I want her to be safe."

"Do you know something that I don't?" I guessed that Dan was referring to the Wickfords. They were the primary private account that we were offloading during this visit.

The Wickfords were idiots, assholes, and cowards.

During the handoff meetings, they'd made veiled threats about undermining my credibility with corporate clients. I wasn't expecting the temper tantrums.

But they weren't violent, which was probably why Dan was questioning my compulsion to have a team of three guards following Janie everywhere she went.

"No. You know everything. I just want her safe." I glanced at the display panel. I still had eight minutes left in my warm-up pace of six miles per hour. "Anything else happen?"

"Not on the ground. I have a few items as part of the daily status update. Speaking of, how are the negotiations going with the Wickfords?" He finally came out and asked.

I grimaced and thought about how to answer without using only expletives. "Better yesterday than the day before."

Extracting my company from the private security business had proven challenging over the past four months. In other words, it was a pain in the ass.

Powerful families were like spoiled children; they required coddling and didn't respond well to change.

"Those people are a piece of work," Dan said. "Do you remember three years ago when I assigned myself to the grandson because he kept having accidents and run-ins with the O'Toole crew? That prick wanted us to get him hookers."

"I remember," I said.

"You should have dropped the family then."

"They pay well."

"Yeah, they're also assholes. I'm glad you're cutting all the families loose."

"So you've said." The treadmill display told me I had another five minutes.

"So, the Wickfords don't like their replacement security? Is that the deal?"

"That's part of it. The other issue is they're nervous about all the intel we've gathered over the years."

Dan chuckled. "They should be. They all should be."

"They want assurances."

"They can kiss my ass." Unlike me, Dan hadn't shed his south Boston neighborhood accent. This sounded more like *Dey kin kiss ma a-a-se.*

I agreed, but I didn't need to make enemies, not with some of the world's richest families. "They'll come around. Let's talk about tomorrow."

"Right. Tomorrow night. The party, the shindig thing. You, Janie, Steven, and me are all on the guest list. They've approved our security detail, finally. Nothing like waiting till the last bloody minute."

"And you've looked over the guest list." I stated this rather than asking.

"Of course, they've been cross checked. A few previous clients will be in attendance, mostly nothing to worry about."

"Mostly?"

Dan hesitated, then he let out a weary sigh. "Remember Damon Parducci? The guy who drugged Janie in Chicago at the Outlandish club—or whatever the hell that stupidass place is called. His parents will be there. And they're still unhappy about you ending their contract after that mess. Damon's sentencing is next month, and all signs point to maximum prison time."

I grunted. My blood pressure spiked, but I kept my tone even. "That little fucker got what he deserved. He had the coke in his possession; we just tipped the cops as to when and where. I told them we weren't in the business of protecting rapists and drug dealers, even before what happened to Janie."

"I know. I just thought you should know, be prepared. Also...." Dan sighed. Again.

"What is it?" I was down to thirty seconds.

"Niki Kenner is going to be there."

I blinked at the display, trying to place the name. "Why does that name sound familiar?"

"You banged her in Los Angeles for a coupla weeks a few years ago. Then she went apeshit and made the rest of the month out there hell."

I grimaced. That bitch was crazy. "Maybe we won't go."

"No. You have to go. At least ten of our corporate liaisons will be there, including the Grinsham corporate account. I know you and Janie are meeting with the security liaison today, but you know how these Brits are. They want to see you socially before they trust you and they know you're on the list. It's the main reason for this trip."

He was right. "Maybe I won't take Janie."

"Take Janie. She'll make you look good. And it'll look weird if she's not there after they meet her today during the specs meeting. She's good for business. And when she's not making you look good, she can make me look short...and good."

"No, no...I don't want—"

"Yes, yes. You don't have to say it again. Steven and I are tired of hearing it. You don't want our extraction from the private clients impacting her in any way. I know this already. She'll have a good time. It'll just be a charity party thing for her. She'll get to dress up and shit."

I grunted again. "I'm serious."

"You're always serious."

"I have to go. We'll go over the daily status report after my meeting this afternoon. I want to know what's happening with Watterson."

"No change with Senator Watterson, and it's fine to go over the rest of the report later. Things are pretty quiet anyway. I'm going back to sleep."

My time was up. I was already a full minute over my warm up, but I had one more thing on my mind.

I needed to ask Dan to be my best man. I briefly thought about waiting until I could do it in person. I decided against that. Better to just ask and get it out of the way.

"One more thing." I took a deep breath, cleared my throat. "We're engaged." Then I added unnecessarily, "We're getting married."

Without missing a beat, Dan responded. "That's great. Do I know him? Was it everything you dreamed it would be?"

I rolled my eyes. "Shut up, asshole."

"Did he get down on one knee?"

"Dan...."

"Both knees? Wow. You're lucky."

I cracked a smile and shook my head. "I'm hanging up now, douchebag."

"Does he know you're not a virgin?"

"Keep talking, fuckface. You're going on knitting group duty when we get back."

"Tell Janie I said she's too good for you."

"Bye." I disconnected the call before he could make another smartass remark. I would have to ask him to be my best man later.

One of the nicest things about working with my best childhood friend is that I can always count on him to tell me exactly what he thinks.

One of the worst things about working with my best childhood friend is that he's always going to tell me exactly what he thinks.

***

JANIE WAS ON the phone when I got back—the hotel phone.

Even though she'd had the cell phone for going on six months, I still couldn't get her to use it voluntarily. She'd text me infrequently, but she didn't like using it for calls. Something about inconclusive research surrounding cell phone radiation exposure and brain tumors.

I stepped behind her, wrapped my arms around her waist. She was wearing only a bathrobe. Torturing myself, and hopefully her, I slipped my hand inside the opening at her chest and massaged her breast. I barely contained my groan when she arched her back at the contact, her bottom pressing against my groin.

I didn't know who she was talking to, but it sounded like business. If it had been one of her friends, I might have continued. But I'd found out a few months ago that she didn't like it when I distracted her from business calls.

She said I was being unprofessional.

Which, for her and given the fact that I was her boss, was basically a crime against humanity.

So I kissed her neck, withdrew my hands to her hips, then stroked her through the terry cloth one more time. I left her and headed to the shower, planning to make it a cold one. I turned to take in one last look at her.

Janie glanced over her shoulder at me, covered the phone receiver, and whispered *psst*. She had a small smile on her full, pink lips, and she mouthed, *Thank you.*

I let my eyes roam over her body, back lit by the window, and promised myself I'd mess up her makeup tonight in the limo.

On that cheerful thought, I showered and dressed in a rush. I was leaving just as Janie finished her call.

"You're leaving?" She turned her wide, amber eyes to me. She held the bathrobe shut at her neck. This was fucking adorable.

"Yeah, I have a meeting at nine with a private client. I'll be back around noon to pick you up for lunch before we meet with Grinsham's people." I took a kiss from her soft, stunned mouth, and shrugged on my overcoat.

The Grinsham group—of Grinsham Credit and Banking Systems—was the only corporate client we were meeting during this trip. Janie had already done an amazing job on the specs and account itemization. All that was left was winning over their security liaison.

"Oh. Okay." She nodded and pressed her fingertips to her lips. "I have everything ready for the specs meeting. I guess I'll see you at noon."

"Sounds good," I called over my shoulder and reached for my suitcase.

My hand hovered over the button to call the elevator when I stopped.

I set the case on the floor. I turned to her. I closed the distance between us in five steps, backed her against the wall, and gave her the kiss she deserved, every place she deserved it.

When I finally left, it was with deep satisfaction of a job well done, and the knowledge that I was going to be late.

***

TEN MINUTES LATER, I was three steps out of the hotel before I realized I'd left my phone upstairs in our suite. I should have been annoyed. After all, I was already late.

Instead, I smiled.

Janie would be out of the shower by now, and she probably thought I was long gone.

An image of her towel drying droplets of water from the white, soft skin of her stomach, her generous breasts, the sweet spot between her thighs flashed through my mind. Her hair was probably still wet.

My body tensed and hardened. I glanced at my watch, turned, and walked back to the elevator. Once there, I jammed my thumb against the button. The doors immediately opened, and I boarded it for the fourth time that morning.

Leaving her was never easy, and even more difficult this morning. She was going to be my wife. What better way to celebrate than an idle morning in bed with Janie and her soft, pliant body.

I was going to be very late.

I reasoned that I didn't have to be present for the pre-meeting. Steven's plane arrived this morning. He would be jetlagged, but he didn't need me there. He'd be surprised, but he'd handle it. Strategically it would work to my advantage. I'd been spending too much time with the Wickfords over the last few days anyway. Tactically it made sense to show them that I already considered our relationship less of a priority.

I was careful to keep my steps quiet as I exited the elevator that opened directly into our suite. I paused, listening for the shower, and heard only silence.

I removed my shoes and strolled to the bedroom, smiled even as my body readied with anticipation of her soft submission.

The door to our room was ajar. I pushed it slowly open. It made no sound. I leaned inside to see where she was, my eyes scanned the master bedroom. I found her squatting on the floor in the same white, terry cloth bathrobe from before.

She was next to my bag.

She was going through my bag.

She was digging, searching.

I could barely believe my eyes and spoke her name automatically. "Janie?"

She bolted upright, jumped away from my luggage, and stared at me with stunned alarm.

I glanced at my suitcase, the spot where she'd been rummaging, then back at her. "What are you doing?"

"Nothing." Her eyes were wide, plainly rimmed with guilt and alarm.

I stepped into the room but didn't cross to her.

"Janie."

"What?"

"Are you going through my things?"

She shook her head; then she offered a delayed, "No."

My gut flooded with displeasure and something else—something like fear. I stared at her, waited for her to tell me the truth.

When I said nothing, she added, "I wasn't. I promise I wasn't going through your things."

I ground my teeth and focused on keeping my voice soft and level because the fear was starting to resemble panic. "You're lying."

Did she suspect? Or did she know already about the private clients? Did she know how I'd built my business? What was she looking for?

No. If she knew for sure she'd have left already, or she'd likely be looking at me now with suspicion instead of guilt. Just the thought made my breath catch.

"No, Quinn, I promise I was not going through your stuff. Really." She started to move toward me, reach her hand out, but then quickly halted and hid something behind her back. "Really, I swear."

I forced myself to stay calm, study her, and listen to her words instead of jump to conclusions. She was ashamed, but her words and expression were honest. She was telling the truth. Yet the fact remained that I'd just walked into our room and found her crouched over my suitcase digging through it.

I subdued the spike of adrenaline. "Then what were you doing in my suitcase?"

"Nothing."

That was a lie.

Her neck and cheeks were red. She was blushing like a pole-dancing virgin.

I stalked slowly toward her. "Why were you going through my bag, Janie?"

She shook her head, obviously torn, her face a grimace. "I...I don't want to tell you."

"Tell me." I stopped three feet from her, close enough to catch her if she tried to run.

Abruptly she blurted, "As able consumers we must be accountable for our purchasing practices. It's not just enough to buy local; we must also be certain that farmers employ responsible techniques, both in the use of labor and the land itself." She shut her eyes, her hands still behind her back, hiding something.

She was hiding something from me.

Panic, a new kind of panic, coiled in my stomach and chest, the kind that drives a man insane, the kind that is fueled by jealousy.

I worked daily to suppress my baser instincts. But I couldn't yet control my selfish nature or the accompanying possessiveness.

I knew owning a person wasn't possible, but I wished it were, because I would have given anything to truly own Janie. I wanted every part of her—all her love, loyalty, fears, secrets, desires—even if that made me a bad guy.

I allowed my voice to betray some of my concern and lack of patience. "What's going on?"

"Seven hundred and eighty million dollars a year spent on chemical products that can cause devastation to ecosystems and…."

My patience snapped and I charged her, took advantage of her closed eyes, and reached for her wrists.

She sucked in a breath, and her eyes flew open just as I wrenched the hidden item from her grip. My other hand pinned her in place, crushed her against me. She landed against my chest with such force that an *oof* escaped her lips. I lifted the item out and away from her reach.

I looked at it.

I blinked at it.

I frowned at it.

I rubbed my thumb over it.

What the hell…?

I glanced down at Janie and found her head bowed against my chest. I could tell that she was holding her breath.

"Janie, this is underwear."

"Yes," came her muffled reply. She sounded downright despondent.

I stared at the top of her wet head. My panic dissipated. I required several seconds to find my next words.

"Why were you trying to hide underwear from me?"

Her hands now gripped the front of my suit as though she was afraid I'd leave her.

"Gah!" was her response.

I glanced at the underwear again. It was white cotton, surprisingly soft, modestly cut. I could find nothing nefarious about it.

"What is going on?"

She suddenly lifted her head, but her hands still held my jacket front. "I just love it so much."

"The underwear?"

"Yes! The underwear! The cotton is organically produced in North Carolina. It's so soft, and it only gets softer each time I wash it, which doesn't make any sense! How do they do that?"

"But…." I searched her face, my brain, the room, the ceiling; I was so confused. "What does that have to do with my bag?"

She heaved a defeated sigh. "When we packed for this trip, I hid several pairs in your bag, in the zippered compartment I know you don't use. I've been…." she paused, chewed on her lip, "I've been putting them on after you leave in the morning. I've been changing out of the lace panties and wearing the white underwear instead. Then, before you get back, I put on the sexy panties again."

"But, why there? Why my bag?"

"Because I suspect that you go through my stuff—which, honestly, I don't care if you do and I've accepted this strangeness about you because I love you—but I knew you would never search your own bag. And, I want to be sexy for you, I want you to think of me that way, not as someone who is always wearing granny panties. And, dammit Quinn, you have a deplorable habit of hiding my underwear!"

I stared at her anguished face, her golden, pleading eyes, and I couldn't think of a single thing to say.

God, how I loved her.

CHAPTER 5

●●●○○ Cipher 📶   5:03 p.m.   77 % 🔋

‹ Messages   **McHotpants**   Contact

Friday, March 14, 4:41 p.m.

Tea joke 1: How does Moses make his tea? Hebrews it.

Tea joke 2: Can't we all just get oolong?

Friday, March 14, 4:54 p.m.

I love you.

I love you, too <3

📷 Text Message   Send

Janie

STEVEN WANTED high tea.

He'd heard of this boutique hotel near the British Museum that had *absolutely fabulous* high tea.

Therefore, after our specs meeting with Grinsham Banking and Credit Systems, Steven and I left Quinn with Dan and we took the Tube. We could have taken a car, but it felt ridiculous when one of the world's best public transportation systems was at our disposal.

Despite his self-proclaimed dislike of people, Steven displayed a good deal of enthusiasm when I proposed the idea of riding mass transit.

My three guards dutifully surrounded us, though they looked less than happy with our choice. It would have been nice to walk freely, without the escort, to experience London like a native or even a typical tourist. Alas, Steven and I sat quietly, exchanging glances instead of talking, while my guards continually swept the train.

We didn't have any real privacy for conversation until we were seated in the tearoom of the hotel.

The hotel was quite small, but it was lovely—exactly the kind of place I would have wanted to stay had Quinn and I been in town for pleasure rather than business.

The lobby was petite, but decorated in black and white. The floor was black and white marble, and four high-backed chairs were covered in black and white fabric with a scrolling flowers design.

A sitting room off to the right was appointed with luxurious antique furniture and red velvet upholstered chairs and sofas, and the wooden floor beneath creaked its welcome as we were ushered up four stairs to the tearoom.

The tearoom was really just three small wooden tables and ten richly upholstered damask chairs in a well-lit space. It jutted out into and looked over a moderately sized garden, and reminded me of an atrium, but not quite. The ceiling was normal and enclosed. Since all the walls were glass, it gave me the sense of sitting in the garden itself, but without the frigid temperature.

Spring flowers were just starting to show signs of life. A stubborn looking pale pink rose bush positioned just beyond the windowpane nearest our table proudly displayed five giant blooms. The yellow rose bush next to it was larger, yet contained only three buds.

"We'll have the Empress tea, please." Steven winked at me as he ordered for both of us. It was a running joke between us that I'd forgotten how to order for myself.

"And what champagne?" Our waitress smiled prettily at Steven. Her accent told me she was from Eastern Europe. "We have Monet Chandon and…."

"We'll take a bottle of Henri Billiot, because I think we're celebrating a momentous event." Steven wagged his eyebrows at me then winked again. Wagging eyebrows plus a double wink meant that Steven's excitement was nearing critical mass.

I was actually surprised he'd held it in all through the client meeting, Tube ride, and walk to the hotel.

No sooner had she left us than Steven reached for my left hand—without permission—and pulled it to his side of the table for intense scrutiny. "Egads, Sugarplum! That's what I call an engagement ring!"

I laughed at his abrupt focusing of the conversation. "Yes, it's just so…."

He interrupted me. "Give me all the details—inquiring minds want to know. How did he do it? Are you pregnant? Should I not have ordered alcohol? I can't believe it! It seems sudden, but then the Boss never takes very long to make up his mind. Damn, he has good taste. But I already knew that."

"I'm not pregnant, and…."

"But you will be."

"Steven…."

"I'm serious. Quinn Sullivan is a hunter-gatherer. I've known him longer than you have. I've seen how he is in business—and that's just money. How do you think he's going to be with the woman who is his *wife*?" Steven *tsked* and released my hand. "My guess is that he'll be at least as domineering and protective about you—I mean, have you seen that ring you're wearing? Already marking his territory. Has he peed on you?"

"Steven!"

"You're right, it's none of my business." He held up his hands, then reached for his napkin and shook it with a flick of his wrist before laying it on his lap. "You two are going to have the tallest and best looking children. They'll be supermodels, and basketball players, and Navy SEALs."

My stomach warmed with the thought of little Quinn Navy SEALs running around the penthouse, causing mischief and throwing taciturn tantrums. Perhaps executing covert ops to extract cookies from the kitchen. "We haven't discussed that yet."

"What?" Steven placed an elbow on the table, then rested his chin in his palm and gazed at me.

"Children."

"You haven't discussed children?" His eyebrows arched over his gray eyes. "Well, don't you think you need to? Seeing as how you're going to marry the guy. You should find out if he wants an even or odd number—you know, like seven or ten."

"Honestly, he took me completely by surprise. I wasn't expecting it at all."

"But you said yes?"

"Yes. Of course I said yes."

"Why *of course*?"

I sighed, but was forced to delay my response when our waitress returned with lovely little sandwiches and the bottle of Crystal. She assured us that petit fours, scones with clotted cream and strawberry jam, and Earl Grey tea would be forthcoming.

Steven lifted his glass of champagne as she left and encouraged me to lift mine. "Clink me, we'll make a toast later after I find out why you *of course* said yes."

"Well, first of all, I'm in love him."

"You and I both know that's not a good reason. I'm in love with my white couch, but you don't see me getting a marriage license."

I ignored his comment and selected a delicate looking egg salad sandwich with no crust from the serving tray. "Secondly, I like him."

"Ah! Now we're getting somewhere. Care to expand on what you like about him? Other than the obvious."

"The obvious?"

"His face, body, and bank account."

I twisted my mouth to the side and crossed my arms over my chest. "He's more than just a face, body, and bank account." I both loved and liked his face and body. I had mixed feelings about the bank account.

"Well, he's got brains too, I'll give you that." Steven popped a chicken salad sandwich into his mouth and spoke while he chewed; miraculously, all the food stayed within. "You're a sensible girl, probably smarter than he is in the traditional way." He gulped half the glass of champagne to wash down the sandwich then continued. "All I'm saying is that I could find a dozen Quinn Sullivans—handsome millionaire manwhores—but I've only encountered one Janie Morris."

I pressed my lips together to keep from smiling. Steven had the uncanny ability to both compliment and insult while making both sound like a discussion about tax law.

"Do you want me to defend my decision?" I tried my sandwich—found it delicious, took a substantial bite—then sipped my champagne.

"No. You don't need to defend anything to me. I'm one of your biggest fans. I just want to make sure you know why you're marrying him. Because, to me, you're special; you deserve the best."

We exchanged a silent smile while our server placed a layered tray of delectable petit fours, scones, and related accoutrements on the circular table then scurried off with a promise of tea. Steven poured more champagne into my class then refilled his.

"Thank you."

"You're welcome. Now then, why are you marrying him?"

I glanced over Steven's shoulder to the garden beyond, searched for the right words, and thought of viruses.

"You know how a virus works?" I refocused my attention to his and watched as Steven's chewing slowed, his eyes narrowed and clouded with confusion.

"Uh…for purposes of this conversation, let's say no."

"Well, in layman terms, the long and short of it is as follows." I sipped my champagne, placed it on the table, then leaned forward. "A virus attaches to a host cell and sends genetic instructions into the host cell. The instructions recruit the host cell's enzymes—like propaganda—and convince the enzymes to make parts for new virus particles. The new virus particles assemble and break free from the host cell. Then the whole thing starts all over again. That's how the virus spreads until it just takes over."

"O-o-o-kay." Steven placed a scone on his plate and cut it open before applying liberal amounts of clotted cream. "Your point is?"

"My relationship with Quinn is the virus."

Steven frowned at his scone then at me. "That sounds unhealthy."

"Yes, in some ways it most likely is. And, for some relationships, it most definitely is. But it's not for us, not really. Every relationship is like a virus—where two people negotiate and change, stretch and grow, recruit and assimilate until you're two things, but also one thing, one entity, working together."

"So, are you the virus or the host cell?"

"The relationship is the virus, and both Quinn and I, separately, are the host cells. The key is to find a relationship, a virus, that encourages you to be stronger, a better person, but also be able to show weakness without fear of exploitation—a relationship that challenges you, but also makes you happy and lifts you up."

Steven's expression hovered between incredulous and amused. "Don't some viruses cause cancer?"

"Yes." I nodded, ceding the point, and began thinking through the ramifications of the expanded analogy out loud. "And some viruses irrevocably change your DNA. But that's like a relationship too, isn't it? Some relationships can change how we see ourselves for better or for worse—as you say, in chronically unhealthy ways, like a cancer. And some do the opposite. They make us realize our potential."

"Huh," came his thoughtful response. He studied me for a

protracted moment before saying, "I love you, Janie. Only you can compare a relationship to a disease and make it sound both romantic and terminal."

CHAPTER 6

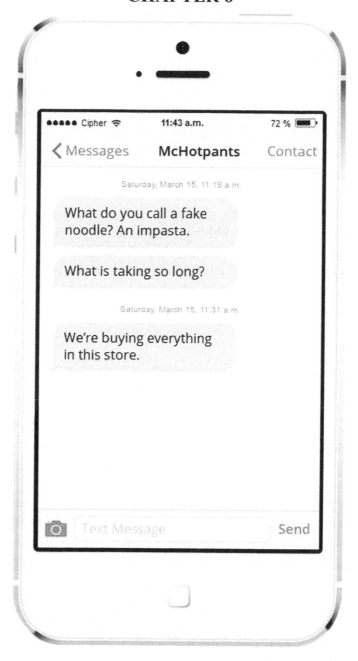

FOR THE FIRST time in my life, I was wearing a ball gown.

It itched.

However, it had also elicited a prolonged, heated stare from my fiancé—likely because it was strapless and necessitated a likewise strapless bustier with a pushup bra. My breasts were distracting even to me, especially when I drew in a deep breath. They kept popping up in my peripheral vision, and I caught myself staring down at my chest wondering who they belonged to.

Given Quinn's preoccupation with them in general, I imagined that to him, my squeezed-in pushed-up breasts were like two pale mounds of hypnotizing flesh.

I'd spent most of the day shopping for necessary undergarments for the gown since I had nothing even close to appropriate. Quinn, to my total shock and surprise, cleared his schedule so that he could come with me. While we were out, he'd also made a point to have me try on, model, and purchase a good amount of bridal lingerie.

I was pleased to see he was taking the wedding planning seriously.

The ball gown was a deep burgundy silk and sequined with dark red and black beadwork. It was fitted through the lower waist then flared dramatically to the floor. It also had a quantity of black feathers—a modest gather at one side of the waist that increased in width and spread down the right side of the skirt like a fan.

I didn't choose the gown. It was sent to Quinn by the foundation hosting the ball after we RSVPed for the event. I didn't discover until later that, along with the RSVP, his secretary—Betty—had sent in a recent picture of me along with my measurements.

All the women in attendance had been instructed to wear the provided dresses, which would be auctioned for the sake of the charity.

Under any other circumstances, beautiful as it was, I never would have worn it. Cleavage issues aside, I didn't know where to put my arms. If they hung down loosely at my sides, the beads of the bodice scratched the sensitive underside of my biceps. If I crossed them over my chest, my boobs went from mountainous to volcanic.

I tried putting my hands on my hips, which worked for a short time, but it wasn't a long-term solution because it made me look like a stern peahen teacher.

I was debating all of this when Dan and Steven arrived. Of course, Steven took one look at me and the awkward no-man's-land placement of my arms and made an obvious suggestion.

"Why don't you wear opera gloves?" He said.

A call to the concierge, and fifteen minutes (of me holding my arms away from my body) later, and we were on our way—with opera gloves.

Yet again, Quinn was Sir McCoolpants Von No Touchy in the limo. I surmised that this time it had more to do with the two other people riding with us than preoccupation on his part. In fact, I was quite thankful for Dan and Steven's presence; limo rides with McHotpants were notorious for throwing carefully applied makeup into a blender of disorder.

One time I walked into a fancy restaurant and my face was clown-town appropriate.

We arrived at the venue, and I quickly I decided that the charity event, which I hadn't actually given much thought to until two hours before it was time to leave, was really just an excuse for rich people to get dressed up.

I came to this conclusion after asking Quinn, Dan, Steven, three random ladies, and two older gentlemen what the name of the charity was—and no one knew. Furthermore, no one knew what the charity supported, even in general terms.

Once we were inside the event space, I modified my theory. Rich people go to charity events to get dressed up, glare at people they don't know, and pretend to have a good time.

The space was magnificent—a gigantic ballroom with a wide, domed stage; a mixture of art deco and neo classical architectural elements; cream colored walls, marble columns, and gold leaf accents. Tables were arranged around a dance floor, and huge, ostentatious centerpieces of flowers, gold and white beaded stars, and ribbon jutted three feet upward in a topiary style.

Tangentially, I wondered how much the event cost to host and, given the grandeur, how it could possibly break even.

The stage was occupied by a small orchestra, and I recognized the piece being played as Mozart. I craned my neck to obtain a better look and spotted several brass instruments—trombones, trumpets, and even a tuba—lined off to one side.

During my neck craning I accidentally bumped into a stout gentleman and watched with mortification as a few drops of his drink spilled to the floor. I withdrew my fingers from Quinn's and reflexively placed my gloved hand on his back.

"Oh, I am so sorry. Please accept my apology, sir."

The man glanced over his shoulder, and I immediately recognized his jowls. It was Mr. Carter, our primary corporate security liaison with Grinsham Banking and Credit Systems.

When he saw me, his eyes widened and he turned completely around, offering his hand. "Not at all, not at all—why…." he paused, white bushy eyebrows lowered over his brown eyes as they ping-ponged over my form. They halted on my hair, which I'd worn down around my back and shoulders instead of up in a bun. I was also currently wearing contacts, whereas yesterday during our meeting I'd been wearing my glasses. "Miss Morris, is that you?"

I took his hand in mine, gave it a firm shake, and released it. "Yes, Mr. Carter. It is I, Janie Morris. I'm terribly sorry about your drink, but I was trying to see the stage. Did you notice that there are several brass instruments not in use?"

He blinked at me, and I wasn't entirely certain he'd heard my question.

Quinn stepped closer to my side. "Mr. Carter," he said, drawing the older man's attention.

"Oh, Mr. Sullivan…of course." Mr. Carter seemed to give himself a little shake before he continued. "Greatly pleased to see you in attendance. These functions are a tax on one's time, but they do allow for additional discourse outside of the office, you know. Your Miss Morris is quite lovely."

Quinn nodded, but said nothing, because Mr. Carter was once again eying the length of me.

Yesterday afternoon, during the meeting with Mr. Carter and his team, Quinn had introduced me as *Ms. Morris, Director of Corporate Accounts, and my fiancée.* At the time, the label had been unexpected and felt a little out of place.

Now, however, I felt grateful that the nature of our relationship had been established, because Mr. Carter's gaze hadn't moved from my bodice for the last four seconds.

I glanced down at the dress, my distracting cleavage, and my hands went to my hips.

"You can buy it," I said.

Mr. Carter's gaze jumped to mine. "I…what…pardon?"

"The dress," I clarified, meeting his gaze and giving him a warm smile. "The dress is for sale, to benefit…the charity." I hoped he wouldn't ask me which charity, because then I would have to admit that I had no idea.

Quinn cleared his throat. I felt his arm wrap around my waist, and he brought me against his side. "We're going to find our table."

Again, Mr. Carter seemed to shake himself before turning his attention to Quinn and responding. "Oh, yes. I believe we're all seated together, table seven. Nice spot. Near the bar. Very convenient arrangement as I should like to discuss with you options for private security for some of our board members and their families."

Quinn's body stiffened next to mine, and I only noticed because we were pressed together. Outwardly, his expression was calm and unchanged.

"I'd be happy to make some recommendations," he said, his voice tempered, measured. "But my firm is in the process of moving out of the private security business."

This statement surprised me. I glanced at Quinn then at Steven, and found the latter issuing me an inscrutable look.

"Oh, well. That's too bad. I've heard your team is the best." Mr. Carter appeared to be markedly disappointed. "Very discreet and all that."

Quinn shifted on his feet, and I knew he was preparing to make an escape. "We've found our considerable talents better suited to corporate security. If you'll excuse us, we'll see you during dinner. I promised my fiancée a better look at the orchestra."

"Oh, yes. Quite!" Mr. Carter nodded and gave me an exceptionally polite head bow paired with an exceptionally cheeky wink. "You're fiancé is a very lucky man."

I returned his head bow with a small nod, but not a wink.

Quinn turned us away and his hand moved to my back. He began steering us through the crowd toward the orchestra, and my thoughts were all muddled. Foremost on my mind was why he hadn't mentioned prior to now that Cipher Systems was moving out of private security.

I knew he was meeting with private clients while we were here; that's where he'd been spending much of his time. But I'd assumed the meetings were benign.

Our party made it maybe ten feet before our path was blocked by a very blonde woman.

Honestly, when I looked at her, the first thing I thought was that she was *very blonde*. Likely, if I reflected on it, many people looked at me and their first impression was that I was *very red-haired*.

"Well, hello stranger," she said, her eyes on Quinn.

I forced myself to look away from her very blonde hair coiffed in a style reminiscent of Marilyn Monroe, and studied her gown: a white halter-top with a fitted bodice and a skirt that bloomed into fullness at mid hip. I had no way of knowing what the fabric content was without touching, asking, or looking at the label.

I refocused on the conversation just in time to hear Quinn's huff. I knew that huff. It was a huff of irritation.

Dan stepped in front of Quinn and placed his hand on the mysterious, very blonde woman's arm. "Hi, Niki, let's go for a walk."

"Get your hand off me." She smiled as she said the words, and her voice was light and pleasant. "Or I'll scream."

Dan let his hand drop, but stepped more fully in front of me. "No problem. Wasn't looking forward to touching you anyway."

Quinn leaned close to my ear and whispered, "Will you get me a drink?" Then he lifted his chin toward Steven.

I glanced at the very blonde woman then at the back of Dan's neck where his swirled tattoos were just visible above the collar of his shirt and jacket; my eyes then darted to Steven, then to Quinn. I wasn't the best person at reading social cues and body language, but even I could feel the coiled potential for drama.

I hated scenes. As much as I was curious about who the very blonde woman was, the thought of being part of a mid-ballroom spectacle made leaving sound like a very good idea.

Therefore, I acquiesced, thankful for the escape. "Sure. Whiskey?"

He nodded, gave me a small, grateful smile, and passed me to Steven.

When I say that he *passed me to Steven,* I mean Quinn tucked my hand around Steven's arm, into the crook of his elbow, and issued him a pointed look.

Then, we were off.

Steven and I maneuvered to the bar. At one point, we had to walk single file to make it through a cluster of ball gowns. I used the opportunity to glance over my shoulder and saw that Quinn was standing next to Dan, his hands in his pants pockets, his face a mask of boredom. I couldn't see the very blonde woman's face as her back was to me.

"You looked surprised."

Steven's voice drew my attention back to our current task as we stopped at the end of the line for the bar. I studied his features for a moment, looking for a clue regarding which subject he was referencing.

"I looked surprised?"

His gray eyes narrowed. "Yes. You looked surprised when the Boss told Carter that Cipher Systems was pulling out of private security."

"Oh. Yes." I frowned. "I was surprised." I knew that Quinn had been meeting with private clients during the trip, and that his meetings had been running longer than he'd anticipated, but I didn't realized he'd been meeting with them to terminate the contracts.

"He didn't tell you?"

"Tell me what?"

"We've been outsourcing private clients to new firms."

"No. He hasn't mentioned it yet. How long as this been going on?"

Steven studied me, his lips pinched, his expression tight. "Janie, how much has Mr. Sullivan told you about the private clients?"

I tugged the glove higher on my upper arm. "I know the specs, the accounting side of things."

"Do you know what we do for them?"

"Yes. Actually, more accurately, I know what we bill for."

"Hmm." Steven crossed his arms over his chest and regarded me for a long moment. We took a step forward to advance our position in the line. Then, as though he couldn't hold on to the thought any longer without bursting, he said, "You need to ask him about the private accounts. Promise me you'll grill him about the subject — and I mean *grill him* like a steak until you know absolutely everything. Don't let him put you off."

"Is there something you want to tell me, Steven?"

He opened his mouth as though to respond, then snapped it shut and shook his head. "No. Nope. This is none of my business. I'm not getting involved. But, as your friend, I'm encouraging you to ask him, and don't stop asking him until you're sure you know everything."

I suppressed my next question, as it was our turn at the bar. I ordered top shelf whiskey for Quinn and Dan, and a glass of champagne for myself. Steven also ordered a glass of champagne.

We stood in silence until our drinks arrived, though I tried to hurl questions at him using just my eyes. He, in turn, peered at me, his gaze a like a gray, stony wall.

We gathered the glasses and moved toward table seven. I waited until we were several feet from the bar and clear of the crowd before resuming my questioning.

"Are you trying to make me nervous, Steven?"

"No."

"Are they...?" I glanced over my shoulder at Quinn and Dan then leaned into Steven's ear to whisper my question. "Is it something illegal?"

I drew away to study his face before he responded. "No. Not *illegal*."

"I don't like how you said that."

"Said what?"

"*Illegal.*"

"How did I say it?"

"Like it isn't illegal, but it should be illegal."

"Well, it's neither of those. At least, I don't think it's either of those."

"Then why are you being so vague?"

Steven didn't get a chance to answer because Quinn and Dan arrived just at that moment, Dan's voice cutting through our exchange.

"What's Steven being vague about?"

"Janie and I were just talking about viruses," Steven said, deflecting.

I glared at Steven, which caused him to glower.

"Viruses?" Dan took the whiskey from Steven, his eyes moving between us. "Do I want to know?"

Quinn accepted his drink when I offered it to him, but instead of drinking it, he set it on our table. "Thank you," he said to me. I got the impression he wasn't referring to the whiskey.

"You're welcome." I studied him over my champagne glass.

"It's the secretive viruses you have to be careful around."

We all turned and looked at Steven. I felt the first hint of a blush spread up my neck. He was being purposefully cryptic, the stinker.

"Secretive viruses?" Dan squinted at Steven. "What are you talking about?"

"The stealthy ones." Steven took a large swallow of champagne before continuing. "The stealthy ones blind your genetic code with propaganda so you don't pay attention to the details."

"Are you drunk?" Dan said.

Steven gulped down the rest of his champagne. "No. But I am hungry. Let's go find some miniature food so these two kids can talk."

Dan cast a suspicious glare at me then Steven. In the end, he shrugged, obviously still a little harried from the encounter with the very blonde woman. "Fine. Let's go. Lead the way."

I watched them depart and felt acutely troubled.

Steven was right. I should know more about the private accounts. Other than help implement the new billing software for the private clients, I knew very little about that side of the business. I hadn't thought it terribly remarkable since I'd been so busy bringing in new corporate partners, but every time I'd asked Quinn about Cipher Systems, he'd deflect or steer the conversation in a different direction.

I think the fact that he'd deflected bothered me most of all. He knew I was easy to distract and had taken advantage of my weakness.

I turned my attention to Quinn, pondered his profile. He was scanning the ballroom with an assessing glare. He'd entwined his fingers with mine. His other hand was at my hip.

"Looking for anything in particular?" I asked.

Either my question or my tone brought his attention to me.

Quinn studied me for a moment before responding. "I'm sorry about earlier…about…." He sighed, and again I noticed that it was laced with irritation. "I'm sorry about that woman."

Curiosity about the very blonde woman warred with my disquiet about the private client accounts. I decided that a proper discussion about the clients was necessary and, therefore, the ballroom of an event to benefit a phantom charity was likely not the best place to initiate the issue.

I decided to press him about the woman. "How do you know her?"

His expression didn't change, but he did glance over my shoulder as he spoke. "We met a few years ago on the west coast."

"She seemed angry. What did you do to her?"

Quinn narrowed his eyes at me then leaned forward and whispered against my ear causing my back to stiffen. "Don't be nice to her."

"What?" I flinched away to read his face. "What does that even mean? *Don't be nice to her.* I don't make a habit of walking around being mean to people."

"I'm serious, Janie; don't go out of your way to talk to her. She's crazy." The hand that was on my hip was now rubbing slow circles on my upper back, beneath my hair, drawing me to him. It felt nice.

I frowned, a tad concerned. "Was she institutionalized?"

"No…." He hesitated, as though he were going to add something. Finally, he just said, "Nothing like that."

"Then why do you…?" My frown eased, though I was certain it was replaced with an eye squint of confusion. He glanced beyond me as I studied his features. To anyone else, he was outwardly calm—aloof even—but something about the set of his jaw and the way he looked away from me was perplexing.

"Who is she?" I asked.

"No one."

Since he was so close, I whispered, "How do you know her, Quinn?"

He reached around me, picked up his glass, gulped the whiskey then asked, "Do you want more champagne?"

I shook my head; he studiously avoided my gaze. "Quinn, who is she?"

He glared at me, and I realized he didn't want to answer.

And just like that, I knew who she was.

My mouth fell open, and I announced my discovery. "Oh! Oh, I get it! She was one of your slamps!"

CHAPTER 7

"Shhh." Quinn glared at me, though it looked like he was fighting laughter.

I lowered my voice to a whisper. "Sorry, sorry. I didn't mean to yell. But I'm right, right?"

He didn't respond, not with words. However, the answering hardness in his stare told me I was right.

"I've never seen one before." I craned my neck to look around the ballroom, hoping to catch a glimpse of her again. To my delight, she was at the bar, and I had a mostly unobstructed view. I studied her, really looked at her this time, and tried to see her from Quinn's perspective. "She's really pretty. And she seems so classy."

I heard Quinn cough, and I turned to face him. He must have been mid-swallow when I said my last sentence as it appeared that he'd choked on his whiskey. He brought his hand to his mouth to cover his cough.

"Are you okay?"

"Classy?" He rasped.

I held my hands up. "Oh, no offense meant, and no judgment either. I'm sure they're all very classy and you had very excellent taste in slamps. It's just that I was not expecting...I don't know what I was expecting."

He suppressed another cough and shook his head. On the Quinn scale of appearing ill at ease, he looked to be about a seven—not as uncomfortable as me discussing my menstrual cycle, but more uncomfortable than my recent tirade on perceived gender and how male sea horses gave birth to their young.

Before he could respond, I continued. "Actually I do know what I was expecting. I was expecting...the chorus of prostitutes in the stage production of *Les Misérables*. Maybe some missing teeth. I don't know why. I mean, I know that it's perfectly acceptable as part of our culture for two people to have multiple sexual partners at the same time—even at the same moment. I just wasn't expecting her to look so normal. I mean, gorgeous, but normal. So

I guess your slamps were normal people, huh?"

"Yes. They were normal people."

"And she has a job? I mean, other than being your slamp."

"Janie, I never paid her."

"I know—gah, sorry that sounded bad. I meant she had other interests outside of being your slamp?"

"I guess so."

"She's not British. She sounds like she's from the States."

"She's from Los Angeles."

My eyes skated over him, and I hesitated only a fraction of a second before asking, "What does she do?"

He shrugged, looking bored. But I knew better. Boredom in this case was a cover for his ill-at-ease level seven. "Something in fashion."

I nodded, my eyes losing focus over his shoulder. "I can see that. She's remarkably well maintained and groomed."

"Maintained and groomed?"

My attention moved back to him. "Yes. She has that shiny, just unwrapped quality about her. Or, more accurately, that fresh coat of paint aura."

The corner of his mouth pulled upward, a nearly imperceptible tilt. "That's a good description."

"What did you two talk about? I didn't know you had any interest in fashion."

"I don't. We didn't talk."

"You didn't talk? Like, ever?"

"No."

"No?"

"No."

His expression was as flat as his tone.

I surveyed him. Something in my face must have increased his ill-at-ease level, because his eyes darted to mine, away, then back again. He smoothed a hand down his tie, cleared his throat. He was almost fidgety—approaching ill-at-ease level eight.

Finally, he blurted, "You're the only one."

"The only what?"

"The only one I've wanted to talk to—that I've...conversed with."

"I'm the only female you've conversed with?" I struggled repeating the words because they sounded preposterous.

He sighed. "Of course I talk to women all the time. I talk to Shelly on a weekly basis, but she's my sister." He tugged at his tie, looking a tad frustrated, yet his voice betrayed no irritation. "You're the only woman that I've been involved with and also wanted to have a conversation with. What I meant was she was boring, even irritating, whereas, I like talking to you. You're interesting, easy to be around. You're knowledgeable about things that matter; your interests are varied and unusual. You're good to talk to."

I nodded, my movements subtle, and I absorbed this information. I translated it in my head and spoke it at the same time. "So, what you're saying is that you like me."

The frustration marring his forehead ebbed, leaving his features warm and his gaze entirely focused on me. "Yes. I like you. I like you a lot."

We shared a smile. Like most of his expressions in public, it was subtle. But, unlike most of his expressions in public, it was a vulnerable display of sincerity.

My smile was considerably wider, and I couldn't help but blurt, "I like you too, Quinn."

He shrugged an arrogant shrug and said, "I know."

This made me laugh, which likely would have made him at least chuckle if he hadn't decided to hide it with another swallow of his whiskey.

My eyes caught the very blonde woman, his former slamp, in the background. She was smiling widely at two men and seemed to be enjoying herself. I indicated my head in her direction. "Well, she looks nice."

"She's not."

My frown returned. "She's not?"

"No. She's crazy." He finished his whiskey.

"So you keep saying. Why is she crazy?"

"When I called things off with her, let's just say she didn't take it very well."

I mulled this over. If and/or when Quinn broke things off with me, I imagined I wouldn't take it very well either. "And that makes her crazy?"

"I don't want you talking to her."

"You don't want me talking to her?"

For Quinn, his tone was soft, coaxing. "You know what I mean."

"Hmm...." I regarded him for a moment then added, "I'll take your wishes under advisement."

"Janie...."

"I will. They're in the advisement folder. I will consider them before I make my decision."

His eyes narrowed as they moved between mine. Then, quite unexpectedly, he smiled at me, and his voice held false warmth. "Janie. You're not talking to her."

"Oh, really?" I laughed lightly, mirroring his expression, and issued him my slow, assessing head bob. "Just so you know, I just mentally shredded the advisement folder and your wishes are no longer being considered."

His smile grew and he looked both frustrated and amused. "That's not nice."

"Then don't order me around. You know I don't like that."

"Yes you do."

I breathed in through my nose and did my best to hide any physical manifestations betraying the surge of pleasant adrenaline at his words. "You're right. Sometimes I do, specifically when we're bereft of clothing. But when we're at a party and I'm curious about this very unusual and interesting opportunity, I don't like it so much. And I may never get another chance to talk with one of your slamps."

He made a low growling sound in the back of his throat and glanced from his empty glass to me. "Please do not call her that to her face."

"I...I wouldn't do that." I responded as though the idea was preposterous, even added an eye roll, but I made a mental note: *Do not call her a slamp to her face.*

"Janie, I'm serious. She wouldn't like it. It would make her...she'd go nuts, try to rip your hair out, or worse." His expression turned dark as his eyes drifted over to the bar, and I wondered exactly how crazy she was. Abruptly, he touched my arm, his eyes locked on mine, and gave me a soft squeeze. "Listen to me. Now I'm asking nicely. Don't approach her."

***

TO BE FAIR, I didn't *technically* approach her.

I rescued her.

Well...I didn't exactly *rescue* her. More precisely, I helped her. It happened in the bathroom.

I'd been followed to the restroom by one of Quinn's team. He waited outside, situating himself by the door so that he could intimidate anyone entering to use the toilet. I hadn't yet grown accustomed to having someone wait for me to finish my business, and it irked me.

When I had a guard, as soon as I entered a public restroom, I felt like the clock was ticking. Usually, I'd rush through and end up with my pants buttoned but unzipped, or sink water down the front of my outfit.

Tonight, however, I told the guard that he could expect a long wait; this was because I wasn't quite sure how to manage lifting the heavy skirts of the dress without losing my balance, falling in, getting stabbed by feathers, or wrinkling the whole thing beyond repair.

The venue had one of those fancy washrooms with an adjacent sitting area. The room was spacious and richly—yet too sweetly—decorated in brocade light pink wallpaper, pink velvet upholstered chairs, and pink curtains. As well, a huge, ornate, lighted mirror with a thick glowing white frame ran the entire length of the walls.

Crystal chandeliers hung from the ceiling.

Suffice to say, the room was bright, shiny, and pink.

And sitting in one corner of the sitting room was the very blonde slamp.

I paused a half second when I saw her, but then I was spurred into action by my bladder and sprinted for the toilet. Perhaps it was because I was distracted by her presence and, therefore, couldn't overthink my technique; or perhaps it was because I didn't feel rushed as I'd prepared Pete—my guard—before I entered to expect a delay, but using the facilities went remarkably smoothly.

I was out of the stall in record time and was drying my hands with a soft cotton towel when I heard the very blonde woman from the other room.

"Shit," she said.

It sounded frustrated and maybe a little desperate. I knew that feeling. I especially knew that feeling while in a bathroom.

I'd laid my gloves around my neck as a scarf, to keep them out of germ's way, so I pulled them from my shoulder and drifted hesitantly into the pink room. She was still in the corner, but now she was standing up. A glass of something that I deduced to be soda water was sitting on the table beside her, and she was rubbing at her white dress with a cloth.

I tried to tiptoe closer, but recognized this immediately as an exercise in futility because my skirt rustled like a cornfield in a windstorm whenever I took a step.

She glanced up, her blue eyes connected with mine, and they turned from frustrated to bitter. "What do you want?"

"Can I help?" I glanced at the place she'd been rubbing. "Oh, see, that's not going to work. Soda water doesn't help with red wine—is that red wine?"

She frowned at me, and her gaze flickered to the stain marring the otherwise pristine gown. "Yes, it's red wine, but I don't need your help...."

"Yeah, that's too bad. Most people don't know this, but you should have used salt. Even then, depending on the fabric, it might not have made a difference. Then again, the stain is quite small and localized—may I touch your dress?"

"What?"

"Touch your dress, to determine the fiber content."

She blinked at me, her mouth opened then closed. Finally, she said, "Go ahead!" Her arms flailed from her sides in the universal sign for *I'm exasperated.*

I sat next to her on one of the velvet stools and rubbed the thick material between my fingers. "Oh. Silk." I *tsked* and shook my head as I considered the stain at her waist. "That's not coming out. If only you had something to cover it…."

My gaze drifted around the room, searching for a quick fix. I wondered if the venue would notice if I tore a piece of pink velvet from the bottom of one of the drapes. Then, my eyes caught on the black gloves in my hands.

"Ah ha!" I jumped up and held the gloves in front of her stunned face. "My gloves!"

"What?"

"My gloves." I sat down again and lifted up my skirt, revealing a row of ten safety pins. "I thought it best to bring safety pins. One never knows when they'll be needed. Also, I'm terribly accident prone, and this skirt is so big. The chances of me tearing something tonight were pretty high, so I brought pins."

"Pins?"

"Yes, pins." I took one of the gloves and formed a loose spiral, pinching one end. "I'm not very crafty, but I've been learning how to crochet recently, and I also learned how to make a fabric flower. The gloves are black silk, so if we just connect them like this…" I pinned the two gloves together. "…and fasten them in place, we can hide the stain and make it look like you have fabric roses at your waist. What do you think?"

I lifted my chin to look up at her face. She was staring down at where I held the two hastily assembled flowers.

"Yes, that's—that's perfect. You're a genius!" Her wide eyes moved to mine, and I was pleased to see she was smiling.

"Thank you. I'll have to put my hand under your skirt and against your stomach so I don't stick you."

"Oh, go right ahead. I'm wearing those Spanx with the slit and I work in the fashion industry. I'm used to hands up my skirt."

"Spanx with the slit?" I set to work pinning the roses in place.

"You know, Spanx? It's like body armor and a girdle all wrapped in one. They hold everything in. And the slit is at my vag, so I don't have to take off the Spanx in order to go pee or...you know...."

I paused my pinning and glanced up at her. Her lips were pressed together and her eyebrows were high on her forehead.

Finally, she finished the thought. "You don't have to take them off in order to have sex."

"Oh. Well...that's convenient." I nodded and resumed my pinning, pleased that women's girdles had graduated from a virtual chastity belt to an open invitation. Then I tried to imagine myself having sex while wearing constricting underwear, and I became preoccupied with where Quinn would place his hands. If I'd been wearing slitted Spanx on Thursday night, he wouldn't have torn off my underwear.

Then I decided that he likely wouldn't go for slitted Spanx because, more than anything, he seemed to want me as naked a possible when we were physically intimate.

"Don't take this the wrong way, but you could totally be a plus-sized model. You're, like, exactly the right dimensions. You could wear stuff off the rack."

Her words pulled me out of my thoughts, and I leaned back to consider my handiwork. "No offense taken. I know I'm a big girl."

"No, you're not a big girl. You're a tall girl with big boobs. I'm not talking about a plus-sized catalogue model. I'm talking about high fashion, runway stuff. In high fashion, a plus-sized model is really just a normal model but with tits and ass for when the designers need a model who looks like a woman instead of a hanger."

"Oh." I let her skirt drop and struggled with how to respond to her statement, which felt like a compliment, but I couldn't be sure. I would need to discuss it with Elizabeth in order to be certain.

I felt her eyes on me for a beat then she turned to the mirror and pivoted side to side as though to test the sturdiness of the applied flowers. "Wow, these are great. They look like they belong on the dress. Thank you."

"No problem." I tugged at the top edge of my gown, as my aforementioned big boobs needed to be tucked back in a bit. They were precariously testing the boundaries of my bodice what with all the bending and pinning I'd been doing.

"So…." She sat down on the stool next to mine and glanced at me from the corner of her eyes before opening a small white clutch and withdrawing some lipstick. "You're with Quinn?"

I stared at her for a beat and thought about how best to answer. I decided it wouldn't be untrue to say that I was. "Yes."

She watched me, and several seconds passed. She seemed to be debating whether to continue.

Then, as though she couldn't hold her tongue any longer, she blurted, "He's not a good guy, hon. He's a user and an asshole. And you seem like a real nice girl…." Her eyes drifted over me, her eyebrows pulled low on her forehead, then her gaze moved back to mine. "Way too good for Quinn Sullivan. What are you even doing with a guy like him?"

I opened my mouth to challenge her label of Quinn, not liking that she'd called him an asshole, but didn't get a chance as she paused only to take a breath and turn back to the mirror.

"I mean he's just going to chew you up and spit you out. I can tell you with one hundred and ten percent certainty that he's not interested in anything long term, not *ever*, not with *anyone*. If he tells you that you're the only one he's with, I guarantee you are *not*."

"How do you know?"

"Because I used to be *with* him." She snorted before adding, "Biggest mistake ever."

"Did he tell you that he wanted something long term?"

"Well…no." She pooched her lips and began applying the lipstick; her eyelashes fluttered. "He never…that is, he told me from the beginning that there were others, but I thought he'd cut them loose when we were together."

"So, he lied to you."

"He never lied, like out loud. *But*, it was implied that I meant something to him. I didn't, and he's a cold-hearted bastard, because when I told him I wanted to—you know—I was ready for things to progress to the next level, he dropped me! He said he didn't date!"

I continued watching her, and my face must have betrayed my confusion and skepticism. I found it hard to believe that Quinn would ever lead anyone on.

Then again, he did have a history of being technically honest.

Then again, everything he'd told me about his previous Wendell lifestyle indicated that he was never the aggressor; he was never the one doing the chasing.

Then again, Quinn and I didn't talk much about his slamps, even though I was still eager to learn about the logistics.

She, however, misread the cause of my skepticism, because she said, "I know! Right? I couldn't believe it either."

"How long were you two together?"

She pursed her lips, her eyelashes again fluttering. "Like, I don't know, a few weeks."

"And then you told him you wanted to be exclusive?"

"That's right!"

"And he responded by telling you he didn't date."

"Yes, the asshole."

"And that was the first time he'd given you any indication that he didn't date?"

The lip pursing, lash fluttering increased. She *tsked*. "Like I said, he told me there were others when we met. After that, he didn't want to do much talking." With this last statement, she issued what can only be described as a smug, catty look.

I felt that it was extremely misplaced, as she'd just admitted that he didn't want to converse with her.

"Yes. So he said." I nodded.

"What did he say?" Her head whipped toward mine, her eyes narrowed. "What did he say about me?"

I quickly processed whether admitting that he disliked her conversation would be a breech in trust. I decided against framing it quite that way.

"He just said that when you two were acquainted, you hardly ever spoke."

Her mouth fell open and her cheeks flushed. "Oh my. He said that to you?" She looked pleased. This further confused me.

Maybe Quinn was right. Maybe she was crazy.

"I can't believe you're with him after he told you that. Us girls need to look out for each other, and I'm telling you, he will use you and abuse you, and I'm telling you, you are too sweet." Her eyes and the soft, sympathetic shake of her head told me she felt sorry for me. "You're a sweet girl. You need to get away from him."

"Looking at this objectively, if you don't mind, may I just summarize what you've said? This will help me understand."

"Go ahead. I know this must be hard. Go ahead if talking about it will help."

"Thank you." I gave her a small smile because she seemed like a nice person. But I wanted to reiterate the facts so I could make a determination on her level of crazy. "When you and Quinn first got together, he told you he was with other women. Then, the two of you engaged in very little conversation. Then, later, when you told him that you wanted to be exclusive, he responded that he didn't date. Do I have that right?"

"Well, yeah...."

"And that makes him a bad guy because...?"

"Because good guys do not have multiple girls on the hook. Good guys don't do those kinds of things. He is a user."

"But...he's an honest user, yes?"

"Just 'cause he's honest about it doesn't change the fact that he uses people."

"Hmm...you have me there. That's an excellent point. I'll file that away for later contemplation."

Her gaze moved over me again, this time a bit more assessing than before. "I assume he's told you that there are others, right?"

Because I was still marinating in her *user* comment, I responded without thinking of the ramifications of my words. "No, he hasn't. Actually, we're engaged."

She didn't purse her lips, and her eyelashes didn't flutter. In fact, she didn't move at all for a good twelve seconds. Then, as though pulled, her eyes lowered to my left hand, resting on top of my knee.

She blinked just once, as if she expected the ring on my finger to disappear. When it didn't, she breathed, "No shit!"

Her stare moved back to my face, and I struggled to remember the last time I'd seen a person so shocked.

"Oh my God...." she said, then she repeated it with varying pitch and inflection. "Oh my *God*. Oh. My. God."

"Do you...need a glass of something?" I offered, because she looked truly distressed.

"You're his fiancée?"

I nodded. "Yes."

"And you know that I used to *have sex with* Quinn and you're in here patching up my dress and calmly discussing my relationship with him."

"Well...yes."

She stared at me, her expression complete befuddlement. "Aren't you jealous? Pissed off?"

"Jealous of what?" I titled my head to the side, tried to think back over our conversation to determine what part of it should inspire jealousy. "Because Quinn had sex with women before we met? I'm glad that he did. It's provided him with a great deal of useful life skills."

Useful life skills is how I decided to refer to his talents in the bedroom...and airplane, and desk, and shower, and bathtub, and et cetera.

"You should be pissed because...." she started, stopped, then sighed. "I guess I don't know."

I gave her a small smile. "Quinn's relationship with individuals from his past doesn't need to have any bearing on my interactions with the same individuals now and in the future. You needed help.

I like to help. You're a nice person."

Her blue eyes moved over my face and her painted mouth tugged to the side. "You're a nice person, too. You're too good for him."

"We're good for each other," I countered softly and stood. "Thank you for answering my questions. I've never met one of his past sl...um...one of his previous relationships. I really enjoyed our discussion."

"Wait a minute." She rummaged through her clutch and took out a thin plastic card. "I'm Niki. Here, this is my business card. I work for a modeling agency. Give me a call if you're ever interested in doing some work on the side or ever need anything or..." she shrugged "...just want to talk."

"Thank you, Niki. I'm Janie. I hope you don't mind, but I need to put this in my bodice. I didn't bring a purse."

She laughed lightly, her eyes merry, and shook her head. "I don't mind in the least! Just don't forget it's in there."

CHAPTER 8

Quinn

JANIE WAS QUIET.

She'd been quiet for most of the night. I could see that she was deep in her own thoughts; she seemed to be working through a problem.

I hoped it didn't have anything to do with crazy Niki.

Dan and Steven left us in the lobby. Janie and I took the private elevator to our suite. She was silent and stood off to one side.

As soon as the doors opened, she exited, kicked off her shoes, and walked to the bedroom. I did an automatic sweep of the outer room while I loosened my tie and took off my jacket. I trailed her into the bedroom and hovered at the door.

She was standing with her back to the full-length mirror and her neck twisted toward it. She was trying to unfasten the twenty or so buttons that held the top of her dress together.

"Let me do that." I went to her before she could say no and pushed her hair over one shoulder, grazing my fingertips down her spine. She stiffened then relaxed under my hands. I heard her sigh.

"Thank you." Her head fell forward and I began undoing her dress.

We were quiet as I worked the buttons from their loops. I stole glances of her profile in the mirror and fought the urge to lift up her skirt, cup her bottom. Maybe bend her over the loveseat tucked into a corner of the room....

"Quinn."

I blinked, found her watching me in the mirror.

"Yes?"

She turned to face me, holding the top of her dress to her chest to keep it from falling to the floor. Her eyes moved between mine, then she said. "I don't like you how exploit my weaknesses."

I frowned, watching her. I hoped she'd continue without me having to ask her to explain. But she didn't, so I asked, "I exploit your weaknesses?"

"Yes, you do, Quinn. You know I'm easy to distract, and so, when you don't want me to ask you questions about a topic or probe too deeply, you distract me."

"Janie…you hide your underwear in my suitcase so I will think you wear black lace panties all day."

"So? What does that have to do with anything?"

"You do the same thing."

She frowned at me. Her frown was thoughtful, not troubled. I could see her analyzing my words.

Finally, she nodded. "Okay. You've got me there. But can I ask a favor?"

"Anything." My attention moved from her face to the sagging dress she was clutching to her chest. I fit my hands in hers and lifted them away, and the gown crumpled to the floor.

This made me smile.

"When I ask you about a topic that is important and that might impact my desire to continue our relationship, you need to tell me the truth and not distract me."

I frowned again, but quickly wiped all expression from my face. "I promise."

Holding her hands, I helped her step out of the circle of the dress and released her so that she could bend to pick it up. I balled my hands into fists instead of grabbing her from behind—because I sensed this conversation hadn't reached its conclusion—and sat on the edge of the bed.

I would wait until she came to me. Or, I would wait until I could wait no longer.

Janie hung up the gown. Then, facing me, she loitered in the doorway of the closet. "Are you aware of the research that says our willingness to trust can be altered by the application of oxytocin?"

She was stunning—long legs, the dramatic slope of her waist, the soft, ample curves of her breasts, which were basically spilling out of the bustier. Fiery red hair framed her porcelain shoulders and face. Her amber eyes were wide and watchful, earnest.

"No," I said, drinking in this vision of her. "I'm not."

"Oxytocin is sometimes called the bonding hormone and is released during pregnancy as well as when a woman breastfeeds. Interestingly, a recent study showed genital tract stimulation also results in increased oxytocin immediately after orgasm."

I swallowed, but tried to keep my expression blank. Janie had learned early in our relationship to cite peer reviewed research relating to sexuality if she wanted to get me hot. It always worked.

It was working now.

"Interesting." It was interesting. I licked my lips, let my eyes wander over the curves of her body, now highlighted by the red and black bustier, and framed by her thigh-high stockings.

Janie twisted her hair into a loose braid and slowly crossed the room to stand in front of me. "Quinn, do you think I trust you so much simply because you've given me so many orgasms?"

My eyes flickered to hers and found them serious, questioning.

"I hope that's not the reason," I answered soberly, but couldn't stop myself any longer. I needed to touch her. I reached for her waist and pulled her forward so that she was standing between my legs.

"Quinn, I need to talk to you. We need to talk." Her hands settled on my shoulders for balance.

I fingered one of the straps on her corset that held her stockings in place. "What do you want to talk about?"

"I want to talk about the private accounts."

I stared unseeingly at her lace-clad stomach. The room went completely silent, and I held my breath. I absurdly wished that we were back in the tower of London and she was tied to the rack.

The last time I was scared was when Janie showed up at one of my vacant apartments and found me shirtless and barefoot with her bitch sister—the same bitch sister who pissed all over my shoes then stuck a lit cigarette into my shirt necessitating the removal of both articles of clothing. I then ran after Janie and into her apartment just seconds before three men with guns broke down the door.

I'd been scared of losing her, and now, that visceral fear was hitting me again, gnawing my insides. But this time her crazy sister wasn't to blame. I was.

My chest felt tight. I needed a drink. More than that, I needed a minute to think.

I set her away and stood from the bed, crossed to the wet-bar and reached for the first available bottle.

"Quinn?" Her voice behind me was tentative, uncertain. I didn't like how it sounded.

"Do you want something to drink?" I poured myself two shots in a single tumbler then glanced at the label; it was scotch.

"No. Thank you." She crossed the room and stood by my side. I felt her eyes on me. Instead of returning her gaze, I kept mine fastened to the glass.

She glanced from me to the tumbler. "Are you going to answer me?"

"You haven't asked a question."

"Will you please tell me about the private accounts?"

"No."

"No?"

I nodded then swallowed half of the scotch.

"Quinn...." She hesitated, then covered my hand with hers. "Please talk to me about this."

I huffed a laugh—felt the bitterness of it through the burn of alcohol coating my throat. "Janie, it's really better if you don't know."

"I don't like that answer."

I cut my eyes to hers, and whatever she saw in my expression made her flinch, which made me curse.

I turned to face her, rested my hip against the sidebar, and tried to ignore the fact that she was wearing nothing but a black and red lacy bustier with matching panties, and thigh-highs.

Tried and failed.

Faced with temptation, I kept my arms crossed over my chest so I wouldn't touch her, and gritted my teeth. I needed focus.

"Why the sudden interest?" I wasn't going to lie, but I didn't want to tell Janie more than she wanted or needed to know.

"Why the evasion?" She lifted her chin as she countered my question. She was sexy as fuck when we battled wits, and I felt a primal urge to bite the tops of her breasts. Then she added, "You're hiding something from me, which feels really close to technical honesty."

We exchanged stares, my jaw still ticking. Unable to help myself, I lifted my hand to her shoulder and traced the line of her collarbone with my thumb down to the slope of her chest.

"You're right. I am."

"Why? Don't you trust me?"

I did trust her. If it came down to it, I would tell her everything and hope she could see past the man I used to be to the man I was trying to become. Part of me reasoned that the entire conversation was irrelevant since I was ending my association with those people.

I didn't answer right away. Instead, I shifted a step closer. She was forced to tilt her head back to maintain eye contact.

I said, "We're getting married."

"Yes. We are." She lifted her hands to my chest, placed her right palm flat over my heart, and gripped the front of my shirt with her left. "And that's why I need you to trust me, completely. History and classical fiction are polluted with story after story, example after example of the downfall of relationships because one or both parties didn't speak openly, or hid a secret that didn't need to be hidden. In fact, I am given to understand that the majority of popular fiction revolves around avoidable misunderstandings as a central theme. I can name ten instances of related Greek tragedies."

"Please don't."

"I will, if you don't start talking."

My hands were on her waist, and I abruptly realized that my grip was likely bordering on painful and had already crossed the line to aggressive. I forced myself to loosen my fingers, but pulled her more completely against me and turned her so her back was to the bar.

I briefly considered using my tie to bind her wrists and my belt to immobilize her feet. If she couldn't leave me, if she were physically incapable, I would breathe easier.

These thoughts I filed away under *crazy* and *desperate*.

Instead, I mentally prepared for her reaction to the truth. I didn't know how else to be other than evasive or blunt.

With my heart in my throat, I said, "I use the intelligence I gather while I provide security to persuade wealthy and powerful people. I use the information to persuade them to make good decisions."

Janie's eyes narrowed and stared straight ahead; she lost focus as she internalized and examined my statement. She was silent for several long seconds, and I moved my knee between her legs to press my torso more completely against hers. I thought about re-examining the *crazy* and *desperate* file.

At length her eyes flickered back to mine. "You blackmail them."

I shrugged but kept my attention fixed on her features, looking for clues as to how she was going to react.

"For money?" She sounded like the words choked her. "Do you blackmail them for money?"

"No. I use the information for influence."

"What does that mean, influence? To do what?"

"Real change comes from knowing the wrong people *and* the right people." I watched her lips part in surprise. I wanted to kiss her. Instead, I continued. "I make sure information goes to the people who can do the most good with it."

"So…the police?"

"Not always." I didn't know how much she wanted to know, and I wasn't sure how much I should tell her. Therefore, instead of telling her that I'd sometimes used criminal organizations as a means to administer justice, I answered only the questions she asked.

Her eyes lost focus as she worked to grasp the truth. "That's why everything is behind those steel doors at the office. That's why the private security servers are not connected to the Internet and behind encrypted security. That's why you won't use open source development apps."

"That's part of the reason." My tone was flat. I'd told her the bulk of it; now it was just about clarifying the details. "The other is because part of the security we offer to private clients is to hack into their personal systems, cell phones, and bank accounts to assess security risks."

She blinked at me and her eyes moved to my mouth. Her next words were full of dawning comprehension, yet lacked judgment. "You store their private information on your servers. They pay you to keep them safe, and you use their secrets against them."

I almost laughed. She was so smart, yet frequently missed the obvious.

Her eyes cut to mine—they were without emotion, but far from emotionless. "This is not legal, Quinn. Does Steven know? Why would you do this? Quinn…." She shook her head, her eyebrows drawing together. "After what happened to your brother, why wouldn't you turn any information over to the police?"

I absorbed the blow, the reminder of my culpability in Des's murder. I met and held her challenging and assessing glare straight on and did my best to explain my actions, but was careful not to defend them.

"These aren't petty criminals, Janie. These are powerful people. I could do more good and make a bigger difference using them and their information than I could if these people were behind bars for tax evasion and recreational drug use. They would just be replaced, and I'd have no leverage."

"Leverage to do what? You said you use the information to persuade them to make good decisions? What kind of good decisions?"

I thought of some examples. Many were selfish, like using powerful families to administer revenge against the crime organization responsible for my brother's death. I hadn't stopped until that organization had been completely dismantled and all the heads of the business had been severed—literally or figuratively. I didn't care which.

Others were less selfish, like using a large campaign contributor to put pressure on a senator. In this case, the pressure was meant to hold a particular CEO accountable for the pilfering of employee pension funds.

Although, that too had been selfish in a way, because my secretary Betty's husband had worked for the company and lost everything, all of his retirement. I supposed it was also revenge.

This didn't cover the few people whose information I'd immediately passed through to the FBI or CIA, because their crimes were beyond reprehensible.

I finally said, "It's complicated. I had a big part in dismantling the organization responsible for my brother's death, but it was all about putting pressure on the right people."

She was frowning now, but she didn't try to move away. "What concerns me is that you got involved in the first place, especially after what happened with your brother."

"Of course I'm involved." The words escaped before I could stop them or the flare of temper. "The only way to make a real change is by *getting involved*, not by burying your head in the sand."

She flinched, her eyes darted away, and her eyelashes fluttered. I silently reprimanded myself and inhaled a deep breath, my hands moving to her arms.

When I spoke next, my words were measured and carefully calm. "Yes, Janie, my hands are dirty—because I've been cleaning up messes."

"What kind of messes?"

"All kinds," I said through gritted teeth. I didn't want to tell her what kinds of messes, because sometimes you had to prioritize one mess over another. When this happened, someone always lost, and it was usually someone who was innocent.

She pressed her lips together and swallowed, the lovely, pale column of her neck working with the effort. Still avoiding my eyes, she said, "You're not Batman, Quinn."

"Like hell I'm not."

"Really?" Her gaze lifted to mine again. "Are you telling me you've never personally profited from these business ventures?"

"Yes, I've profited. And if Batman had been doing it right, he would have profited too."

Her mouth fell open and her forehead wrinkled with disbelief. "You can't justify using people for gain."

"I'm not. It's not about the gain, Janie." I shook her arms a little and I inwardly cringed at the edge in my voice. "Do you believe— knowing what you do about me, the part I had in Des getting shot—that I was just going to let these people walk away?"

"Is this revenge?"

"In a word? Yes. Or at least it started that way."

I watched her for a long moment, studied her expression and body language. To my surprise, she didn't look repulsed. She looked sad and confused.

As much as I wanted to bind her to me, tie her up and restrain her, I knew I was going to have to let her go eventually.

She needed to make a decision: either I was worth the investment, or I wasn't. Either I was redeemable, or I wasn't.

I inhaled through my nose and stepped away, her hands fell from my chest. Losing the warmth of her, it felt like I'd abandoned a part of me. I left it with Janie to do with as she saw fit. For safekeeping, or to throw away.

Reaching around her, I grabbed the half-empty glass of scotch and swallowed the remainder, then moved to her side to refill it.

"What is it now? It started as revenge, which—by the way—is just as well documented as being a central theme in Greek tragedy as avoidable misunderstandings. But what is it now?" She asked; she'd wrapped her arms around her middle, like she was holding herself.

"Now…." I glanced at the ceiling. "Now I'm done."

She turned her head to look at me, paused as though processing my words. "You're done? Done with what?"

"I'm done with private clients and playing Batman. I'm getting out of it. That's what the first part of this trip was about. I'm passing over my UK clients to new firms."

"Is that why I've had three guards with me the entire time we've been here?"

"No. That's about me needing to know you're safe."

"Am I in some kind of danger?"

"I don't believe so." She wasn't, no more than any random person. What I didn't say was, even that small unknown felt like too much.

"Is this going to continue in Chicago? The guards?"

"No. It shouldn't. Some of these people can be...." I searched for the most truthful description of the private clients as a group. "They can be unpredictable, but they're rarely violent. Most of the US group has already been handed off. I'm only keeping a few. Just a small number of clients that are trustworthy, that have nothing to hide."

I met her stare and took another swig of scotch.

"Can you do that? Can you just hand them off?"

"I don't know. But for you, I'm going to try."

Her eyes darted between mine. "For me?"

"I told you, you make me want to be a good guy." Because I couldn't help myself, I placed my hand on her cheek, let my thumb brush against her full bottom lip. Touching her was torture because I didn't know if she still wanted me.

"Quinn...." She held perfectly still, staring at me with her large amber eyes.

The thickness in my voice betrayed how badly *I* wanted *her*, but I wasn't going to tie her up. "I'm trying to be a good guy."

CHAPTER 9

Janie

"OH THANK GOD!" Steven threw himself into the plush leather chair of the private jet and stroked the armrests lovingly. "I've missed you. Did you get my flowers? Please let us never be separated again."

I watched through narrowed eyes, though I couldn't help my smile, as Steven spoke to the interior of the plane as though it were a lover and not a 46,000-pound piece of aviation machinery.

"You took one commercial flight, Steven. One."

"Shhh!" he pressed his finger to his lips and loud whispered, "He'll hear you."

I glanced to my right and left. "Who will hear me?"

"Manuel, the plane."

"You've named the plane Manuel?"

"Don't ruin this for me, Janie. I've been thinking about this moment for over a week. Just let me have it." His fingers flexed into the leather, his eyes beseeching.

Smiling at his silliness, I decided to give him a moment of privacy with the plane and walked to the back of the cabin to use the facilities before takeoff. Total airtime for our Heathrow to Chicago Midway flight would be just over nine hours, and I liked using the bathroom when I didn't have to fight against turbulence to stay upright.

I was preoccupied with making a mental note to discover the brand of soap stocked in the lavatory when I exited and collided with Quinn.

The man who'd just admitted to me last night that he blackmailed people in order to bend them to his will.

My fiancé.

The man I was going to marry in less than three months.

"Oh—sorry." I reached for and held on to the lapels of his jacket even though I was in no danger of losing my balance. I did this for four reasons.

First, we'd gone to sleep last night with silence between us and nothing resolved. He'd shut down, and I'd turtled into the cozy corner of trivial facts. Rather than actually think about the ramifications of his admission, I'd let my mind wander.

Second, he'd barely touched me. In fact, he'd avoided me in bed, turning away from me while we slept.

Then he'd left me this morning and hadn't returned. He also hadn't returned my phone calls, even when I used my cell phone. Therefore, having him there, in front of me now, within my reach, made me want to superglue myself to his body.

Lastly, he smelled good—like, really good—much better than the soap in the lavatory.

His hands automatically lifted to my upper arms as though to steady me, and his tenebrous blue eyes settled on mine then darted away.

"No problem," he said.

My heart pinged with hurt because he was so aloof. His hands fell away. I pressed my lips together and waited for him to return his eyes to mine.

After a long moment of me gripping his jacket front and him standing there like a statue, he lifted his hands to mine and tried to pry them from his lapels, but I held on tight.

"Janie, I need to get in there."

"Okay," I said, but I didn't move out of the doorway. "Where did you go this morning?"

"For a run then…on a ride."

"On a motorcycle?" My heart ping-morphed into a heart seize. I knew he liked riding, but—irrationally—it made me anxious each time he did it. "Where did you find the bike?"

Finally, his eyes met mine. Though his features were stone, his gaze was piercing and heated. "I borrowed one."

He stopped trying to remove my fingers from his jacket and, instead, he held out his hands between us, palms up, showing me that they were covered in a layer of dirt and grease.

"I need to wash my hands. They're dirty."

"Oh." I took in his appearance and realized that he was uncharacteristically disheveled. His cheeks and nose were pink, his hair was windblown—which meant he'd been riding without a helmet—and his suit lacked its typical sleek meticulousness. Also, he was wearing no tie.

"I got some on your sleeve…" He was frowning at me and I followed his gaze to the upper arm of my white shirt. His hand had left a greasy imprint when we'd collided.

"Oh," I said again then returned my attention to his face. He was staring at the stain, and he looked frustrated and angry.

On a sudden impulse, I leaned forward and pressed three kisses onto his white dress shirt—one on the collar and two near the placket of buttons. I leaned back to study my lip-work, pleased that I'd chosen to wear a shocking shade of pink that morning.

"There," I said, touching the new stain near his neck. "Now we're even."

He glanced down at himself, his eyebrows pulling low, then he lifted just his eyes to mine. I was pleased to see that the earlier frustration had ebbed. However, in its place his gaze had grown sharp with a familiar intensity. My heart and stomach tried to out-flutter each other.

Quinn nodded once, slowly. Other than his eyes, his expression betrayed nothing. But then his hands came to my hips, and he walked me backward into the lavatory.

And I let him.

Once we were inside, he closed the door behind him and turned me so that my bottom was against the sink.

"What are we doing?" I asked, all at once breathless, even as I reached for the front of his pants and unbuckled his belt.

Quinn brushed his lips against mine as his hands slipped under the hem of my skirt and hiked it to my waist.

"We're having make-up sex," he growled.

Then he kissed me. I moaned because it felt so good and right, and we hadn't kissed in over twenty-four hours—not since before the ball for the phantom charity, not since we'd gone lingerie shopping.

His mouth separated from mine. He licked and bit a path over my jaw to my ear. I tried tilting to the side to give him better access, but my head connected with the paper towel dispenser.

"Were we fighting?" I asked, though I had no idea how he was going to answer because I was violently pressing his face into my neck—because I just could not get enough of his mouth on my skin. My other hand reached into his boxers and gripped his length, my hips rocking forward in answer to his arousal.

He gripped my waist and lifted me onto the counter. This caused the button for the faucet to be pressed which caused the water to turn on. I felt the spray against my backside and I squeaked.

He lifted his head from my neck, his eyes dazed and questioning, his breathing labored. "What? What is it?"

"Nothing. Kiss me. And take off your pants." I reached for the band of my white cotton underwear and wiggled my bottom until I could pull them down my legs.

Quinn took a step back and pushed his pants to the floor. I reached for him as I tried to rid myself of sensibly breathable fabric and caught him smirking when he spied granny panties around one of my ankles.

"Nice underwear, darling," he hissed, likely because I held his erection in my hand and I was stroking it, stroking him, coaxing him toward my center.

"Thank you. It's also a socially responsible choice, if you recall."

Quinn lifted his eyes to mine and his face split with a smile, which quickly ebbed and became something else entirely—something beautiful and visceral and reckless—as he entered me. He sucked in a breath, his forehead resting against mine, his hands gripping my bottom, his eyes closing as though he were overwhelmed by his senses.

"We're getting married," he said. It sounded like an order.

I nodded. "Yes," I said, my legs wrapping around his, my breath hitching.

He opened his eyes and moved his hips, setting a slow, tortuous rhythm. "And when we get home, you're going to put on that corset from last night, and I'm going to take you over the sofa."

I moaned at the image his words conjured, tried to encourage him to increase his pace, but only succeeded in getting myself hot and bothered and breathless.

"Say you love me." One of his hands slipped into my shirt, under my bra, and cupped me, squeezed, kneaded in time with his thrusts. I didn't care that his hands were making me dirty.

"I love you."

This earned me an increased tempo and a pass of his thumb over the center of my breast. "Tell me you trust me."

I felt my brain clear as our eyes met and I stroked my hand down the side of his face; he turned his lips into the palm of my hand and kissed it.

"Quinn, I trust you."

"Tell me I make you fearless." He whispered, still holding my gaze.

"You make me fearless." I didn't hesitate.

My fingers reached around his neck and pressed against the back of his head until his mouth fit over mine. My legs trembled with the beginning of my orgasm and I arched my back while my hips simultaneously tilted forward. He must've sensed I was close, because he shifted his position, giving me more of himself.

My heels pressed ruthlessly into his thighs, my nails dug into his jacket over his shoulders, and he captured my scream—because I was a screamer—with his mouth.

Then, as I tumbled back to earth and he came with a tense groan, I returned the favor and worshiped his mouth with mine.

I tried to impart with my kiss and with the eagerness of my body all that I felt for him. I hoped he knew that I believed in him, that I believed in us.

Quinn and I stayed like that—wrapped in each other, kissing—for as long as possible. But then, the inevitable knock sounded at the door accompanied by a polite clearing of the throat.

"Mr. Sullivan...uh, sir, we're almost ready to take off whenever you, uh, and...whenever everyone is in their seats."

I recognized the voice of Donna, the flight attendant, and heard her retreating steps. Both sounds pulled me back to reality and brought my surroundings into focus. A substantial blush instantly claimed my chest, neck, cheeks, and ears. I was sure the top of my head was bright red. Good thing I wasn't bald.

Before Quinn could speak, Dan's voice whispered from the other side of the door. "Just so you know, we've all formed a high-five line outside the bathroom."

I buried my face in Quinn's neck and moaned my mortification.

I felt Quinn's rumbly chuckle and his kiss on my hair before he responded to Dan. "If you try to high-five me, I'll punch you in the throat."

"The high-five line is for Janie, not for you, Dummy."

Quinn pressed his lips together to keep from laughing, and I was sure that if no one had died yet from awkwardness, then my autopsy report would be the first of its kind.

"I'm kidding. I can feel her embarrassment from out here." Dan continued to whisper. "Listen, I have new clothes for you both hanging just outside the door along with two towels, and I've drawn the curtain so you can't be seen when you open the door. I just spoke to the pilot. They've moved us back in the take-off queue. You've got fifteen more minutes, and you're welcome."

I closed my eyes, sent up a silent prayer that Dan would find someone worthy of his awesomeness, and snuggled closer to Quinn's body.

This always happened when we made love. I always seemed to forget where I was. I didn't think of myself as an exhibitionist, nor did I take any pleasure in the possibility of being caught. Rather, when I was tangled up in Quinn, I existed in a blissful alternate universe, and everything else just…ceased.

Quinn grabbed several paper towels in quick succession. He shifted away, but continued to support my forehead on his shoulder. He pressed the paper towels between my legs and waited until I took over, then he threaded his fingers through my hair.

As usual, they got stuck in the curling snakes, and he used the leverage to lift my face from his neck. His eyes skated over my features before pinning me in place, and I saw that his expression was dreamy and content, one of wonder and worship.

"How do you do that?" His question was quiet, reverent.

"Do what?"

"How do you make everything better?"

My forehead wrinkled as we studied each other. "What did I make better?"

"After last night, I thought you…." He exhaled, frowned, shook his head. Then his mouth pulled to the side in a barely there smile. "You make me better."

I returned his smile and leaned forward an inch to kiss his nose. "Quinn, we're going to settle this. Tomorrow, at home, we're going to discuss everything until we both feel good about it. And then, you're going to help me decide what shade of ferns we're going to use for our centerpieces."

He blinked. "Ferns?"

"Yes. Ferns are much more environmentally friendly than flowers. Also, there are hundreds of varieties, and they come in a vast array of colors."

My smile grew because his eyes widened with alarm.

CHAPTER 10

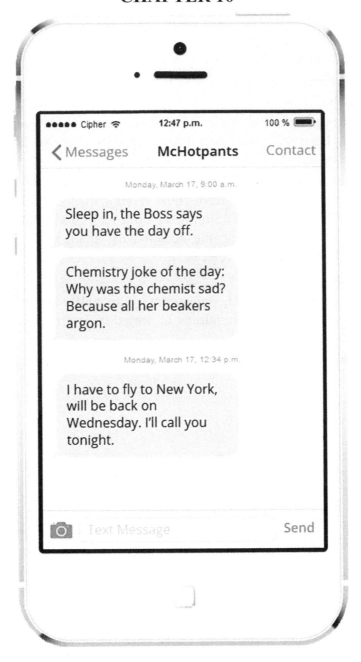

IT WAS TUESDAY night, and nothing was settled.

We arrived home late Sunday night. He carried me from the limo to the apartment to the bed, and undressed me while I lay complicit and dozing. I awoke Monday mid-morning to the chiming of my cell phone. Quinn must have found it in my luggage, charged it, and placed it on my bedside table at some point.

I gave the noisy device a dirty look and cursed it. Nevertheless, I glanced at the screen then bolted upright in bed. The alert was for three text messages from Quinn. The initial texts sent back-to-back at 9:00 a.m. made me smile.

The third message made me frown.

Part of me wondered if the New York trip was just a way to avoid discussing the wedding plans. On the flight home, his eyes had glazed over whenever I tried to show him pictures of centerpiece ferns and groomsmen tuxedos.

Regardless, Quinn had called briefly from New York on Monday night, just long enough for me to determine that he was dead tired and needed to go to sleep. He also texted then called me Tuesday morning for a quick *I love you* and *I miss you* that made my knees weak and my brain witless.

Therefore, nothing was resolved.

Yes, we'd attacked each other in the bathroom of the airplane.

Yes, the oxytocin it released into my system had gone a long way toward re-affirming our bond within my brain. At some point I would have to sort through how much of the bond was brain chemistry and how much of it was corporeal. For now, I was going to assume it was mostly corporeal.

But, no, we hadn't yet talked through the ramifications of Quinn's admission about the private clients.

Instead of obsessing over whether or not I'd displayed good judgment by seducing my fiancé rather than talking through our issues *then* seducing my fiancé, I decided that I would focus my energy on sorting through the situation as it currently stood and define a list of action items.

First, I was going to write down all of my concerns and questions related to Quinn's admission and our impending marriage.

Then, when he came back from New York, we were going to sit down and review all the concerns and questions.

After that, I was pretty sure I was going to seduce him again.

And, lastly, I was going to force him to go through an entire wedding magazine and discuss whether the cake should be white with white frosting or chocolate with white frosting.

One thing I was sure of based on every wedding cake picture I'd seen was that wedding cakes should have white frosting.

But first I had to break the news of our engagement to my knitting group.

I decided to show up late to knit night for a few reasons. Mostly, I wanted everyone to find out at the same time rather than one at a time as they arrived. I would tell them as a group, they could have their reaction, and then we could move on to other topics rather than dragging it out.

I had no idea what to expect.

Therefore, I emailed Marie from work that I would be one hour late. I stopped by a shop to pick up two extra bottles of red wine, mentally rehearsed what I would say, and worried a little that they wouldn't be supportive of my decision. After all, Quinn and I had only been together for a few months.

Turns out, I needn't have worried.

As soon as Marie opened the door to her apartment, I was greeted with a very loud, cheerful chorus of "SURPRISE!"

They were all standing in the small entryway wearing hats and blowing noisemakers, and smiling at me like I'd just told them I'd solved world hunger.

I opened my mouth to respond, but didn't get to do anything other than puff out a breath as Elizabeth pulled me through the door and I was surrounded by a six-woman group hug.

"I'm so happy for you!"

"Let's see the ring!"

"Give her a minute."

"How did he do it?"

"Did you bring us anything from London?"

"Nice shoes! Can I borrow them?"

They ushered me into Marie's crowded apartment, all speaking at once, and I started to laugh—and cry.

Elizabeth, the first to notice, shushed the group and pressed my hand between hers. "Janie? What's wrong? Are you okay?"

Through my tears and laughter, I managed to splutter, "It's just...you just all...." I sniffled and pressed my lips together to keep my chin from wobbling as my gaze moved over their happy, slightly perplexed, somewhat worried faces. "I was nervous about telling you and you already know and it's such a relief and you're all so happy for me and I am just so lucky that you're all my friends."

"Aww." Ashley's arms encircled my shoulders from behind. "Of course we're happy for you!"

"We all are," Fiona added, giving me a sincere smile. "You deserve every good thing."

"And we brought presents!" Sandra's eyes were huge and excited, and she wagged her eyebrows as she added, "Spoiler alert, I bought you edible underwear. Also, further spoiler alert—they're a matching his-and-hers set."

Everyone burst out laughing, and Kat covered her face—which had turned beet red.

"Come in and sit down." Marie pushed me to the sofa while everyone else settled in around me. "We have champagne and lemon drops. I didn't know which one you preferred."

"A lemon drop sounds great, and I brought wine too." I held up my bag, which was promptly confiscated and passed to Marie.

The barrage of questions began again, and I held my hands up. "Wait, before I tell you the how and when, what do you already know? And how did you all know?"

Elizabeth sat forward. "It was me. Remember a few weeks ago when I met you and Quinn at the bathroom fixtures shop?"

"The one on West Lake Street? With all the sinks on the wall?" Fiona asked. She added with a faraway look, "I love that place."

"Yes, that's the one. Well, Quinn told me about his intentions then. I helped him pick out the rings in exchange for a heads-up when he asked."

"So, Quinn told you?" I was astonished, both that Quinn and Elizabeth had worked together, and also that Elizabeth had been able to keep the proposal a secret for so long. Then again, even though we were technically roommates, we hardly saw each other anymore. Since moving into the building just over a month ago, I usually spent most of my days and nights at Quinn's place.

"Yes. He texted me Friday at, like, one in the morning—which I guess would have been seven in the morning in London."

"What did he say?" Ashley asked. "You never did show us the text."

Elizabeth rolled her eyes and said in a droll tone, "All he texted was *it's done*. Of course I knew what he was talking about, but a few more details would have been nice."

"How did he do it, Janie?" Sandra bounced in her seat next to me. "Leave nothing out. We want all the juicy details."

So I told them.

When I came to the part about the glass case filled with rings, Elizabeth chimed in.

"That was my idea! He came across an estate sale—or, I think his secretary did—where some ancient family in Scotland was auctioning off all their jewels. He had over two hundred to choose from, so it was hard to narrow them down to one. Do you like it?"

I nodded and held my hand out so everyone could see. "Yes, it's perfect."

"He thought so, too. I narrowed it down to five, and he picked out that one. I'm so glad you like it."

"I love it," I admitted. "I feel somewhat uncomfortable about loving a material thing so much. I worry it's unhealthy."

"More than your shoes?" Ashley asked, "I know how much you love your shoes, because I love your shoes."

I responded without hesitation, "More than my shoes."

"Whoa." Ashley's eyes were huge. "That's a lot."

"Yeah," I agreed.

"Makes sense to me." Fiona's words caught my attention. "It's a symbol, the ring. Really, it's him you love. The ring is symbolic of him and everything you are to each other. Of course you love the ring."

"I like that," Kat interjected, a soft smile on her face, her eyes a little dazed. "It's so romantic, him taking you to London to see the Crown Jewels, then giving you a priceless, antique ring from a noble Scottish family." She sighed as she leaned back in her chair.

"Is that how you want to be proposed to?" Marie asked Kat, handing me my lemon drop and placing a pitcher full of liquid happiness on the coffee table.

Kat's eyes lost some of their dazzle. "Honestly, I'd settle for someone who's honest, doesn't rely on emotional blackmail to solve arguments, and treats me like I matter more than who my family is. I sometimes wonder if guys like that exist."

"They do." Fiona reached over and squeezed her leg. "You just need to find your own version of Quinn, but maybe not as grumpy, and nicer to your friends."

I was about to ask Kat to explain her concerns, as I had no idea who her family was, but Sandra spoke before I was able to.

"Everyone be silent so we can hear the rest of Janie's story!" Sandra commanded, waving her hands through the air. She then turned to me, her elbow on her knee, her chin propped in her hand, and a giant grin plastered on her face. "Okay, go on. What happened next?"

I continued with my story—about how Quinn was called away and how I was led to the torture device room—and Ashley guessed that he hadn't actually been called away for a phone call, but rather to get the ring out of the case so he could propose.

This theory was met with nods of approval and more shushing from Sandra.

Then, I told them about the rack, and the room broke into chaos of laughter, gasps, high fives, and whooping.

"That sly dawg!" Ashley giggled, slapped her knee, and lifted her drink toward me. "What an opportunist. I love Quinn."

"That's so amazingly awesome. That's how I want it to happen. I want to be on the rack when I'm proposed to. Someone make a note!" Sandra hugged me as she made this assertion.

Elizabeth rolled her eyes. "Of course. Of course he proposes while you're incapacitated. Typical McHotpants."

"I think it's sexy." Marie clinked her glass with Ashley's. "I like his entrepreneurial spirit. Maybe if David had asked me to marry him while I was tied up, I might have given him a different answer."

Her statement shocked me. David was Marie's boyfriend and they'd been dating for more than five years. I was tangentially surprised to learn that he'd asked her to marry him; this was the first I'd heard of it. Again tangentially, I wondered whether Marie was at all interested in marriage; she seemed to value her independence above everything else.

Fiona merely shook her head and chuckled to herself. Kat gaped at me with wide eyes, obviously stunned.

Rather than asking Marie to clarify about David, I finished my story. I told them about the dinner on the river Thames and our agreement to have a big wedding, but I left out the frantic tent interlude because it felt like that would be oversharing.

"He wanted to get married today? As in, less than a week after he proposed?" Fiona frowned at me, perplexed.

"That was my reaction too. And, as it turns out, he's in New York right now, called away on a trip, and we would've had to postpone the ceremony in any case."

"I'm confused." Marie leaned forward and withdrew a knitting work in progress from her bag. "Let me see if I have this right: he wanted to get married immediately, you then negotiated the timeline, and now you're getting married in three months? And you insisted on a big wedding?"

"Yes, except it's two months and twenty six days."

"I'm really surprised." Elizabeth reached for my now empty lemon drop glass and refilled it. "I didn't think you'd want a big wedding."

"It's not that I want a big wedding; it's that I think Quinn and I need to experience something other than dating bliss before we get married."

"I don't understand." Fiona glanced from me to Elizabeth then back again. "What does that mean?"

"It means we're having a big wedding so we can be miserable together before we're happy together. We've never been miserable before. How can you make a decision to marry someone if you've never been miserable with them?"

"Janie...." Fiona's face scrunched in confusion. "Happiness is not fleeting if you accept it. But if you keep looking for ways to postpone your own happiness, it will always be elusive."

I frowned, blinked at her. "I'm not trying to postpone my happiness. I'm trying to make sure we're solid before we make promises."

"So...." Elizabeth raised a single eyebrow at me, her chin dipping to her chest. "Are you going to do that thing where you stop having sex prior to the ceremony?"

"Elizabeth...." Fiona's voice held a note of warning. "Be nice."

Elizabeth gave Fiona her very best *Who, me? I'm completely innocent!* look. I knew that look well. It didn't work on me anymore, and considering Fiona's stern eyebrows, I didn't think it was working on Fiona either.

"No, really. It's a real thing." Marie nodded. "Elizabeth's wanting to torture Quinn aside, I read an article about it in *Cosmopolitan*. Since so many couples are having sex before marriage these days, abstaining while planning the ceremony is supposed to be a way to make the wedding night special."

"By making the bride and groom go insane?" Fiona asked, glancing away from her knitting. "Planning a wedding is stressful enough without having to abstain from physical intimacy."

My mind snagged on the idea, picked it up, turned it over, and began assessing it from all angles. Then, my mind ran with it.

Rather than belt out, *Eureka!* I asked without thinking, "Do you really think abstinence would dramatically increase the level of stress prior to the wedding?"

Fiona's eyes narrowed into suspicious slits as she studied me. "Janie, you make it sound like you *want* the wedding planning to be stressful."

"I do," I admitted, nodding emphatically. "I do want it to be stressful. Quinn and I have only been together for five months. Like I said, we have to fit years of the worst into approximately two months so we can both say our vows with our eyes open."

Fiona stared at me, her mouth agape, her expression plainly shocked. "That's craziness. You're crazy, Janie. I can't…I can't even…."

Elizabeth laughed. "I've never seen Fiona speechless before."

"Well, I think it's a good idea." Sandra shrugged and lifted her chin in my direction. "I can't imagine marrying someone I've only known for five or six months. Good for you, making him wait another twelve weeks before tying the knot, and you're a smart woman for introducing some hardship—even if it's contrived— and being honest about your concerns. Granted, this is coming from the girl who makes all her first dates cry and whose longest relationship was in high school…so…grain of salt."

"I'm afraid to voice an opinion," Ashley volunteered, her eyes focused on the scarf she was knitting. "On one hand, I see your point, Janie, and I think your plan is very pragmatic; it would make logical sense if feelings weren't involved. On the other hand, you two crazy kids are in love with each other. Maybe it's the romantic in me, but applying logic to love is like buttering a pig before you slaughter it."

"You have a romantic in you?" Sandra teased, fighting a smile.

"Yes I do, Freud," Ashley responded, issuing Sandra a look of mock dissatisfaction. "I just save my love for fictional characters and my knitting group, and God knows why I put up with you."

"What about you, Kat? What do you think?" Elizabeth nudged Kat with her elbow, prompting her out of her silence.

"What do I think?"

Elizabeth nodded then turned her sweater to begin a new row. "Yeah, what's your take?"

Kat's wide eyes glanced around the room. "Uh…." She cleared her throat then turned her attention to me. "It might sound like a cop-out, Janie, but I think you need to follow your heart. And if your heart is uncertain of Quinn, and as long as you're being honest with him...." She ended the unfinished thought with a shrug, and her soft brown eyes told me she'd support me in whatever I decided.

"It's not that I'm uncertain of him. It's that I want our marriage to be built on a strong foundation. Right now, we've only had good times. We haven't been tested. I haven't been tested."

"Withholding your body for the next several months certainly would be a test for Quinn." Elizabeth gave me an evil grin, even though her words sounded like a warning.

"Well, I wouldn't do it unless he agreed to it." I crossed my arms, my attention shifting to a spot over Elizabeth's shoulder as I thought through how to convince Quinn to go without sex for the next eleven-ish weeks. "If we're going to be together for the rest of our lives, then abstinence for the next three-ish months shouldn't be that big of a deal." After I said the words, I wondered if I could actually last that long without his hands and mouth and...other parts.

"Good luck with that!" Marie shook her head and lifted her glass in my direction. "If you can manage to convince Quinn to go without physical intimacy while you're planning the wedding, then I might hire you as my agent—because your powers of persuasion would obviously be magical."

"I think everyone is overlooking the most important part of this whole situation, which is Janie's insistence that she have a traditional wedding." Sandra glanced around at us, her green eyes wide and serious.

"What is that?" Ashley sighed. "And you better not say bridesmaids dresses because, as much as I love Janie and will wear whatever she tells me to wear, I have never seen a bridesmaid dress that did anything but make the wearer look like Molly Ringwald in that movie *Pretty in Pink*. Was that not the ugliest dress? Why did she think she'd look good in that dress? That didn't make any sense."

"Someone cut her off," Elizabeth said, looking pointedly at Ashley. "I think she's had too much to drink." She moved to take Ashley's glass.

Ashley lifted her knitting needles in a very threatening way. "If you touch my wine, I will stick my Hiya-Hiya circular needle up your nose, and it's one of those extra pointy ones."

Elizabeth backed off, holding her hands up, palms out.

"No, not the dresses—although Ashley makes a good point about the bridesmaid dresses. We really should all sit down and come to a consensus before any decision is made." Sandra spoke with a surprising degree of earnestness regarding the theoretical bridesmaids' attire.

Then, suddenly, her entire expression changed to one of intense excitement. "I'm talking about the bachelorette party. Vegas, baby!"

Part 3: Planning the Wedding

CHAPTER 11

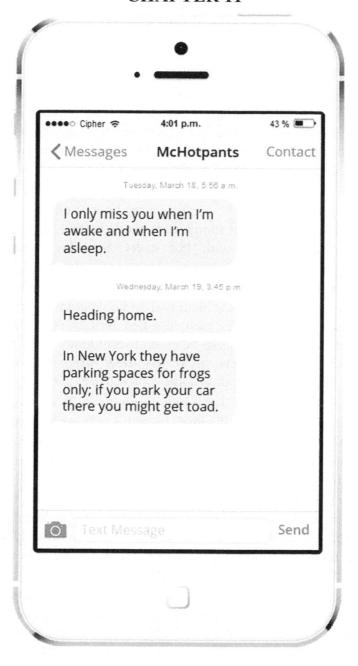

I FOUND AND purchased a three-ring binder wedding planner Wednesday afternoon during lunch.

In addition to the list provided within the planner, I made an additional list of all the Quinn-Janie specific issues and plans that needed to be discussed and settled prior to the wedding.

Of course, the unresolved issues relating to the private clients were at the top of the list. Other major issues included meeting the parents, discussion of children (how many and how soon), prenuptial agreement, a voluntary period of abstinence before marriage, and riding his motorcycle without a helmet.

I felt pretty confident about the fact that Quinn would want me to meet his parents; the only question was how soon. I'd met his sister, Shelly, and we got along very well. In fact, Quinn and I typically had breakfast with her every Saturday morning at Giavanni's Pancake House.

I sent an email to my dad and told him about the engagement. I made sure to offer to pay for his travel so he wouldn't worry about the burden of expense. As well, I asked him to send me some possible dates for us to visit so he could meet Quinn. Reluctantly, I also asked him if he knew where my older sister was. I hadn't spoken to her in years and didn't know how to get in touch.

I assumed Quinn would agree that a prenup made a lot of sense, because it did make a lot of sense. In fact, I was a big advocate of prenuptial agreements in general and felt that the state should hand out a template with every marriage license application.

I was still uncomfortable with the fact that he was very rich, but it was no longer about the disparity in our circumstances. I wasn't keeping score of gifts and favors, and neither was he. We did what came natural. I paid half the rent for the apartment with Elizabeth because, technically, that was where I lived. All my comic books were still there, as were the bulk of my shoes.

But the fact remained, he was very wealthy. A prenup would draw a visible protective circle around his money, and it would always be *his* money, *his* business. Therefore, I wouldn't ever have to take ownership for it. I didn't want ownership of it. I didn't even like thinking about it.

I guessed that he wanted children. This guess wasn't based on any actual data, just a feeling I had. Therefore, on this point, an explicit confirmation was required.

Regarding abstinence before marriage, however, I was pretty sure I'd have to develop an extremely compelling and persuasive argument with graphs, citations, and figures if I had any hope of securing his stamp of approval. In all honesty, part of me wanted him to completely reject the idea.

Nevertheless, I was committed to my plan of manufacturing as much stress and hardship as possible during the next few months. At the very least, the conversation would be an excellent experience for us both. Perhaps it would even escalate into an argument.

Quinn found me at the kitchen table that evening surrounded by my bridal binder, wedding magazines, laptop, and miscellaneous citations and notes relating to waiting before the wedding.

I thought I heard the door, but I didn't hear his footsteps, nor did I expect to. He was stealthy.

I imagined I *felt* his eyes on me, but his hands brushing away the curtain of hair from my back was my first tangible evidence that he was home. He placed three languid kisses on the center of my neck and then—pulling my shirt to one side—he kissed the top of my shoulder.

"Hi." The single word greeting was more of a rumbly breath against my skin than sound; it made me shiver.

"Hi," I responded, and turned my face toward his to request a kiss, which he supplied; yet I pulled away before he could deepen it, purposefully not meeting his eyes.

If I met his eyes then I would be hypnotized and witless. Then we wouldn't talk and I would grow increasingly agitated until I unfairly lost my marbles over something ridiculous—like an inadvertent inaccurate reference to string theory as a science.

I cleared my throat, pressed my lips together, and found my Quinn-list of conversation topics. "Welcome home. I hope your trip was satisfactory."

His hand stayed on my back, his arm on the back of my chair, as he claimed the spot next to mine. Quinn used it to pull my seat closer to his, the wooden legs making an abrupt sound against the tile floor, and turned my knees so that I was facing him.

I was wearing an A-line grey wool skirt that ended just below the knee. On a normal sized person, the skirt would have ended mid-calf. Beneath the skirt I wore black tights. Quinn's hands snuck under the hem and caressed a path to my thighs, his fingers searching.

"These go all the way up." He sounded disgruntled at this discovery. There was a visible frown in his voice. I wasn't looking at his face because, again, hypnosis. Instead, I was scanning the list of issues and mentally reorganizing them based on importance and conversation flow.

I nodded because I assumed he was referring to the fact that I was wearing warm tights befitting the cold Chicago weather and not lace-topped thigh-highs. "Yes. Are you hungry? I made chicken and saved some for you in the fridge."

"No, thanks. I grabbed something on the way home." His hands continued their path upward. "Why are you wearing so many layers of clothing?"

"Because it was cold outside today. I think the high was twenty-four."

"Are you cold now?"

"No."

"Then…." Quinn paired this non-thought with a swift tug-yank that landed me on his lap. His fingers had already inched my tights and cotton underwear down a few inches before I could protest.

"Wait! Wait a minute!" My hands gripped his shoulders mostly due to instinct, and I squirmed away. His mouth was once again on my neck, and he gifted me wet kisses along the column of my throat.

"I need my wife." His words were hot and possessive, causing me to shudder both inwardly and outwardly. I knew this shudder. It was the hypnotized shudder of cautionless desire.

"I'm not your wife, I'm your fiancée." I arched my back, offering him more of my neck.

"Same difference," he mumbled between kisses. He'd

successfully pulled my tights to my upper thighs.

I grabbed his hands and held them still. "But we need to talk."

"It can wait," he whispered, leaning back to catch my eye, but his hands didn't move.

I, stupidly, met his gaze and nearly forgot my name.

Witless.

Then his hands tugged again, and I shook myself, trying not to be overwhelmed by all the heat and promise of his stare. "No…no it can't." My voice was unsteady and breathless. "It's important."

His eyes searched mine, his glare probing. "Did something happen? Are you okay?"

"Nothing happened."

"Then nothing is more important right now than me rediscovering every inch of your perfect body."

"Actually," I said, gripping his hands harder and tightening my fingers, "it's about that, Quinn—about all the inches of my body and about not having intercourse before the wedding, and waiting 'til the wedding night…."

Quinn flinched, and his eyes abruptly narrowed into sharp, piercing slits; my heart rate doubled as did my avalanche of words.

"…And other things as well, such as the private clients, because that issue isn't really resolved, and you need to wear a helmet when you ride a motorcycle. Also the prenuptial agreement status, because I'm sure you'll want one, because I want one, and also when I can call your parents for a visit, and whether or not we should wait to have children for a few years or get started right away, and how many you want, because I'd like to have at least two and then reevaluate at that point, but I'd like a commitment from you for two…children, that is…."

We stared at each other for a very long time, during which neither of us moved. I was resolved not to speak, because if I did speak first, I would start spouting data related to pre-wedding abstinence, and I felt we should wait to discuss that issue until the private clients issue was resolved. Also, I hadn't yet prepared my graphs and citations list.

But not speaking was becoming increasingly difficult. Quinn's eyes seemed to grow hotter with each passing second, though the rest of his face was a stoic mask. I was a little concerned that a bolt of lightning or a nuclear blast or some other plasmic inferno was going to burn a hole through my skull.

At last, after a pointed swallow and a moment or two of teeth grinding, he said, "We're not getting a prenup. Don't bring it up again."

I winced at the glacial vehemence of his tone, and my heart seized in shock—I imagined this was what it would feel like to be stabbed.

"But...but I thought...I mean, I think that you should consider our differences in...."

Quinn stood, his abrupt movements causing me to stumble from his lap. He moved his hands from my legs to my shoulders and waited until I'd regained my balance before speaking. "Don't."

I blinked up at him. "I can see that you're serious. But I don't understand why we can't even discuss it. If you would just listen, I think you would see that...."

"No." He shook his head, removing his hands and crossing his arms over his chest.

"Why not?"

"Because, just thinking about it makes me want to throw this table out that window." He pointed to the table then the window in turn, emphasizing the coolly spoken threat.

I frowned and tried to surreptitiously put to rights my underwear and tights. "That's ridiculous. A prenup is meant to...."

I didn't get to finish, because Quinn turned away from me and stalked to the bedroom, pulling his suit jacket from his shoulders with rigid, stiff movements. I stared at his retreating form for two beats then finished fixing my tights and followed him.

He was angry, really, really angry, and I couldn't fathom why. Of all the topics I'd covered, the prenup was the very last one I thought he'd take issue with.

I suddenly realized that this was a fight. We were having a fight, a real fight. Logically, I recognized that it was a good data point.

But I didn't like it, because my throat felt tight and dread was coursing through my veins. My neck was hot and my scalp itched.

I'd never felt like this before, hot and cold, angry and anxious. I wanted to apologize, to escape this uncomfortable sensation, but my stubborn resolve wouldn't let me because I didn't feel like I was in the wrong.

I lifted my voice as I chased him into the bedroom. "A prenup is meant to protect you, your business, your assets in the event that our marriage ends. It's a good thing, Quinn! There is nothing wrong with defining terms for divorce now so that our future break will be as seamless and painless as possible."

Quinn spun on me, backed me into his dresser, and everything about him looked furious. "There isn't going to be a future break."

"You don't know...."

"Yes, Janie, I do know. And the fact that you even brought it up...are you trying to hurt me?"

My mouth dropped open and I flinched, because I was completely astonished by his accusation. "What? No! No, Quinn, I'm doing this because I care about you."

"Are you going to leave me?"

"What? No...!"

"Then drop it." His eyes sliced through me, and he turned toward the closet, moving like a panther.

I gathered a deep breath and glanced at the ceiling for help. Unsurprisingly, it offered none. Since I couldn't bring up any of the other very important issues until he calmed down—as they would likely be tainted by association—I decided to take a different approach.

"It occurs to me...." I inhaled another steadying breath, hoped it would even my tone so I didn't sound quite so shaken. "It occurs to me that this is our first fight. How we move forward from here, what we learn from this interaction, how to talk to each other in particular, is very important. Therefore, it would be really great if we could discuss this calmly."

I couldn't see him because he was inside the walk-in closet, but I heard him huff an extremely bitter laugh just before three drawers slammed. An instant later, he was standing in the doorway, his arms braced on the trim, his large body filling the entire space.

"You're driving me fucking crazy," he said.

My eyelashes fluttered due to his bluntly spoken proclamation and his use of the f-word—since he rarely cursed, at least in front of me—and I instinctively crossed my arms over my chest.

"Well, if you're expecting me to apologize for doing absolutely nothing wrong, then you'll be waiting for a very long time. I honestly have no idea why you're so upset."

"Doing nothing wrong?" His usual outward façade of indifference was completely shattered. I was having difficulty adjusting to all the emotions twisting his features. "You're planning the end of our marriage."

"I am doing nothing of the sort!"

"Do you not trust me? Is this what this is about? How long is it going to take? What do I have to do?" Quinn's voice rose with every question until he was full-on shouting at me. "Just tell me what to do, Janie. What other tests are required?"

I sighed and my eyes stung because his words hurt. In fact, my chin wobbled and I couldn't stop it. It made my words come out as watery and strained. "None of this is about testing you, Quinn."

"That is complete bullshit! That's what all of this is about."

I stepped toward him, surprised that my voice also arrived as a shout. "Can't you understand that I want to protect you? Even from my future self, I want you to be safe. I come from a long line of crazy women. We cheat on our husbands, abandon our families, use our sisters' boyfriends as ashtrays and toilets. I started therapy before I was a teenager."

He winced, his hands dropping from the closet frame, and I noted that his expression had softened, but I wasn't finished.

"I'm a ticking time bomb of crazy—you just said so! I drive you crazy. Maybe it'll never happen—maybe I won't go nuts; I'd like to think I won't. But I'd feel a lot better if I knew you were protected. You know I like labels. I like clarity and defined expectations, because without them I'm lost. It's *your* money. I don't want it. A prenup for you isn't about me not believing in you. It's about…."

"Shh, Janie, that's enough." Quinn's voice was soft as he crossed to me in four steps and wrapped me in his arms—which were now bare along with his chest. He'd removed his shirt while in the closet.

I gripped his biceps and snuggled against the warmth of his skin, pressing my cheek to his chest so that I could feel his heartbeat.

"I don't want a prenup," he said, giving me a squeeze. "I don't want it, and just thinking about it makes me...." I felt him swallow before he finished his thought. "It pisses me off."

I nodded, pressed closer. "I trust you. You have to know that. None of this—the wedding and related tribulations—none of this is about not trusting you. It's about us repeating vows with certainty and knowledge of what we're promising. Love through suffering."

I felt his chest rise and fall before he answered. "I know."

"And the questions I have about the private clients aren't about not trusting you; it's just that I'd like to understand better what your past involvement means for your safety and for us moving forward."

He nodded. "That makes sense."

I was on a roll, so I moved my hands from his arms to the hard plane of his back. "Your safety is going to be my safety and our children's safety—and speaking of children, I'd like at least two with an option for more."

Quinn's light laugh dispelled some of my lingering anxiousness. "Well, I want more than two. I was thinking four or six."

I stiffened and lifted my head to catch his eyes, to gauge whether or not he was serious.

He was serious.

"Four or six?"

"I like even numbers. Growing up it was always Shelly and me against Des. This way our kids can pair off to torture each other in teams."

"Hmm...." My mouth twisted to the side as I considered this. "Can I think about it?"

"Sure. But for now, I think your plan—two then reevaluate after we have them—makes a lot of sense. And I'd like to wait a few years before we start our family."

"How many?"

"Three or four, but start before you turn thirty."

"I can agree to those terms."

His mouth hooked to the side, and his expression was now the polar opposite of the glacial inferno from just minutes prior. I marveled at how quickly the discussion had escalated, reached volcanic, then subsequently plummeted back to baseline.

"This was our first fight," I said.

He nodded, his eyes searching my face. "It was."

"I don't like fighting with you."

"I don't like fighting with you either."

"Good." I kissed his chest. "We should try to figure out how to avoid fighting in the future."

"It's going to happen. We can't avoid it completely."

"I know. But if we can decrease the number of incidences, I think that would be ideal. It seems like the key is to assume the best of each other. To...not assume that the other has malicious intent."

Quinn dipped his mouth to my neck, bit my jaw, and whispered, "I've also heard it helps to only fight while naked."

"Then we would never fight," I responded distractedly. "I would just stare at you and drool and you'd win."

"You'd drool?"

"You know I drool. What do you think those stains are on my pillow? Drool during sleep can be indicative of poor digestion or eating too late, but it can also be saliva manufactured during sex dreams."

He blinked at me. "Your drool is because of sex dreams? You have sex dreams?"

"Yes, of course...don't you?"

"Yes!" He responded as though the mere question were a slight against his manhood or a question of his sanity.

"Well, good. It's normal, you know, to have sex dreams. It's reported that they're more common—that is, they occur with more frequency—in men than in women until the age of thirty-one. Then women out-pace men until thirty-eight. Then it's about even."

He stared at me for a long moment. I thought about telling him that women's sex dreams were usually about foreplay and erotic situations, whereas men's sex dreams typically involved penetration, but decided against it. Maybe I'd share that later.

At length, he sighed as if he was confused and frustrated. He kissed my neck and shoulder, nibbled my ear, then pulled away. Setting me away with obvious reluctance, he released another heavy sigh. "What were the other things?"

"Other things?"

"Yes. The other things, when I came in. Because I really want to spend several hours tonight giving you material for future sex dreams, and I don't want you distracted or suddenly asking my opinion on ferns."

I blinked at his bare chest dumbly for ten seconds; I was having difficulty seeing anything other than the hard ridges of his stomach framed by the V of his hips. This of course made me think about touching him, which made me think about him touching me, which made me think about having sex, which finally made me remember the *other things*. "Oh, yeah…the other things."

He reached for the buckle of his belt, and I backed up two steps, crossing my arms in order to keep my hands to myself.

"So…?"

"Well, one of them was, uh…." I bit the inside of my lip, debated which topic to tackle. "About the private clients. I don't feel like the conversation we started in London was resolved. I'd like to have a better understanding of that side of the business."

Quinn pulled his belt from the loops of his pants and placed it on the dresser behind me, his expression thoughtful.

The he said, "I'm done with it—done with them. They're not going to be a part of our lives moving forward."

"So there is no chance they'll impact us at all?"

He studied me, his jaw ticking, but his expression was a mask, revealing nothing of his thoughts. At last, he said, "You already know. Everything else is details—who they are, logs of activity, bank account transactions. Knowing the details isn't going to give you any additional information about the workings of that side of the business."

"I'd like to know the details, and I'd like to make that decision for myself."

He frowned. "I'm not sure that's a good idea."

"Why not?"

His frown intensified, and his eyes lost focus as he moved them to some point over my shoulder. "Let me...let me think about it."

"Can I ask what that means?"

Quinn tilted his head to the side and seemed to be choosing his words carefully. "If you really want to see the details, I think what I'm going to do is pull a few files, show you some examples, and review the decisions made for each. I believe this approach will answer your questions without placing you in...in an uncomfortable position. I just ask one thing in return."

"Okay, what is it?"

"I don't want you having contact with these people. You can look through the files, but you aren't to speak to any of them. And if you have any questions, you have to promise to ask me—not Carlos, not Steven, not Dan—only me."

I quickly considered this request and decided it seemed more than fair. "Ok. I reserve the right to request more information later. For now, I can agree to those terms."

His small smile was wry. "That's the second time you've said that today."

"We're discussing terms, aren't we? And I have three more issues to discuss."

"Go ahead." Quinn unbuttoned his pants then regained the two steps I'd retreated and lifted my sweater over my head.

Obligingly, I raised my arms. "I want to meet your parents."

His hands reached for my shirt, but stalled for a beat when I spoke. His eyes didn't lift to mine when he said, "I haven't spoken to my parents in a long time." I recognized that his voice was carefully emotionless; it made my heart hurt.

"That's true. But you're getting married now. We'll be starting a family in a few years. They'll have biological grandchildren, assuming neither of us has any fertility issues. I think about my upbringing, what I wish were different. I didn't really have a mother; not really. And the stories you tell about your family, about growing up—your memories are good ones."

Quinn seemed to be looking at me sideways, like he was bracing himself, as he admitted quietly, "I do have good memories. They were good parents."

"See? Maybe a little part of this is that I'd like to have someone in my life in that role, especially if we're going to have kids. I have my dad, but he's...he's never been present or very interested. I know it might not make sense, but having a mother seems like it would be nice. I think it would be a good idea to at least make an attempt, extend an olive branch, but not an actual olive branch. Maybe a jar of olives. In Greek mythology as well as early Christianity, the olive branch symbolizes peace and tribute."

He seemed torn, undecided.

I placed my hands on his hips, my fingers dipping into the grey band of his black boxers. "I could always call them if you...if it's too difficult or you don't have time."

He nodded once. It was a non-committal nod, and I recognized that I wasn't going to get a definitive yes or no.

"What are the other two things?" He began unbuttoning my shirt.

"I...uh...it's about your riding the motorcycle."

His eyes flickered to mine then back to where his hands were working on my buttons. "What about it?"

"I realize that you like riding your bike, and I'm going to have to be ok with that. The only thing I ask is that you wear a helmet, all the time, no exceptions."

"Makes sense. Fine. Deal." He was down to the last three buttons.

The backs of his knuckles were brushing against the skin of my abdomen, sending lovely ripples to my chest, up my neck, to my fingertips, and down into my belly. My ability to concentrate was waning, as was my desire to bring up the last item on my list.

In fact, I was just talking myself into staying silent on the subject when Quinn said, "What's the last thing?"

I licked my lips, my thumbs rubbing circles over the skin on either side of his belly button, my nails hooked into the side of his hips. He felt hot and smooth beneath my hands, and I didn't want to stop, didn't want him to stop.

"Janie?"

I had difficulty thinking back to a time when touching him wasn't possible. The thought of willingly giving that up, giving up his body and the intimacy we'd established, felt like cutting off a limb.

"Nothing." I shook my head. "It was nothing."

He was looking at me now, his gaze questioning, his fingers pushing the edges of my shirt to the side and revealing my torso. I was wearing a red lace bra that we'd purchased during our London lingerie-shopping day. His eyes dipped, snagged on the bra, met mine again, and then he removed his hands.

"What was the last thing?"

"Don't make me say it," I blurted, shaking my head harder.

He watched me for a long moment, and I could tell he was trying to think back to my original tirade, when he'd pulled me on his lap at the kitchen table.

At length, he tilted his head to the side and his eyes narrowed. "We talked about the prenup, kids, meeting the parents, the private clients, and wearing the helmet while riding."

"Yep. That's it."

"No. There was something else."

"Quinn...." I removed my hands from his pants to unzip my skirt while I lifted on my tiptoes and placed a kiss on his mouth. "It was nothing, really—nothing worth discussing."

I witnessed the precise moment he remembered my earlier words, surprise flickering behind his gaze as his eyes refocused on my face.

"You want to wait?" He said the words slowly, like he was inspecting them. "You want to wait until our wedding night?"

"No...."

I kissed him again. My zipper was stuck.

He wasn't touching me, but he allowed the kisses. "You said something about not having intercourse until the wedding night."

"I meant discourse, like conversation and debates about the parliamentary system of government."

He laughed, more of a laugh-huff, and his eyes danced over my features. His mouth smiled the big grin, the one that sent my stomach to my toes.

I decided his new nickname should be Sir McSwoonypants.

Disgusted with my stubborn zipper, I gave up and whipped off my shirt, wrapped my arms around his neck, and pressed my body against his.

Quinn kissed me once, really just a chaste press of our lips together, then untangled my arms from his shoulders. "Now, wait a minute. Not so fast—this idea has merit."

"What idea?"

"Waiting until the wedding night."

I stared at him for a beat then said, "Fine. We won't engage in discourse about the parliamentary system of government."

He laughed again, but subtly shook his head. "No. Maybe we should wait 'til our wedding night."

I'm sure I looked like I lost control of my facial muscles, because I could feel my eyebrows do this weird, wiggly thing on my forehead. Also, my mouth opened and closed, my nose wrinkled, and I'm pretty sure I hissed at him. I might have also said, *Booooo!*

This only made him laugh harder.

When he had finally reigned in his laughter but was still holding his stomach, he took two steps back, leaned against the wall, and crossed his arms over his chest.

Shirtless, pants unzipped, boxers pulled low—he was chocolate cake with chocolate sauce and chocolate ganache, with chocolate mousse and chocolate cookie crust...so delicious.

"How about this?" He paused, an evil glint in his eye, his smile persisting. "How about we make a bet. If you can hold out the entire time, we'll do the big wedding with all the extra stuff at the end. But...."

Quinn sauntered forward—yes! Sauntered!—and invaded my space, his lips hovering just over mine, his fingers drawing a line from my shoulder to my breast and down my stomach.

"But, if you give in at any point over the next few months, we'll cancel the wedding and elope within twenty-four hours."

I warred against my body's very loud and insistent inclination to surrender, right now, this minute. Because, honestly, I didn't think I would be able to last.

I stalled by clearing my throat and asking unnecessary questions. "So, you mean that you'll be trying to seduce me for the next few months? And if I give in then we get married within twenty-four hours?"

"More or less."

"What do you mean, more or less?"

"I mean that I have no plans to seduce you, but otherwise you've got it right."

"Really?" I eyeballed him. "No seduction plans?"

"That's right."

"Then...what's off limits? I mean, what *can* we do?"

"Just kiss."

I'm pretty sure my eyes looked like they were going to pop out of my head, and I know the volume of my voice was inappropriately loud when I said, "JUST KISS?"

If possible, the glint in his gaze turned even more sinister. "That's right."

"No touching at all? Like, what you're doing now?"

Something passed over his features—maybe apprehension, more likely reassessment of the terms—and he conceded. "Kissing and touching are fine. But no...."

"Penetration?" The word emerged as a squeak.

He nodded, watching me closely, and added, "Or oxytocin-releasing genital arousal."

I studied his features, rolling my lips between my teeth and contemplating the offer. A thought occurred to me. "But this means that you'll help with the wedding—cheerfully—no complaining or being disinterested about the color of ferns. You'll voice your opinion."

He didn't respond immediately and his gaze hardened, grew distant. Finally, he said, "Okay. Fine. Do we have a deal?"

I pressed for more. "And we'll go to your parents' house in Boston for a visit."

His mouth became a tight line, but he answered, "Fine."

"Ok, then…." I nodded my head and doubted the veracity of my own words when I said, "I can agree to those terms."

CHAPTER 12

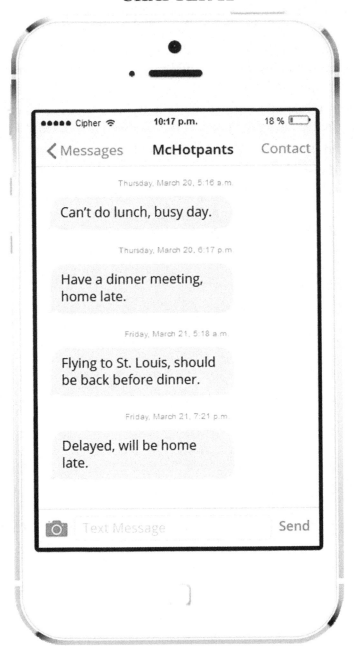

A BRIGHT SPOT in the wedding-tainted sea of stress came just two days after I made the bet with Quinn when I was able to establish contact with his mother.

I called her.

It was a Friday evening, and I was on my way to the penthouse, riding in the back seat of a black Cadillac Escalade. It was chauffeured by Jacob, my guard until I arrived home.

Quinn and I usually left work together, but he'd indicated—via text—that he would be working late. I wondered if he were avoiding me. The thought was depressing.

I dialed the number I'd requested that Betty, Quinn's secretary, look up. I hadn't asked Quinn for it, partially because I doubted he had it. The other reason was because he looked sick to his stomach every time I mentioned his parents.

"Hello?" A woman's voice sounded from the line, and my brain went blank.

I don't know why, but I wasn't expecting her to answer the phone. Perhaps it was because I was used to playing phone tag with wedding vendors. I'd prepared a message; in fact, I'd typed it out, printed it, and now held it in my hand ready to read to her voicemail. Therefore, when I heard her answer live, I felt unprepared and almost hung up.

"Hello?" She asked again, not sounding irritated.

I cleared my throat and forced out a greeting. "Hi! How are you?" Then I cringed when I realized I forgot to introduce myself.

"I'm…fine. And how are you?" Her tone was tempered with suspicion. She likely thought I was a telemarketer. In a way, I kind of was. I was trying to sell myself to her, and maybe sell her on the role of being grandmother to our children.

My throat felt tight. I didn't know how to talk to women who held a maternal role unless they were my coworkers and my interactions with them occurred within a clearly defined set of parameters, like it was with Betty. Motherly types made me nervous.

I gathered a deep breath and closed my eyes. "Hi." I repeated, shook my head. "I'm Janie Morris. Is this Katherine Sullivan?"

"Yes. This is Mrs. Sullivan."

"Right. Sorry, Mrs. Sullivan. I'm…." I held my breath, my heart galloped wildly, and I wondered why I suddenly felt like I was throwing myself off a cliff. "I'm Janie, as I said, and I'm engaged to your son, Quinn. In fact, it just happened about a week ago, the engagement, so it's all very new. And I'm calling because…." I glanced down at my typed speech and began to read. "…because I was hoping you and your husband would be amenable to future interactions, including but not limited to meeting me sometime before the wedding, having dinner, speaking over the phone, or exchanging emails. As well, I'd like to gauge your level of interest in becoming involved in the wedding in some capacity, perhaps with the planning, but no pressure either way. I understand that you might have some reservations, as I'm basically a stranger and my understanding is that historically, interactions with Quinn have been justifiably strained. Nevertheless…."

"Wait…wait a minute." She sounded perplexed, shocked, and tense. Her interruption was followed by a long period of silence. I heard some rustling in the background. If my heart hadn't already been in my throat, it would have jumped there now.

At last, when she spoke again, her voice was impossibly soft and warm. "Let's start over. I'm Katherine—please call me Katherine."

I pressed my lips together because my chin inexplicably wobbled. I had to look at the ceiling of the Escalade to keep from crying, and I didn't know why I was so close to tears. "Hi, Katherine…." I paused to chase the watery quality from my voice. "I'm Janie. It's nice to meet you."

"It's nice to meet you, Janie."

I heard a smile in her voice, and maybe also a little waver in her inflection. I wondered briefly if she, too, were fighting tears.

"So…how…?" I gave her some time to collect her thoughts. It also allowed me to take several deep breaths. After a pause, she continued. "So you and…Quinn? How did that happen?"

"I work for him, for his company."

"Oh?" She sounded a little wary, but her next question was pleasant enough. "What do you do?"

"I'm an accountant, although my background is in architecture. To be more accurate, my degree is in both mathematics and architecture, but I've always been an accountant, never an architect. What do you do?" I closed my eyes again, worried that my question might have come out as rude.

"I'm a teacher. I teach high school calculus." She answered simply, her tone reflecting that no offense had been taken.

"Oh!" I smiled. "I loved my high school calculus teacher. He's one of the main reasons I started tutoring kids in math and science. He could teach integrals to anyone, at least I always thought so."

She laughed lightly, a pleasant sound that made my stomach feel warm. "That's a great skill to have."

I began to relax into the conversation. We mostly spoke about ourselves, our likes and dislikes, our hobbies and favorite foods. She didn't knit, but she crocheted. She also knew how to sew and was an avid quilter. I also learned that she was five years away from retirement, but hadn't decided whether she actually wanted to.

At no point did she ask directly about Quinn nor did she say his name again. However, whenever I mentioned him or Shelly, she'd grow very quiet, almost like she was holding her breath. Then, when I finished, she'd press me for more information on whatever subject I'd just covered.

I knew that Quinn hadn't spoken with his parents since his brother's funeral. I also knew that Shelly didn't speak to her parents either. I'd never pressed either of them for more information. I'd accepted the situation at face value: Quinn's parents had blamed him for their oldest son's death. Shelly had stopped speaking with her mother and father. I guessed this was a way to show solidarity with Quinn.

But now, after a half-hour phone call with the woman, I started to think there was more to the story. Either that or this family had been separated by tragedy and the rift had been fostered by lack of communication.

We ended the call with a plan to email about dinner, a dinner that was to take place sometime over the next two weekends, and my promise to call her again within the next several days—*just to talk,* she'd said. Then, before hanging up, she asked me what my favorite dessert was.

The dessert question threw me off, so I deployed evasive maneuvers, told her it was too hard to choose, but that I'd let her know when we spoke next. That night I spent several hours researching whether or not desserts, or ingredients in desserts, had any hidden symbolism. For example, I didn't want to tell her that I liked key lime pie if it meant that she'd think I was a tart.

I finally settled on chocolate cake with chocolate frosting, mostly because I missed Quinn and chocolate was a proven, although woefully inadequate, replacement for intimacy.

***

THE NEXT MORNING I awoke to an empty bed and a text from Quinn indicating that he'd gone for a motorcycle ride wearing his helmet. He went on to state that he would meet Shelly and me for our usual breakfast at Giavanni's around 10:00 a.m. I checked twice for another text message, hoped for a joke or pun. To my dismay, there was nothing new.

Quinn and I would be sharing our big news with Shelly over pancakes.

She told me the first time we met each other that everything was big news over pancakes.

She and I had hit it off immediately. She was markedly weird, prone to intermittent tangents or periods of silence, and didn't seem to be able to sit still for very long. Her eccentricities never bothered me. I actually found her fascinating. Part of it was because Quinn was completely devoted to her—in fact, I was 99 percent certain that he supported her financially—and the other reason was because she didn't seem to care about other people's opinions as they related to who she was or the decisions she made.

Ever.

Not ever.

In fact, I wondered once or twice if she lacked empathy, but dismissed this theory after we spent more time together. Shelly, although detached with most people, cared deeply for Quinn and had several causes she championed, mostly to do with cruelty toward animals.

As I came to know her, I realized she was one of those people who felt more comfortable in nature than she did in society.

I, however, felt equal parts uncomfortable in both places.

Shelly sometimes spent Saturday nights in the loft Quinn had purchased on her behalf and exclusively for her use. This was the same loft where he'd taken me after finding me drugged at Club Outrageous.

Most of her time, however, was spent in a large farmhouse three hours south of Chicago. She had four horses that she boarded for a rescue foundation, three dogs of various breeds and ages, seven cats, and a parrot named Oscar who only said curse words. Apparently, his former owner had a limited vocabulary.

She was also a sculptor, mostly large-scale metalwork, and a car enthusiast.

I'd only been to the farmhouse once, but I was struck by how many vintage cars she owned in various stages of repair. After she fixed them up, she donated them to charities benefiting animal shelters.

As far as I could tell, she had no interest in men—or women for that matter—and didn't seem to need or seek relationships outside of the weekly check-in and breakfast with her brother. This struck me as unhealthy, but I kept this opinion to myself.

I also wondered—if I had grown up with a sibling who fostered my strangeness rather than challenged it—if Shelly's existence was a mirror to an alternate dimension version of me.

I'd been forced by necessity to go to college, get a job, interact with society. Shelly had attended the Art Institute of Chicago, but never held a job—not a real one, at least, with a boss who held her accountable for her work.

If all my bills were paid and money wasn't an issue to my survival, would I lock myself in a farmhouse with Internet connection, or within walking distance of a library, and just gorge on information day in and day out?

I couldn't answer this hypothetical question, because both answers—yes and no—felt dissonant with who I was and who I wanted to be.

Therefore, I embraced Shelly as a friend and found I didn't have to try very hard when we were together. She didn't seem to mind my presence during her Saturday mornings with Quinn—quite the opposite. I'd missed one breakfast because I thought she might want some alone time with her brother. She made Quinn call me, and refused to eat until I showed up.

Honestly, it was kind of nice to be the least eccentric woman at a meal.

On this particular morning, I was the second one to arrive at Giavanni's. Shelly was already there and was building a tower of Styrofoam cups at the counter—but not in the way most people would do. She wasn't stacking the cups. Rather, she'd cut them into strips and added slits, and was using them like one would build with Lincoln logs. She had used the circular portions for design elements.

As usual, the line to get breakfast was out the door and, as usual, I bypassed the line and claimed a stool marked *reserved* next to my soon-to-be sister-in-law.

She was dressed in brown cargo pants and a very thick brown wool sweater with large wooden buttons. On her head was a green fleece cap that barely covered a long mass of brown hair that seemed to have a mind of its own. Her blue eyes—the same shade as Quinn's—flitted to me when I claimed my seat then moved back to her tower. Upon closer inspection, it looked more like a complicated gate than a tower.

"You're engaged," she said. Her deeper than was typical for a female voice held some amusement.

I nodded, studied the sharp angles of her face. Physically, she was the female version of Quinn, but without the muscles. Certainly, she was fit—likely due to all the physical labor involved in caring for animals, welding metal, and fixing cars—but she was thin, willowy, and two inches taller than me.

Tangentially I noted that she wasn't pretty—just like Quinn would never make a pretty female—but something about her was striking, beautiful. She was like a lady-hawk. At least, I thought she was beautiful.

A very small smile curved her mouth. "It's about time. When is the wedding?"

"June 14."

Usually when I told people the date of the wedding, they assumed I meant June 14 in one year and several months. When I explained that it was June 14 less than three months away, they always responded with shock.

Shelly also responded with shock, her gaze moving to mine, holding it. "Three months? So long? Why the wait?"

I smiled at her typical atypical response. "I insisted on a big wedding."

"Why would you want to do that?"

"Because Quinn and I get along so well. I thought it would be a good idea for us to experience a degree of suffering prior to taking vows."

She gave me a once over, her expression flat, then she grunted. "You're weird. I ordered you pancakes."

"Thanks. What are you building?"

"I don't know." She dropped her hands to the counter and frowned at the Styrofoam creation. "Some kind of gate, I think."

"That's what I thought it might be. It reminds me of a gate I saw when I went to the Victoria and Albert museum in London. I like it."

"Hey."

We both looked up at the sound of Quinn's voice and I gave him an automatic welcoming smile, which he returned. He paired it with that softness, the dreamy quality in his eyes that I usually found so disconcerting. Today, however, after not seeing the expression for several days, it felt like a cool, soothing balm to my itchy, uncomfortable, overactive imagination.

Quinn placed his helmet on the counter then cupped my jaw with a gloved hand, kissing me. It was a socially acceptable kiss for our surroundings, yet I couldn't help but want more.

He pulled away, his eyes holding mine, a gentle smile on his features, then shifted his attention to his sister.

"Hey, Shelly. Nice gate."

"Thanks. I like it. I think I'll build it for real and give it to you guys as a wedding present."

Quinn frowned—just a slight frown—and glanced at me. "You already told her?"

"No, I…."

"I took one look at her and guessed. She looked like she was preparing to tell me some big news." Shelly gave me a wide smile and the expression looked out of place on her face. For a second I thought she was going to tussle my hair with affection as if I was a dog.

"Ah…." Quinn nodded and took the stool next to me.

His leg—hip to knee—pressed against mine. It was the closest we'd been in days. He smelled good, like Quinn. If we'd been alone I would have attacked him.

"How was the drive up?" He signaled for Viki, our usual waitress, as he addressed his question to Shelly.

"Fine."

"Are you staying tonight?"

"No."

"Did you order already?"

"Just for Janie and me. I didn't know if you were going to eat pancakes with us or stick to that egg white omelet crap." Shelly said this with no malice. In fact, for her, it was almost tender.

Viki approached, gave us all a wag of her unibrow, then rested her eyes on Quinn. "What'll it be, handsome? The usual?"

"I'll have the same as Janie. Blueberry pancakes, right?"

Viki nodded, scribbled on her notepad, poured coffee into our cups, then left.

I assumed all engagement talk was over and was about to change the subject to Shelly's horses. But she surprised me—likely both of us—by asking, "Are you going to tell them?"

Quinn stiffened. I felt the change in him where our legs were pressed together. Then I watched him stall by sipping his coffee more slowly than usual. Finally, with no other way to avoid responding, he asked, "Who?"

"Mom and Dad. Are you going to tell them about Janie?"

I opened my mouth to inform them of my conversation with their mother, but Quinn spoke before I had a chance to. "Yes."

"Don't." Shelly shook her head, her expression hard. "Don't tell them."

"Why not?" I blurted, leaning back in my seat so I could watch them both at the same time. "Why not tell them?"

Shelly didn't look at me when she responded, her glacial glare boring into Quinn's profile. "They don't deserve to know."

Quinn's shoulders rose and fell with a deep sigh, though his back straightened. "You need to let it go, Shell. Des, the funeral...it was a long time ago."

Her expression grew dark, agitated. "They disowned you, Quinn—at our brother's funeral. You said they told you to leave, they kicked you out of the family, said you were dead to them. Why would you even consider sharing Janie with those people?"

Shelly's words made me flinch, and my heart hurt for Quinn as unbidden images of him suffering surfaced in my mind's eye. Quinn, no older than twenty-one or twenty-two, being kicked out of his brother's funeral; a brother he loved; a brother whose death he felt responsible for.

I tried to reconcile Shelly's words with the woman I'd spoken to on the phone, the one who taught high school calculus, who wanted to know what my favorite dessert was and insisted that we schedule dinner as soon as possible. The woman who wanted me to call her on the phone, and requested that I refer to her as Katherine.

Quinn's eyes flickered to mine, then to his coffee cup. "It's up to Janie."

I studied them both, horrified with myself, wondering why I'd never thought to ask Quinn about the circumstances surrounding his prolonged separation from his parents before now. I wanted to hug him, kiss his neck, and tell him how I loved him. I wanted him to know how much he meant to me.

So I did.

He grew rigid again when my arms tightened around his torso, but he relaxed when I placed several quick kisses on his neck and whispered in his ear, "I love you, Quinn Sullivan. You are precious to me, and I will love you always. And if I die before you, I plan to haunt you."

He glanced at me over his shoulder, his eyes sad but warm, and stole another quick kiss from me. "Ditto," he said.

I ensnared his gaze and suggested, "Perhaps you could learn to make pottery so that posthumously we can use the wheel together in a sensual, mystically transcendent display of affection."

I was rewarded with a grin and an expression that was considerably less melancholy when he responded, "Consider it done."

**

I WAITED UNTIL Shelly used the bathroom to tell Quinn about my conversation with his mother. Shelly usually took fifteen minutes or more, which I felt was odd. I wondered what she did in there. It felt like a big mystery. I'd never asked her about it.

She excused herself, leaving cash on the counter for all three of our meals, "Can you watch my hat, Janie? I'm going to leave it here."

I nodded. "Your hat is safe with me."

"I know." She said, then turned and walked away.

I watched her go then slipped my hand under Quinn's arm into the crook of his elbow. "I have to tell you something. I was going to tell you last night, but you came home so late. Then, I was going to tell you this morning, but you left early."

"What's up?" he asked, not addressing his coming home late or his leaving early.

I decided to ignore both for now and just get to the point. "I spoke to your mother yesterday."

His face went completely blank and something shuttered behind his eyes. After a beat, he said, "I see."

"Was that okay? I thought it was, because on Wednesday you and I discussed it and you said 'fine,' which I figured meant 'yes, that's fine.'"

"Yes. It's fine. You said you were going to do it."

I released a breath and studied him; still no expression in his eyes or inflection in his voice. He may as well have been a robot.

"Do you want to know what we talked about?"

He shrugged, like he really didn't care. "If it's relevant."

"Relevant?"

"If I need to know."

"You never told me that she's a math teacher. She teaches calculus."

He nodded, just once. "That's right."

"Quinn...." I twisted my mouth to the side, my eyebrows pulling low as I searched his face for something, anything other than complete ambivalence. "Your mother and I scheduled a dinner; it looks like maybe two weeks from today. Is that okay?"

His eyes moved to my right, to the wall behind me. "That should be fine. I have some projects in Boston I should check on any way."

I frowned at him, at his complete lack of emotion, then reached for his hand with both of mine and pulled it to my lap. It was warm even though his countenance was cool.

"We don't have to do this, you know. I didn't realize about the funeral; I didn't understand about Des, what they said to you. I could just cancel and tell her I made a mistake."

His eyes came back to mine then moved over my face in that way he frequently employed as if he was memorizing every detail. "It's fine. We should do it."

I was about to give him another out, at the very least a suggestion of postponement, when he used the hand I was holding to tug me forward and give me a kiss. This kiss was less appropriate than the one he'd given me when he arrived. He removed his hand from mine, gripped my hips with both of his, and pulled me forward until I was standing between his legs.

His mouth devoured mine, right there at the counter of Giavanni's Pancake House, as if he was starving. I knew he wasn't starving because he'd eaten all of his pancakes and half of mine.

When he finished, and we were both breathing with some difficulty, I hid my face on his shoulder and wrapped him in my arms.

"That was really nice," I said. My voice was a little shaky. It was more than nice. It was necessary. After a week of almost no touching, it felt like a moral imperative.

He cleared his throat, but he didn't respond. I felt his fingers dig into my hips.

"I thought you said you weren't going to seduce me," I whispered against his neck.

"I said I had no plans to seduce you."

"But now you do?"

"No."

"So what was that?"

"Just a kiss."

I huffed a laugh. "That was not just a kiss."

"It wasn't?"

"No. That was a big, hot, wet kiss—with lots of tongue. I think there was even some groping. If judges were present, they would rule that a seduction attempt."

"And where does one hire a seduction judge?"

"Well," I glanced to the right and considered the logistics of a *seduction judge*; "I don't think there is any central authority, but-"

Quinn shook his head, cut me off with his movements, and gently pushed me a step away. He guided me onto my stool. His eyes were cautious, but most definitely simmering with something that resembled wicked delight.

Smirking, he placed one hand on my leg and his other arm along the counter at my side. Leaning close to my ear, his whisper scorching, sending shivers down my spine, he whispered, "When we're married, I'll show you the difference between *just a kiss* and a big, hot, wet kiss…with lots of tongue."

CHAPTER 13

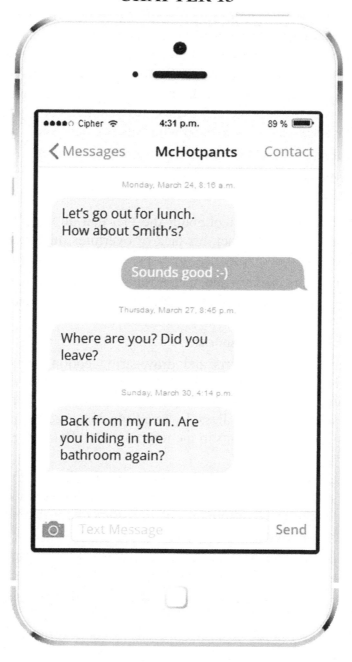

I SPENT A lot of time in the bathroom over the next two weeks.

In fact, I started hiding my personal laptop in the cabinet under the sink, and when Quinn would walk around the apartment in only his boxers, I'd excuse myself to the bathroom and read about Lyme disease and the pollination of vanilla flowers in Madagascar.

I trusted his insistence that he had no plans to seduce me. The problem was that his mere presence was enough for my body to react like a sex-starved sex-fiend who was sex-deprived.

Other than existing, he was taking it pretty easy on me.

Or maybe he wasn't.

It was hard to tell.

I didn't know how to feel about the fact that he wasn't making seduction overtures. In fact, his lack of overtures might have been worse than overt attempts.

We kissed every day—but never for very long and never very deeply—and we started wearing pajamas to bed, whereas before, we'd slept naked.

I was in tank tops and shorts.

He was in black t-shirts and draw-string cotton pants, Hanes brand. I knew they were Hanes brand since I checked the tag. I don't know why I checked the tag; maybe because his pajamas felt like my adversary. Regardless, I was a little surprised by his simple choice in PJ's since he was in the top point zero five percent of the wealth distribution curve.

Admittedly, I began to feel a measure of spite for the Hanes clothing company. The loss of his nudity was a travesty and part of me—the completely irrational, needing-someone-to-blame part— held them accountable.

He was also touching me less in general. Fewer hugs, fewer incidental caresses, no more cuddling or spooning in bed.

Another byproduct of the big wedding was that we seemed to talk about nothing *but* the wedding. Certainly, at work we talked about work. At home however, we talked about ferns, appetizers, and ribbons.

Ribbons!

Before Quinn, the lack of engaging conversation wouldn't have affected me much.

But now, I'd grown used to sharing my random facts with him, having him ask me questions, discussing the broader ramifications of the information and how it might be applied to future situations and the interpretation of data.

Maybe I wasn't sex-deprived as much as Quinn-deprived, and the lack of quality Quinn time—or Quinnime, which is Quinn + time—was messing with my head.

After we made the bet, the first two weeks were terrible. We talked often, but I began to feel lonely.

Marie called me one day out of the blue and offered her services for whatever I needed. She actually helped a great deal. As an artist, she had an eye for color and design that I lacked. She almost made me want to have an opinion about centerpieces, cake toppers, and chair covers.

I assembled a list of vendors in the Chicago area and left messages for photographers, videographers, caterers, venues, jazz quartets, DJs, and fireworks display professionals.

Unfortunately, the bad news rolled in immediately.

My dad didn't think a visit was a good idea. He said he'd think about coming to the wedding as long as it didn't interfere with any other plans. This was disheartening, but not a surprise. As well, he said he hadn't spoken to June, my older sister, since she jumped bail for her latest conviction. Like me, he didn't know where she was or how to reach her.

My dad…goodness, I didn't know what to think about him.

He wasn't a bad guy.

Really, I think about my childhood in terms of my mother. There was never a time where she wasn't the focus of my dad's life or ours. Before she died and after she died, she was the alpha and omega, the zeta and tri-delta.

Actually, she was literally a tri-delta. She was in the sorority when she met my father, and he was a humble mechanical engineering student. I'm pretty convinced that my oldest sister, June, and my youngest sister, Jem, both have a different father.

There's also a high chance that my father is some anonymous, unknown sperm donor.

Regardless, my dad never turned my mother away. He paid for our daycare, dropped us off, and picked us up every day. He may not have tucked us in at night or made any attempt to calm us when we had nightmares, but he did put a roof over our heads and food in our mouths.

When we weren't spending weekends with my mother's mother, a pill-popping head case as well as a former beauty queen, we were running amuck around the neighborhood.

Now my relationship with my dad consists of him sending me email forwards, mostly jokes or chain mail or both, along with fifty other people on the To: line. The few times each year that I call him, he seems confused at first as to who I am. Then he seems confused as to why I've called.

Therefore, the call I made to him went accordingly.

The other bad news about the wedding was that almost every place in Chicago was already booked; I was forced to move down the lists to my third, sixth, and tenth choices. It was extremely stressful—which was satisfying as an outcome—and I spent a good amount of time with Quinn lamenting my inability to secure any meaningful part of the event.

Compounding matters, I couldn't send out the invitations because I couldn't finalize the reception location. This meant I would have to find a printer for the invitations who would be able to turn them around in two days or less, which was basically impossible.

Therefore, when Sandra insisted on taking over all activities relating to my bachelorette party, I gave in immediately and allowed her to do so. I then promptly forgot about it, figured she was bossy enough that I could trust her to tell me what to do, where to go, and when to be there.

Additionally, I wasn't sure how to feel about Quinn's parents. I did feel a good deal of guilt that I'd pushed him into the visit. My mind didn't like feeling guilt, so it wandered to less uncomfortable topics—like what class of plastics corresponded to each recycling number.

Katherine continued to be lovely and gracious and even funny during our phone conversations. Desmond Sr., Quinn's dad and his brother's namesake, surprised me by joining our third call. He said almost nothing while Katherine and I discussed the difference between plastics denoted with the number 1 (PET—Polyethylene Terephthalate) and plastics denoted with the number 2 (HDPE—High Density Polyethylene).

But then, at the very end of the call, he said in a voice that sounded eerily similar to Quinn's, but with a much thicker Boston accent, "We're really looking forward to seeing you Saturday."

I hung up feeling dazed and confused and maybe a little overwhelmed by what I'd initiated.

Everything was set and scheduled for our trip to Boston. But as the time approached, I couldn't help but wonder if my insistence on meeting his parents had more to do with my wanting non-ambivalent parental figures in my life—most especially a maternal figure—or that I honestly wanted what was best for Quinn.

Signs of my distractedness and physical-and-intellectual-intimacy-Quinn-starved-addled-brain-disease presented at knit night just a few days before we were set to leave for Boston.

We were all gathered at the apartment I technically shared with Elizabeth, but she hadn't arrived yet.

I thought I was covering pretty well. I even made margaritas for everyone, and they were good margaritas. I credited the addition of Limoncello and agave nectar.

Marie was discussing the wedding plans and lamenting our inability to secure a venue.

"Can't Quinn help?" Sandra asked, "He does security for all those fancy places, like that club where he rescued you."

I smoothed out the wrinkles of the Wonder Woman apron I was wearing. "I didn't want to ask him to do that."

"Why not? It's his wedding too," Fiona pointed out and sipped her margarita. "You should ask him to help. Men like to help."

I thought about how his eyes glazed over every time I asked him for an opinion on floral arrangements or main course options. It was a mere three weeks since our engagement, and I dreaded every discussion he and I had to make about the wedding.

I sighed. "I don't know...."

"You can do it, Janie!" Sandra shouted before gulping some of Kat's drink. Kat was distracted, but I noticed. "Start this way— here, watch me—pretend I'm you." She cleared her throat and fluttered her lashes. "Oh, Quinn, I am existentially flubbered."

"I don't think flubbered is a word," Ashley interjected.

"Yes it is. It's flustered and befuddled."

"Wouldn't that be fluddled?"

"Shh, you're messing me up." Sandra frowned at Ashley's interference and turned her attention back to me. "What do you call each other? What are your pet names? Dearest? Turtledove? Thor? Herr Handsome of my heart? Lizard of my labia? Captain of my clitoris?"

I rolled my lips between my teeth, but it was no good. We all burst out laughing.

"Lizard of my labia? What the heck?" Kat chuckled and reached for her drink. Still, she didn't notice that one third of it was depleted let alone that Sandra was the culprit.

"You know, lizards and their tongues flicking." Sandra glanced around the room. "I think it's a nice term of endearment."

"No." I shook my head. "No, I do not call him that. Other than Sir McHotpants, which I rarely use and only to illustrate a modification in his mood, I don't have a pet name for him."

Sandra frowned. "Not even in bed? Not even when the two of you are going at it? Not even *baby*?"

To be certain, I thought back over our times of physical intimacy. "No. We don't talk much during sex."

Sandra's mouth fell open. "You don't talk during sex? You don't dirty talk? Like, at all?"

I shook my head. "No. Not really. Before, during foreplay, I might quote a few interesting and relevant studies relating to arousal or stamina. But we're both mostly silent during the act." I nibbled my top lip. "Sometimes he'll say *move* or *bend over* or some other instruction regarding the placement of my body, but nothing like a term of endearment. Recently he told me what to say while we were engaged in the act—or rather, he made requests."

"Like what?" Sandra looked confused. "Like dirty requests? A la, 'Tell me how much you want my big co....'"

"Sandra! I think we all get your point." Fiona exchanged a look with Sandra then peered at me before speaking. "You don't have to answer her questions, Janie."

"No, it's ok. Quinn said stuff like, 'Tell me you love me.'"

"Aw...that's sweet." Fiona smiled at me approvingly. "That's not dirty talk, that's lovely bedroom talk."

"Thanks." I returned her smile. "I have limited experience so, to be honest, I'm not sure what is considered normal. This conversation is actually quite helpful and—if all of you are comfortable with the topic—will allow me to gather data on what kinds of things are said in the bedroom between normal, well-adjusted adults."

"I don't mind," Ashley chimed in. "I'm ok with dirty talk in the bedroom—to a point. For example," she glanced upward, setting her knitting on her knee and seemed to search the bookshelf behind Fiona for the right memory. "This one time, in college, my boyfriend started calling me a whore while I was...well, you know, fellatiating."

"Fellatiating?" Sandra made a confused face.

"The art of administering fellatio," Ashley clarified.

"Ah...continue."

"And it was a complete turn-off. I feel like, with that kind of stuff, the girl has to invite it. Like, I need to be the one to say, 'Call me a ho!' or else it feels degrading."

"I agree." Sandra nodded. "I mean, I'd never say to a guy while he's savoring my goods, 'You're a slut!' Right? That's not okay."

"What else do people say during sex that's considered dirty talk?" I asked. "Other than calling each other names, I mean." I wondered if they'd think it was very strange of me to take out a piece of paper and jot down some notes.

There was a pause while they all considered the question.

Surprisingly, Marie was the first to respond. "I don't have much experience either. But the guy I was with before David was always asking me if I liked what he was doing, but not as though he really wanted to know—not a survey—more like," she paused, then lowered her voice to imitate a man, "You like that, dontcha? You like it when I do that, dontcha? You want it all the time, dontcha?"

"Hmm...." Sandra nodded thoughtfully. "I was with a guy who did that. He seemed to need a lot of praise to sustain an erection, so I figured out quickly that it was a good idea to say, "Yes! Yes! God, yes! Don't stop!""

We all chuckled a little at Sandra's theatrics, and Fiona turned her smiling eyes to me. "Dirty talk in the bedroom can be fun, especially if you're with someone you love and who loves you. Don't be afraid of sounding weird or turning him off. Believe me, anything you say or do—as long as it's unselfish and about bringing pleasure to *both* of you—is good."

"Look at you, Ms. Sex Therapist." Marie winked at Fiona. "You and Greg are the cutest coupled; of course you guys have everything figured out."

Fiona turned her attention to her work in progress. "No one has *everything* figured out."

"Any chance you can make more of those margaritas?" Ashley smiled at me over her empty glass. "They're amazing, Janie."

I nodded and stood. I was the only one who didn't knit; therefore, I enjoyed being the bartender. "No problem. I'll be right back."

Distractedly, absorbing this information, I walked back to the kitchen and began mixing another batch.

I decided that I wanted Quinn to have a pet name for me. I heard some commotion from the living room, but only peripherally as I was caught up in the idea. Suddenly it felt very important, and I began listing then rejecting possibilities.

I was still tallying and assessing my preference for different terms of endearment when I walked from the kitchen and found that the commotion was Elizabeth's arrival. I smiled when I saw her, because I missed her and she was one of my most favorite people in the world—definitely in the top three.

I lifted one of the margaritas I was holding. "Do you want a margarita? I'm making them with Limoncello and Petron."

"Yes. I will have margaritas." She returned my smile. It was good to see her smile. Usually, at least when I saw her, she was walking around half asleep from exhaustion.

Even though she was my best friend, I would never ask her to help with the wedding. In fact, when she'd offered weeks ago, I told her absolutely not.

She never got enough sleep, was always picking up extra shifts at the hospital. Helping with my wedding—a wedding I was only planning in order to manufacture stress—was out of the question. She didn't need more stress. She needed rest.

"Okay, two more coming right up." I nodded, passing a glass to Ashley and the other to Sandra. I hoped it would keep Sandra from sneaking any more sips from Kat's beverage.

I was happy to resume my drink mixing as it gave me more time to consider endearment terms. Honestly, I couldn't think of many that didn't sound creepy or that didn't convey inappropriate connotations if examined closely. My problem, as ever, was that I examined most trivial things too closely and most important things not at all.

When I again emerged from the kitchen, the ladies were discussing one of Elizabeth's hospital pranks and the ramifications of her poor decision making. I thought her pranks were funny, but most likely a way to keep others at arm's length.

Someone mentioned something about wrinkles just as I was mulling over the possibility of dog breeds as potential endearment terms.

Therefore, I felt it appropriate to volunteer, "Several breeds of dogs have wrinkles, like the Pug and Shar Pei." I sipped my margarita and licked at the excess salt on the rim.

No one responded for a moment, and I dismissed the idea of Quinn calling me Pug as a sign of his love and devotion.

"Janie, your left-fielding skills are very impressive. You are the most impressive left fielder I've ever met." Sandra said this as she sneaked another sip of Kat's drink.

I frowned. "You mean the baseball position?" I sat back in my chair, wondering if I could somehow turn left fielding, or another baseball position, into a pet name. "I've never played baseball."

"No, hun. I'm talking about someone who says stuff out of left field. I never know what you're going to say or where you're going to take me. I'm just happy to be along for the ride." Sandra blew me a kiss. I liked it when she demonstrated overt signs of affection. She was a big cuddler and always seemed to want everyone to feel good.

I thought about this impulse of Sandra's as the conversation continued. She was a romantic and would likely be a good source of ideas for pet names, especially if I instructed her to take the assignment seriously. I was pondering how to get her alone to solicit some ideas when Sandra swiped Kat's margarita and was caught.

"It's okay," I said to Kat's outraged expression. "I'll make some more and bring out a pitcher." I stood and reached for Sandra's empty glass. "But since Sandra is being greedy, she has to come and help me."

Sandra stood. "Fine. It's a fair punishment."

"I'll come too," Elizabeth volunteered and began bundling her hand-knits into a ball.

My heart both sank and lifted. It sank because I couldn't ask Sandra about terms of endearment in front of Elizabeth. Elizabeth would likely want me to call Quinn something that referenced his domineering tendencies. However, I was happy to have her along because she was lovely and one of my aforementioned favorite people.

"I love this kitchen." Sandra's voice from behind me sounded wistful. "It's a kitchen for cooking."

I glanced at her, saw how she gazed longingly around her, and offered my agreement as I mixed together the tequila and lime juice. "I approve of this kitchen. I like the placement of the dishwasher relative to the sink and the refrigerator relative to the stove. Sandra—can you start squeezing more limes? They are in the bottom drawer of the fridge."

"These are really good margaritas, Janie. Well done." Elizabeth gave me a bright smile, which made me feel a bit better. I missed her as we'd been spending barely any time together—especially since the engagement.

"It's the Limoncello and fresh lime juice, I think. I also used agave nectar instead of sugar." I finished adding the necessary ingredients. Replacing the lid, I shook the shaker, enjoying the sound of the ice as it slid around the inside of the canister.

Elizabeth said, "You should make these when we go to my reunion in Iowa next week."

I stared at her, my movements stalled, and I felt the ground tilt beneath me.

Elizabeth's high school reunion.

I'd completely forgotten.

I was a horrible friend.

"Janie? Are you okay?"

"I completely forgot. I completely forgot about your reunion." I lowered the canister to the counter. My heart gave a twist, it felt like a cramp, as I noted Elizabeth's face fall.

"Did you make other plans?"

I glanced beyond her, trying to find a solution to the problem. "I'll—I'll find a way to…I'll think of something."

I tried to think of a solution. The dinner with Quinn's parents was Saturday. I wondered how I could be in both places at once. Maybe I could change the dinner with Quinn's parents to Saturday morning breakfast then fly to Iowa for Elizabeth's reunion in the evening. I could even bring pancakes. Certainly, it wouldn't be ideal. But I hated to cancel on Quinn's mom, especially since this was the first time I was meeting her.

Also, I still wasn't certain how Quinn felt about the whole thing. I didn't want to push him on it; I trusted him to tell me if I was overstepping.

Everything about the situation was worrisome and stressful, and now I'd just let down my best friend.

"What plans did you make?" Sandra's voice interrupted my contingency planning. "Maybe I can help?"

I attempted to keep the despondency out of my tone as I explained the problem. "We're—Quinn and I—we were planning to go to Boston to see his parents. I was going to meet his parents, but...." I glanced at Elizabeth, found her expression still downhearted. "I completely forgot about the reunion since you and I planned the trip so long ago."

"I'm confused. Isn't Quinn estranged from his parents? Didn't they, like, disown him? Don't they blame him for his brother's death or some such nonsense?" Sandra picked up the canister full of half-mixed margaritas and began shaking it.

I nodded. "Yes, they did. I'm not sure if they still do. I called his mom a few weeks ago and introduced myself. I told her I was marrying her son and explained that I planned to give her grandchildren at some point."

Sandra's hands ceased mid-shake. "You what?"

"Well, I know this separation from his family, from his mom and dad, contributes to some measure of his broodiness. I thought I could offer them grandchildren in exchange for forgiveness."

Elizabeth nodded in understanding, but Sandra stared at me like I'd just morphed into a wrinkly pug. Silence stretched. Elizabeth took the opportunity of Sandra's stillness to take the canister from her hands and continue to mix the contents.

"I—I can't believe you did that." Sandra finally sputtered. "You're using children—"

I shook my head and tried to explain. "No. I'm not using children. We're going to have kids anyway, and I thought why not use the idea of these future kids to persuade his parents to make the right decision now?"

Sandra made a choking sound then leaned on the kitchen counter. "You're not going to—you're not going to use the kids are you? Later? Once they're born? You're not going to manipulate his parents into...."

"No. Absolutely not." I was horrified by the thought. "I would never do that. I just—I just want his mom and dad to give him a chance. I just want them to make an effort. He's so...He's so...."

"Grumpy?" Elizabeth said and poured the margarita into

Sandra's glass.

I scowled at Elizabeth's inaccurate assessment of Quinn. "No. Not grumpy. He's sensitive. He doesn't show it to many people...."

She snorted. "You mean he only shows it to you."

I didn't want to debate the point, so I ignored her comment and continued explaining the situation to Sandra. I think part of me needed to justify my meddling and pushing regarding his family.

"But he is. And he misses his family. And they're his family. And I want to meet them. I've never had a mother, not really, and his mom sounds great, except for the whole—you know— disowning her son thing. And why shouldn't my children have grandparents?"

Elizabeth surprised me a little by saying, "They should. I completely support you in this decision."

"Thank you, Elizabeth. Your support means a lot."

Sandra was still frowning, seemed to be mulling over the situation, when she asked, "Well then, what about the reunion? I imagine it took a lot for you to get these people to agree to the visit, right?"

My attention moved from Sandra to Elizabeth, and I didn't know how to respond. I couldn't think of a solution, not one that would allow me to be in Boston and Iowa at the same time. My chest tightened uncomfortably because I knew the right thing to do was to cancel the dinner with Quinn's family.

Maybe this was a sign. Maybe I wasn't supposed to have initiated contact with his mother. Maybe, in the end, I would see that my efforts had been a mistake.

Before I could express this, however, Elizabeth surprised me by saying, "You should go to Boston." She lifted her eyes to mine. "Really. Go to Boston."

I shook my head. "I can reschedule. You can't reschedule your reunion."

"I'll go." Sandra's sloppy declaration—sloppy because it was somewhat slurred—surprised us both.

I blinked at her. "To Boston?"

"No, Wonder Woman, I'll go to Elizabeth's high school reunion. I'll go with Elizabeth, and you're off to Boston with your McHotpants to go make babies for those awful people."

I looked at Elizabeth. Elizabeth looked at me. Elizabeth looked at Sandra. Sandra looked at Elizabeth. I looked at Sandra. Sandra looked at me.

Sandra lifted her glass again, winked at Elizabeth, and toasted us both. "To friendscorts. Like escorts, but without the cash."

CHAPTER 14

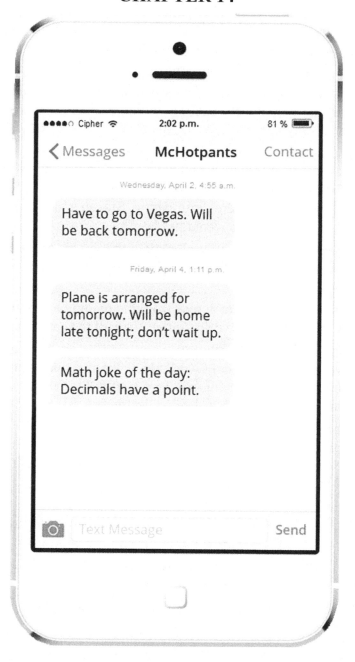

WE WERE ALONE on Quinn's plane.

Well, we weren't completely alone. The pilot, Eve, and the flight attendant, Donna, were also on the plane. But, they didn't really count because they tried to be basically invisible.

We planned to spend five days in Boston. Saturday evening, today, would be spent with Quinn's parents. Sunday we had no plans. Monday through Wednesday would be spent with corporate clients in all-day meetings. We planned to fly back to Chicago on Thursday.

Dan had flown ahead of us two days prior, and we'd arranged for Steven to video conference on days when he was needed. Since the private client numbers were diminishing, Steven and I were splitting up the corporate accounts.

Therefore, Quinn and I were alone together on his plane, and Quinn's plane was the last place we'd be together—as in *together together*—for several days.

He was sitting in his seat across from me reading a report like he didn't have a care in the world—other than all the cares that were currently making him frown.

But I wasn't thinking about work cares. I was thinking about the no-touching cares…the being-so-close-to-him-but-not-kissing cares…the he-didn't-seem-to-be-at-all-affected-by-our-lack-of-intimacy cares.

I was also thinking about the increased frequency and vividness of my sex dreams as well as the resultant saliva on my pillow. I'd had to change the pillowcase four times in a week.

Four times!

Add to his apparent apathy—at least for all things me—was the fact that I didn't know how to bring up the subject of his family without feeling like a conniving charlatan, and I felt a little overwrought, sexually stunted, and nauseous.

Make that a little nauseous and a lot stressed out.

"Hi," he said.

I blinked at him several times in rapid succession, bringing his face into focus. I'd been staring at him. But I wasn't really looking at him. Looking at him these days hurt a little. Therefore, I'd begun the practice of starting at one thing on him—like the scar above his eyebrow, or the top button of his shirt, or a single red stripe on his tie.

"Hey." I shifted in my seat, realized I'd been gripping my iPad too tightly, and loosened my fingers.

"Are you alright?" He asked this question as if he already knew the answer, as if he knew I was starving and he'd just asked me if I wanted to lick the frosting off his cupcake. It was a little irritating.

Therefore, I didn't answer his question.

Instead, I said, "I think I need a pet name."

"Pardon?"

"I think you need to give me a pet name—a term of endearment."

His face was its typical impassive mask, but I could tell that I'd surprised him.

Finally, he said, "Like…*babe*?"

"No—that feels awkward and wrong and has undertones of pedophilia. I'm thinking of something more age appropriate, yet affectionate."

He considered me, my request. I was pleased to find that he appeared to be taking it seriously. "Cupcake?" he asked.

"No food."

"Why not?"

"Because I'm not edible."

"I disagree."

My eyes widened before I could control my body's response to his bluntly spoken statement, mostly because I didn't want to delve too deep into the matter for fear that I would haul him back to the lavatory to prove that I was edible. Instead, I said, "Okay…I'll take food under advisement, but I think we should continue the search."

"Dove?"

"Dove? No."

"Why not dove?"

"Too close to ostrich, and falcons eat doves for lunch."

"So?"

"So, I think of you as a falcon. And, although we've established that you consider me edible, I don't like the mental image of you killing me for a meal, my feathers strewn about in a bloody mass of...."

"Alright, not dove. What about sweet pea or lamb?"

"Meh."

"Meh?"

"They don't feel right."

He placed his report on the chair next to him, rested his elbows on the armrests, and tented his fingers. "You suggest something then."

"Okay...what about Medusa?"

He grimaced. "Medusa?"

"Yes."

"No."

"Why?"

"Because that's not giving me a good mental image."

"What? Why? Poseidon thought she was lovely."

He sighed, frowned, and shook his head. "How about kitten?"

Kitten? "Kitten?" I thought and said the word at the same time.

"Yeah. Try this on—" Quinn paused, his eyes moved from mine to my mouth, neck, chest, then up again; the return pass left his gaze half lidded and lazy. All of this effected a leisurely inspection that might have been lewd if attempted by anyone else. But, as Quinn was my fiancé and the man I was head over heels in love with, the perusal made me a lot agitated (in the best and most frustrating way possible).

Then, low and intimate, he said, "Hey, Kitten."

"Guh," was my automatic response. Actually, it was barely a sound, more just an inadvertent rumble of lady-feels. My stomach flipped and heat blossomed in my chest. I think I'd like anything he said using that voice.

His eyes danced between mine then landed on my lips. His mouth curved slowly into one of his slow, sexy grins. "I like this. This was a good idea."

I had to swallow twice before I could speak. "Why?"

"Because you just purred like a kitten," he responded, using the same low, sexy voice.

I wondered for a brief moment what the hell was wrong with me. I could be married to this man, right now—right this minute. Instead, I was sitting across from him, not touching him, and nearing volcanic levels of sexual frustration just because he'd called me *kitten*.

"I need a drink." I choked. I was desperate, and self-medication with alcohol seemed like a pretty good idea. As well, I was sweating. My neck was damp and my stomach and chest were hot.

"Not a cigarette?" he asked and, damn him, he grinned.

"No. Not a cigarette." The words may have emerged a bit grumpily—mostly because he was just sitting there, cold as an icicle, and I was melting.

I set my iPad on the seat next to me and peeled off my jacket, then unbuttoned the top two buttons of my blouse. I didn't care if he knew he made me hot. He did make me hot. That was truth. We were getting married, and I might as well own the fact that, when he wanted to and sometimes when he didn't want to, he affected my internal temperature, heart rate, blood pressure, and endorphin levels.

"Are you warm?" he asked, looking only mildly interested.

"No, Quinn. I'm hot. In fact, I'm burning up, in case you didn't already know." Throwing caution to the wind, I stood and released a third button, pulled my shirttails from my skirt, and fanned the fabric, trying to encourage air flow. "You have an incendiary effect on me, and I'm quite uncomfortably aroused right now. Your biometrics might be completely unaffected by my presence, but all you have to do is call me *Kitten* and I experience vasomotor symptoms."

"Vasomotor symptoms?"

"A hot flash," I said simply. "But it's not a real hot flash, not like the kind brought on by menopause. If it were then I'd have to go get my pituitary gland inspected. Hot flashes are typically associated with the hormone changes that occur during menopause, but…in some women…."

Quinn cut me off by sliding his hands to the back of my legs and up my skirt, and pulling me to his lap. I basically crashed into him, and he took advantage of my stunned flailing to caress me, cup me through my panties.

"Guh," I said and paired it with a gasp, every nerve ending abruptly on fire. Quinn grabbed a fistful of my hair with the hand that was not pressing against my center, and—quite roughly— tugged my head back to expose my throat.

He sucked on my neck. Then, he bit me. Like, *bit* me. It was painful and fantastic, and tangentially my mind told me that it would leave a mark. At once, I was aware of a few things.

First, he was hard—in a way that I imagined was quite painful— beneath my bottom. Even through the clothes that separated us, I felt how markedly his biometrics were affected.

Second, his fingers were pushing my underwear out of the way and entering my body. I was so ready for his invasion—I was beyond ready. If ready were the Illinois-Iowa state line, I was doing circles around the moon.

Third, we were no longer alone.

"Mr. Sullivan, the pilot wants to know—oh my God! Sorry!" I heard Donna's voice over my shoulder. I stiffened.

Quinn removed his mouth from my neck just long enough to issue the command, "Go away."

The next sound I heard—other than my own frenetic breathing— was Donna's shoes scurrying down the aisle back to the galley.

His kisses felt both frantic and methodical, as did his fingers between my legs, which were beginning to shake. I shifted on his lap, my hips bucking, my hands searching for purchase, and bursts of light rimmed my vision. It didn't take long before I was ready to explode.

Then, I did explode. At least, it felt like an explosion, and this time he didn't capture my mouth with a kiss to deafen the sound. Instead, he just let my moans turn into screams—because I was a screamer—until my throat was sore and I was completely spent.

I collapsed against him, curling into his body, gripping whatever part of him I could.

Quinn released his hold on my hair and wrapped me in his arms, though he made no attempt to put either of us to rights. My skirt was around my waist, my underwear halfway down my hips; and at some point, my shirt had been pulled open and several buttons were missing.

I swallowed, my throat a tad sore from my expressive appreciation, and I placed several kisses on his neck and jaw.

It occurred to me that the bet was over, that we would be getting married within the next twenty-four hours, that I could say goodbye to all the manufactured stress. It was an amazing feeling. I smiled and nipped at his chin.

"So…I guess the wedding's off," I said, my voice raspy.

Quinn nuzzled my ear, licked it, made me shiver. "Why would you say that?"

I pulled away so I could look into his eyes. "Because I lost the bet. I couldn't last."

"You didn't lose the bet."

I frowned. "I didn't?"

He shook his head. "No."

"But…but we…."

"No. We didn't. I did." He kissed me quickly then slid his nose along mine. "The bet was that you had to last, but we said nothing about me lasting."

My frown deepened. "Wait—perhaps I don't understand the terms. You mean…you mean…what do you mean?"

"You still haven't touched me," he said simply, then added in his *kitten* voice, "but I couldn't go another minute without touching you."

I sighed despondently even as I shivered, a lovely involuntary response to his tone and words. "That's not equitable," I said. Actually, it might have been a whine. "The bet should be over."

"Nope. Wedding is still on, unless…."

"Penetration." I supplied the word, scowling at him.

I wasn't angry with Quinn. I was annoyed with myself because

I'd been happy to hand my decision-making reigns over to his capable hands—no pun intended. Quinn, being Quinn, handed them right back to me. This should have made me feel empowered. Instead, I felt irritated.

But then, just as suddenly, I felt grateful and…certain.

Quinn and me were always going to be Quinn and me. I could go through the motions, but the end result was going to be the same. Postponing the inevitable was making me miserable, and being miserable wasn't okay with me anymore.

In fact, I wasn't okay with being just okay anymore either, not when I could take a simple action and grab happiness by the scrotum.

As Fiona had said, happiness doesn't have to be fleeting if you accept it. I think in a lot of ways, I had difficulty allowing myself to be happy. Maybe I thought I wasn't deserving enough to be happy, that I hadn't earned it. Maybe I thought it wouldn't last, and I was frightened of one day facing the end of my happiness. Maybe I associated it with selfishness, because my mother always seemed to choose her own happiness over everyone else's wellbeing.

More likely, I didn't think it was possible to just be happy.

Just…happy.

No one else was in the wings, suffering because I was happy.

No rigorous minefield of proof was necessary.

No litmus test of worthiness.

No secret handshake.

My eyes were open. I was in love. I wanted to be happy.

I didn't surrender to it. I grabbed the reigns. I loved Quinn without condition.

I chose happy.

I jumped off his lap.

"Take your pants off." I motioned to his pants with a flick of my wrist, straightened my skirt and underwear.

Quinn lifted a single eyebrow at me, a cautious smile pulling at his lips. "Janie…."

"Take them off." I whipped my shirt from my arms, tossed it

over my shoulder, and unhooked my bra, casting that aside as well.

Quinn's eyes immediately went to my breasts and I thought I heard him growl. He reached for me, brought my bare chest to his mouth, and lavished my skin with hungry bites and kisses.

"Pants. Off," I repeated, arching against him and slipping my hands down his stomach to his belt.

"Why, Kitten? What are you going to do?"

I smiled, kissed him quickly, sank to my knees, and said, "I'm getting married."

***

SUFFICE TO SAY, both Quinn and I were very relaxed when the plane touched down in Boston.

He was smirking. It was the worst kind of smirk, too—a smug, arrogant, proud smirk, and I didn't mind one bit. Yes, I'd abandoned my plans for a big wedding. Yes, I would have to break the news to Marie that all her good advice was for naught. Yes, I was a quitter.

But I didn't care, because I was happy.

I did feel sorry for our flight attendant, however. If anyone was waiting in the wings suffering due to our happiness, it had to be Donna. Technically, she wasn't in the wings; she was in the galley. I found her there just before the plane landed.

When I apologized profusely, she was very gracious about it, said that she was happy for us, and then she also apologized. I suggested we work out some kind of signal, like the seatbelt sign on commercial airlines, for future trips. She seemed to think this was a good plan.

Pragmatically, I knew this flight was not the last time Quinn and I would be intimate on the plane. As such, I would have to work on my loud sex noises.

I also thought noise-cancelling headphones would make a great gift for her birthday and made a mental note to pick up a pair.

The plane landed. We changed clothes. Dan was waiting for us in the limo.

As soon as Quinn saw him, everything about his demeanor

changed. The smirk disappeared, his eyes shuttered, and a coolness seemed to radiate from his pores. It was like someone had yelled "I need a tampon" in a sports bar.

Scootching farther on the bench seat, I glanced from Quinn to Dan then back again.

"Hey, Dan the security man," I said, giving him a half wave as the car pulled away from the airport.

"Hey, Janie," he responded, a tight smile on his face, then he turned his eyes back to Quinn.

Quinn met his gaze and held it for a few moments, and something passed between them that I didn't understand. It was some secret guy code or telepathy. At length Quinn moved his attention to the window and the landscape beyond.

The limo was basically silent during the entire ride.

At one point I said, "Boston is fairly unusual because it's the most populated city in Massachusetts and also the state capital. Very few state capitals are also the most populated city in the state."

Quinn glanced at me as I spoke and for a few beats afterward. Then, with no change in his expression, he returned his gaze to the window.

Dan grimaced. I thought I heard him mutter, "Fucking Boston…."

Where Quinn looked ambivalent, Dan looked uncomfortable.

I began to understand why Steven didn't like riding in limos with Quinn. I thought back to a conversation Steven and I had had some months ago, the day I learned Quinn was *The Boss*.

Since I was nervous and the interior of the car was completely quiet, my mind began to wander with complete abandon. Therefore, when the limo pulled to a stop and the engine cut off, I was a little surprised that we'd arrived.

"Are you ready to do this?" Dan's eyes were narrowed on Quinn, and I heard the faint sound of the driver's side door shutting.

Quinn stared at his friend, and for several seconds made no outward sign that he'd heard Dan's question, then shrugged his shoulders. "Sure."

Something like frustration or worry cast a shadow over Dan's expression, and his eyes shifted from Quinn to me.

"Call me if...." He started, stopped, gritted his teeth. "Just call me."

I nodded. The back door to the limo opened revealing a sidewalk, a black wrought iron gate, and cement steps leading to a blue-gray row house with white trim.

As usual, Quinn exited first. He'd changed into a new suit on the plane after I'd annihilated our bet. It was dark gray, his shirt was white, and his tie was a gradient of black to gray with a single red, diagonal stripe. I liked this tie. It was strange to think that I would have an opinion on a man's tie, but I did.

On top of his suit, he wore a black, cashmere overcoat. He looked quite dashing.

He held out his hand. I took it then held on to it as the driver closed the door behind us. I glanced at Quinn and saw him conducting a sweep of the street, his eyes taking in every detail with his typical aloof precision.

My attention was drawn to the three-story row house in front of us, the potted plants that lined the steps, and a cluster of new tulips giving the otherwise cold, gray day hope for the approaching spring.

"Is this where you grew up?" I studied the house in front of us. It was old but well maintained. The white trim was newly painted, as was the red door.

He nodded, still glancing around the street.

I briefly wondered if he were actually still surveying our surroundings or just postponing having to face his childhood home.

Eventually, I was the one who took the first step toward the house, tugging him behind me. "Come on. It's cold out here."

I was nervous.

I was a tad nervous about meeting Quinn's mom and dad in person. I worried a little that they wouldn't like me or would think I was strange. I'd conducted a self-examination of these feelings and believed they were typical reactions to meeting one's new in-laws. These feelings weren't overwhelming; just present enough to be noticed.

More than that, much more than that, I was nervous for Quinn. He'd shut down every time I'd tried to talk to him about the situation with his parents. I wanted him to be okay. Actually, I wanted him to be happy. I hoped that today wouldn't undermine that.

If it did, then I would make it up to him. Maybe we would get a puppy, or maybe a new biometric watch that recorded your heart rate, steps taken, and calories burned. Or, maybe I'd go a week without wearing underwear.

Or maybe all three.

I glanced down at my outfit as I climbed the steps, fiddled with the large brass button of my dark navy coat and thought about the average height of steps. Step height—as well as the currently accepted depth and width—were determined in 1927. Humans have grown taller, their legs longer, and I wondered when construction norms would be re-evaluated to account for the increase in stature.

Beneath the coat, I wore a light blue button down shirt, a cream pencil skirt, and cream stockings. I'd paired the outfit with navy blue and off white stilettos. They were really pretty shoes.

We reached the top of the stairs, and I pushed thoughts of construction norms from my mind, tried to focus on the present. I gave Quinn a reassuring smile even though his face was as impassive as I'd ever seen it.

I attempted a swallow, but found it a bit difficult. With a shaking hand, I reached for the doorbell and pressed the button, flinching when the chime sounded from within the house.

I stepped back, waited, then blurted to Quinn in a rushed whisper, "I'm really nervous."

His hand squeezed mine, his lips suddenly at my ear, and he whispered in response, "Don't be. They're going to love you."

I didn't get a chance to tell him that I wasn't nervous for me.

Part 4: Meeting the Family

CHAPTER 15

Quinn

I WAS DREADING this moment.

How do you face the people whose son you murdered? How do you greet your parents when you played a large part in the death of your brother?

I didn't hold the gun or pull the trigger, but criminals had been free to shoot my brother Des because I'd helped them walk free.

I knew Dan being in the limo when we landed was his way of showing me support. He'd been there when it all went down. I still needed to ask him about being my best man, but it would have to wait.

Telling Janie about the death of my brother hadn't been in my plans. I hadn't expected to tell her; when I did, I thought she'd say the same thing everyone else said: it wasn't your fault, you can't hold yourself responsible, you couldn't have known.

That was all bullshit.

I knew what I was doing. I knew I was putting people in danger. Even worse, I was a smart kid who came from a good family, and I knew better.

I knew better.

What she'd said was, "I understand why you blame yourself."

Her words were a revelation. She didn't try to make me feel better about it. She didn't try to feed me a line. She looked at the situation with cold logic and concluded that the blame I carried made sense.

That's why, when I asked her if she blamed me, her response was important, because her honest answer would be meaningful.

She'd responded, "I blame the bad guy who actually pulled the trigger and killed him. In this situation, you sound like a person who has recognized the error of his ways and attempted to change. If you recall, that is the difference between a good guy and a bad guy."

And that made all the difference.

Her response was a rational analysis of the situation. She had nothing to gain, and she wasn't the type to offer empty words meant to absolve me of my responsibility.

What I didn't expect was that she would recognize that I needed to be held accountable.

I needed it.

I needed accountability so that I could change. I needed to make different decisions. I never would have made different decisions without taking responsibility for what I'd done.

I was responsible. I needed to be held accountable.

But none of that, no amount of restitution, would bring Des back.

That's why meeting my father's eyes was just as difficult as it had been on the day of my brother's funeral.

But I did it.

The door opened and they were there. My father's eyes found mine first. He looked older, shorter than I remembered—but that's not to say that he was small. He was exactly my size now; when I was a kid, he'd just seemed so much larger.

My brother took after my mother, blonde hair and light brown eyes, medium build. But Shelly and I looked like my father. Janie said I reminded her of a hawk. If that was the case, then my father was an eagle—big and proud, and quiet until just before the kill.

He was also the most patient man I knew. He could out-wait a statue. Reading him had always been difficult, unless he wanted you to know what he was thinking. That's probably why he was such an excellent police detective.

My mother was speaking to Janie, Janie had let go of my hand to accept a handshake, and still my father and I looked at each other, sharing nothing. The interaction was numbing.

I didn't know what he was looking for—maybe remorse. Whatever it was, I couldn't give it to him because it would never be enough. Nothing I would do would ever be enough.

"Quinn?"

I glanced at Janie, her upturned smiling face, her expectant amber eyes.

"Yes?" I said.

"Did you know that comity of handshaking originated in remote antiquity? At that time, human beings lived on hunting. If they happened to meet a stranger, they would throw their hunting tools aside and open their hands to show the person that they weren't a threat."

As she spoke, my attention flickered to my mother who was watching Janie with rapt attention. As soon as Janie finished, my mom stepped forward and touched her elbow.

"I was just cutting carrots, but I have no other weapons on my person." She was smiling at Janie. She was smiling at her as though she liked her.

"Oh, me neither," Janie responded with a warm smile. "But I imagine Quinn probably has a gun. But don't worry, he has a license for it."

My parents' attention turned to me, and I had no choice but to stand still under their scrutiny. An uncomfortable moment passed while Janie glanced back and forth between us. I noticed her neck had flushed red and splotchy.

I knew what would come next. Janie would try to fill the silence with more facts.

But no gushing of information arrived, because my mom stepped out of the house. She stood directly in front of me, gave me a half smile, and wrapped her arms around my waist, her cheek pressed against my chest.

Startled, I glanced from the top of her head to Janie.

Janie's eyes were wide, and she lifted her chin to my mother. When I frowned at her, Janie mimed a hugging motion and lifted her chin more urgently, mouthing the words, *Give your mother a hug!*

So I did. I wrapped my arms around the woman who'd raised me, who'd loved me until she didn't, and she responded by sniffling against my jacket and squeezing tighter.

I swallowed a building lump in my throat and, for no reason in particular, my attention turned to my father. His stone-faced expression was gone as he looked at my mother's head tucked against my shoulder, then his eyes lifted to mine.

They were wet.

The world tilted on its axis because this was the closest I'd ever seen my father come to crying.

***

NAVIGATING THE NEXT hour was like being on a movie set from my childhood with no script.

My mother hugged me for a long time. This only ended after Janie, unable to contain herself any longer, lunged at my father and gave him a hug too. He was so surprised he started to laugh, which made my mother laugh. Then Janie laughed and gave my dad a kiss on the cheek.

"What was that for?" he asked.

"For laughing at me. I've never liked the sound of my laugh so much," she said, then stepped back and apologized for being forward, and tried to explain that hugging—in some cultures—was more intimate than kissing, therefore she should have asked permission first.

My father responded by grinning at me and scooping her back into his arms. The hugging on the front porch finally culminated in a group hug between my fiancée and my parents, which I was forcefully pulled into by both Janie and my mother.

Then I was led into the house, my overcoat and suit jacket were taken, a beer was placed in my hand, and we were standing in the kitchen of the house where I grew up.

I didn't know where to look. I didn't know what to say, or how to talk to these people. Janie seemed happy to fill the silence, standing at my side with her arm around my waist and her hip against the counter.

She talked about her inability to knit, the origins of knitting, fiber as an art, the cultivation of carrots, the origins of the Easter Bunny, variations of rabbits, the reprehensible treatment of Irish immigrants in the United States during the Industrial Revolution, the largest rodents, the plague, modern viruses.

Janie was nervous. But as I glanced at my parents, this time really looking at them, I realized that she wasn't the only one. I saw my mother looking at me as though I might disappear. When I caught her, her expression turned anxious and sad.

I tried giving her a small smile. She returned it with a larger one.

My father appeared to be absorbed in all the information Janie related. Occasionally, he'd stop her and ask a question, request clarification on a point or a fact.

When Janie had told me that she'd contacted my parents, all I'd felt was shame and a growing sense of dread. I don't know what I was expecting when we arrived, but it wasn't this.

Eventually, Janie separated herself from me, tied on an apron, and began helping my mother with dinner. They spoke about elementary number theory, about how Janie had been taking a free masters course online offered by Stanford University.

My attention caught on a picture held by magnets to the refrigerator and, upon recognizing it, my lungs hurt like I'd inhaled smoke from a fire. Without premeditation, I crossed to the fridge and stared at the picture.

It was of me when I was twelve. Next to it was another picture—of me, Des, and my father—taken on my first fishing trip. Another hung next to it of Shelly and me when I was six; she'd painted both of our faces with makeup.

The fridge was covered in pictures, and none of them were recent.

I felt rather than saw my father stand next to me. He didn't speak at first, just watched my profile.

Then he said, "Do you remember that trip? You caught the largest fish."

I nodded, staring at the photograph. "I remember."

"You look confused, son," he said; his blunt words were not a surprise. For better or for worse, he was always blunt. He was also always careful with the words he used.

My eyes narrowed on the picture then slid to the side to meet his. He was watching me like he knew what I was thinking, like he was just waiting for me to say it out loud.

"I am confused," I admitted. "I thought you would have...." I didn't finish the thought because it felt disrespectful to say out loud that I thought my parents would have burned all pictures of my image, or cut me out of them.

If the roles had been reversed, I would have done that.

He studied me for what seemed like a long time. His hair was almost completely gray now, and deep frown lines had carved themselves between his eyebrows.

"I regret...." He started, stopped, cleared his throat before continuing. His voice was low so as not to be overheard by the ladies present. "I've regretted for a long time what happened, what I said to you, when your brother died."

I stared at him. My shock must've been plain because this man of few words kept speaking.

"Your mother and I were blinded by grief, but that's no excuse. It was wrong what we said, how we acted. It was dishonorable, and we both regret how we treated you. I hope you can forgive us."

My throat tight, I responded automatically. "No. There is nothing to forgive. I deserved it."

"You didn't."

"I did. I may not have...." I glanced over his shoulder. "I was responsible."

"You weren't."

I met his eyes again, was surprised to see his expression full of remorse.

I shook my head, said between clenched teeth, "You did nothing wrong."

He placed his hand on my shoulder, his head shake mirroring mine. "We did, and we're sorry for it. And we'd like to make it up to you, if you'll let us."

"I'll eat almost anything, but my friend Elizabeth hates mayonnaise." Janie's voice was at my back, her hand on my hip. "Excuse me, guys. I need to get out the mayonnaise for the deviled eggs. I was just telling Katherine that I'll eat almost anything, but that Elizabeth hates mayonnaise. I think it must have something to do with the texture, because she also doesn't like pudding. I'm not implying that she has a sensory processing disorder; it's just that soft, gelatinous foods make her gag."

My dad's hand dropped and he stepped away. His eyes arrested mine for a beat then moved to Janie. "Sensory processing disorder?"

"Yes. Extreme sensitivity to textures—in food or fabric or really anything that has a texture." Janie pressed on my hip to move me out of the way. She smiled at me as the fridge door opened, hiding us from my father's view. "Sometime people just need some time to process the way things feel—to get used to it before making a judgment about it."

I narrowed my eyes at her. I was still disoriented by my father's words, but I pressed my lips together in order to communicate that I understood her heavy-handed attempt to speak of both Elizabeth's aversion to mayo and my present discomfort.

She shrugged, wrinkled her nose. "I've tried pushing her into eating it, but it never works. So I've learned to be less pushy."

"You're still pushy," I said, taking a swig of my beer. After what my father had just admitted, I needed something stronger.

"I'm not *that* pushy…am I?"

I let my eyes travel over her face, enjoyed the shape of her eyes when they were wide and curious, noted that she wasn't wearing any lipstick. This meant I could kiss her later without any evidence.

"Yes. You are that pushy."

Her mouth twisted to the side, and I knew she was biting the inside of her lip. She let the fridge close and held the mayo jar between both of her hands.

Then she blurted, "But you must like it if you want to marry me."

"I do like it." I stepped closer and gave her a quick kiss, momentarily forgetting where I was.

Or maybe I didn't forget. Maybe I wanted just such a moment in my parents' house with the woman I loved as if we belonged here, all of us together.

When I looked up, I caught my dad glancing at my mother. He was smiling.

***

MY FATHER DIDN'T bring up my brother again. He said almost nothing leading up to dinner, which was typical of how things were when I was growing up. He was never a talker. I'd learned from him early on that the less you spoke, the more people listened.

But quiet in this house was atypical. Between my brother Des, Shelly, and my mother, the house was never quiet.

Everything here was the same—the furniture and carpets, the pictures on the walls—and nothing felt right. I kept thinking about the last time I saw my parents. My mother couldn't even look at me without crying.

My father's apology felt too fast, too soon, and—as Janie would say—dissonant with reality. I trusted that he meant it, but I didn't understand it. I'd lived with the guilt of my part in my brother's death for ten years. Since walking into the house, I was choking on it, and the apology only compounded it.

The only thing that kept me from bolting out the door was Janie. I think her presence created a buffer for my parents and me. She was the necessary conduit through which we could co-exist. I saw her as a reminder in this house full of history and memories that things had changed and would continue to change. I was no longer a selfish, dumbass teenager. I was trying to be more.

Janie and I were setting the table. She followed me with the silverware as I set the plates and glasses on the table. I could tell she wanted me to talk about what I was thinking, but she didn't push. She seemed to sense that I needed some time with my thoughts.

My mother brought out dinner. I realized once all the food was assembled that she'd made almost all of my favorites: sausage with gravy and mashed potatoes—otherwise known as bangers and mash—deviled eggs with ham and pimento, butternut squash, carrots with brown sugar, and homemade brown bread.

The smells made my mouth water and I was bombarded with memories. During grace, I could feel my mother's eyes on me, so I glanced up.

She was a mixture of anxiety and hope. She made no attempt to hide her emotions.

I wanted to say, "I don't merit your hope or your worry. I don't deserve to be your son."

Instead, after grace, I said, "This all looks really great. Thank you."

Her smile was immediate and her response sounded a little breathless. "Well, it's not every day we get to…I mean, we're just so happy you're here. Both of you."

A brief moment of silence stretched, because I didn't know what to say. Again, I wanted to ask her how she could be happy that I was there. I wanted to know how they could possibly think that I deserved an apology. Part of me wanted to shout at them, ask how they could stand the sight of me.

"I'm happy to be here," Janie blurted. "I hope I set the silverware right. I forget if the spoon goes on the inside or the outside of the knife. Usually, at home, Quinn and I only use the utensils needed for any given meal, so, usually just a fork, unless we have steak or chicken, then we also have a knife. Of course, soup needs a spoon." Janie scrunched her face, looking a little frustrated. "Sorry, that's all very obvious."

"Do you know what you're serving for the wedding?" My mom asked Janie in a gentle voice.

Janie sighed. "I've come to the conclusion that I'm not suited to plan a wedding, not a real one. I think I told you the last time we spoke on the phone that I still haven't found a location for the reception. Everything, all the other parts, really revolve around the reception location."

"You don't have a place reserved yet?" My mother exchanged a glance with my father as Janie cut into the sausage on her plate.

"No. Honestly, nothing has been accomplished. Planning a wedding is like organizing a beauty contest for cats. It feels like the ultimate effort in futility."

Then, a second later, Janie mumbled mostly to herself, "I guess I shouldn't say that, because there is a feline beauty contest in Bucharest, Romania every year." She turned to my father and added, "Over two hundred cats participate, and the winner gets a little cat crown. Although, I have no idea how they secure it to the cat's head…." She picked up her wine to take a sip.

I couldn't help saying, "Maybe you should enter the kitten contest."

Her eyes flew to mine, widened, and she covered her mouth before the wine she'd just sipped ended up on the tablecloth. I felt bad that I'd made her choke, but I was pleased to see the first signs of a blush spread up her neck.

"Do you have a kitten?" my mother asked.

"Yes," I said.

"No," Janie croaked.

Then, addressing my mother, but still holding my gaze, Janie quickly added, "I'm sorry, you were asking me about the wedding."

"Oh, yes. Well…I know that this is your special day, and it's about the two of you—the love you have for each other—but…." My mother hesitated, and her eyes caught mine. "But if you haven't already found a place in Chicago and you don't have your heart set on getting married there, I wonder if you would consider getting married in Boston."

I masked my surprise by chasing a bite of mashed potatoes with a large gulp of beer.

"In Boston?" Janie asked; her tone made her surprise obvious.

"Yes. I'm sorry if I've overstepped. I was thinking about it after our last call. So I checked with the Irish Club and they're holding the date for me, just in case. If you had the wedding here, we could have the entire family, and I could help with the planning."

"It would mean a lot to your mother." My father said this to me, though his eyes were on his plate.

"It's not about me," my mom said, a frown directed at my father. She shifted her attention back to Janie. "It's about you and Quinn. It's about starting your life together and celebrating with all your friends and family, who should be there to support you. And of course your family must be taken into consideration, so if Boston is too far then just forget I said anything."

"To be honest, my family doesn't need to be taken into consideration. I'm not saying this to be unfeeling; it's really just the way things are." Janie said this with no malice. In the past, she'd remarked that her family's dysfunction was one of the laws of thermodynamics.

"What about your parents?"

"I'm sure my dad will come, if given enough notice and we reimburse his travel expenses, regardless of location. My younger sister is a sociopath, and I don't know where she is. Quinn might know. But I don't think we want her there..." Janie shook her head at the thought, and I suppressed a grimace at the mention of Jem.

Janie didn't notice. "My older sister can't come. The last I heard she skipped bail on a conviction for prostitution; she was running an escort service on the West Coast. Besides, June often turns what would typically be a normal event into an awkward and uncomfortable function. She came to my college graduation and tried to solicit my favorite professor. We don't really keep in contact."

"You and your sister, or you and your favorite professor?" My father asked.

"Neither. I'm afraid that bridge was burned when she cornered him in the men's room."

My mom stared at Janie for a long moment, absorbing this information, then asked, "What about your mother?"

"She'd dead."

My mother's eyes widened. I read both sympathy and shock on her expression. "I'm so sorry."

Janie gave her a smile meant to ease her mind. "Thank you, but she wasn't around very often when I was young. I have very few memories of her that don't involve the botched preparation of vegan dinners."

My mother's gaze drifted to and searched mine. She appeared troubled. She also appeared determined.

"Speaking of dinners, these sausages are delicious." Janie's voice was a little higher pitched than usual, and I knew she was trying to change the subject. Discussions of her family—really, the aftermath of discussions and people's reactions—always made her agitated.

"My partner gave them to me. You remember Tom?" My father

asked me, spooning more mashed potatoes on his plate. "He goes moose hunting in Canada every year, always brings back sausages."

"M-moose?" Janie asked.

Something about the tone of her voice caught my attention, and I glanced at her, did a double take as she'd suddenly become pale.

"Yep. Moose."

Janie set down her fork, one hand going to her stomach, the other to the water glass, shaking.

I frowned at her, tried to catch her eye, especially since she was now turning green.

My mom also noticed, because she asked, "Are you okay, Dear?"

"Deer too?" Janie's eyes grew wide and she'd firmed her chin. "Deer and moose? Any other woodland animals included in the sausage? Beavers maybe?"

"No," my mother said, "just moose. I was calling you Dear. There are no deer in the sausage."

"Oh...." Janie blinked. I could see her throat working; she was struggling to swallow.

"What's wrong?" My concern was escalating to alarm. I'd never seen her this way before. She looked like she was going to be sick.

"It's just...." She lifted her eyes to mine, and I saw she was panicked. She covered her mouth and shook her head.

"Janie," I started to stand but she lifted her hand, staying my movements, keeping me in my seat. "Janie, what is wrong?"

She shook her head again, closing her eyes. "I don't want to say." Her words were muffled because her hand was still in front of her mouth.

My mother looked at me imploringly.

"Say it," I said. My heart rate spiked, and I was pulling out my phone. I didn't know who I was going to call—maybe Elizabeth. She was a doctor and Janie's best friend. She'd be able to tell me if I should call an ambulance. Maybe she could talk her through this crisis.

"It's just...." Janie buried her face in her hands, her elbows hitting the table. "It's just that moose carry a strain of mad cow disease, but it's not mad cow disease, it's mad moose disease."

"Mad moose disease?" my father asked, his fork halfway to his mouth with a piece of moose sausage speared on it. He glanced between Janie and the bite of moose meat.

"The moose go mad, break off their antlers, just crazy moose running around in the forest. They can weigh seven hundred pounds or more, so you can imagine the devastation. And there is no cure—not for the moose. And if you eat moose meat, you can get it—assuming the moose you eat has the disease—and you won't know because it doesn't present for ten years, or thereabouts, after you've consumed the moose meat. So we could all be infected and our brains could melt and we could all go mad…in about ten years."

The end of her tirade was punctuated by deafening silence. Then, the silence was followed by a muffled burst of laughter from my mother. I looked at my mom, found her trying to contain her giggles with a napkin covering the bottom half of her face. But her eyes shone with mirth, and try as she might, she couldn't stop laughing.

I looked to my father and found his shoulders shaking. He was doing a better job of hiding his amusement, fighting harder against it, because his eyes were closed and his hand was clamped over his mouth.

Even I was grinning and shaking my head.

Janie was peeking at us from between her fingers. Her face and neck were every shade of red, but a weary smile tugged at one side of her mouth as her eyes moved between my parents. Her hands fell away.

"So I guess…." She shrugged her shoulders, looked pained but also reluctantly pleased with herself, and took a deep breath. "We should just make the best of the time we still have left!"

CHAPTER 16

Janie

QUINN AND HIS father did the dishes.

As soon as dinner was over, Quinn stood, began collecting the dishes, and left the dining room with his father as if it was imprinted in his genetic code. I watched them come in and out, these two giant men, clearing the serving plates in silence while Katherine spoke to me about one of her favorite students.

I debated whether to stand, made up my mind to do so, but Quinn shook his head when I pushed my chair back and indicated through our developing means of silent communication that I should stay and chat with his mom.

When the last of the items was taken, I turned to her, leaned close, and whispered, "Does Desmond always do the dishes?"

She glanced at the doorway to the kitchen and nodded. "Yes, if I make dinner then he does the dishes. If he makes dinner then I do the dishes. It's how we've always done it. It's also nice because, since it's tradition, we both know what's expected of us, which leads to fewer dirty dishes and less nagging."

"Oh." I started to stand.

"Where are you going?"

"To help with the dishes."

"No, no. Stay with me, you helped with dinner and, if you don't mind, I appreciate your company." Her smile was warm, affectionate and therefore felt maternal, which made me a little uncomfortable. But Katherine reached for my hand, squeezed it. "You know, you remind me of Shelly a little."

"I do?" I grinned at the thought. Other than being tall, awkward, and loving Quinn, I didn't think we had much in common.

"Yes. It's the curiosity, I think. She was the most curious kid I've ever met, always taking things apart, wanting to know how they worked, putting them back together—but never in the way they were before. Always in a new way."

"I am curious. It's true. That's a fact."

"And also the goodness. She felt everything so deeply as a child and as a teenager. We once found a dog running around the neighborhood with three legs. She was only eleven, but she fashioned a prosthetic limb for the animal out of wood and old car parts Desmond had laying around. It rolled, had a wheel, so the dog could run with the others."

I could imagine serious Shelly—because she was always serious—wanting to help as many strays as possible. She was still that way.

"But the two of you are different in important ways as well." Katherine's smile lost some of its luster as her eyes lost some of their focus. "She's not...open to new things, and she never did well with change. She wasn't ever very affectionate, didn't respond to hugs, that sort of thing."

"No, you're right. I once tried to hug her and she put her hand on my face and pushed me away. Then she just kept talking like nothing had happened."

Katherine gave me a sympathetic smile, then gave a bantam laugh. "She doesn't like outward displays of affection. She told me when she was fourteen that she preferred sacrifice as a demonstration of love rather than hugs and kisses."

I don't know why I asked my next question, but I felt driven to it. "Was that hard for you? When she was growing up?"

Katherine's gaze searched mine and she seemed to be considering the question. Finally she responded, "Yes and no. I always looked for and expected the best in my children. I learned to love everything about them, but I didn't always like it. I didn't like that Quinn worked for criminals when he was a teenager, but I loved that he was smart and enterprising. I didn't like that I couldn't hold my daughter without her pushing me away, but I loved her fierce independence and individualism."

"And what about your oldest, Desmond Jr.?"

She smiled at me, but it was a smile that made my heart break. "I don't know...I think when you lose a child you forget everything you didn't like. When I think of Des, I think of him laughing all the time, his loyalty to his family, his sense of honor, his sweetness. But I'm sure, when he was with us, he drove me crazy too."

I tried to return her smile but managed only a half mouth tilt. Her grip on my hand shifted and she fit my fingers between both of her palms.

"And now we have you," she said.

"Me?" My eyebrows lifted then lowered. "What about me?"

"Now we have you to discover, to love, to like."

"I'm weird. You should know that, if you don't already."

"I'm weird too. I like math jokes too much and have opinions about people who do crossword puzzles."

This was surprising. "Studies show that they're exceptionally good for keeping your brain active, retaining memories."

"Those studies were probably conducted by people who do crossword puzzles."

I lifted a single eyebrow, contemplating the possibility of investigator bias. "I honestly don't know...."

She chuckled, shook her head. "I'm so glad you called me. I'm so glad I get to know you."

I glanced at our entwined fingers. She was holding my hand and I was holding hers. Even though it might have been premature, it felt so strange, but also right and natural to have a woman with wisdom and experience who looked at me with trust and affection. I knew I lacked a mother in every way that mattered and was curious about the dynamic of mothers and daughters.

But I didn't know until that moment, sitting at Katherine's kitchen table, holding hands, how desperately I wanted this relationship. I think I'd already fallen in love with the idea of her. Rationally, this was concerning because I didn't know her very well.

We both shifted our attention to Quinn and Desmond as they walked into the room. Quinn's shirtsleeves were rolled up to his forearms and he was in the process of drying his hands with a towel. Desmond came in behind him holding a pie and plates.

Quinn's gaze met mine, held for a beat, then shifted to where his mother and I were holding hands. His expression didn't change.

Except for two or three breaks in his façade, he'd been wearing basically the same expression the entire time we'd been there.

Impassive.

This didn't worry or alarm me, especially now that I saw Quinn was a carbon copy of his father. Their eyes shone with intensity and were often the only outward sign of a shift in thoughts or feelings. Truly, it was fascinating to see them together.

But I saw glimpses of his mother in him as well, especially the goofy jokes and dry wit. As well, Katherine was a toucher: she showed a good deal of her affection through light caresses, squeezing of shoulders, brief embraces. She'd cupped my cheek, smiling into my eyes several times while we'd been making dinner, and I'd noted the way she was always looking for excuses to touch her husband, scratch his back, smooth her hand down his arm.

She did these things in a way that reminded me of her son, and it warmed my heart. I would have to thank her later for passing this personality trait to Quinn, as it was definitely one of my favorites.

"What's going on?" Quinn's gaze was still on our hands.

"We were just talking about whether or not investigator bias is present in memory trials involving crossword puzzles," I said, which was mostly true.

Quinn's eyes narrowed as they moved back to mine, assessing the truth of my statement.

I was struck with a sudden thought.

"Uh—Quinn, could you join me in the bathroom for a minute?"

He blinked at me once. "In the bathroom?"

"Yes. In the bathroom."

I noted his parents exchanged a look before his mother said, "If you two need to talk, we can…."

"No, no. I prefer the bathroom. I do my best thinking in there." I stood from the table, gave Katherine a nod of my head, and grabbed Quinn's hand. "We'll be right back."

I led him blindly out of the dining room in no direction in particular—just out. He quickly took over and steered us through a hallway lined with family photographs to a small half bath under the staircase.

Once we were inside with the door closed but before the light could be switched on, I pressed him against the wall and kissed him. He liked this, because he immediately turned me so that my back was against the wall. At first, everything—every touch, grope, bite, lick—felt frantic, urgent, necessary.

Then, after maybe a full minute, his weight shifted against me and the movements of his mouth slowed, savored. He used his hands to tilt my head this way and that, angling me how he liked, and kissed me with an unhurried meticulousness until I was well and truly dizzy.

At length, he dipped his chin so that our foreheads connected and we inhaled each other.

"Thank you," I said.

"You're welcome," He said.

His response, so serious, made me smile. We were still surrounded by darkness, which made our softly spoken words sound louder and more intimate.

"Quinn…I want you to be happy," I said, and my hands moved from where they gripped his arms to his waist.

"I am."

"And I want to marry you as soon as possible."

He nodded, moving his face to nip my jaw, nuzzle my neck. "Good."

I gathered a deep breath of courage and—though it was nearly pitch black—I closed my eyes in preparation for the words I would speak next.

"And, I think that *as soon as possible* is still June 14, and here is why: I think we should have the wedding here, in Boston." I felt him stiffen at this news, so I tried to speak faster. "I think we should let your mother plan it, or as much of it as she wants to plan. I think we should have a large family wedding. I think I should wear a white dress, and underneath I should wear the bridal lingerie you picked out in London. Because I think it would mean a lot to your parents—not the bridal lingerie, the family wedding—

and we don't really care about the details, and if it's within your power to give another person great joy at little or no expense to yourself—or even at great expense—then you should, especially when you love that person. And, in the interest of full disclosure, I think I might be a little in love with your mother...."

"Okay," he whispered against my ear, one of his hands caressing from my shoulder to my waist, then up to my breast.

I opened my eyes in the darkness. I could just barely discern the outlines of his form towering above me.

"...Okay?"

"Yes."

My face was commandeered by a huge smile. Quinn moved against me in such a way that ignited sparks along my spine and made my lower stomach twist. My body instinctively reached out to his, to him.

"Thank you." This time my words were a bit breathless.

"No, Kitten." He lifted his head, brushed his lips against mine twice, then touched his nose to mine. "Thank you."

CHAPTER 17

Quinn

ALL HELL BROKE loose on Wednesday.

After a long day of dealing with idiot assholes, all I wanted to do was make love to my girl. Then I wanted to listen to her voice as she described the best way to extract essential oils from peppermint leaves, or whatever the hell topic she decided was most interesting at that particular moment.

Instead, I came back to our suite at the hotel and found Dan, his asshat brother Seamus, Janie, and my mother sitting in the living room having tea.

Fucking hell.

We had seen my parents every day since dinner on Saturday.

We went to church with them Sunday morning then out to eat. My father and I talked about a fishing trip over the summer. Shocking both of us, I asked for his advice on two new properties, corporate client accounts that my company would be managing at the end of the summer. After the discussion, I decided to ask him later if he was interested in consulting.

Janie spent the rest of Sunday talking about wedding plans with my mother, conferencing in her friend Marie from Chicago.

The next days in Boston were filled with corporate client meetings. At night, we went back to my parents' house for dinner. By Tuesday, being around them was finally easier, but I was ready to climb the walls. I think it helped that they didn't try to apologize again. But every time we were together, I wanted to tell them I was sorry.

I didn't, because the idea of apologizing felt inadequate. I wasn't sure that I was ready to be forgiven. So I kept quiet and swallowed my guilt.

This morning, which was also the last morning of our last full day in Boston, Janie and I split after breakfast. I needed to tie up loose ends with former private clients. She said she needed to run some wedding errands with my mom, whatever that meant.

I hadn't expected those errands to include tea with local thugs.

Seamus—Dan's money-laundering no-good asshole of a brother and Jem's ex-boyfriend, the same ex-boyfriend who'd tried to kidnap Janie several months ago—was on my list of top three sonsabitches I'd like to disappear.

Right now though, the first person I was going to murder was Dan. After that, Seamus. After that…maybe Janie. Probably not.

I did a quick scan of the room, surprised to find two of my local lieutenants, Carl and Stan, standing at either end of the perimeter. Their eyes met mine. One look told me they were less than pleased with the current situation.

Once I was certain that the room was secure, I shut the door with a little more force than necessary and waited for the occupants to notice me. They did, immediately and all at the same time, glancing up from their conversation in unison.

The room fell silent.

I glared at Dan. He glared back. I saw he was pissed, and I knew he was the one who had called Carl and Stan. Dan was the only one not drinking tea. He was on the edge of his seat looking tense and uncomfortable between Seamus and the ladies.

I shifted my glare to Seamus. He gave me a shit-eating grin. I decided that he was now number one on my list of people I'd like to make disappear.

"What are you doing here?" Instead of pistol-whipping him, I set my briefcase by the door, began pulling off my leather gloves.

"I heard you were in town, thought I'd stop by for a friendly chat." His greasy smile widened, and he looked at Janie. The bastard winked at her.

Seamus shouldn't breathe the same air as my mother or Janie, much less share teatime.

I tossed my gloves and overcoat to a nearby chair, my eyes never leaving Seamus. "What are you doing here?" I said it slower this time.

The smile dropped from his face as his eyes flickered to mine. He looked nervous.

My mother set her tea on the table and stood. "I invited him in."

Before I looked at my mother, I let Seamus feel the threat behind my stare.

She seemed weary. "I had two choices, Quinn. Invite him in or turn him away. One way or the other, he wanted to talk to you. But more than that, he wants to make a statement."

"I don't know what she's...." Seamus said, but my mother cut him off.

"You forget, Seamus, I changed your diapers. Don't try to bullshit me." She then turned back to me. "And you also forget that I know Seamus. He and Dan used to come over after school when they were kids. Seamus got an A in my trigonometry class."

"Right before he dropped out," Dan piped up. His tone told me he was close to losing his shit.

"Listen..." Seamus glared at his brother, then his eyes flickered to my mother. He had the nerve to appear ashamed. "I'm sorry if I interrupted anything."

"You did," she said. "And I know you're not sorry. You knew we were here—Janie and me—and that Quinn was not." I studied my mother. She seemed to be searching Seamus's face for something, as if he were lacking some much-needed character trait, and her sigh was defeated when she looked at me again. "Janie and I are leaving. We have an appointment with a dressmaker."

"Mrs. Sullivan, I am sorry. Please don't leave on my account." Seamus tried again, his voice surprisingly sincere.

"If you want to tell someone you're sorry, Seamus, I have your mother's phone number. Maybe you'd like to give her a call."

He dropped the act. His expression flattened, his mouth formed a grim line, and he stood silent under my mother's disappointment.

She allowed just five seconds for her point to sink in. Then she reached for her purse. Janie stood and my eyes immediately locked on her.

It felt like getting punched in the stomach, she was so beautiful. She looked curious and composed, but not frightened, even though she'd been uncharacteristically quiet throughout the whole thing.

She was also wearing some kind of light pink wrap dress, the kind that reminds me of a bathrobe, except the ties are connected. I knew, because I had previous experience with one of her other wrap dresses; all I had to do was pull the tie and the dress fell open.

I fucking hated Seamus.

I gritted my teeth and exhaled, fought the urge to order everyone out so that Janie and I could be alone. The only reason I didn't was because my mother was right. Seamus wanted to make a statement. He was nothing but an irritating blip on my radar. If he didn't put on his show now, it would be later.

My mother passed by me first, gave me a small smile, and squeezed my arm. Then she surprised the hell out of me with a gentle peck on the cheek.

I felt twelve years old again. It made me feel forgiven.

Carl followed my mother. I was still shaking off my disorientation when he gave me a curt nod; I knew he would take care of them.

Janie trailed behind, hesitant, waiting for a cue on how to act. She was so fucking smart it killed me. I grabbed her hand as she passed, settled for an irritatingly chaste kiss on her cheek. When she leaned close, I noticed that she smelled different, like perfume or a new soap, and I wanted to know why.

Stan was last and muttered as he passed, "We'll take them home."

My eyes slid back to Seamus before I said, "You do that."

I heard the door shut.

Then I walked to the bar and poured myself a whiskey, turning my back to the room. I was in no hurry now, and since I was in a bad mood, I was happy to share it with someone I disliked.

I downed the first glass with one quick swig then poured two more generous fingers.

"No thanks, I don't want anything," Seamus called.

"I didn't ask and I'm not offering." I turned and glanced out the window of the presidential suite to the skyline of Boston beyond.

"That's not very nice." Seamus whined, sitting down again. "After I did that solid for your girl."

My eyes slid to the side and I glared at him.

"He *gave* you all the money Jem stole." Dan said this to his brother, shaking his head. "You didn't do him a favor."

"I let her go, didn't I?"

"And Quinn could have busted open your operation with one phone call. You'd be rotting in prison right now, right?"

"What are you doing here?" I asked the question slower this time, pausing menacingly between words.

Seamus shifted in his seat, increasingly uncomfortable. "Didn't know you were going to be so rude."

"Stop fucking around, asshole. Just spit it out." Dan huffed, leaned back in the large leather club chair, and shook his head. He looked embarrassed.

Seamus was many things, but he was not stupid. He was resourceful, clever, and if he worked half as hard at a real job in a legit industry as he did laundering money, he'd be very successful. But he didn't. He was the ruler of a modest empire, one that I allowed to exist.

Or, rather, one that I *had* allowed to exist. Because if I knew who needed money laundered on the East Coast, then I had valuable information.

But I didn't deal in information anymore, or at least I was trying to get out of it. This meant Seamus's current position as the ruler of his realm was precarious at best.

And, right now, finding him in my suite, winking at Janie, and keeping me from learning more about essential oil extraction methods, I was pretty sure Seamus's reign was coming to an end.

"I heard a rumor about you," Seamus said, making a desperate show of his aggression.

I just looked at him, because he hadn't yet given me any reason to speak.

Seconds ticked by and he grew more agitated.

Finally, he blurted, "You're one cold bastard, Quinn. I thought we were friends."

"No you didn't."

"So, is it true? Are you cutting everyone out?"

I waited for a moment. Then I strolled to the couch and sat down, stating the obvious. "This is a waste of my time."

"Are you going to cross me now?"

I squinted at him. "Why would I do that?"

"Because, if you're not looking for influence, you don't need my info."

"Seamus, I don't know what you're talking about. I run a security firm. I provide security for corporations—businesses, banks, hotels, et cetera. As far as I know, you are not affiliated with a corporation. You and I have nothing to do with each other."

His eyes narrowed and he studied my face like it held the key to his continued existence. "Just know this: you come after me, I come after you."

Dan muttered a sacrilegious curse. He then followed it with, "What are you even doing here, huh? What are you going to do? Send more guys to Chicago to get stabbed with knitting needles? Just let it go, Seamus." He huffed in exasperation.

"I can't," Seamus said to his brother, but his eyes never left mine.

"You need to because Quinn is out; he's been out for almost a decade, and everyone he cares about is untouchable."

"That's a load of shit, Dan." Seamus turned to his brother. "He isn't out. He's been building an empire, a global fucking empire of contacts, of people to use. He is the master of *using* people. I think I'm an excellent delegator, but I'm nothing, *nothing* in comparison. Now he wants to wash his hands? Too bad! Hands that dirty don't get clean."

"Nothing we do is illegal." Dan threw his hands up and yelled this to the ceiling.

"Yeah, except the part about knowing. Your guy here is an accessory to hundreds of felonies because he *knows*."

I was bored. Seamus's dramatics were boring.

"Get to the point." Dan sliced his hand through the air. "What do you want?"

"I want assurance that your decade of squeaky clean information gathering isn't going to come back and bite me in the ass, that's what I want."

Seamus wasn't the first person I'd had this conversation with. The first question most of my private clients had after they found out I was offloading their account was, "What assurances do I have that you're going to keep my secrets?"

What they didn't know was that if the secret was bad enough, I'd already spilled it. People with reprehensible secrets weren't used; they were exposed.

If the secret was drug distribution, human trafficking, or any other form of mass destruction or exploitation of an individual, that information had already been passed to the right people, people who could make it stop without my involvement being revealed.

I knew with certainty that my involvement would never be known because the right people—the people who ultimately made the bad guys pay—didn't know I'd been the one to provide the evidence.

Luckily, very few of the private clients were of this type. Most of them were of the hiding funds offshore type, the tax evasion type, the recreational drug user type, or the cheating on their spouse type. Their secrets ranged from embarrassing to potentially life and career devastating, but very rarely—in my estimation—consummately evil.

"Seamus, you're an idiot." Dan was out of patience.

I glanced from one brother to the other. Physically, they were very similar, six foot, stocky, brown eyes. They could have been twins. My brother Des and I didn't even look related. We were approximately the same height, but he was blond and took after my mother.

Des had been my hero; just like Seamus had been Dan's hero. But whereas Des's values of honor and courage were easy to admire, Seamus was a selfish asshole.

Seamus glared at his brother. "Get off your fucking high horse…."

"That's enough." This conversation was going nowhere and it needed to end. "Seamus, I have nothing to offer you other than assurance that I am entirely disinterested in your existence."

Seamus sniffed, scowled, but nodded. "Yeah. Okay…good."

I waited a moment, allowed him to relax, get comfortable in the promise of my indifference.

Then I added, "Don't give me a reason to become interested."

***

JUST WHEN I thought the day couldn't get any worse, more hell broke loose.

I walked into my parents' house and found Jem.

Actually, I walked in on my dad slapping handcuffs on Jem. She was lying face down, her cheek pressed into the wood floor of the entranceway. He had one knee on her back, pinning her in place, though, giving credit to her crazy, she was doing her best to break free from his hold.

"You haven't read me my rights, *pig*," she shouted as she squirmed, thrashing her long legs.

"Fuck a duck, look who it is." Dan stopped short just inside the door then glanced at my dad, "Sorry, Mr. Sullivan."

My dad heaved a sigh; otherwise, he appeared to be completely composed.

"Where's Janie?" I asked, craning my neck to check the living room.

"Not here," my dad answered. "They left this afternoon, aren't back yet."

Worry surged in my gut, and I pulled out my phone. I turned away to call Stan.

"Boss." He answered on the first ring.

"Where are you?"

"Beau Boutique."

I frowned. "What the hell is that?"

"The hell if I know. I've never seen so much pink in my life. How many dresses does she hafta try on? And they're all white! The ladies are drinking champagne outta glasses the size of my thumb. But don't worry, Boss. They don't have beer. I asked."

"Jesus Christ, Stan…."

"I know, right?"

"No." I hit my fist against the door jam. "You were supposed to bring them home."

The line was silent for a moment then Stan whispered, "You want me to take champagne from your mom?"

I rolled my eyes, thought about telling him to get his ass back to the house, but then I imagined Janie and my mom's reaction if I tried to dictate their comings and goings. It was better that my mom stay and drink her champagne. Under the circumstances, it was probably good the ladies were out.

"Fine. They have one hour. Text Dan the address."

I ended the call and turned, found Dan standing behind me.

"Everything okay?"

I nodded, glaring at him. Then, because all hell was breaking loose and Dan was keeping his shit together, I decided now was the moment.

"Will you be my best man?"

He blinked at me. Then his eyes narrowed and he looked abruptly irritated. "Of course. Why the hell you even asking that shit? I've already talked to your mom about the tuxes."

"Good." I tried to frown, failed. "Let's go."

We walked back to the entranceway where my dad and my handcuffed future sister-in-law were still on the ground. I nodded once to my dad, communicating silently that Janie and Mom were fine, then shifted my attention to Jem. She was intermittently mumbling to herself then screaming. She had just tried to bite my dad's arm, and was being giant a pain in the ass.

She wasn't supposed to be in Boston. She wasn't even supposed to be in the States. I'd dropped her in Rio with a hundred thousand dollars in cash and a new passport. She promised me that she would disappear. I didn't really believe her promise, but I hoped she would never be my problem again.

I stepped into her line of sight, leaned against the wall, and rubbed my forehead. I was getting a headache. She looked tan, which—for her—meant very freckled. It also meant her eyes seemed lighter, not amber like Janie's looked against her pale skin. Jem's looked almost yellow.

"I just left Seamus," I said.

Panic flickered behind her eyes. She quickly clamped down the flare of emotion and lifted her chin defiantly. "So? What do I care?"

"So, if you don't stop kicking, biting, and pissing me off, then I'm going to call Seamus and ask him to come pick you up."

Considering the fact that Seamus wanted Jem dead, I felt this threat would be most effective.

Her eyes fired shards of yellow glass at me. "You wouldn't. Janie would never forgive you."

"You know Janie. She's very pragmatic."

Jem huffed, growled, screwed her eyes shut, then stopped kicking. Her legs fell to the floor with a *thud*.

My dad glanced at me, cocked an eyebrow.

I considered which version of the truth to tell him and finally settled on, "Seamus is her man."

The corner of his mouth quirked up. "And Dan is your second in command, and Janie is your woman...." His eyes narrowed slightly, and I could see that he was assembling an invisible relationship diagram. "Small world."

I shrugged, decided to tell him later that I'd first noticed Janie in Chicago at the Fairbanks building because I thought she was Jem. I uncomfortably realized that, in a way, Jem was partially responsible for Janie's and my relationship.

I dismissed the thought.

For the second time in less than as many hours, I found myself asking an individual on my list of top three people I'd like to have disappear the same question.

"Why are you here?"

Her eyes were still shut, but the muscle at her temple jumped when I spoke.

"Tell your douchebag doppelganger to uncuff me."

"Nope," my dad responded. "I'm arresting you for something. I just haven't decided on the full list of charges yet. No need to uncuff you if I'm just going to do it again in five minutes."

"I'm not going to jail!" she screamed, her eyes flying open.

"Why are you here?" I repeated, my fingers digging into the space between my eyebrows. I needed an ibuprofen.

"Listen...." She licked her lips, her eyes darting around the room. "I've been in town for two weeks, heard you were here with my sister. I need to speak to Janie and...I need money."

"What happened to the money I gave you?" I asked, not caring what conclusions my dad would draw because, at some point, I knew I'd be able to set him straight. This thought caught me off guard and I wondered at what point over the last several days I'd started taking for granted that I would have a future relationship with my parents.

"I ran out," she said. "It wasn't enough."

"You ran out."

"I need to talk to Janie!" she shrieked.

"That's not going to happen," Dan said, shaking his head, his arms crossed in a wall of defiance.

"I'll tell Janie you want to speak to her," I said, I wanted to outright deny her request, but it wasn't my place to do so. "It's up to her."

"Just...just let me talk to her and give me some cash, and I'll leave you alone, I swear."

"She was holding this when she broke through the window." My dad chose this moment to withdraw a .22 pistol from the back of his pants. "I thought she was Janie at first, so I didn't shoot."

I let out a frustrated bark of laughter. Thank God my mother had made an appointment at Beau Boutique so Janie could try on white dresses.

"Listen, freak show," Dan said; he had reached the end of his tether, and I wasn't surprised. He knew Jem a lot better than I did. "You're going to jail. You see this guy, Mr. Sullivan? Quinn's dad? He's the real deal, sweetheart. You broke into his house. He's Boston PD. He's a detective. That means he's a badass. You're going to jail for breaking and entering into a badass police detective's house...*with a gun* you crazy bitch."

Dan waited a moment, giving her time to start plotting a way to weasel out of the situation, then he added, "Not even Quinn can save you from that."

Jem's heavy breathing was the only sound in the room. Tears filled her eyes. No one was impressed.

Then, my dad read Jem her rights.

Just then my phone rang. I turned from the scene relieved for the distraction. I walked to the dining room. It was a New York number, but I didn't recognize the owner. I debated a half second whether or not to answer.

Nothing could shock me at this point, so I picked up the call. "Yes?"

"Hi. Is this Quinn Sullivan?" It was a male, smoker, late twenties or early thirties, who sounded vaguely familiar.

"Who is this?"

"Uh, Elizabeth Finney gave me your card. I'm Nico Moretti, and I'm in need of a new private security firm."

CHAPTER 18

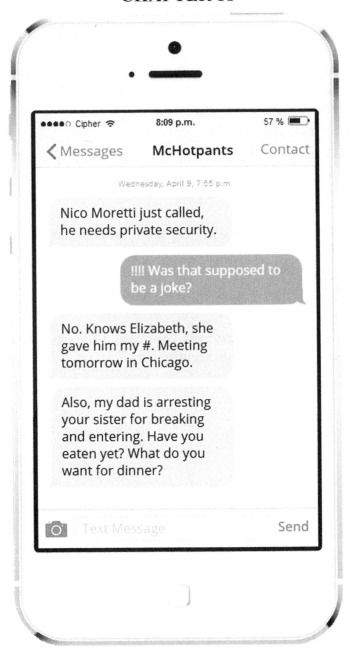

●●●●○ Cipher 🛜   8:09 p.m.   57 % ▭

‹ Messages   **McHotpants**   Contact

Wednesday, April 9, 7:55 p.m.

> Nico Moretti just called, he needs private security.

> !!!! Was that supposed to be a joke?

> No. Knows Elizabeth, she gave him my #. Meeting tomorrow in Chicago.

> Also, my dad is arresting your sister for breaking and entering. Have you eaten yet? What do you want for dinner?

📷   Text Message   Send

Janie

"NICO MORETTI? THE comedian?" Katherine glanced from me to Quinn, her face a mixture of delight and disbelief. "That good looking guy who gets naked at the end of his show?"

"How do you know he gets naked?" Desmond's hands stilled, his pizza slice halfway between his plate and his mouth. He was frowning at his wife with a very Quinn-esque glare of displeasure.

It was after 10:30 p.m. and we were just finishing dinner. I'd been starving; thus, I was quiet through most of Dan's recitation of the evening's events. I got the impression that he blurred the facts surrounding Seamus's visit—likely for Quinn's parents' benefit— but held nothing back when recounting Jem's arrest.

Apparently, we'd missed quite a lot while I was trying on wedding dresses.

I was surprised by Jem's attempt to break into their house, but then again, nothing she did really surprised me anymore. I hadn't decided what to do about her request to speak with me. Therefore, I delayed my decision. It's not like she was going anywhere.

I felt annoyed and guilty about the whole thing. I was annoyed because she was once again mindlessly casting her insanity and poor decisions all over the place and into my life. She was like an insane chef, tossing globs of rancid tomato sauce around a restaurant then telling everyone that dinner is served. The analogy made just as much sense as her behavior choices.

I felt guilty because I felt annoyed. Part of me would always hold out hope for her, for a relationship, and I wanted to feel more than annoyance for my little sister.

I'd tried to apologize to Desmond and Katherine but they waved me off, said that I was not responsible for the decisions of other people.

I think Katherine in particular just wanted to know more about Nico Moretti. Dan was happy to recount Quinn's call, even though he hadn't heard both sides of it. He also didn't try to hide his excitement about Nico. It seemed Dan was a fan.

Katherine rolled her eyes at her husband's expression then turned to confide in me. "He's very hot."

I smiled but didn't comment, even though I agreed.

Quinn had been quiet during dinner. As far as I knew, if he accepted Nico Moretti as a client, this would be his first celebrity and his first new private client account in over four months. I wondered what he was thinking, but didn't ask.

Quinn leaned back in his chair and picked up his whiskey. He seemed to be studying the contents of the glass as though he was pondering the manufacturing methods of Texas distilleries.

Therefore, I was surprised when he announced rather loudly, "I'm sorry."

We all looked at him. I noted Katherine and Desmond shared a glance of confusion then shifted their attention to me. I looked to Dan. He also appeared to be perplexed.

"What's that, dear?" Katherine asked, a gentle smile on her face.

"I'm sorry about Des. I'm sorry it happened and that I could have prevented it." Quinn's gaze moved between his parents.

A long moment followed. Katherine's smile waned, her face fell, and a flash of pain cast a shadow over her features. Desmond held Quinn's gaze, his expression stone, but that didn't signify anything. Like Quinn, his thoughts were private and his emotions were like ghosts.

Quinn swallowed, his throat working with effort, and I was surprised to see that he made no endeavor to hide his anguish. I'd never seen him so transparently desolate, and my heart reached out to him. I didn't realize it, but so did my hands and my arms. Before I quite understood that I'd moved, I was embracing his shoulders and holding him tightly.

He repeated on a whisper, "I'm so sorry."

Katherine pressed her lips together and lifted her chin. Her eyes shone, and I knew she was holding back tears.

"Quinn...." she started, stopped, cleared her throat. "You couldn't have known."

He shook his head at his mother and asked on a tortured sigh, "Why don't you hate me?"

A pained understanding claimed her features, like something in her broke and mended at his words, as though pieces of a puzzle finally fit together, and the picture they revealed was dreadfully wrong.

"Baby, I could never hate you. We have *never* hated you. We may have been lost to our grief, we may have lashed out at you in despair, but we never hated you—not ever. Loving unconditionally brings only joy. You are our son, and when Des...when Des...." Her chin wobbled and two tears rolled down her cheeks.

Katherine quickly wiped them away and swallowed before continuing. "When Des died, our hearts were broken, and so was yours; so was Shell's. We should have taken comfort in each other instead of mindlessly casting blame. That's on us, baby. That's not your fault. And I am so, so sorry we didn't do something about it before now." The end of her sentence was lost on a sob and she buried her face in her hands.

Quinn shook his head, but before he could challenge his mother's words, his father reached over and gathered his wife in his arms, pulled her to his lap, and tucked her head against his shoulder.

Then he turned his eyes to Quinn. I heard and felt Quinn's small intake of breath at his father's expression, perhaps because it was so full of love and compassion.

Then Desmond spoke. "Blame is a thief. It robs us blind while it wastes our time, time we could be spending as a family, making memories, supporting each other. Your mother and I don't want to miss another day with you, or your sister, or Janie. You need to cut that shit out. You need to let go of it, because your mother needs you...I need you. And I think you might need us too."

***

IT WAS PAST midnight by the time we finally made it back to the hotel. I was tired, but Quinn was exhausted. Therefore, on the ride home I demanded that he rest his head on my lap in the back of the limo. I traced the curve of his eyebrows, the slope of his nose, the line of his jaw with my fingertips until he fell asleep.

I was sad to wake him, but relieved at the possibility of stripping naked and wrapping myself around his equally bare body, skin to skin, as we both fell into a deep slumber surrounded by each other's warmth.

When we arrived at our room, I was surprised to find Dan just leaving the suite. He'd been with us throughout dinner, but left shortly after Quinn's apology and the subsequent heavy discussion.

"Hey…." Dan stopped just outside the door, gave me a small but sincere smile, and nodded once at Quinn. "I did a sweep of the room. Everything looks clear. I've got four guys coming up in a few minutes for the night shift; two will be inside, two will be out here. Also, I've notified hotel security that we're taking extra precautions."

Quinn nodded once. "Thanks. Goodnight."

Dan lifted his chin in acknowledgement then walked past us to the elevator. I didn't see him depart because Quinn was pushing me into the hotel room. He promptly kicked the door shut then reached for the tie at my waist.

With one tug, the dress came unraveled and fell open. Quinn's appreciative groan made me smile, and my grin only broadened when he said, "I knew it. I love this dress."

I laughed as his hands reached inside, parted the fabric, and gripped my waist. He brought me forward and against him, claimed my mouth, and began walking us into the bedroom.

Where he led, I followed, my feet shuffling backward with trusting steps, my hands on his shoulders as his roamed over my body. He didn't touch me in order to ignite desire. His caresses were possessive rather than purposeful, like he'd been denied my skin for an unreasonable period of time, and he was merely taking his due.

When we reached the bedroom, he kicked another door shut— the bedroom door—and guided me to the bed, knelt over me and shifted my body until I lay beneath him. The dress still covered my shoulders and arms, but the open front framed my torso, hips, and legs.

We kissed. And then, abruptly, we were no longer kissing. I opened my eyes to find Quinn staring at me and a frown drawing his features, made more severe by the dim light illuminating our bedroom.

I blinked up at him, searched his face for a clue to his thoughts. "What is it?"

"I told you I would show you an example of a private client file. I haven't done that."

I watched him for a beat, waited for him to continue. When he didn't I threaded my fingers through his hair and lightly scratched the back of his neck.

"We can do that when we get back."

His eyes narrowed on me, studying me, contemplative. He shifted his weight to his side and brought me to his chest, encouraged my leg to fit between his, my head on his shoulder.

Then he said, "You smell different."

I lifted my head and peered at him, a little surprised he'd already noticed as I'd just purchased it earlier in the day. "Oh, yeah. I bought some perfume."

"Why?"

"I read a study yesterday about perceived attractiveness. It stated that men find a woman approximately twenty percent more attractive when the woman smells good."

"How…how would a study like that even work?"

"I believe they used the same woman in all test cases, but different men. The men rated the woman on her attractiveness after…"

"Never mind that. What I want to know is why *you* are wearing perfume."

I lifted an eyebrow at his repeated question because I thought I'd already answered it. "Because, although you seem to be smitten at present, I recognize that you will eventually become inoculated to my looks, perhaps even bored of them. I thought smelling good and changing it every so often would give me a twenty percent advantage—approximately."

Quinn watched me for a moment then closed his eyes and sighed. "You drive me crazy, and I don't have enough energy right now to argue with you about how nuts you are."

I smiled against his chest then moved to unbutton the front of his shirt. "Good. You should take your clothes off."

His hands came up and closed over mine, stilling my

movements. "Before we do that, before we go to sleep, I need to talk to you about one of the private clients."

"It can wait until morning."

"No." He shook his head on his pillow, his eyes still closed. When he spoke next, his words were slurred with fatigue. "It's about that night at Club Outrageous when you were drugged. That guy, the one that drugged you, we provided security for that family."

Now he had my full attention.

"Oh...?" I thought about this information then asked the next question that popped in my head. "Is that how you had him arrested? You used one of his secrets against him?"

"Kind of...yes." Quinn yawned, and I wondered if he would remember this conversation in the morning. He already seemed half-asleep.

"Quinn, why do you want me to know about this client?"

"Because...Parducci...they're a good...example of...what I do...."

A few seconds passed as I waited for him to continue. Instead, he lay completely silent, his chest rising and falling with steady breaths.

"Quinn?" I whispered—and waited.

It was no good. He was asleep. I let him sleep. But I did undress him. This was like trying to put a diaper on an elephant. He was all long, heavy limbs; and he was passed out, dead weight.

After I finished, I went through my evening routine then joined him in bed, reminding myself to ask him about this good example of a private client in the morning.

Before I surrendered to unconsciousness, I thought about what his father had said, about blame. I made a silent promise to myself that I wouldn't allow blame to steal time from me, from us. The little thieving bastard would have no place in our marriage.

But my last thought, just before I drifted off to dreamland, was an echo of what Katherine had said earlier that evening; specifically, *loving unconditionally brings only joy.*

CHAPTER 19

LEAVING BOSTON WAS bittersweet.

We'd said our goodbyes to Quinn's parents the night before, but boarding the plane and watching the city fall away felt wrong. It felt like I was leaving home or a piece of myself behind. I decided to tuck that thought away for examination at some point later.

However, I missed my friends. I missed my knitting group and, strangely enough, I missed Steven. I was used to seeing him every day, hearing about his dating tribulations and quest for perfect furniture.

I reflected on how much different my life was now than it had been before, when I was with Jon.

I recognized now that Jon had been an enabler of my behavior. He'd encouraged my reclusive tendencies. He'd never pushed me outside of my comfort zone. In the end, when our relationship dissolved, I realized he'd never pushed me because he'd been afraid of losing me.

I was learning that fear has no place in a healthy relationship.

Sometimes it felt like all Quinn did was push—push me to feel, to think, to act, to want, to need. He also made me wish and dream for more than Cub's tickets, comic books, and shoes.

I wasn't running—in my head or by foot—from uncomfortable thoughts as much as I used to. I was still hiding in the bathroom, but that didn't feel as bad for some reason. Maybe because I was confronting fears and concerns. This felt good, healthy, like a positive change.

Dan was on the flight with us and seemed to be walking with a new spring in his step. Seeing him with his older brother Seamus reminded me of my relationship with my sisters. As a result, I felt a little closer to him and a good deal more comfortable around him.

That's why I allowed myself to tease him about his man-crush on Nico Moretti, especially after we landed in Chicago and Dan requested to come to the meeting.

"I'm sure he'll be your best friend if you just ask," I said, trying to give him a guileless smile. The three of us waited together at the appointed restaurant at the appointed time. Nico was two minutes late.

Dan gave me a frown that was not at all convincing. "I don't want to be his best friend. Guys don't have *best friends*." His gaze flickered to Quinn's and they shared a weird look, then their eyes darted away.

I took note of it and filed it for later analysis.

Dan added, "Well we do, have best friends…I guess. But we don't talk about that kind of shit."

"What kind of shit?" I pressed.

He shrugged, his eyes searching the restaurant. "Friendship ranking, not like girls do. They're always either talking about it or thinking about it."

"About friendship ranking?"

"Yeah, but not just with friends; with any kind relationship—drives me crazy. Girls always want to know how they rank. The thing is, if you can't tell how a person feels about you, then you probably don't want to know."

I considered this statement, found it had a great deal of merit. But before I could spend too much time scrutinizing my current relationships—friendships and otherwise—based on this new theory, Nico Moretti came strolling into the restaurant.

Actually, a more accurate description of his gait would be *swagger-saunter*. But it wasn't one of those purposeful swaggery saunters. It was like he couldn't help it. He was the swagger; the swagger was him. And, together, they must saunter.

Dan stiffened and sat a little straighter in his seat; he must've seen Nico walk in as well. Quinn's back was to the door and, though I was sure he was aware that Nico had just entered—because Dan's rapt attention was a dead giveaway—Quinn didn't turn in his seat.

Rather, Quinn continued to look over the menu with pointed intensity.

"He's here," Dan said unnecessarily.

"I know" Quinn muttered. "I can tell because you're drooling."

Dan gave Quinn a perturbed glare. "Shut up, Assface. Don't be a douche."

I listened to Dan and Quinn's exchange, though my attention was completely transfixed by what was occurring at the hostess stand. Part of me worried that the two women who'd flocked to Nico Moretti (as though their internal organs were magnetized to his gravitational pull) were going to faint.

So I voiced this apprehension and likely sounded as concerned as I felt. "Those women look like they're going to faint."

Dan suppressed a laugh-snort. "Yeah. Either that or take off all their clothes."

"I hope not. It's thirty degrees outside and not much warmer in here." It was true. I'd opted to leave my jacket on. I was cold.

At length, the women pointed at us and both personally guided Nico to our table—one of the ladies in front, one behind.

I studied him as he drew near. He was smiling, his eyes moving over our party of three. Our gazes met, held, and his smile widened. I got the distinct impression that he knew a secret about me...like what color underwear I had on, or that orcas were my favorite species within the oceanic dolphin family.

Dan stood, reached out his hand first. "Hi. Daniel O'Malley. Pleased to meet you. Call me Dan."

"Hi, Dan, very nice to meet you." Nico gave Dan a friendly nod and turned his attention to me, extending his hand. "You must be Janie Morris." His expression was warm and open and enigmatic and completely engaging. I decided I liked him, and it was the strangest thing because I knew him not at all.

"Yes. I am. I am Janie Morris...that's my name. Janie...Morris." I accepted his handshake and his grin, returned both. I was smiling so wide my cheeks hurt. I'm sure I looked and sounded like a doofus.

Quinn finally glanced up from his menu, looked at our hands, which were still bobbing up and down in an endless handshake, then stood. Actually, his standing was more like a slow, menacing unfolding, and it necessitated the end of my contact with Nico, because Quinn basically blocked me from sight with his body.

I heard Nico say, "And you must be Quinn Sull…."

"Sit." Quinn gestured to the seat next to Dan and across from me. "You're late. We haven't ordered."

Nico moved to claim the chair, his omnipresent smile now just a curve of his lips, pressed together like he was trying to hide it. His eyes flickered to me once more then immediately away and back to Quinn.

Quinn was now glaring at his menu like he wanted to murder it.

"Congratulations," Nico said, still watching Quinn.

Quinn slid just his eyes to the side, met Nico's friendly gaze. "What?"

"Congratulations on your engagement. Elizabeth told me that her best friend had just become engaged." Nico gestured to me but didn't look at me when he said this.

"Thanks," Quinn said, his eyes narrowing.

"How do you know Dr. Finney, I mean, Elizabeth?" Dan asked pleasantly, seemingly unperturbed by Quinn's frigid reception of our guest. Like me, Dan was obviously under this man's spell.

Nico's attention moved to Dan, and he paused as though considering how to answer the question. His smile fell away and his eyes glowed with intensity. The change was so abrupt I could feel my eyebrows rising with surprise.

After a short silence, he said, "We grew up together, we're in love, and she's going to marry me."

Quinn choked on the water he'd just brought to his lips, drawing everyone's attention to him. He recovered quickly, replaced the glass, and stared at Nico as though he were an alien.

"You're marrying Elizabeth? When did this happen?"

Nico shrugged. "She doesn't know about it yet." He then picked up his menu and began reviewing the options, asking, "What's good here?"

As soon as the words were out of his mouth, I realized who he was.

Nico was *the Nico*. He was the boy Elizabeth had told me about when we first met in college. He was the best friend of her childhood sweetheart, Garrett, and *the Nico* she'd lost her virginity to when she was sixteen.

He was *the Nico*.

And he loved her.

I had a feeling that life—in particular, Elizabeth's life—was about to get very, very interesting.

***

I LIKED HIM.

Dan liked him.

And, eventually, Quinn liked him too. But it was clear to me that Quinn liked him with extreme reluctance, as though liking him was compulsory and done against his will.

Quinn's grumpy mood was the only reason I didn't object when he ordered my food for me, but I made a mental note that I would most definitely have to speak to him about it. Granted, he'd found out what I wanted first, but then when the waiter came he didn't give me a chance to speak. We'd been together over six months, and it still bothered me. I was going to have to put an end to the weird, misplaced chivalry.

Nico explained his situation and described the problems he'd had with his previous security team. Apparently, his niece needed infusions once every eight hours as part of a cystic fibrosis clinical trial. Elizabeth, my best friend and the woman he'd decided was going to be his wife, was his niece's treating physician during the trial.

He also noted that his niece and his mother—who was the guardian of his niece—were staying in a hotel near the hospital. He felt this set-up was less than ideal.

As well, Nico couldn't stop talking about Elizabeth. He brought her up almost constantly. At first I thought he was doing this on purpose, as each time he waxed poetic about my best friend, Quinn seemed to relax a little more.

But then Nico did it so much that Quinn became irritated at Elizabeth being the constant focus of conversation.

Listening to Nico and all these facts, I realized that the solution was obvious. Nico needed to move into Quinn's building.

Quinn's building was secure and safe. Nico wouldn't have to worry about keeping a security detail with him while he was in the building.

Also, his family would be in a real home instead of a hotel, and—since Elizabeth *also* lived in the building and as long as the hospital didn't object—his niece's transfusions could occur at their new home instead of at the hospital. I didn't know the details of the study, but it was worth a try.

It was the clear logical solution to all the problems presented.

Dan agreed immediately. Quinn agreed reluctantly. Nico waited for Quinn to agree, then gave me a huge, grateful smile.

"I guess I'll be Elizabeth's neighbor," he said. His eyes, which I just noticed were a light shade of olive green, actually twinkled like twin shining stars of mischief.

"Should make your eventual proposal a lot easier," Quinn said, a subtle—reluctant—smile tugging his mouth to one side.

"Yes, much easier…." Nico nodded, his gaze shifted to some spot over my shoulder, the mischievous glint increased. He appeared to be deep in thought. I had the distinct impression he was plotting.

Looking amused, Dan glanced at his watch. "Well, we should get over to the building. I'll ride with you, Mr. Moretti."

Nico agreed, pulled out his wallet and phone, placed several large bills on the table. "Call me Nico. You should know my real last name is Manganiello. I imagine you'll need it. Moretti is a stage name."

Quinn nodded. "How did you get here? Do you have a car?"

"No. I took a taxi."

I noted Quinn suppress an eye roll then turned to Dan. "Call a car; have one assigned to Mr. Manganiello."

"Nico. Call me Nico," he said again, distracted by his phone. He frowned at the display then stood. "Sorry, excuse me. This is my mom; it might be about Angelica, my niece."

Nico left the table to take his call, and Quinn heaved an audible sigh. He frowned at Dan and collected the bills Nico had left behind. "You're going to have to follow him and give him his money back."

"Sure. Fine." Dan stood. "He's nice, right?"

I nodded enthusiastically. "He is! I like him."

"He's alright. He smiles too much," Quinn grumbled.

Dan grinned at Quinn then turned to go, calling over his shoulder. "You're just upset because, for once, you're not the nicest piece of man eye-candy in the room."

***

"I LIKE HIM!" I said, stripping to my new bra and underwear set. Honestly, I was kind of proud of it. It was handmade by artisan lingerie crafters in London, made from responsibly farmed silkworms, and it fit like it was made for me. Nothing feels quite as nice as a lacy bra that fits and matching underwear that flatters.

"Who?" Elizabeth asked. She appeared to be a tad overwhelmed as she fell to our couch.

Elizabeth's state of overwhelmedness made sense given the present circumstances.

After our lunch, we'd taken Nico to Quinn's building for a tour of the second penthouse and several other apartments that might suit. I'd given him a key to the apartment I shared with Elizabeth so he could see the floor plan. When Quinn and I arrived, we found Elizabeth and Nico caught in a moment.

And, by moment, I mean they were just about to maul each other.

Basically, Elizabeth was in her underwear because she was in the midst of a panty dance party. Nico, having come upon her, looked like he was going to throw her down on the nearest surface and *charisma* a promise of marriage out of her.

And, by charisma, I mean use staggering sex appeal and raw emotion until she surrendered.

It might have worked if not for our interruption.

Now, Elizabeth and I were alone, as Quinn and Nico had been dismissed. I was the one who did the dismissing because I knew my best friend.

As soon as I saw her trying to hide her body—from Nico—behind a pair of throw pillows, I knew something major was amiss.

As I watched her interact with Nico, I realized she was drowning in a kerfuffle sea of self-imposed angst and neuroticism.

I'd never seen her so discombobulated, and I'd definitely never seen her make such an overt and violent attempt at modesty. She'd never been modest, not as long as I had known her.

We needed to talk.

"Nico. Mr. Manganiello." I said. "He's nice."

"Yeah. He's nice." She sighed, appeared to be lost in a labyrinth of thoughts. Abruptly she asked, "When did you get back from Boston?"

"Just today, this morning actually. Nico called Quinn last night and made arrangements to meet us today, to arrange private security, and that's when I suggested his family move into the second penthouse." I walked to her phone, scrolled through the selection of boy band albums. I was stalling because I was trying to find a way to steer the conversation back to Nico. "Have you abandoned your plans with the Dr. Ken Miles?"

Dr. Ken Miles was the latest guy Elizabeth was fooling herself into sleeping with. She hadn't slept with him yet, but this was her modus operandi ever three years or so. Since college, I'd watched as she forced herself to become interested in a guy, usually someone who was hot as Hades but lacked depth: a Gooch.

Predictably, she'd sleep with Mr. Random Gooch then lose interest. I came to understand that she only pursued men who were shallow Gooches because then her feelings would never grow beyond shallow.

But Nico was not shallow. And if Elizabeth had feelings for Nico, then she was probably freaking out.

"No, not really. Not yet. Maybe. I don't know." Her non-answer fueled my suspicion.

I waited for a moment, unsure how to proceed, then blurted, "Nico seems like a really nice person."

She cleared her throat. I could feel her staring on me. "You already said that."

"Yes. I just wanted to reiterate the fact that he is a really nice person."

"And why do you want to reiterate that fact?"

I turned, met her eyes, and debated how much to say. I believed Nico when he said he loved her. I also, as I may have mentioned already, liked Nico. Elizabeth's history would make it difficult for them to move beyond the hurdle of his depth of character and real feelings.

I'd been so preoccupied with Quinn and me and the wedding planning that I hadn't even noticed the change in Elizabeth. She'd been there for me, without fail, since we met. She'd counseled me, guided me, given me advice, allowed me to talk through my weirdness and work through my issues. Yet, she'd never really needed the same from me in return.

I was determined help.

I finally settled on, "Because I'm ninety-seven percent certain he is in love with you."

She continued staring at me, her anxiety clearly evident as she said, "Why ninety-seven percent?"

"A three percent confidence interval is standard."

"Why would you think he's in love with me?" Her tone was defensive, as though she felt guilty.

"You know what I'm talking about," I said, wanting her to stop pretending that she didn't know.

"No, I don't."

"Yes, you do. He's *the* guy. He's the guy from Iowa, Garrett's best friend. He's the one that you were friends with as kids, then hated, then didn't hate, then lost your virginity to. I just met him this afternoon, and I, the queen of missing the obvious, couldn't help but notice. He talked about you basically nonstop, Quinn found it irritating, but I thought it was charming. Also, he looks at you like he wants…well, like he *wants*."

My tirade only served to make her breathless. "What did he say?" she asked, looking more alarmed with each passing second.

I thought about telling her that he flat-out admitted he was in love with her, but decided against it.

I wanted to help Elizabeth, not frighten her away from someone who so obviously cared about her and so obviously was worthy of her care in return—obvious even to me.

"He talks about you like you invented penicillin. Like you—like you're an angel. It's rather disconcerting, to be honest."

She frowned; it was a very sad frown. "Because I'm so awful?"

"No. You're not awful; what a ridiculous thing to say." I'm sure I was scowling, and my annoyance was obvious. I was annoyed by her assumption, but I was also annoyed with myself. Instead of being there for Elizabeth, I'd been planning a wedding I didn't even want.

Eventually I said, "It's disconcerting because he's so smitten, and you don't—well, you know. You don't have relationships, after what happened with Garrett."

She covered her face with her hands like she couldn't stand anyone looking at her. "Oh, Janie, I don't know what to do."

This behavior worried me. I walked to where she sat on the couch and sank down close to her, placing my hand on her back. "What's wrong? Did I say something wrong?"

"No, but I've really missed you." She sniffled like she was going to cry.

My heart twisted in my chest at the sadness of her tone.

Thank goodness I'd come to my senses and thrown the bet to Quinn by depantsing him on the plane. Thank goodness I'd chosen to be happy now instead of postponing my happiness indefinitely. Thank goodness Katherine seemed content to take the wedding reins away from me, because I needed to focus on what was important.

Like living and working through *real* struggles with Quinn, not manufacturing stress.

Like forming lasting relationships with my in-laws.

Like enjoying giving and receiving support from my friends.

And, right this minute, Elizabeth needed my support.

"I'm here now," I said, "Do you want to talk about it?"

And that's when Elizabeth started to cry.

CHAPTER 20

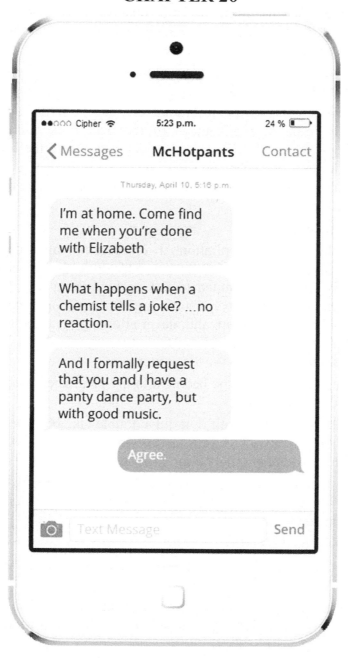

QUINN WAS RUNNING on the treadmill when I got home. This was unusual as he normally ran outside when the weather permitted it. I gave him a questioning look, and he held up three fingers. This was his sign that he had three minutes left.

I blew him a kiss and was pleased to see the barely-there smile claim his features as a result.

Since we'd gone to the restaurant directly from the airport, I decided I would take advantage of the next three minutes by unpacking my luggage. However, when I moved into the bedroom I found the bustier, panty, and stocking set from the night of the (still-unknown charity) ball laid out on the bed with a note that said *Wear Me.*

I squinted at the note.

Struck by sudden inspiration, I crossed to my side table, withdrew a scrap of paper, wrote *Wear Me* on it, then affixed it to one of his ties. I still wanted to talk to him about his irrational display of manners—always ordering for me, opening doors without fail like I was an invalid, never allowing me to pull out my own seat—and felt like my clever table turning using his tie would be an excellent segue into the discussion.

I was just placing it on the bed next to my prescribed outfit when he walked into the room.

I turned, smiling to myself, but did a double take because he was shirtless and sweating, leaning against the door frame, watching me with his trademark quiet Quinn intensity.

My first thought was that I couldn't wait for him to release oxytocin into my system. My second thought was that even the tie was too much clothing.

"Hey, Kitten," he said.

I think I also said hey, but maybe not. I might have purred or grunted…or meowed.

Whatever I did put a small smile on his face. His eyes moved up and down my outfit, but I got the impression he wasn't looking at my clothes.

"Did you have fun with Elizabeth?"

I nodded, the question and the topic a life preserver, allowing me to climb out of my lust fog. "Yes. I'm trying to be a good friend, and I'm looking forward to getting back to things that matter."

"Instead of…?"

"Instead of planning a wedding neither of us wanted." I gave him a wry smile. "You were right about that, and it's important to me that you know that I know that you were right."

His eyes squinted as he tried to follow the train of my thoughts. "Thank you…I think."

"You're welcome." I gathered a breath as I smoothed my hands over my skirt, lifted my chin, and prepared to broach the subject of antiquated manners. "And, while we're on the topic of things that matter, I want to talk to you about something."

"The Parduccis," he said.

I frowned. "The Parduccis?"

"Yeah, the private account I mentioned last night." Quinn stepped away from the door and moved to where his laptop sat on the table in our room. While he crossed to his computer, he towel-dried sweat from his chest and neck.

I watched him and was mesmerized by his movements. This happened to me whenever he was shirtless, and also when he was pantsless, or really all the time regardless of the amount of clothing he had on. He mesmerized me witless, every time.

I began to mentally recite the numbers that followed the decimal point of pi in order to keep my head above Ida's influence.

He threw the towel into the dirty laundry bin then grabbed the laptop and motioned for me to come to him. "I have some of the details here, but you can look at the entire file at the office whenever you like."

I walked to his side and peered over his shoulder. "So…who are these people?" It felt a little strange, now that I was faced with what I'd requested, like an invasion of privacy.

"They're modern day industrialists, very wealthy, huge contributors to Senator Watterson's campaign, and likely the reason he's a third-term senator."

I bit my lip and started reading one of the surveillance logs he'd pulled up. Distractedly, because I was trying to read and talk, I asked, "You said their son was the one who drugged me?"

He straightened, turned to me, caught and held my gaze. "Yes. Their son's name is Damon Parducci, and he is both the secret they tried to keep and the reason my company ceased providing security for them six months ago."

"Why? What happened?"

Quinn recited the facts like he was giving a report to his supervisor—no embellishments, just stark details.

"We realized Damon was trouble soon after we secured the account, but he wasn't within the scope of our operations. We were assigned to provide security to just the husband and wife. None of the children—all grown—were within our purview. However, we intercepted several phone calls between Mr. and Mrs. Parducci and their son. He is a drug abuser, and they were attempting to push him into a rehab program. This is what we do. We gather information, store it, flag it as potentially useful. Their son's drug problems were flagged. We started trailing Damon because he appeared to be the main source of potential leverage over his parents. However...."

Quinn's jaw ticked and he glanced away briefly; when he returned his gaze to mine, his face was somehow harder. "However, once we began trailing him, we discovered that he was dealing in a large amount of product—a very large amount. Also, we found that he was drugging young girls and raping them."

My eyes widened. "You—you let him...?"

"No." Quinn's hands reached for my arms as though to stay any potential retreat. "No. Pete was trailing him that night and stopped Damon before he could do anything more harmful than filling the girl's system with benzodiazepines. But we believe that she was not the first."

"God...what happened?"

His voice turned monotone once more, his expression grim, but he didn't release me. "I confronted his parents with the information we found, showed them the evidence of their son's misdeeds, and told them that I would have to turn him over to the police."

I waited for him to continue. He didn't, so I asked. "Unless...?"

He shook his head. "No. No unless. It wasn't about leverage. I told them it was going to happen and explained why I had to end our professional relationship."

"But...weren't they upset? What did they do?"

"Yes, they were very mad, and they tried to bribe me, to bury it. Then, they threatened me."

"What did you do?"

He shrugged. "I told them that I was also aware of their off-shore holdings and eleven prior years of tax evasion."

"And...they chose their offshore holdings over their son?"

"Yes."

"Why didn't you turn the parents in? If you were already exposing the son, why not the parents as well?"

"When we discover something like exploitation, rape, drug distribution, we don't hold on to it, we pass it on to the police through an anonymous tip. Sometimes we provide tangible evidence, like video, audio, or pictures. In this case, Damon was arrested possessing a very large amount of cocaine with intent to distribute, which is a felony and an automatic fifteen-year sentence."

"And the parents?"

"Their tax evasion is insurance against retaliation." Quinn's eyes narrowed and he took a deep breath. "Honestly, though, I think they were relieved. Their son had been a pain in the ass for a long time."

"But...what about the girls?"

"Since we stopped him before he violated the girl, the drug charge carried the heavier sentence. I passed on as much of the rape evidence I had; that way, if any women come forward, their stories can be corroborated. I stepped up the timeline for his arrest after I found you in the Canopy room."

I nodded, thought about this, then asked for additional clarification just in case. "You always pass this kind of stuff through to the police? Always?"

"Yes. Always. In fact, I've pulled a few other files for you to see—they're at the office waiting for you. Nothing as bad as Damon Parducci, but similar issues where we've turned the bad guys over to the cops."

"Who makes the determination? Who decides if the misdeed is bad enough to turn over or…not bad enough to use as leverage?"

Quinn inhaled, his gaze steady, but his jaw tight. Finally, he said, "I do."

I studied him. This wasn't a revelation so much as verification of my educated guess. I analyzed his confirmation from several angles. The responsibility he'd saddled himself with was a terrible burden, especially since it wasn't his to begin with. Laws, courts, judges, and juries existed to administer justice.

He was a superhot vigilante.

"Oh, Quinn…." I gave him a sympathetic smile. "You really are Batman."

He breathed a small laugh and closed his eyes. "Something like that. But, you were right, I've benefited from the information I've gathered." His lids lifted and his gaze felt somehow determined, sharp. "It was all about revenge at first, gathering as much information as I could so that I would be able to destroy the people who killed my brother. After that…."

I wanted to prod him for more, but waited.

Quinn's hands dropped from my arms and he glanced over my head. "Let's just say I'm talented at using people."

I watched him for a long moment. It was too much to absorb. All this detail sharing led to more questions. I needed to get my head out of the weeds and think about the big picture, what he'd ultimately done with information he'd gathered, what information he still possessed that should be turned over, what would happen if he did pass it to the police.

What were the broader ramifications—not just for us, but for the victims of these bad guys?

I couldn't ignore the fact that Quinn used secrets to persuade people to do what he wanted. I called it blackmail when he first told me that night in London. The line between persuasion and blackmail was a thin one; it might not have been technically illegal.

Technical honesty and technical legality were concepts that were dissonant with right and wrong. I liked my labels, which meant I didn't like relativistic morality.

Eventually he brought his gaze back to mine, his head tilted to the side, one of his eyebrows raised. "You wanted to talk about something else."

I was still deep in my hamster wheel of analysis. "What?"

"When I came in, you said you wanted to talk about things that matter, but it wasn't the private clients."

I shook my head slowly. "No. It wasn't the private clients. Although, admittedly and in retrospect, what I wanted to talk about feels a bit ridiculous."

"What was it?" He asked this question gently, like nothing about me was ridiculous.

"I'm only going to tell you because I need some time to think about what you've just shared with me, and this other topic—it is ridiculous. But it will provide a distraction." I paused, took a quick survey of my thoughts on the subject, then added, "I think I'm going to need a lot of time to think about what you've just shared."

"Take all the time you need." Quinn brushed the hair from my shoulder.

"I'll have more questions."

"I expected you would."

"But you trusted that I wouldn't overreact?"

He nodded. "Yes. After our conversation in London, and what happened on the plane after…and when you let go of the idea of a prenup, I trusted that you wouldn't overreact."

"Hmm…." I gave him a little smile, just a little one, then gathered a deep breath to tell him how I felt about his inappropriate gentlemanliness.

"Quinn, I don't want you to open doors for me anymore."

He looked at me, his expression blank, and I didn't know if that meant he was angry, annoyed, or confused. So I continued.

"I feel like it's inappropriate for you to order my meal. I am fully capable of speaking to waiters and waitresses. Also, I can pull out my own chair."

"You're upset because I have good manners?"

"It's that, you don't do these things for other people. I've never seen you pull out a chair for anyone else. You do these things for me because I'm a woman."

The skin around his eyes crinkled as though he were smiling. He wasn't smiling, but he wasn't frowning either. "I was not expecting this."

"Well...it's how I feel."

He leaned against the arm of the chair behind him, folded his arms over his chest, and looked at me like I was the most adorable thing he'd ever seen.

Then he said, "Kitten, have you ever considered it's my way of telling both you and the world that you matter to me? It's not about you being a woman. In fact, it's more about me than you. Doing these things, even though they're small, give me an outlet to show how I...what I think about you."

"But it also makes me feel like I'm showing the world that I'm weak. By your logic, I should be holding doors for you. We can't both be holding doors all the time. We'd never make it into a building."

"You're not going to start holding doors for me; that's not going to happen."

"Quinn, it makes me feel like a hypocrite. I want equal treatment. If I want the same salary as a man in a similar position, then that means I can open my own door and put on my own coat. Accepting these gestures, simply because I'm a woman, is not equal treatment."

"It's not *because* you're a woman. It's because you're *my* woman."

"Quinn...."

"Okay." He lifted his hands to stop me, then said, "Think of yourself as a 1964 mint condition Ford Mustang with all original parts."

I squinted at him and huffed through my nose. I thought I knew where he was going with this, but I wasn't sure I should feel good about being compared to a car, even if it was a 1964 Ford Mustang, the coolest car ever of all time.

"Okay…."

"Now, if I had that car, I'd take really good care of it, right? In fact, I'd be careful taking it out. I might avoid certain parts of town that had potholes. I'd make sure it was treated well, and I'd make sure it was safe when I wasn't driving it, right?"

"But I'm not the coolest car of all time. I'm a person."

"Yes you are. You are my person. And I'm yours."

I squinted at him, felt like I was missing something obvious. "What are you trying to say that I'm not understanding?"

He reached for and held my hands with his, his smile soft and cherishing. "You do so many things for me because you love me, just to show me how much you care."

I could see where he was going now, and it was an excellent point.

I nodded, biting my lip, and conceded. "Yes."

"I would never ask you to stop doing those things."

I countered, "You would if the things I did made you feel like a weak hypocrite."

Quinn paused at that, considered me, then said, "You told me once that intentions matter."

"That's right. They do." Gah! Another good point.

"It's not my intention to make you feel weak. I would never want to do that."

He was winning this argument. Rather, it wasn't really an argument. It was a debate. He was winning this debate. I was now on the fence. He was an excellent persuader.

I opened my mouth to challenge him again, just because I wasn't ready to admit defeat without trying once more, but then he said, "I wish it didn't bother you. I wish you would let me continue to show you how much I respect you by giving you deference. I know you can pull out your own chair, but I like doing it. I like showing the world you matter to me, that you matter most."

Part 5: Vegas, Kitten. Vegas.

CHAPTER 21

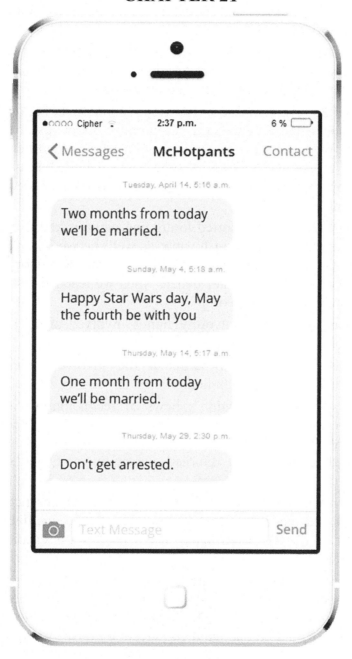

●○○○○ Cipher 🔋 2:37 p.m. 6 % ▭

❮ Messages **McHotpants** Contact

Tuesday, April 14, 5:16 a.m.

Two months from today
we'll be married.

Sunday, May 4, 5:18 a.m.

Happy Star Wars day, May
the fourth be with you

Thursday, May 14, 5:17 a.m

One month from today
we'll be married.

Thursday, May 29, 2:30 p.m.

Don't get arrested.

📷 Text Message Send

As it turned out, Nico Manganiello was right. He and Elizabeth were in love, and they did become engaged. But that's a different story for a different day.

Lots of things happened over the month and a half that followed our week in Boston with Quinn's parents. Many were noteworthy—for example, I learned to crochet.

Also, after several rounds of intense negotiations bordering on fights, Quinn and I came to a compromise about his antiquated manners. We made a list of gentlemanly behaviors, and I chose the top three things that I found irksome; these included speaking for me in any capacity—like ordering food—opening doors for me, and pulling out my chair.

In the end, once we resorted to arguing while naked, we agreed that he would stop ordering for me; as well, he would sometimes open my door, and sometimes I would open my own door. But he won the pulling-out-the-chair debate when we reached a stalemate and a coin had to be flipped.

But none of these noteworthy things involved artificial stress brought on by wedding planning.

However, one event in particular did involve actual stress brought on by wedding planning.

Shelly did not take Quinn's news of reconciliation with his parents very well. We told her the Saturday after getting back from Boston. She walked out of Giavanni's Pancake House, abandoning her pancakes, and hadn't returned any of my or Quinn's phone calls since.

She also wouldn't take any of my calls, and her absence in our lives bothered me. I didn't understand why the reconciliation had upset her so deeply. Then again, her behavior was erratic at the best of times.

We decided to give her some time, then corner her at her house in a few weeks. Actually, I decided we would corner her at her house in a few weeks. I hadn't told Quinn about my plan yet, but I was sure he would be one hundred percent on board when the time came.

I also decided to ignore Jem's request for contact. Quinn got her a good lawyer—which was somewhat awkward since she'd broken into his parents' house—and I washed my hands of the situation. I was in a good place, I was happy, and I just wanted to stay in the happy zone for as long as possible.

Katherine, Quinn's mom, had taken over the planning like a champion. I didn't know if there were such a thing as a wedding planning championship; but given the fact that Bucharest had a yearly feline beauty contest, I thought the chance of a competition for best wedding planner was highly possible.

She actually seemed to enjoy it. Marie also helped. Basically, she served as the style consultant. I got the impression that Marie's happy abandon and dedication to the wedding had everything to do with the fact that she was determined to never get married.

Marie informed me of this one knit night while the two of us were in the kitchen mixing lemon drops.

Between the two of them, I'm not sure who was enjoying themselves more.

Probably Marie. She seemed to take a certain glee in spending Quinn's money, whereas Katherine was always trying to stick to a smaller budget.

Regardless, I was happy to hand it over and forget about it. To be honest, once I was done picking out a wedding dress, I did kind of forget about it.

That's why, when the girls showed up at my office on a Thursday afternoon during the last week of May, I was confused.

I glanced up from my computer expecting to see Steven or Quinn. They were the only two people in the office who never knocked. Instead, I was greeted by Sandra, Ashley, Kat, Fiona, and Marie.

I looked at Sandra; Sandra winked at me. I looked at Ashley; Ashley grinned at me. I looked at Fiona; Fiona lifted her chin in greeting. I looked at Kat; Kat smiled shyly at me. I looked at Marie; Marie gave me two thumbs up.

I frowned at them.

"Um…." I said, glancing at the clock. "It's Thursday."

"Yep!" Sandra stepped forward and sat on the edge of my desk.

"Did we move knit night?"

"Nope." She started swinging her legs back and forth, and her wide green eyes were distressingly excited. At least, I found the excitement in them distressing. It was never a good sign when Sandra was this excited.

"Then…what's going on?"

"We need to get a move on if we're going to make our flight."

My eyebrows jumped. "Our flight?"

"That's right, Sexy-Brains. Bachelorette party—it's a tradition! It's two o'clock Thursday, May twenty-ninth, and we have permission to kidnap you for the next three days. So, turn that computer off, get your ass up, and prepare thyself for Vegas."

***

ELIZABETH MET US at the airport. Apparently, she'd packed my bag for me. This was worrisome as she was always trying to force me to dress like a harlot.

It should be noted that no judgment is implied by the term *harlot*. Harlots dress to sell their body. Therefore, the clothes they wear accentuate the areas of their body that are most desirable to customers.

I did not want to sell my body. Therefore, I did not enjoy it when people looked at me like I was for sale.

I was both pleased and alarmed to find that we were not taking Quinn's private jet. Instead, he'd purchased all the tickets in first class on a commercial carrier and, per Sandra's request, lemon drops were waiting for us as soon as we stepped aboard.

I had four during the flight only because I was trying to keep pace with everyone else.

A limo—of course—was waiting for us when we arrived. This was actually a good thing, because we were all drunk. I thought I recognized the driver as one of the guards who took me dress shopping with Quinn's mother in Boston, but I couldn't be sure.

Because I was drunk at five in the afternoon.

Luckily, we were in Las Vegas. I contemplated the fact that being drunk in Las Vegas was like being sober everywhere else in the world. So…normal. As well, I briefly wondered what it would take to determine the percentage of people on the strip who were sober at any given hour.

I guessed the number would be as fascinating as it was shocking, but likely not surprising.

When we stumbled into our hotel room, everyone gasped, myself included.

It was enormous.

It must've been one of the largest hotel rooms in the world. I wouldn't know for certain until I'd measured the square footage.

The entrance opened to a waterfall behind glass that was lit from the ceiling. To the right was a huge bar with every type of liquor imaginable. To the left was a hallway. Behind the waterfall was a giant living room with four couches, seven chairs, and a panoramic view of Las Vegas as seen from the forty-ninth floor.

The suite reminded me a 1970s lounge, if everything in that lounge had been brand-new, lacked wood paneling, was oversized, red, orange, and gold, and felt like heaven.

The red couches were soft. The orange shag carpet was softer. The bearskin rug in front of the fireplace was even softer.

We spread out, looked around, and found eight bedrooms. Each had its own bathroom, and each bathtub was worthy of tubinn time (tub + Quinn).

"At some point I'm getting naked on this rug," Sandra said, rolling around on the bearskin. "I might even try to take it home with me in my suitcase."

I sat in one of the large chairs, and Fiona handed me a bottle of water. "Keep hydrated," she said, smiling.

"It won't fit in your suitcase." Ashley's voice carried from where she was standing behind the bar, going through all the alcohol choices. "This place is off the chain. They have a bottle of Royal Salute up here."

"Holy crap!" Marie walked over. "That's like a thousand dollars."

Elizabeth walked in, flopped into the chair across from mine. "What is Royal Salute?"

"It's thirty-eight-year-old scotch," Ashley responded, then

whistled. "I'm not touching it. I don't even have a thousand dollars in my savings account."

"How many ounces is it?" I asked.

"It says seven hundred milliliters."

I did the math in my head, converting milliliters to ounces and dividing the bottle cost by number of shots. "That's sixty dollars a shot."

"Well, hell. I can afford that." Ashley grinned.

Elizabeth winked at me, and I smiled even though I was starting to feel a little unsettled. Maybe it was because the lemon drops were wearing off.

I glanced down at the huge antique ruby ring on my finger and, in my brain, I took a long look around me and thought about the last few hours—the room, the limo ride, the first class tickets—and realized that this was my life now.

I was marrying Quinn, but I was also marrying his bank account.

The thought didn't fill me with excitement. It filled me with dread.

***

WE CAUGHT A show that night. Then we gambled and drank and danced in the club on the top of the casino. Then we passed out. No one objected to sleeping late the next morning.

I crawled out of my room around 12:30 p.m. and was the third person up. Fiona and Ashley were also awake, and they'd already been to breakfast, the pool, shopping, and returned. Neither of them were typically big drinkers so it made sense that they didn't have much of a hangover.

I didn't have a hangover either, but sleeping in felt good. We'd gotten back to the hotel room after 3:00 a.m. and, without sleep, I was like a malfunctioning Internet search engine. You could ask me a question about moon phases, and I'd come back with information about how to make homemade marshmallows.

Everyone else joined the land of the living over the next half hour, at which point I was informed that we all had an afternoon and evening of bliss planned at the hotel spa. Again, the entire spa had been reserved. I felt a lot spoiled and a little irritated that I was the only one who seemed to be experiencing dissonance with the level of luxury.

I'd never been to a spa before. I'd never had a massage or a facial, and I'd certainly never been waxed anywhere. Sometimes I'd painted my own nails or given myself a pedicure. I usually thought of grooming as standard maintenance, like cleaning out and vacuuming your car. I supposed a day at the spa was like getting a tune-up or an oil change.

Regardless, this experience felt extreme and a little like being a piece of meat prepared for dinner. I was stripped, plucked, cleaned, tenderized, seasoned, boiled, and dressed.

When we arrived, we were told to take off everything but our underwear. The attendant gave us plush terry cloth bathrobes and slippers, lovely against the skin. Everyone was on a different schedule. I started with a ninety-minute massage. Next, I had a soak in a mud bath, a mineral bath, a body scrub, then eyebrow waxing and a facial.

I was disoriented and dizzy, a mixture of relaxed and overwhelmed, when I was shown into a large room and told to sit in a very official looking chair with a tub at my feet. I was glad to see that all the other girls were already there getting pedicures and wearing similarly dazed expressions.

Except Sandra.

She was beaming and talking animatedly. I caught the tail end of the conversation, "…article where they placed jewels around it. Jewels! Can you imagine? It's called vagazzled."

"That's crazy." Ashley was knitting while her feet were being pampered. "And stupid. Who would want jewels glued to their skin around their vagina?"

"Maybe some women have ugly vaginas," Sandra shrugged, sipped her water.

We'd all been drinking water since over consuming the night before.

"To a heterosexual man, there is no such thing as an ugly vagina," Elizabeth interjected. "Although I personally find them very strange looking."

"Okay, show of hands, who here gets their junk waxed?" Sandra asked and raised her hand.

I glanced around, saw that Kat, Marie, and Elizabeth had also raised their hands.

Sandra squinted at Fiona. "Really? Greg doesn't complain? He doesn't want you to skin the peach?"

"Skin the peach?" Fiona lifted an eyebrow at the phrase.

"Yeah, skin the peach, peal the kiwi, groom the cat, mow the lawn, trim the topiary, clip the hedge, scale the tuna?" Sandra's recitation of waxing euphemisms impressed us all.

"I prefer to say shearing the sheep," Ashley said.

"That's because you're from Tennessee and like farming references." Sandra, I knew, was purposefully trying to heckle Ashley. Ashley, of course, knew it too. She ignored the attempted heckle.

"No, it's because it's a knitting reference. Get it? Shearing the sheep? Carding the wool?"

"Oh! That's a good one." Elizabeth smiled and lifted her water bottle like she was toasting Ashley.

"What about defuzzing the sweater?" Kat added, looking thoughtful. "You know, when sweaters get those balls of fuzz."

"Wouldn't that be de-pilling the sweater?" Sandra asked.

Elizabeth shook her head. "Doesn't have the same ring to it. I like defuzzing the sweater better."

"I feel like Zamboni has a place in this conversation...." I said, trying to think of a good waxing euphemism including a Zamboni. "But I just can't think of how it could be used."

"De-icing the rink?" Marie offered.

Everyone shook their head then stared thoughtfully at nothing.

Then Kat broke the short silence and said, "Another way to say vagazzled is lighting the landing strip."

"That's good!" Sandra nodded enthusiastically, "I'm going to use that. Maybe figure out how to add the word cockpit to it."

"What was your original point?" Fiona lifted her eyes to Sandra.

"Oh, I was saying, doesn't Greg complain about your hairy-kari?"

Fiona shrugged. "When would I have the time or opportunity to worry about harvesting the wheat and leaving decorative crop circles? I have two kids. I'm lucky if I shave my legs."

"Harvesting the wheat!" Marie gave Fiona a long distance high five then added, "Genius!"

"What about you, Janie?" Elizabeth narrowed her eyes at me. I didn't know if she did this to see me better, try to be intimidating, or because she was still drunk from the night before.

"What about me?"

"Are you going to start vacuuming the carpet now that you're getting married?"

I frowned, twisted my lips to the side, and considered the question.

I had no idea.

I hadn't thought about it. Aside from my lust for sexy shoes, I was exceptionally low maintenance. I shaved, but had never considered waxing.

"Maybe. I'll try anything once." I shrugged at last.

"Anything?" Sandra's smile paired with her eye squint made me nervous.

"Almost anything," I amended.

Then she asked, "What about a sperm facial?"

"Sandra!" Fiona looked and sounded shocked.

"Is that what the kids are calling it?" Marie said, smirking.

Fiona wasn't done. "Really, is that necessary?"

"No, really, it's a real thing! I promise!" Sandra held her hands up, her eyes wide.

Then one of the lovely ladies giving us our pedicures spoke up. "It's true. It's a real thing. Heather Locklear gets them. We have them here. We use whale sperm."

The room was silent for a very, very long moment as we all wore mirrored expressions, except Sandra. She looked vindicated.

"Whale sperm?" Kat sounded horrified. "Whale...*sperm*?"

"But how...." I tried to imagine the logistics of whale sperm extraction. "How do they get the sperm out of the whale?"

"Wetsuits?" Marie offered between giggles. She glanced and Ashley and they both burst out laughing.

"This is disgusting." Fiona shook her head, but the effect of her indignation was ruined by her poorly hidden laughter. "I can't...I can't even...."

"Have you lost your ability to can?" Sandra asked Fiona.

"Actually, it makes sense." Elizabeth, like me, wasn't laughing. She was glancing at the ceiling, and I could tell she was thinking critically about sperm facials. "Spermine, which is a component of semen, is high in anti-oxidants. It makes sense that it can be used to smooth out wrinkles. It's high in proteins, too."

Ashley made a gagging sound then said, "Cockroaches are also full of protein, but you don't seem me mashing them up and putting them on my face."

"But the type of protein matters," Elizabeth said, defending her position.

"See, this is why Elizabeth and Janie are BFFs." Sandra winked at me. "Janie wants to know the mechanics of the process, and Elizabeth is critically thinking about the medicinal benefits."

"Can we please talk about something else?" Fiona shivered, her face a grimace. "Someone, quick, change the subject."

Sandra shrugged. "I've also heard of a spa treatment where they use fish to eat the dead skin off your feet."

"Oh my God! Stop with the spa treatments!" Ashley glared at her knitting like it was offensive, her hand movements jerky. "No more. No more discussion of weird spa treatments allowed. You're harshing my mellow with talk of whale sperm in the face and skin-eating fish."

The room plunged into silence except for the sound of splashing water and knitting needles clicking. I glanced at Elizabeth, and we shared a small smile. Then I looked at Sandra and knew, I just *knew* she had one more weird spa-related treatment to share. I wondered if she'd made a point to look them up before we left.

Just when I thought she was going to let it go, Sandra blurted,

"Then I guess I won't bring up the nun urine."

"Sandra!"

CHAPTER 22

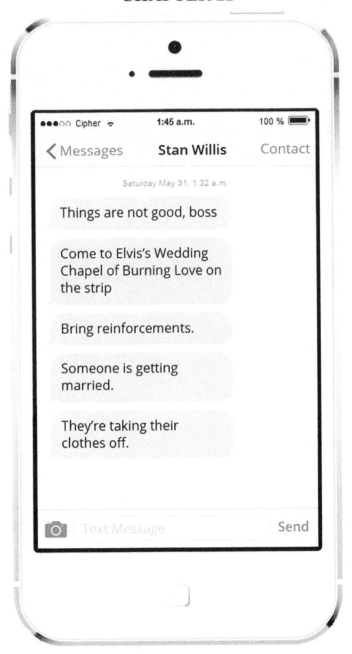

●●●○○ Cipher 🔕   1:45 a.m.   100 % ▬▬

< Messages   **Stan Willis**   Contact

Saturday May 31, 1:32 a.m.

Things are not good, boss

Come to Elvis's Wedding Chapel of Burning Love on the strip

Bring reinforcements.

Someone is getting married.

They're taking their clothes off.

📷 | Text Message   Send

Quinn

WE WERE IN the desert shooting machine guns when I got the first text.

I glanced at the screen of my phone. When I read the message, I secured my weapon, placed it back on the stand, and walked out of the shooting range.

Then four new messages arrived all at the same time. Each one was more strange and alarming than the one before it.

The texts told me that the ladies were on their way to Elvis' Wedding Chapel of Burning Love. According to Stan, someone was getting married and he needed help. Also, they were taking off their clothes.

I didn't hesitate.

I tried calling Stan for a status, but he didn't pick up his cell.

"Shit." I glared at the text messages, reading them again.

Nico came up behind me and stopped at my side. He glanced from me to the phone. "What's going on?"

"I don't know. Read this." I showed him the texts. His eyes narrowed when he read the last two.

His eyes lifted to mine. It was one of the few times I'd seen him frown. "We should go."

Ten minutes later Dan, Nico, and I were aboard the helicopter and on our way back to Las Vegas. The trip took less than twenty minutes. Nico checked his watch fifty times.

I instructed the pilot to land on the Circus, Circus helipad instead of the one on the Excalibur. Google maps told me the older casino was just a block from Elvis's Wedding Chapel of Burning Love.

We were still in our fatigues. I took off my outer shirt, and the other guys followed suit, leaving us in camouflage cargo pants and green T-shirts. It was hotter in the city than it had been in the desert. Also, the button-down long-sleeve shirt suddenly reminded me of a straightjacket.

We jogged from the helipad, down the stairs and straight to the elevator. Dan, who'd been quiet the whole time, was pacing the small box the entire ride down.

He only stopped to say, "What the hell is going on?" Then he hit the mirrored elevator wall with an open palm.

I was continuously speed-dialing Stan's cell but it kept clicking over to voicemail.

I wasn't panicked.

I was irritated.

Assigning three guards instead of one was my initial plan. I should have listened to my instincts.

I didn't think they were in danger from other people, but—all together, in Vegas, likely drunk—they were definitely a danger to themselves. Stan's radio silence concerned me most. My guess was that he'd been separated from his phone by one of the ladies.

Nico bolted out of the elevator as soon as the doors slid open. Dan followed. I was last. The sounds and chaos of the casino made me flinch. These places were mazes, meant to keep people on the floor, spending their money.

As soon as we were outside, Nico glanced at me for direction. I pointed and we jogged toward the chapel. I was a faster runner than the other two, and when the sign came into view, I sprinted.

I pulled open the door to the chapel, bracing myself. I didn't know what to expect, but I suspected that it would be crazy.

I was right.

Everyone, including Elvis, was wearing their underwear, and Stan was nowhere in sight. They were all dancing, and irritating boy band music was blaring from the sound system.

My eyes searched for Janie and found her. She had on a veil, a sash that said, *I'm getting hitched*, a white lace underwear set, and zebra print stilettos. She was laughing and she was drunk.

Seeing that she was unharmed, I took stock of the situation.

Elvis and Kat were dancing, and he was holding her waist.

Sandra was standing on a pew and lip-synching. Next to her was a man I didn't know and had never seen. His hands were all over her, and he wore a shirt that said *I married Sandra Fielding and all I got was this lousy T-shirt*. He had stripped down to his boxers—no pants.

Janie and Ashley were dancing with each other...and they were touching.

I groaned then grimaced.

It was innocent touching—holding hands, hugging, bumping their asses together—but it was still happening, and I saw it.

I was now grateful that Janie sent me away from her panty dance parties. I don't care how devoted you are to your woman, you see two ladies as hot as Janie Morris and Ashley Winston in lace underwear dancing with each other, it's going to leave a lasting impression.

Marie and Elizabeth were also dancing together; it looked like the tango, and Marie had the lead.

"Oh my goodness!" This sounded like *Ermergoodnish* because Sandra slurred it. She pointed at me and yelled above the music, "You came in costume!"

I glanced at my T-shirt, cargo pants, and boots. Just then, Nico and Dan flew into the room, stopped short, and looked around.

I glanced between Sandra and Kat, tried to decide which one to extract first. Dan charged over to Elvis and made the decision for me.

"Get your hands off her," Dan snarled, pushing him against the wall. He stared at him for a moment before turning to Kat and lifting her in his arms.

This left a stunned Elvis with his hands raised in surrender. "Hey, hey—sorry."

I gritted my teeth, glared at Elvis. "Turn off the music."

The impersonator, still in a posture of surrender, skirted along the wall toward the sound system controls. I was gratified that he moved quickly.

While he did this, I took three large steps and lifted Sandra off the pew and away from the unknown male. She didn't protest, but he did.

"Hey—hey, man."

"Shut up." I passed Sandra to Nico, then turned back to the man and sized him up. He was already scrambling down from the bench.

He was in his late fifties, approximately five foot eleven, and unnaturally tan. His skin looked like it had been painted on. He wore a large diamond stud in one ear, and his blond comb-over reminded me of Donald Trump.

"I don't know you," I said. "You don't touch her."

"Hey man, we're married."

The music stopped; the chapel was abruptly silent.

"What did you say?" I said, stalking closer.

He swallowed and his eyes ricocheted around the room. "I, uh, said…uh, we're married…?"

As he said this, he held up a piece of paper. I snatched it out of his hand and read it. He was right. It was a marriage license, and Sandra's name was printed in the bride box. She'd signed it.

I lifted just my eyes to the man then ripped the paper in two. "Not anymore. Put on some pants and get the hell out of here."

He flinched then nodded, edging away.

My eyes flickered over him before I added, "And leave the shirt."

He nodded faster and pulled the shirt over his head, tossed it to a bench, and grabbed his pants but didn't put them on before he ran out the door.

All eyes turned to me, and I studied each of their faces.

Alarm twisted my gut. They didn't look drunk. They looked stoned.

I crossed the room to Janie; she was leaning against Ashley. I took her chin in my fingers and peered into her eyeballs. As I suspected, her pupils were dilated.

"What the hell…?"

Marie stumbled forward. "Heya Quinn, whatzup?" She slapped me on the back. "Areya here for the wedding?"

I glared at her. "What did you take?"

Sandra burst into a fit of giggles, and would have fallen on her ass if Nico didn't help her sit on bench. "I think it was…the *shocolate.*" She covered her face with her hands. She was still laughing.

Nico moved to Elizabeth and was studying her eyes too. "Hey, Bella, are you okay?"

Her head nod was over exaggerated. "I'm grrrrrrrreat!"

"Are you really here?" Janie asked. Her question brought my attention back to her. She twisted her arms around my neck. The amber of her eyes was almost invisible. I cursed under my breath.

"Janie, what did you take?" I pushed her hair from her face.

"It was the chocolate, I'm pretter sssure." Sandra stood, staggered like she was going to fall, then walked to me. She stopped three feet away, placed her fists on her hips, and lifted her chin. "With ab-snythe…arbsooth…absinthe—absinthe…yep."

"Absinthe? This isn't absinthe." Dan set Kat on the bench then knelt in front of her. He cradled her face in his hands. "This looks like LSD."

"Or LDS." Sandra shrugged.

Elizabeth giggled. Sandra looked at Elizabeth. Sandra and Elizabeth burst out laughing. Soon, all the ladies were laughing. Janie laid her forehead against my chest and gripped my arms. She was consumed by a fit of giggles.

"No…." Nico wrapped his arm around a laughing Elizabeth, frowned at her. "Not LSD. No hallucinations."

Marie sat on the floor. "I can't—I can't…." I figured she was trying to say, *I can't breathe* but was laughing too hard.

Kat pointed at Elizabeth as Dan sat next to her. I saw she had tears in her eyes as she said between snorts, "Too bad we don't know any doctors."

And the room erupted again.

I closed my eyes for a moment, shook my head. This was crazy.

Sandra was the culprit, I was sure. I walked Janie over to the bench and sat her next to Dan. I then turned to Sandra and placed my hands on her shoulders.

"Sandra." I gripped her arms and shook her a little to get her attention. "What did you give them?"

Her laughter tapered off and her eyebrows lifted. Her eyes

moved over my face like she was trying to place me.

"Sandra, what did you give them?"

I saw a flicker of lucidity in her gaze and she wrinkled her nose. "Amsterdam absinthe. It's harmless."

"Ohhhh...." Dan said. I looked at him. He rolled his eyes. "It's hash, Quinn. *Amsterdam* Absinthe is a nickname for hashish."

My stare slid back to Sandra.

She looked at Dan, and her eyes were squinted like she was confused. "No, no, no. I specifically remember. I wanted Absinthe-flavored chocolate because it's supposed to be like...like...like a clear-headed drunkiness."

"You got hash," Dan said. He was fighting a smile.

"No. The chocolate—it's Amsterdam Absinthe chocolate. And, besides...." Sandra pursed her lips and crossed her arms over her chest. "Hash is *illegal*. Absinthe is not."

"Should we take them to the ER?" Nico lifted Elizabeth into his arms.

"Oh, Nico...." Elizabeth said, and she pressed her forehead and nose into his neck. "I love you."

Janie and Kat leaned against Dan, who said, "Nah, if they were going to have a bad reaction, it would've already happened. Let's just...." He was juggling Kat to keep her from falling, all while trying to be a good guy and not touch her bare skin. "Let's just get them dressed and get outta here."

"Dan the security man," Janie said, and her arms went around his neck, her lips against his ear. "You're cute but you're short. Don't listen to Randy Newman, Dan. You have lots of reasons to live."

"He's not short." Kat fell forward. Dan was trying to keep her upright, and somehow she ended up in his lap. "You guys are the same height. If he's short then you're short."

"Valid point. You're not short, you're perfect." Janie reached forward and tried to give Kat a high five. The attempt went wide, and she fell forward onto Kat. Now they were both on his lap and laughing again.

"Damn it—can we please find their clothes?" Dan sounded like he was in pain.

I watched this exchange and was surprised that I found it funny. Seeing Dan uncomfortable always ranked high. The irony of his discomfort, surrounded by beautiful women in their underwear, one of which I was going to marry in two weeks, only made it funnier.

"Yeah," I said, returning Nico's grin. "Yeah, let's get them out of here."

"We can't. We can't go yet," Marie called from her place on the floor. "Someone has to get married."

"What?" Nico, Dan, and I said in unison.

"It's true." Ashley was swaying to invisible music. "We made a pact. We must act to follow the pact—we can't redact."

"Rhyme!" Sandra pointed at Ashley and—surprise, surprise—everyone started laughing again.

"No-no-no," I said. "No one is getting married."

"What happened to Donald?" Sandra glanced around the room.

"Who is Donald?" Dan asked.

"I think we got married."

"Donald is gone. Forget about Donald." I needed to get them dressed and in a car.

"He left me? Was he crying?"

"No. No crying." I frowned at Sandra's strange question. "But he's gone."

"Well…I guess we'll just have to find someone else."

"No one is getting married." I said it louder this time. "You all need to put on your clothes. We're going back to the hotel."

"No-no-no." They all called in unison. The ones who were sitting stood and moved toward each other. Then, as a group, they charged toward me. At least, they charged as much as they could considering they were stoned.

"It's happening! We're not leaving until someone gets married."

"Sandra…."

She turned to look at me, blinked, then pressed her lips together.

"You scare me." She didn't look scared. She also didn't sound scared. "And you're grumpy. Why are you always so grumpy? Tell me about your relationship with your mother. It's ok to cry. I'm used to it."

Ashley loud whispered and drunkenly draped herself over Sandra's shoulder. "It's true. She is. They always cry."

"Enough. We're leaving."

"No! It's the last thing on the list." Elizabeth held up a list. It was a numbered list of ten items. All but the bottom one was crossed out.

They began calling to me in a chorus, tugging at my shirt. Janie made her way to the front, pressed against me, and whispered in my ear. "Please, please, please...."

"A little help here?" I looked to Nico.

He shrugged. "I don't know how we're going to get them out of here unless they're willing."

"Fine." I gritted my teeth and said, "Janie and I will get married."

"You can't get married," Nico said, trying to dissuade me with a vigorous headshake. "It'll break your mother's heart."

I squinted at him. "What do you know about it?"

"I crochet with the girls every Tuesday. I know all about it." Nico looked around the room then said to the Elvis impersonator, "What do we need to do to get married here?"

Elvis, who'd been standing like a statue, shook himself and stuttered, "Uh-uh-uh...."

"Who is getting married?" Dan asked over the continuing chorus of protests from the knitting group.

Janie was still rubbing against me, and I was starting to return her kisses. Fuck if she wasn't driving me crazy. I'd never seen her so uninhibited. I was equal parts turned on and exasperated. She had me on fire.

"I'll take one for the team. Elizabeth and I'll do it." Nico rubbed his hands together. He was smiling. It didn't look like this was going to be a sacrifice.

Dan shook his head at Nico. "She is going to be pissed tomorrow when she finds out."

"Finds out? She's here, isn't she? She's awake, isn't she? And look…." He pulled a box out of his cargo pants, opened it to show us a diamond engagement ring and two wedding bands. "I even have the rings."

Dan glanced from the rings to Nico. "Did you plan this?"

Nico shook his head. "No. But I'm going to take advantage of it."

"She's stoned out of her mind."

"Tomato, tomah-to."

"Fine," I said, putting my hands up because it was the easiest option, and Janie's continuing assault had become overwhelming. I needed to put a stop to it or I needed to get her alone. I couldn't leave with just her, and I wanted easy. I needed to get them home, and arguing with six mostly naked knitters was the opposite of easy. "Fine. We'll have a wedding. But everyone needs to get dressed first."

"Yay!" Janie smiled up at me and the assault was over. They moved away in a sloppy mess of limbs and bare bodies, hugging each other.

"Clothes on. Wedding after," I reminded them.

The next several minutes were spent sorting through their clothes. Janie gave Elizabeth the veil. Once they had their clothes on, things didn't get much better. They each seemed to be trying to out-do the other for the shortest skirt.

Janie easily won, but this was only because her legs were longest. Elizabeth's blue dress and Janie's red one didn't have straps. Sandra was the only one in pants, and they were leather pants. The outfits looked more like wrapping paper than clothing.

Nico finally got Elvis talking, though Dan kept shooting the man dirty looks. I guessed Dan was still thinking about finding him with his hands on Kat. I didn't want to know what was going on there, between Kat and Dan. I knew, based on the background checks I'd done on all the ladies, that Kat was more than just a secretary at an architecture firm, but I hadn't shared the information with Dan, and he hadn't asked.

The girls didn't seem any more sober, but with the wedding to look forward to, they took direction better and sat in the pews when instructed. Random bouts and snorts of laughter erupted periodically.

I was going to have to get a sample of Sandra's Amsterdam absinthe chocolate and get it tested just to make sure they hadn't ingested anything stronger or dangerous. But none of them looked sick. So Dan called for a car, and we made the ladies promise to leave as soon as Elizabeth and Nico were married.

It was decided that Dan would be the best man and that I would walk Elizabeth down the aisle. I protested when the group wanted Janie to be the maid of honor because she wasn't walking in a straight line very well. I was overruled.

An organist appeared from someplace. He was in his eighties at least and walked into the chapel as if he'd been planning to show up all along. He sat down and began playing "A Big Hunk O' Love." I guessed that the impersonator usually sang along. He didn't. He stood at the front, not looking anything like Elvis.

Nico and Dan also stood at the front. I watched Janie take slow steps away from where Elizabeth and I were waiting at the back of the small building. Amazingly she didn't fall.

"We're so lucky," Elizabeth loud whispered at my side.

I glanced at her. "What?"

She peered at me. "We are lucky. I am lucky to have Nico. You are lucky to have Janie. He gives meaning to the beating of my heart. You and I...we despise almost everyone, which means we save all our love and affection for a small few. I don't know how they put up with the intensity of it, but they do."

I searched her face. She was still stoned out of her mind, which might have meant that her walls were down and she was speaking honestly.

She continued. "I really do like you, Quinn. You love her like she deserves. You should let her love you back."

"I do," I said. Then, because she was being so honest and she probably wouldn't remember any of this in the morning, I added, "Janie makes me a better person."

She gave me a small smile before she turned to the front of the chapel. "You make yourself a better person. Janie is just a reminder of why it's worth it."

I blinked at her, taking in this nugget of wisdom. But before I could say anything else, we were walking down the aisle. I glanced at Janie. She was still high as a kite, but she was beaming at her friend. Nico was watching Elizabeth. He looked like he was about to float out of his shoes.

We reached them in five steps, and I handed Elizabeth to Nico. I then took a seat in the front pew, the one closest to Janie so that she was standing directly before me. If I wanted to, or if she started to fall, I could reach forward without standing and bring her to my lap.

Mercifully, the organ music stopped. I almost moaned my relief. Elvis cleared his throat to get everyone's attention, and then he began in a singsong fashion, "Dearly beloved...."

He read the words from a piece of paper and didn't look up once during his recitation. This was probably because Dan was still giving him the evil eye.

I glanced at Nico and Elizabeth and got the distinct impression that they no longer saw us; they weren't at all aware of the shitty Vegas chapel or the lack of flowers and decorations. They saw only each other.

That's how it's supposed to be, I thought.

I understood why some people wanted to get married in a beautiful church, temple, or mosque. They wanted to exchange vows surrounded by the presence of their maker. They wanted the experience to be sacred. They wanted beauty around them as they pledged their life together.

I thought I would be more like Nico when the time came. He looked at Elizabeth, and she was the only beauty he saw. It wouldn't have mattered if they'd been in St. Peter's Basilica in Rome, the Siddiqa Fatima Zahra Mosque in Kuwait, under the sky, in a tent, or in a piece of shit chapel in Las Vegas, Nevada.

Nico didn't care.

"I, Elizabeth Heather Finney, take you, Niccolò Ludvico

Manganiello...."

"To be my husband," Elvis prompted.

But Elizabeth didn't repeat after him. She swayed forward a little then repeated his name. "Niccolò Ludvico Manganiello...."

Elvis looked between the two of them, cleared his throat. "That's right. Now say, *to be my husband.*"

Elizabeth ignored him. She started jumping up and down. "Manganiello...Manganiello...Manganiello!" Each time she said his last name it was louder until she was shouting it. I knew Elizabeth had trouble saying Nico's last name. But her shouting of *Manganiello* was ridiculous.

Nico laughed and shook his head. "Tutto questo è ridicolo. Quel che conta è che il mio cuore ti amava ancor prima di incontrarti e ti amerà sempre. Sii mia e lascia che io sia tuo."

Nico had told me once that Elizabeth went crazy when he spoke Italian to her. This was information I considered irrelevant.

Regardless, he was right. Sitting in the front row of the chapel, I saw the evidence clear as day.

Elizabeth swayed again, her hands lifted to Nico's shoulders. The ladies all sighed loudly. I glanced at Janie and found her looking at me like she was starving and I was fried chicken. I lifted my eyebrows at the intensity of her gaze.

I needed to learn Italian.

Elizabeth, her nose now an inch from Nico's, moaned and said, "Oh, screw it. Just say husband and wife already!"

Elvis looked between them, then to me. I shrugged.

"Uh...husband and wife," he said.

Elizabeth jumped into Nico's arms, her legs wrapped around his middle, and swallowed his startled laugh when she kissed the hell out of him.

***

THE CAR DROVE us back to the casino hotel where the ladies were staying. When we exited the car we split up the girls; each of us helped two make it into the hotel.

"This is like herding cats." Dan was carrying a passed out Marie over his shoulder, fireman-style. His other arm was around Kat's waist, stumble walking with her.

"This is worse," I said.

It was worse. It was torture.

Janie was snuggled against my chest and her hands were roaming. She hadn't stopped looking at me like I was a meal since Nico's little performance. Twice I'd pulled her fingers out of my pants while we walked across the floor of the casino. Janie's exploration would have been nicer if Sandra hadn't been on my back.

The only way I'd been able to keep Sandra from running off was by giving her a piggyback ride. Her legs were around my waist, her arms around my neck. Every few minutes she'd dig her heels into my sides, arch her back, and say, "Yee haw!" or "Get a rope!" or "Save a horse, ride a cowboy!"

"It's not so bad." Nico said. "Chi s'accontenta gode."

Nico's arms were full of Elizabeth and Ashley. He was the only one who was smiling. Ashley was surprisingly docile. She seemed content to lay her head on his shoulder and quietly follow where he led. Elizabeth had her arms around him and was kissing his neck and face. She also followed him without question.

"What does that mean?" Dan frowned. "I don't speak Italian."

"It means a contented mind is a perpetual feast," Nico said. "Similar to a burden that one chooses is not felt." His hand around Elizabeth slid down the side of her body and grabbed her ass. "Enjoy yourself, and you might find that the task is not so difficult."

"That's easy for you to say." Dan gritted his teeth and walked around a slot machine. He was propping up a mostly asleep Marie while Kat was tonguing his ear. "You're holding your wife. If I enjoy myself I'm a scumbag."

We finally reached the elevator. Nico pressed the button. We waited.

My attention flickered to Dan. Kat leaned in to him, pressed her body against his, and kissed his jaw. "You're cute," she said, and her hand slid from his neck to his chest, then lower.

I cocked an eyebrow at them.

"Fuck...." Dan gasped. His eyes lifted to the ceiling of the casino. "Fuck. Fuck. Fuck. Hurry up."

"I think she likes you." Nico grinned between Elizabeth's kisses.

"No." Dan's voice was tight. He tried turning from Kat, but she was plastered to him. If he moved away too far or too fast, she would fall. If he let go of Marie, *she* would fall. "Kat would never do this if she were sober. Can one of you help me out? Move her hand?"

"Sorry." Nico didn't sound sorry. "My hands are full."

Dan looked to me. Sandra giggled in my ear and bucked, smacking my ass. "This is fun!" she said. She slurred her words, making it sound like she'd said, *Thishun.* Then she slumped, her body dead weight. I had to lean forward and grip her legs to keep her from falling.

The movement revived Janie. She turned more fully against me, kissed my neck, and pulled my shirt completely out of my pants. She whispered in my ear, "I want you to talk dirty to me and call me Kitten so I can scratch your back and eat your...."

I straightened and pulled away before she could finish. Otherwise, I would probably dump Sandra on the floor, grab Janie, and find a stairwell.

Instead, I glared at Dan and said, "You're on your own."

CHAPTER 23

Janie

THE NEXT MORNING I woke up feeling like death.

Then the world slowly came into focus.

I realized I was in bed.

And I was lying on a man's chest.

And I was topless.

"Oh shit!"

Startled and completely horrified, I tried to jump up and out of the bed but succeeded only in falling to the floor in a tangled mass of sheets.

"Janie?"

I blinked from my position on the floor, sitting completely still. I even held my breath.

The voice that said my name sounded like Quinn's. I licked my lips, forced myself to breathe, then peeked over the edge of the bed.

Quinn was lying there, his head propped up on his hand, his elbow on the bed. He wasn't wearing a shirt, but he had on camouflage cargo pants. I squinted at the pants then I moved my gaze back to his.

His hair was askew as it was a little longer than usual, and his eyes were sleepy.

I closed my eyes then opened them again. Sure enough, he was still there.

"...Quinn?" I was surprised by the sound of my voice. It sounded raspy, and my throat hurt. I blinked at him again. "What...who...how...why are you here?"

Quinn's gaze moved over me as he sat up. He seemed to be studying me or waiting for me to say something.

But I had nothing to say. My mind was oddly vacant, and my head hurt. I tried to think, tried to recall my last memory, and found the only thing I remembered was getting ready to go out the night before.

After the spa, we came back to the hotel room. Fiona was flying back early, so we all said our goodbyes then got ready for our last night.

I remembered putting on a red dress that Elizabeth had picked out and thinking it was scandalous.

I remembered the girls putting a veil on me and a white sash that read *Getting Hitched.*

I remembered Sandra passing out chocolates and Ashley passing out drinks and us making a toast to Las Vegas.

Everything after that was a void of unknowns.

"Kitten."

My eyes refocused on his, and I stared at him. He looked pensive and…watchful.

"Yes?"

"What do you remember?"

I pressed my mouth into a line and shook my head, my eyes drifting shut. "Please, please, please don't tell me that I was drugged again."

I heard him sigh and I knew the answer.

I thought about freaking out. I decided against it. Instead, I attempted to sit perfectly still and just…wait. I would wait for the memories to return or to wake up from this bad dream. I didn't realize it at the time, but sitting perfectly still and denying the existence of reality was—by definition—freaking out.

Then someone screamed. Actually, it was more like a shriek.

My eyes flew open and I glanced toward the sound.

Quinn looked at the door, looked at me, then fell back on the bed. He covered his eyes with his forearm. I thought I heard him laughing; it sounded both irritated and amused.

"Are you…?" I tried to swallowed, but I was so parched that nothing went down. I needed water. "Are you going to see what that was?"

"Nope."

I watched him. When he said nothing else, I scooted closer to the bed. "Do you know what that was about?"

"Yep."

Another shriek sounded from beyond the door. I frowned at him. He still wasn't moving.

I stood with the intent to walk out of the room but remembered my half-nakedness. Also, I was dizzy. I spun in an unsteady circle trying to find something to wear. Finding a man's green T-shirt—presumably Quinn's, unless there was another man lurking about that was Quinn's size and smelled like him—I pulled it on and walked to the door.

"Don't, Janie."

I glanced over my shoulder at him. He looked exhausted and had a very strange expression on his face. "Why not?"

"Because once you open the door, you let the world in. Just come back to bed. Elizabeth's crisis can wait."

My eyes widened and I flinched. "Elizabeth's crisis?"

Quinn sighed again, groaned, cussed, then pulled the covers over his head. Despite the muffling effect of the sheets, I heard him say, "Just be thankful that *we* didn't elope last night."

I frowned at the lump he'd become under the covers, trying to make sense of his words. When no sense could be found, I opened the door and stumbled out of the bedroom.

I heard voices coming from one of the bedrooms so I made a beeline for the sounds. Within one of the rooms, I found Elizabeth sitting on the bed, white as the sheets she sat on. On one side was Ashley; on the other side was Marie. They were all dressed in the same clothes they'd worn the night before.

But Elizabeth had on my veil.

"Hey. What's going on?" I tiptoed toward the bed, searching the room for danger and finding none.

Elizabeth turned saucer-round eyes to me and held up her left hand. "Look."

I crossed the room, squinting because I'd forgotten to put on my glasses. I was almost on top of her before I realized she wore an engagement ring *and* a wedding ring. Last night she'd had neither, because, although she was engaged to Nico, they hadn't yet chosen a ring.

I gasped.

"I know! Right?" Elizabeth groaned then regarded the ring with evident despondency.

"What the...? Well, where did those come from?"

"I don't know!" Elizabeth shook her head, her hand dropped to her lap, and I saw she was trying to take the ring off. It wouldn't come off.

"How did it get there?" I asked, looking between Ashley and Marie. They looked equally confused.

"I don't know!" Elizabeth shrieked. She was tugging the rings with more force and panicking.

I opened my mouth, closed it, opened it again. "What happened last night?"

"We have no idea." Ashley's voice met my ears. "It's like one minute we're all toasting your wedding and the next minute we're standing here with dead rodent breath, looking like hades, and Elizabeth is married to...someone."

Elizabeth groaned and fell backward onto the bed; she covered her face with her hands and curled into a ball.

"Could it be Nico?" Marie sounded hopeful. "I mean, it could be Nico. I don't see any strange men wandering around the suite."

Elizabeth shook her head but kept her face covered. "He's in New York filming all week. Unless he somehow finished early, flew out here, found us doing...whatever we were doing last night, bought the rings, took me to a wedding chapel, and married me, then it's not Nico. Besides, we haven't even set a date yet."

"Also, if it were Nico, wouldn't he be here right now?" Ashley asked the room. "In fact, shouldn't someone be here? I mean, your new husband should be around here someplace."

Elizabeth groaned again and rolled to her side.

"That's not helping, Ashley." Marie shook her head, but she was suppressing a smile.

Ashley exhaled loudly and flopped onto the bed next to

Elizabeth, rubbed her back. "I'm sorry. It'll all work out."

"Who knows if you're even really married." Marie sat on the bed on the other side of Elizabeth. "Maybe someone gave you the rings for safekeeping...."

Elizabeth assumed the fetal position.

"She's married." A voice sounded from the door and we all turned toward it. Elizabeth lifted her head and peeked through her fingers.

Sandra was standing there holding a piece of paper; she looked like a redheaded raccoon. "I found the marriage license on the bar."

There was a pause, and I was pretty sure we were all holding our breath.

Then Ashley blurted, "Don't keep us in suspense, woman! What does it say?"

Sandra looked down at the license and read the name. "Niccolò Ludvico Manganiello."

Elizabeth sat up slowly, her eyes wide and unblinking, her mouth open. She looked entirely befuddled. Then she said, "Nico?"

Sandra nodded and held out a second piece of paper. "He left you a note."

"He left me a note?" Elizabeth breathed; then she repeated, but much louder, "HE LEFT ME A NOTE?!"

I flinched and my eyes darted to Ashley's. She was covering the bottom half of her face, and I could see she was trying not to laugh.

Elizabeth stood suddenly, swayed a little, and marched over to Sandra. She grabbed the note, unfolded it, and read it with, frankly, wild eyes. Through the back of the paper, I could see that only two or three lines had been written. Elizabeth read it several times before a short hysterical sounding laugh erupted from her mouth.

"Don't keep us in suspense, woman! What does it say?" Ashley repeated, although I had the feeling this time she was trying to use it for comic relief.

Elizabeth passed me the note then began to pace the room muttering, "I'm going to kill him...I'm going to kill him...."

I glanced from her to the paper, and read the contents out loud.

Dearest Wife,

Now we don't have to worry about setting a date. You're welcome.

Your Husband, Nico

***

SANDRA WOULDN'T STOP apologizing.

Soon after discovering that Elizabeth and Nico had gotten married the night before and that none of us had any memory of it, Sandra confessed that the chocolate had been spiked with absinthe. More specifically, a type of absinthe called Amsterdam absinthe.

"I can't understand it, though." Sandra held her forehead in her hands, glaring at her coffee cup.

We'd called up for room service and we were all gathered in the large sitting room munching on a buffet of brunch foods.

Marie and Ashley were knitting. Sandra was beating herself up. Dan was by the buffet spooning himself eggs. Elizabeth was zoning out with a dreamy smile on her face. I was sitting on Quinn's lap eating a plate of fruit.

And Kat was not making eye contact with anyone.

"Absinthe shouldn't have made us lose our memory; it's supposed to be like getting drunk but without the fogginess. And it's completely legal! You can even order it online." Sandra sounded despondent.

"Don't tear yourself up about it." Kat reached over and patted Sandra's back, careful to keep her eyes on her friend. In fact, Kat was being careful to keep her eyes either downcast or mostly lowered.

Abruptly, Ashley growled. "I have a confession to make!" She tossed her knitting to the side and covered her face with her hands. "I am so, so sorry, but I think I might also be to blame."

We all exchanged wide-eyed glances—well, everyone but Kat, because she was still avoiding looking more than two inches from the floor.

"Spill it, Ashley." Marie prodded her with her elbow. "What did you do? Spike our drinks?"

Ashley groaned. "Yes! Yes, I spiked the drinks."

Marie's mouth fell open. "You didn't...."

"I did. I asked my brother, Cletus, to send me some hooch. I added it to our drinks." Her shoulders rose and fell with a large breath, then she mumbled, "I added a lot of it to our drinks...."

"What the hell is hooch?" Dan asked, his hands on his hips.

"Moonshine! White lightning...it's nasty." She peeked through her fingers at me. "I'm sorry."

"You dirty hillbilly!" Sandra wrinkled her nose at Ashley, but didn't sound very upset. "I wish you'd told me. I wouldn't have handed out the chocolate."

"I'll need a sample of both, what you put in the drink and the chocolate." Quinn said this between large bites of sausage and eggs benedict.

"Yes, absolutely." Sandra nodded at Quinn's request and huffed an unhappy sigh, her gaze shifting to me. "I'm sorry, Janie."

I shrugged. "No harm done, Sandra."

As soon as I said the words, two interesting things happened.

Kat and Dan glanced at each other then pointedly looked away, Kat turning bright red and Dan clearing his throat.

The other interesting thing was that Elizabeth nodded at my statement. "Hey, we'll all get checked out this afternoon, and McHotpants can have his bat-lab do an analysis to see what was actually in that stuff."

Sandra stared at her, still looking miserable. Ashley was peeking at all of us between her fingers and seemed content to keep silent.

Elizabeth leaned toward Sandra and gave her a small smile. "It's also our fault; we should have known better than to accept chocolate from you. I've never seen you share chocolate."

"It is not your fault. It's my fault, and it's Ashley's fault. We need to learn how to coordinate our druggings next time." Sandra folded her arms on the table in front of her and her head dropped.

"Oh, no. There will *never* be a next time," Marie teased, turning her work, then asked, "What I want to know is how did Quinn,

Nico, and Dan the Man get here?"

Everyone except Sandra, because her face was still buried in her arms, turned their attention to Quinn. He was mid-bite and looked entirely unconcerned.

We waited for him to finish chewing his food before he responded. "We were in the desert shooting machine guns and I got a text from Stan. So we took a helicopter over to Circus, Circus and jogged to the chapel." Then he took another bite as though this supremely odd explanation answered our questions.

Elizabeth looked at him like he'd just sprouted a fin. "Wait—you were in the desert shooting machine guns?"

He nodded.

"With Nico and Dan?"

He nodded.

"How close is this desert where you were shooting machine guns?"

He shrugged, glanced to the left, swallowed, then replied, "About twenty minutes by helicopter."

"Helicopter? You took a helicopter?" Ashley finally dropped her hands from her face.

He nodded.

"Why were you there anyway?" Elizabeth pressed. "Nico was supposed to be in New York this week."

"He was. He just came out for the day."

"To shoot machine guns…?"

He nodded and punctuated it with a "Yep."

Ashley was studying Quinn intently. After several long moments, she abruptly asked, "Were you there for *your* bachelor party?"

He nodded. "Yep."

I looked at Ashley, she looked at me, then we both looked at Marie and Elizabeth.

But it was Sandra who spoke our thoughts. "Can *we* go out to the desert and shoot machine guns?"

Quinn frowned, glanced at Dan. I saw Dan lift his eyebrows then look to the ceiling and sigh. I had come to understand that, for Dan, this was his silent way of communicating that he was dumbfounded.

Some people say, "I can't—I can't even…."

Some people say, "Bitch, you *crazy.*"

Some people say, "I have no words."

Dan just glances at the ceiling and takes a deep breath.

Quinn turned his gaze to me, his eyes searching. "Do you want to go?"

"YES," I said immediately and maybe a little too loud. "YES I WANT TO GO TO THE DESERT AND SHOOT MACHINE GUNS."

His expression softened and his eyes turned dreamy and adoring as they moved over my features. Then he leaned forward and whispered, "Whatever you want, Kitten. Whatever you want is yours."

Part 6: The Wedding

CHAPTER 24

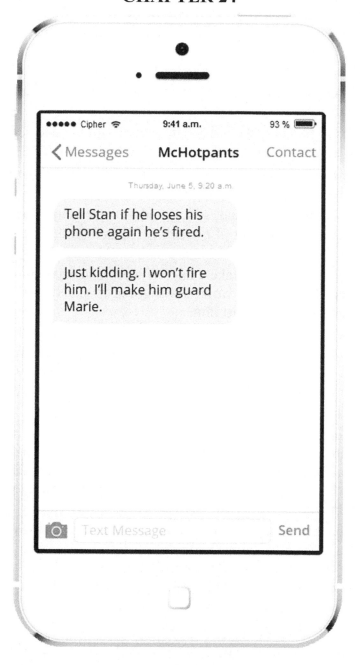

TEN DAYS BEFORE the wedding, my father finally committed to coming. I had Quinn's secretary, Betty, make the arrangements and reminded Dan to have a tux arranged. I was shocked that he agreed to have dinner with Quinn, me, Katherine, Desmond, Dan, Elizabeth, and Nico on the Thursday before the wedding.

He'd been my mother's doormat, and now he was giving me away at my wedding.

But first, I had to make it through dinner with my dad, Quinn, his parents, Elizabeth, and Nico.

A part of me wondered if my dad only agreed to come because he found out Nico would be there.

Shelly, on the other hand, still wouldn't return any of my phone calls. Against every fiber of my being, I'd even texted her. Still no response.

I had no choice but to take a day off work and drive down to the farmhouse. If this didn't work, I was going to sic Nico on her. No one, it seemed, could resist him.

I told Quinn about my plan to drive to her farmhouse. He didn't protest, but he didn't want to go with me, either. He said we should wait until after the wedding when things settled down to normal, then work on her about starting up Saturday breakfast again.

His plan was unsatisfactory.

If Quinn and I had opted to elope or just go to the courthouse, I don't know that I would have minded her absence. But her mother had put a lot of work into the wedding. All of Quinn's family was going to be there as well as my knitting group, and I wanted Shelly to be there, too.

We would be flying out on Monday and staying in Boston for the week leading up to the wedding day. I didn't expect her to come and stay the entire time if she didn't want to. At the very least, I just wanted her there on the day, to share it with us and be a part of it.

It was important to me.

So I sat next to Stan in the front seat on the drive to Shelly's farm and practiced my speech.

I glanced over at him at one point; he was nodding his head

along with The Cars song "Good Times Roll." I discovered The Cars when Nico made a mix-tape for Elizabeth. I then downloaded their greatest hits to my phone.

Admittedly, one thing I didn't hate about the phone was that I could listen to music on it.

Anyway, I soon discovered that all my guards really, really liked The Cars, and Quinn did too. Therefore, when Quinn and I had our own private panty dance parties, they usually started with "Shake It Up" and usually ended with "Drive."

Stan, now bobbing his head along with the music, seemed completely at ease. Therefore, I figured it was a good time to apologize for what happened in Vegas.

"So…Stan."

His eyes flickered to me then back to the road. "Yeah?"

"I wanted to just say…I just wanted to say…." I twisted my hands on my lap. "On behalf of everyone, I am really sorry about what happened, what we did to you in Vegas."

His gaze slid back to mine, held for a beat, then went to the windshield. He cleared his throat. "Don't worry about it."

But I did, and I was going to worry about it. Even though I had no memory of it, it was going to bother me.

According to Stan, Marie had stolen his phone while he tried to stop us from taking off our clothes. She then threw it out the door of whatever chapel we were in—the chapel where Elizabeth and Nico apparently got married. He tried to grab the phone, but Marie told a police officer standing nearby that Stan was harassing us and wouldn't leave us alone.

He was then detained, and must've just missed us when we left the chapel with Quinn, Dan, and Nico.

I shook my head. "I am going to worry about it. I am so, so sorry. I have no excuse for our behavior, and I hope you will accept my apology."

He gave me a small smile. "Nah, it's fine. Things always get a little crazy during that kind of sh- uh, stuff."

"Thank you for being so gracious about it, and please let me know if there is anything I can do to make it up to you."

He shrugged and I thought he looked happy, which I felt was a little strange. Regardless, better that he was happy than upset.

We spent the rest of the journey in mostly companionable quiet listening to The Cars. I watched the scenery change from city to urban sprawl to farmland. Other than mentally rehearsing my speech for Shelly, I let my brain wander.

Surprisingly, my mind meanderings were mostly about my life and about Quinn, almost like a normal person.

I thought about the private accounts and all the details I'd learned directly from Quinn some weeks ago as well as from the files I'd reviewed at the office. The Monday after returning from Vegas, I finally looked over the account documents he'd set aside.

I understood now that Quinn's assertion that he blackmailed people was a gross oversimplification of the issue. It reminded me of how he kept saying things like "I'm responsible for my brother's death" when he wasn't responsible, or how he said, "I'm good at using people," when he didn't precisely use people.

I was coming to understand that Quinn actually, truly saw himself as a bad guy. He was a defeatist; things were black and white, right and wrong, and he'd decided that he was firmly in the not-a-good-guy column.

There was no doubt that he blackmailed people, especially early on in his business life. He'd blackmailed gangsters and criminals, and had been focused solely on taking down those people who most contributed to his brother's death.

But now, from what I'd pieced together, he used information gathered from private accounts to steer his business. He would find out about a plan to open a new club from one of his private clients and then be aggressive about going after the corporate account to provide security. This was especially true if one account—i.e. the club—would eventually lead to a larger account—i.e. casinos in Las Vegas, Atlantic City, and Monaco.

Providing security for clubs led to providing security for hotels, which led to providing security for casinos, which led to providing security for banks. That was the security business food chain.

I found corroboration for his assertion that all crimes involving exploitation of individuals were immediately passed through to the

FBI, CIA, or police. Anything mentioning drugs, rape, human trafficking, fraud, corruption, or the like had a plan attached to it where the client relationship was severed and the evidence was anonymously delivered to what Quinn had called the right people.

I did see that he also used people's secrets to push them, but it wasn't precisely *using*.

One of the files I'd reviewed detailed how a private client was stepping out on her husband. I listened to a recording of Quinn as he showed the client the pictures, confirmed that he wouldn't be sharing the information, then suggested she put pressure on a Senator Watterson to hand down a maximum sentence to a crooked CEO.

Most of the *blackmail* examples were of this type. He would show the evidence to the clients then make a suggestion—like suggest an alternative business practice, one that wasn't corrupt— or he would request a meeting with a high-ranking official in the government, or ask for a meeting with a corporate security liaison for a casino or bank.

He was using people's secrets, but not in the way he thought. He showed them their files, said he wouldn't betray them, then asked for a favor.

These people trusted him.

And that was probably why they were so reluctant to lose his services.

I'd put off reviewing the private account files because a big part of me was afraid of what I would find, especially after Quinn's description of his behavior. But now, I saw the humor in it, the irony. He was talented at using people. He was so talented, they had no idea that they were being used; they trusted him, and they thanked him for it.

I hadn't had a chance to discuss my findings with Quinn since reviewing the files two days ago; I was still marinating in all the details and looking for holes in my theory. But I was finding none.

After I finished talking some sense into Shelly, I would have to talk some sense into Quinn. Somehow, I would have to reason with him, get him to see that he was already one of the good guys.

The SUV rocked as we pulled into the dirt driveway leading to Shelly's farm, and the jarring movement pulled me from my thoughts.

I saw Shelly right away, or at least, all that was visible of her—cutoff jean shorts, work boots, and a tank top. Her brown hair was in a braid down her back, and she had grease smudges everywhere skin was showing. She was bent over a car, her head in the hood.

Stan pulled to a stop in the circular driveway some twenty feet from where she was, and I saw her head lift out of the engine. Her eyes narrowed, and I thought I saw her frown, but instead of coming toward us, she went back to tinkering under the hood.

I firmed my jaw, and with it my resolve, then exited the car.

I was also in jeans, but I was wearing a plain grey T-shirt. I wanted to be dressed for any eventuality—like a food fight or an arm wrestling match. I had purposefully worn my Converse tennis shoes. The farm was no place for Jimmy Choo stilettoes.

"Go away." She said this before I'd reached her.

I continued to walk toward her and the car. "I'm not leaving until you and I discuss some things. Since you won't pick up the phone or answer emails and text messages, you must have known that I would drive down."

I saw her shoulders rise and fall as she exhaled a large breath. "Maybe it means I don't want to talk to you."

"Oh, really? I hadn't thought about that." I rarely employed sarcasm, but made an exception since I'd just driven quite a distance to speak with surly Shelly.

My tone or my words caught her attention, because she peeked at me, her eyes narrowing. "Are you upset?"

"Yes, I'm upset."

She straightened, her gaze flickering over me, and she pulled a towel from her pocket and wiped her hands. "Why are *you* upset?"

"Because I miss you and you won't talk to me." This tumbled out before I could deliver my planned response.

No...that's not right. I frowned because I was deviating from my rehearsed speech. *I'm upset because I want her to come to the wedding. That's why I'm upset.*

But maybe it wasn't.

She blinked at me, and something shifted in her gaze. But like her father and brother, she was almost impossible to read, especially for me and especially since I'd had such limited interaction with her; really, just Saturday breakfasts for five months.

"You miss me?"

"Yes."

"No you don't."

"Don't tell me what I think. If I said I miss you then I miss you." I put my hands on my hips to show her I meant business.

The side of her mouth tugged upward like she was going to smile, but she didn't. "I'm not coming to the wedding."

"Fine," I said, surprising myself.

She squinted at me. "I can't come to the wedding."

I threw my hands away from my sides. "Fine."

She huffed. "Damn it. What do you want me to say?"

"How about you're sorry? How about you're sorry for cutting me out of your life and not telling me why? How about that?"

Shelly glanced at her boots and kicked the dirt, covering a drop of oil that had fallen to the ground.

I glared at her, feeling maybe a little more emotion than made sense, then started to talk stream of consciousness. "I don't know why I'm so upset, okay? I mean, I look at you and your brother and your parents, and I want that. Not the not-talking-to-each-other-for-ten-years part, but the we-have-happy-memories-together part. And you're all so stupid! You have this great family—Quinn is great, your mom is great, your dad is great, you are great—and you don't talk to each other? I have no words! I can't—I can't even...."

I shook my head, paced in a circle, then turned back to her. "Your mother? She misses you. And your dad too. They accept you for who you are, and you're weird! I feel comfortable telling you this because I am weird. Your brother died. You all loved him. But his death doesn't negate the love you all have for each other."

She huffed again, but this time is sounded like a growl. "They kicked Quinn out of the funeral...."

"Yes, they did. And they were heartbroken because their son had just died. People do unimaginable things when they're distraught with grief. You have to understand that. But instead of trying to be a bridge between your parents and their son, you stopped talking to basically everyone. You only give Quinn one morning a week. That's not right. He deserves more than that."

"But I don't!"

We stared at each other and I waited for her to elaborate. I might have been scowling.

When she didn't, I pushed. "What does that mean? What do you mean that you don't deserve more?"

Her blue eyes flashed fierce fire; it was an expression I'd seen on Quinn's face very few times and Shelly's never.

She was angry, but not just upset. She was furious.

"It means that I'm the reason Quinn started working with criminals when he was a teenager. I asked him to do it. I knew he could hide their data. I introduced them and made it happen. I wanted to go to art school in Chicago. He paid for me to go to art school in Chicago. Quinn dropped out of college. Did you know he was accepted to MIT? And when Des died, I didn't go to the funeral. I stayed in Chicago because I had an installation of my work, a sculpture, that I didn't want to miss."

I continued staring at her, trying to assemble the puzzle pieces she was throwing at me as fast as I could.

She turned toward the car like she was finished talking, but then spun back to me. "My parents called me three months after Des died and asked if I could get in touch with Quinn. They wanted to talk to him, to apologize. I told them that he never wanted to speak to them again."

"What? Does Quinn know about this?"

"No." Shelly shook her head, her hands on her hips, and she glanced at my feet. "Then I said that I didn't want to know them anymore either."

"Why would you do that?"

"Because...." She closed her eyes, shook her head. "I was so angry…at my parents for hurting him…at Des for getting himself killed…at Quinn for needing me…at myself for not being there for him."

Now I was watching her with dawning comprehension. Quinn's parents had been staying away because Shelly had pushed them away. They believed that Quinn wasn't interested in a relationship. They'd lost a son and their entire family all at once.

"You're embarrassed." I realized, thought, and said the words in a single moment.

Her eyes flew open, and they were like ice-cold daggers as I continued. "You're ashamed of what you did, of pushing Quinn to work with criminals, of not being there for your family. You're ashamed for pushing your parents away, and you think they'll never forgive you."

She just stared at me without a word.

I exhaled a large breath, hoping it would release some of the tension in my chest. It didn't.

"It's not okay to treat people that way," I said. "It's not okay to cut people out of your life, especially your family, because you're too embarrassed or ashamed to take responsibility for your mistakes. It hurts them."

She didn't move, and made no outward sign that she heard me.

"They didn't push you out, Shelly. You pushed them away. But you should know that your family loves you, and that includes me now. You have a family that will forgive you, but you have to want forgiveness. When you're ready, when you want it, we'll be waiting."

I waited for a full minute, waited for her to say something. She didn't. So I turned and walked back to the car, opened the door, and slipped inside.

Stan got in the car when he saw me approach and had the engine on by the time I buckled my seatbelt.

He pulled out of the driveway, and I glanced in the rearview mirror. Shelly had turned back to the car, her head under the hood like nothing had happened.

Like I hadn't been there at all.

WHEN I ARRIVED home, I turned off all the lights in the penthouse, drew all the curtains, poured myself a glass of whiskey, and sat in the dark.

I took maybe one sip, but didn't actually drink the whiskey. It just made me feel better to hold it.

Growing up I watched a lot of film noir, read a lot of comic books. When a character wanted to brood, they'd sit in the dark, usually in a large leather chair by a table with a single unlit lamp, holding a tumbler of whiskey.

I wasn't a big brooder. I'd done it maybe four times in my life. But today, after my discussion with Shelly, I needed to brood.

I didn't know if I should tell Quinn about Shelly's admission. At the very least, I decided to wait, to brood on it. Maybe I would ask Dan the security man what to do.

The other uncomfortable realization that came out of the conversation was that I needed to talk to my sister Jem. She'd wanted to talk to me, and I'd ignored her. On the off chance that she'd broken into my future in-laws' house with a gun in order to apologize to me and/or forge a healthy, loving relationship, I needed to talk to her. I needed to give her that chance.

Quinn found me this way, brooding in the dark, when he came home after work. Just like in the movies, he walked in and flicked on a light switch, illuminating the lamp next to me and causing me to squint from the sudden brightness.

He narrowed his eyes, his gaze flickering to the glass of whiskey then back to my face.

"Hey…what's going on?"

I gathered a deep breath, closed my eyes, and let my head fall to the chair behind me. "I'm brooding. This is how I brood. You should know this about me before we get married."

"Yes. It's a good thing you told me now." I heard the humor in his voice, though it was his typical deadpan, and then I heard him walking toward the seat next to mine. The leather creaked a whisper as he sat.

"Anything else I need to know?" He took the full glass from my hand and helped himself to a swig.

I opened my eyes and considered his question. I hadn't yet decided whether to tell him what I'd learned from Shelly about his parents. I couldn't decide if it were my place to do so or even if he would want to know that they'd tried reaching out to him only to be lied to by his sister.

Maybe because I hadn't decided to tell him, I had the sudden urge to overshare.

So I said, "I can't pee if I know you're listening."

His mouth snapped shut as he swallowed a gulp too quickly, and he blinked at me as if a speck of dust were caught in his eye. "What?"

"I don't want to have the door open—ever—when we're doing our business in the bathroom. Some things should stay a mystery."

He watched me for a moment then shrugged. "Okay…that's fine."

"And I don't want you to carry my purse—not ever. I hate that, and I actually feel a level of severe moral reprehension about men carrying their spouses' purses. Don't even reach for it. You can have your own purse if you want one, but I don't want you touching my purse."

His mouth was pressed together in a stiff line and eyes were watching me like I was the most fascinating creature he'd ever seen.

"And sounds," I continued. "I know you'll make them, but you need to be cognizant of them, like farting. Try to do it elsewhere so I can't hear. I'll do the same with you. Make an effort, you know? It's like, why share that with anyone?"

"Burping too?"

I thought about that then shook my head. "I'm glad you asked. For some reason I feel like loud, long burps are okay, but little burps are disgusting. So, let's just say no to burps unless we're having a contest."

He stared at me for a beat, nodded. "I can see that. That makes sense. I have a request."

"Sure, go for it."

"Don't talk about your period—ever. I don't want to see evidence of it either."

"Ever? But what about if you want to do something and I'm...."

"Then we'll put it on the calendar. We can have a code for it so I'll know when it's happening. I just don't want to talk about it."

I frowned at that, nodded. "Then I don't want to hear about stomach or digestion problems—unless something is really wrong and you need to go to the doctor."

"Sounds good."

"And," I continued, thinking of another item, "I want you to kiss me when you leave and kiss me when you come home."

Quinn gave me a quick smile then leaned forward and brushed a kiss against my mouth. "I like that one." He settled back against the couch. "Same goes for you. And you should also tell me you love me, every day."

"I love you and I will. That's a good one. You should say it too."

"I'll say it too, and I love you. Anything else?"

I studied him, tried to think of other specific requests, came up empty. At length I shook my head. "I can't think of any more, but if I do I'll email them to you."

He stuck his hand out for me to take, saying, "I can agree to those terms."

I smiled at his hand then at him and shook it. Those were the same words I'd used the last time we'd discussed marriage related issues.

But the last time the issues were much larger, big deal kinds of things. This time, I reflected, the issues were much smaller, everyday kinds of things; but taken all together, maybe no less important.

Quinn's mouth hooked to the side and he released my hand; his eyes moved over my features—forehead, nose, cheeks, lips, chin, neck, then back to my eyes via my hair.

Then he blinked, frowned. "We got the results back from the chocolate and Ashley's hooch."

I quirked my eyebrow, because I never thought I'd hear Quinn say the words *Ashley's hooch*.

"Really? What's the damage? Was it LSD?" I'd done some research after the fact. LSD seemed like the scariest of the options so, of course, I assumed it was LSD. No one likes being drugged or losing their memory. The only thing that kept me from a full-on freak-out was the fact that either Stan or Quinn had been with us the whole time.

"No, it was hashish—in the chocolate—and moonshine in the hooch. But the moonshine was laced with methanol. It looks like the methanol paired with the moonshine and hashish made bad things happen."

"Moonshine and hashish?"

He nodded.

"That sounds like a nineteen seventies sitcom involving a stern but loveable police detective and his sloppy but loveable sidekick."

"It would also make a good name for a band." He gave me a barely-there smile, which I returned with a larger one.

"I'll tell the girls. They'll be relieved to know it was only moonshine and hashish. I may never get tired of saying moonshine and hashish. If we have dogs we should name them Moonshine and Hashish."

"No. We're not naming our dogs Moonshine or Hashish. My father is a police detective."

I considered this then nodded my agreement. "You're right. I'll come up with a list that doesn't involve drug paraphernalia."

"Speaking of dogs and the people who own them, how was Shelly?" Quinn asked this as he studied his glass of scotch, and my heart broke a little.

I decided right then that I would never tell him what his sister had done. It was her place, her sin to confess. Or it was something that might come up eventually with his parents. But I wouldn't tell him.

"She was being stubborn, so I told her that the ball was in her court—which is an idiom that comes from tennis, although some crazy people think it comes from badminton. Of course, this assertion is completely false, because it would be the shuttlecock is in your court, not the ball is in your court."

Quinn's eyes held mine, but his face seemed meticulously expressionless when he said, "Why is it called a shuttlecock?"

"Excellent question—I'm glad you asked. The word refers to the forward and backward movement it makes during the game: it was named after the shuttle of a loom."

"And the cock part?"

My eyes narrowed on him and—by the power of Thor!—I could feel my neck heat. This was entrapment.

I cleared my throat and looked away, picking a piece of lint from my jeans before responding. "It has feathers on it."

"Oh. So it wasn't named after the forward and backward movement of...."

"No! No it was not." I rolled my eyes then closed them.

I couldn't be too mad at him, though, because it was impossible for me to hold a grudge when faced with the sound of Quinn's laughter.

CHAPTER 25

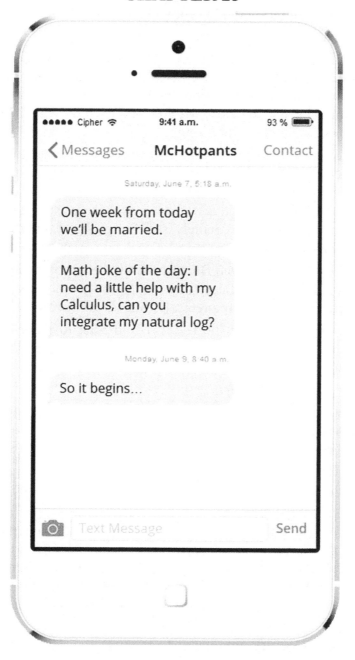

I PROBABLY SHOULD have been more careful.

That stated, Quinn should have knocked.

Really, we were both to blame.

If we'd flown in together then it could have been avoided. What happened was that I took an early flight to Boston on Monday morning so I could have one final wedding dress fitting. Assuming it fit, I would be able to take it with me and try it on with the shoes, veil, lingerie, jewelry—everything.

I was illogically and exceedingly excited by the prospect. I'd never been a fan of fairy tales and related princess costumes— unless they were tales of caution where the beautiful maiden is punished for her vanity and selfishness, as these usually had tragic endings, which I found extremely satisfying—but I couldn't wait to try on the entire getup.

I went directly to the Beau Boutique from the airport and tried on my dress. It fit perfectly. I carefully loaded the gown in the car and drove to the hotel. Or, more precisely, Stan drove me to the hotel.

As soon as we were in the room, I told Stan to make himself comfortable, and I bolted into the bedroom, shutting the door behind me.

Then, I put everything on.

The underwear, bustier with built-in garter belt, and stockings from London; the lovely ivory Vera Wang silk stilettos with beautiful silk embroidered flowers at the heel, the organza silk veil with antique lace around the edge.

I turned to look in the closet mirror, my eyes wide, and I inspected my reflection.

It was a very nice dress, a simple ivory sheath with practical three quarter sleeves and a square neckline, and I looked nice in it. I'd chosen it because it was simple and inexpensive. I didn't want or need anything more. In fact, as I surveyed my reflection, I considered that I might be able to dye it a different color then reuse it, maybe bring the hem up to my calf.

And that's when the unthinkable happened.

Quinn was just suddenly *there*. He was an abrupt apparition, an unexpected face in the mirror, looking at me with a quizzical nonexpression.

I turned, my hands moving futilely to block the dress from his view, and I yelled, "Quinn! What…what are you doing here?"

Then I realized that I was trying to hide the dress from him. I had instinctively bought into the silly tradition of not allowing Quinn—the groom—to see me—the bride—in my wedding dress before the wedding day. I'd ascribed to it without even realizing it.

This made me flustered and confused and embarrassed.

Therefore, I let my arms fall away—even though it felt completely counterintuitive, like using milliliters to measure distance—and let him look at me, in my wedding dress, five days before the wedding.

He was still studying me, his expression temperate and unaffected. "My morning meetings ended early. So, that's the dress?"

I glared at him then threw my hands in the air. "Yes. Yes, this is the dress."

"Hmm…." His eyes lifted to mine and he said, "I really like the veil."

"The veil?"

"Yeah. When are you going to be done? Do you want to grab some lunch?"

I stared at him for a beat and felt…inexplicably disappointed. I glanced down at myself then back to him. I felt the need to defend my dress.

"Did you know that people used to wear wedding dresses in different colors? It was only at the time of Queen Victoria, during her marriage to Prince Albert, that women's wedding dresses became predominately white."

He lifted his suitcase to a luggage rack and asked, "When did marriage become a real thing? Was it with the advent of religion? Polytheistic societies had marriage. Zeus and Hera and their hijinks come to mind."

I frowned at his question. He thought I was discussing marriage in general, and I wanted to discuss wedding dresses in specific, because—I had no idea why. Yes I did—I wanted him to really,

really like my choice in wedding dress, and he seemed a tad bit too unimpressed with it for my liking.

Reluctantly, I answered his question, but then I tried to steer the conversation back to wedding dress history. "Egyptians are credited with the earliest marriages as an institution, similar to the construct we think of today. And, of interest, the wedding dress has always been a major, symbolic part of all marriage ceremonies. Don't you think it's interesting that every society where marriage is an accepted paradigm shares the tradition of a wedding dress?"

He shrugged. "Not really. It makes sense if you think about it. The bride is often considered the prize, the focus of the ceremony. It would follow that—regardless of culture, religion, or era in history—everyone would want the bride to stand out, to look her best."

I glowered. For some reason, and I couldn't have predicted it, his response made me feel worse.

I glanced again at my reflection in the mirror.

Did I look my best?

No. I didn't.

It was a practical dress. I could dye it and wear it again, and feel a measure of peace that I hadn't spent thousands of dollars on a gown that would be worn once.

Then why didn't I feel peace? Why did I feel disgruntled?

Quinn walked up behind me and placed his hands on my shoulders. He met my eyes in the mirror and kissed my temple. "Kitten, I couldn't care less about what your wedding dress looks like. I know what's underneath it. No wedding dress can compete with that."

I gave him a small smile, because I knew he was trying to make me feel better.

But I didn't feel better.

I felt discombobulated and miserable.

Suddenly I hated this dress.

***

BECAUSE I WAS already discontented, I decided to go visit my sister in prison.

When she saw me behind the glass, she stopped, hesitated for a minute, then looked away. I thought she might turn around and ignore me, but instead she eventually shuffled to the seat on the other side of the pane and picked up the phone.

I picked up the receiver on my side and waited for her to lift her eyes to mine before I asked, "What's new?"

Her mouth curved slightly upward on one side. "Oh, you know, the usual: vacationing in Rio. It's so hot there this time of year."

I shook my head. "No it's not. It's their winter. It's mild and dry."

Jem rolled her eyes. "Can't you ever just let shit go? Can't I ever be *imprecise*?"

"Sure. But first I want you to precisely tell me what you were doing breaking into my future in-laws' house with a gun."

Her expression was flat, stoic. She blinked at me twice. "It doesn't matter."

"It matters to me."

"Fine." She sniffed, leaned forward. "I was there because I needed money, and I know Quinn has a shit ton of money, and I wanted you to work on him for me."

I glared at her for a moment then employed Dan's method of dealing with such situations. I glanced at the ceiling and took a deep breath.

It was either that or say, "Bitch, you crazy."

I did say, "I don't even know why I'm here." But I wasn't talking to her. I was talking to myself.

I supposed I should take comfort in the fact that some things never change.

"So…you're getting married?"

My attention flickered back to her at the question. She looked strangely intense, like the answer mattered to her.

I shrugged. "Yes. I'm getting married."

"You and Quinn, huh?"

"Yes. Me and Quinn."

"He's okay. Smart guy—you could do worse." She picked at the chipped edge of Formica on the tabletop. "If he hurts you, I will fuck him up."

Again, I stared at her, then glanced to the ceiling and took a deep breath before saying, "I don't understand you, Jem. Honestly, you make no sense, *no sense* to me."

"What don't you understand, Janie? You're my big sister. I don't want you hurt."

"Unless you're the one to do it?"

Her jaw ticked, her eyes narrowed, and she looked at me for a long time before responding. When she did respond, I was surprised by the intensity behind her words. "You're all I've got, Janie. I need to know that what I do still matters to someone, even when it's crazy."

This statement caused me to flinch, and I opened my mouth to respond but no sound came out.

She looked away, sighed, then added, "They have me on this medication. They started it after I…never mind about that. I feel better. Like, less angry. It's nice."

I watched her for a moment and my heart—silly, silly heart—experienced a twinge of hope. I decided not to press her. I didn't want her to get defensive about it, so I changed the subject and promised myself I'd find out what she was on. Then I'd research the medication. Then I'd see about talking to her doctors to see if I could help.

"Dad is coming to the wedding," I said. "Do you want him to come visit you?"

"Dad?" She looked truly confused. "Why?"

"Why what?"

"Why is he going to the wedding?"

"Because he's my dad; he's giving me away; that's what dads do at weddings."

Her face was contorted with a confused sneer. "Why would you have him give you away? He never had you. He never had any of us. We're not his to give."

I frowned at her statement, but shrugged. "It's tradition."

She stared at me for a long moment then huffed. "Yeah, whatever. You should give yourself away. You raised yourself, and you basically raised me."

I released a humorless laugh. "I guess that answers the question of whether or not I should have kids."

"Fuck yeah you should have kids." She surprised me by looking honestly offended. "You'll make a great mom. You were great; I was the problem. Always breaking shit...." She glanced to the side then down at the table that separated us, picked at the Formica again.

Something was different about her. Maybe it was the medication.

I watched her and a lump formed in my throat. I looked to the side and blinked my eyes against the sudden stinging moisture. I didn't know if she was trying to play me or if she was sincere. It didn't matter much, because she was in prison and was likely going to stay there for a long time.

Rather than show her that the words affected me, I decided to stick to the wedding, mostly because it felt like benign territory. "I'm thinking about getting a different dress, for the wedding."

Her eyebrows lifted in surprise. "Isn't it kind of late? When is this thing?"

"Saturday."

She scoffed then asked, "Why do you want a new dress? What's wrong with the one you have?"

"It's...." I struggled with the right word to describe the dress. I didn't want to tell her about Quinn's non-reaction because that would give her power over me, letting her know how it bothered me. Instead I finally said, "It's plain."

She chuckled. "Of course it is. You're always this way. You're always volunteering to be last. Growing up, you were always giving me your share of potato chips. It makes you an easy mark."

"What would you have me do? Take your chips? Treat you like dirt? Behave like you?"

Jem's eyes held mine as she shook her head slowly. "No, Janie. I wouldn't see you like me for all the world. What I want for you is to stop worrying about what you think you should want, and just do what you actually want. If you want a new dress with fucking…ruffles and shit, then call in every favor, every IOU, and go get a new dress."

I stared at her, my brain working overtime, latching on to what she'd said; specifically, *call in every favor.*

I exhaled a laugh as a plan started forming in my mind. "Jem…you're a genius!"

She lifted a single eyebrow and wiped her nose with the back of her hand. "I know. We were both IQ tested in elementary school."

***

AS SOON AS I was back in the SUV, I pulled out my wallet and searched for Niki's card.

Yes, that Niki, Quinn's former slamp and current fashion industry guru. I had kept her card because we had corporate clients on the West Coast and I thought it might be nice to have a contact out there. Maybe she knew where the knitting groups met.

I didn't think twice about calling her now even though I would have to use my accursed cell phone. I'd helped her with a fashion emergency once, and I was hoping she would have some ideas on how to deal with my problem now. Worst-case scenario, she would say no and I would wear my plain and sensible dress.

The phone rang three times before it was answered. "Talk to me."

I was a little caught off guard by the abrupt non-greeting, but quickly recovered. I also took her request at face value, skipped the salutation, and talked to her. "I need your help finding a wedding dress that is Marie Antoinette levels of completely amazing but without any reference to the fact that she was ultimately beheaded. The main issue is that I only have four days before we get married."

The line was quiet for a beat, then she said, "Who is this?"

"This is Janie Morris. We met in London at the charity event."

"What charity event? For what charity?"

Inwardly, I groaned. "See, I knew someone would ask me that eventually. I have no idea what the name of the charity was. I asked while we were there, but no one seemed to know. I tried to look it up later, but none of the society columns defined the charity. You would think that at least one person would know. It could have been a charity for retired feline beauty contestants for all I know."

"Wait—wait, is this…are you the one who helped me with my dress in the bathroom? You're the jer—um, you're Quinn Sullivan's fiancée, right?"

I tried to discern her mood through her voice. She sounded excited, but it could have been irritated or agitated.

"Yes, this is me. I am her."

"Oh! You should have said so. How *are* you? Tell me everything."

"Oh, well, if you want to know, I'm well. Except Quinn's sister is just not being reasonable. I think she doesn't realize what a gift she has in her family. All she needs to do is apologize and mean it so everyone can move on. I also think Quinn isn't giving himself enough credit and speaks of himself in disparaging terms that are completely unfair. He's a good person. I just wish he'd realize it. Then there's my sister. I just got finished visiting her in jail. She's being charged with breaking and entering my in-laws' house, and she had a gun. I'm not really sure how to feel about her right now. They have her on some medication which I think might be helping, but…."

"Janie, whoa, slow down…!" I heard Niki laughing on the other end. "I meant, tell me everything about the dress problem. You said you need a completely amazing wedding dress, and I think I heard something about Marie Antoinette in there somewhere. What's wrong with your dress?"

"It's very sensible and plain and, I thought it was what I wanted, but it's just all wrong." My eyes flickered to the back of Stan's head. He seemed to be very dedicated to keeping his eyes on the road this afternoon.

"Oh, girl. No woman should *ever* wear something sensible on her wedding day. That's not allowed. It's the one day you get to dress like a princess and blow the knickers off your prince."

"I didn't think I wanted that when I picked out the dress, but now…I feel completely ridiculous admitting this, but—I totally completely want to blow the knickers off my prince." My brain was at war with…my brain. My heart and my body were ambivalent. It was all brain-on-brain brawling. "It doesn't make any sense!"

"It's tradition, girl. You can't half-ass tradition."

"What can I do? I'm in Boston. The place where I got my dress has nothing off the rack in my size, at least they didn't the last time I tried dresses on. Either they're too big or too short. You might remember that I'm very tall."

Niki was silent for a moment. I heard her shift her phone to the other ear, and then I heard nails clicking on a keyboard in the background. "Did you say the wedding is in five days?"

"It's Saturday. So, technically it's more like four and a quarter days."

More silence. More keyboard clicking.

Then, "Ah, ha! I can help you! Have you ever heard of Donovan Charles?"

The name sounded familiar, but I couldn't place it. "I think so…."

"He's a fashion designer, a big deal—or he will be very soon. His haute couture shop is in Boston, *and* I know for a fact that he has several wedding dresses in house. Some are from his latest collection, and they're *fab-bu-licious*."

"Fabulicious?"

"Yes, definitely. He might not sell one to you, but he'll let you borrow it for a day. I'm sure of it. Let me call him. I'll do it now."

I opened my mouth to ask her whether she thought they would fit, or to thank her, or some other thought that hadn't quite materialized, but she clicked off.

Several moments passed during which I held the phone to my ear. I was still caught in the forward inertia of our conversation; my mind hadn't yet adjusted to the fact that she'd hung up or that she'd readily agreed to help me. But just as I was lowering it to my lap, it buzzed.

She'd texted me and, if I interpreted it correctly, it meant:

Donovan Charles was willing to help.

He was sending over some dresses to my hotel on Thursday morning at 11:00 a.m.

I needed to text her back with the hotel address.

Niki was amazing and wonderful.

Quinn had great taste in slamps.

CHAPTER 26

QUINN WAS BANNED from the hotel room on Thursday starting at 9:00 a.m. and for the next eight hours. I didn't know how much time I needed to try on the dresses or if they would arrive promptly at 11:00 a.m.

I needed to be finished in time for dinner. We would all be congregating at a nearby restaurant around 6:30 p.m. It would be the first time Quinn and my father would meet.

I wasn't nervous.

Weirded out was the most accurate description for what I was.

I hadn't seen my dad in years. I didn't know what to expect when Quinn and his parents met him. It all just felt very Twilight Zone-ish.

Add to this the fact that Quinn didn't know he was banned from the hotel room, but Dan knew Quinn was banned and promised to keep it a secret. Furthermore, Dan promised me that he would keep Quinn out of the way for as long as possible.

I didn't tell Dan the reason I needed Quinn out of the way. I didn't tell anyone about the dress mess. This was for a few reasons.

First, I couldn't be certain that I was going to like any of Donovan Charles's wedding gowns. I'd looked him up online, and he seemed to love feminine fits reminiscent of the 1940s. This was good; I liked this style; this was encouraging. But I couldn't find any pictures of his wedding dresses.

Secondly, even if I did like them, I had no idea if they would fit.

And, last, I still hadn't come to terms with my desire to blow Quinn's knickers off with a stunning wedding dress. I wasn't the princess- gown-wearing ribbons-and-bows girly type.

At least…I didn't think I was.

But Jem's advice kept rattling around in my brain.

I decided not to dwell on this contradiction too much as it hinted heavily of an identity crisis.

Therefore, since I'd told no one, I was alone and waiting when I heard a knock on the door Wednesday at 11:00 a.m. sharp. I didn't think twice as I ran to the door and pulled it open. I'm sure my face, at least initially, was a mixture of excited expectation.

Desmond, Quinn's dad, stood in the doorway.

I was startled by his unexpected appearance and tried to rein in my surprise.

"Oh! Desmond…hi."

"Hi."

"I, um…hi. What's going on?" I glanced down the hall behind him and saw Stan just outside my door.

"Can I come in?" Desmond asked.

"Oh, yes…yes, of course. I'm sorry." I moved out of the way, gestured that he should enter. I thought about telling Stan to intercept the dresses, but I decided against it. If I re-routed the dresses, it would feel dishonest, like I was trying to hide something. Quinn's dad wasn't a talker and wouldn't likely stay very long. My mind was reeling as I tried to remember whether he'd said he would stop by this morning. Had Katherine sent him to pick up something for the wedding? I had nothing.

With very little time to contemplate the best course of action, I merely shut the door and followed Desmond to the sitting area.

He walked to the coffee table and set a bag on top of it, and scanned the room. "Place is nice."

"Yes. It's a nice hotel. I like that they have large bathtubs."

He gave me a very small smile. "Katherine likes big tubs too."

"They're excellent places to think."

He narrowed his eyes at me in a way that reminded me of how Quinn looked right before he was about to tease me. "Do a lot of thinking, do ya?"

I nodded, because I did think a lot, but I said nothing else.

I wanted to tell him about brain usage and related myths, but decided against it. Quinn may have appreciated my random bouts of information, but I didn't want to force his family to sit through it.

"What?" He gave me a sideways look. "Did I say something wrong?"

I shook my head. "No. Not at all. I do a lot of thinking. You are correct."

His mouth tugged to the side and he hooked his thumbs in the belt loops of his pants. "You look like you want to say something else."

I shook my head, rolled my lips between my teeth.

He grinned. "Come on. Out with it."

I'm sure my expression betrayed how difficult it was for me to keep from spewing the random information all over him, because my voice was tight when I admitted, "It's weird. I'm weird. And I don't want to bore you."

"Tell me."

I considered him for a split second, then let it out, "Okay, fine. You shouldn't believe the myth that humans only use ten percent of their brain. Most people don't consider the fact that the brain is only three percent of a human's weight—on average—yet uses twenty percent of the energy."

He lifted a single eyebrow. "Really? I've heard that, about people only using ten percent of their brain. It's not true?"

"No. Not true. Some people attribute the durability of the misconception to Einstein; he said something along those lines when people asked him why he was so intelligent. I think he was just trying to make them feel better about their own stupidity and limitations—like, if they could tap into more of their brain then they would be able to understand higher-level concepts. The fact is, we use almost every part of our brain every day, maybe just not all at once. You get the brain you get, and Einstein was both blessed and cursed."

"So there is no hope for stupid people?"

I paused, considered how best to answer this overly simplistic question. I was about to respond with a rephrasing of the question that would hopefully break the issue into several silos defining the types of stupidity and how one might rise above each.

However, before I could, another knock sounded on the door to the suite. I flinched, turned, bolted to the door and opened it.

Standing in the hall was a woman—a very, very stylish woman—dressed in a black business suit with red piping. Her clothes were stunning. Her black hair was pulled into a tight bun, and she wore matching black stilettos with a red triangle at the toe.

"Janie Morris?" She asked, lifting a markedly perfect eyebrow.

I nodded. "Yes. I am her—she. She is me."

"Oh yes. You are quite lovely." She smiled; her eyes moved up and down my body and came back to my face. "It's too bad about the freckles. Photographers hate freckles."

I could only blink at this statement.

She didn't wait for me to invite her in. Instead, she turned and said to Stan, "You there, please help me with this." She gestured to a garment rack on which were hung five large garment bags. Then she turned back to me, linked our arms together, and pulled me into the suite.

"Niki is absolutely *fantastic*. We love her. *Adorable.* So when she called and explained the situation, Donovan simply *had* to help. She promised us that you were stunning; of course she was right. But, no matter either way, we would have helped—of course. However, you can imagine how convenient it is for us that we'll be able to shoot the wedding."

"Shoot the wedding?"

"Yes. Is this the groom?" She stopped in front of Desmond, eyeing him up and down.

"What? No. No, this is my father-in-law."

"Oh." She smiled at him.

He frowned at her.

Then the woman turned to me. "That's excellent news, assuming your groom looks like his father. Well done. Now where will we do this? I'll need light, lots of light."

"Uh...." I glanced at Desmond. He was watching me, and his face was devoid of expression. I closed my eyes, sighed, and lifted my hand to the bedroom. "In there. I can try them on in there. The room has a large window."

"Fabulous!" She said, air kissed both my cheeks then turned back to Stan. He was loitering by the door with the portable garment rack. "You, darling, come with me. Just bring it in here."

I watched her disappear into the bedroom with Stan close behind, and I listened as she called out instructions on where everything should be placed.

Hesitantly I turned back to Desmond. His expression was inscrutable. I felt the deluge of my explanation pressing against my throat, and I couldn't hold it back.

"Quinn saw me in my wedding dress, and it was terrible—not Quinn, the dress. It isn't actually terrible, but it's made from very practical synthetic fibers. Really, it's lovely, but Quinn had no reaction. None. And I was disappointed so I...."

"You called for more dresses?"

"No. I visited my sister in prison and asked for advice, if you can believe that. They have her on medication. I looked it up, a neurotoxin derived from snake venom. It seems to be working for her."

"And your sister...helped you find a dress?"

"No, she said that I should stop worrying about what I think I should want and just do what I actually want. I agree with her in some respects. But I believe, as an overall life philosophy, that it can't be adapted to one hundred percent of situations."

He nodded. "I agree, with her and with your application of her advice."

I smiled at this statement, feeling better for some reason that he'd given me his blessing. "Thank you. That means a lot to me. I just...I just want to be beautiful for Quinn. I want to look my best."

His eyes moved between mine, and I got the sense that he wanted to say something. At length, he exhaled a large breath and said, "Can I give you some advice?"

"Oh, yes. Yes, please do. I could use some advice." My head was bobbing up and down because I really, really wanted someone to give me advice. My whole life I'd been advice-bereft, except for the ladies in my knitting group. I loved advice. It was like free data.

"I'll tell you what I told Shelly when she was going through a hard time in middle school." He returned my smile with a small one of his own. "Be beautiful for yourself, Janie. And only if you want to. If a man is worthy of you, he'll see more beauty in who you are than in what you look like."

I thought about this, saw an enormous amount of wisdom in his words, and subsequently started to cry.

This only made him smile wider. Then he pulled me into his arms and gave me a hug.

"Why are you crying?" he asked softly. I could tell he was still smiling.

"I don't know," came my watery reply. I shrugged, but pressed my face closer to his chest, my hands gripping the back of his shirt. "I guess because that was such a good *dad* thing to say, like how they show dads in TV shows and movies and in great books, and it felt nice."

"Didn't your dad ever give you advice?"

"He likes to forward me funny emails every month or so."

"Not even when you were a teenager?"

I shook my head. "He told me to ask my therapist."

I felt Desmond's chest rise and fall, his arms squeeze tighter just before his hands moved to my arms. He set me a little distance away so he could look into my eyes.

His gaze was impossibly kind as he said, "Then, daughter dear, call me Dad."

I burst into a new bout of tears. This made him laugh. He brought me forward and hugged me again. He let me hug him for a long time. He even hugged like I thought a dad would hug, all soothing and wise and a little awkward because he was so big; like he didn't want to crush me with his ginormous Boston police detective arms, so he held me carefully.

"All right, that's enough," he said at length, setting me away again. "That crazy woman in there will be back any minute, and I have something for you."

I wiped my eyes with the back of my hands and sniffed. "You don't have to give me anything."

He reached for the bag he'd brought and took out a small wooden box. The outside was carved with what looked like Celtic symbols.

"I want to," he said, handing the box to me.

I twisted my mouth to the side and gingerly opened the little treasure box. Inside was a yellow-gold Claddagh ring. I gasped, my eyes lifting to his.

He wasn't exactly smiling, as his mouth was flat. But when I saw the crinkling around his eyes, I knew that for him, this was probably a smile.

"It was my mother's ring, and her mother's before that. Quinn should have used it when he proposed, that's the order of things, the tradition in my family. I'm not asking you to replace your engagement ring. I'd just like it if you wore it and carried on the tradition when the time comes, with your son."

"Of course." My chin wobbled.

His smile was plainly visible as he said, "Don't cry."

I shook my head. "I'm not crying. I just have something in my eye."

"That's the spirit."

"Darling!" The woman in black poked her head out of the door. "Everything is ready, and I'm bursting to get started! Tell your daddy-in-law to wait here. We need an audience for our fashion show."

I nodded, plucked the ring from its home, and slid it onto my right hand middle finger. It fit perfectly.

I whispered to him, "You don't have to stay. This will be boring for you."

Desmond shifted on his feet, glanced at the door, then studied me for a short moment. Abruptly, he turned and sat in a nearby chair. "Nah, I'll stay until after lunch." He swallowed, and I noted he looked resigned. "What am I going to do instead? All I had planned was a pastrami sandwich."

I gave him a closed-lipped smile and tried not to cry or laugh at how uncomfortable he looked. But I decided to accept this gift he was offering me. I crossed to the room service menu and plucked it from the table.

"Here." I handed him the folder. "We'll multi-task. Order two pastrami sandwiches."

***

DESMOND STAYED AND helped me pick out my wedding dress.

To his credit, and perhaps even our mutual astonishment, he was a tough critic and voiced his opinion when I came out in each of the seven options. Of course, his opinion was curt, blunt, and less than ten words. This was glorious for me, because where I would have been polite, he spoke up and insulted some of the more ridiculous elements of the gowns.

Ramona, the woman in the black suit, pretended to be offended, but I could tell she was enjoying the challenge.

I'd read several articles in wedding magazines about the phenomenon experienced by brides when they found *The Dress*. It was like angels singing, they said. A dress that might look unremarkable on a hanger would be put on the bride-to-be and the clouds would part, the heavens would open, and little cherubs would sprinkle magical rose petals from their place in the sky.

I thought this was ludicrous wedding propaganda. Weddings were big business; billions of dollars a year were spent trying to create a fairy tale day in a consumer-driven world. The perfect dress didn't exist. It was a myth, like Bigfoot or string theory—which everyone but wackos knows is more of a philosophy than a science.

That was, I thought it was a myth until I tried on the fifth dress.

The heavens opened, the sky parted, and the cherubs must've gotten rose petals in my eyes because I had trouble believing the reflection in the mirror was me. It was the perfect dress.

My suspicion was confirmed when I walked out of the room and Desmond glanced up from his cell phone, poised to insult with as few words as possible whatever travesty Ramona had put me in now.

Instead, he did a double take, started, stared, his eyebrows meeting his hairline. Then he whistled, but not a catcall. He whistled a single note, low and long.

"Whoa."

Ramona grinned. "Yes. Well said, you beastly man." Then she turned to me. "We have two more to try on, but this one I think will be it."

Then she pushed me back into the room and we tried on the other two dresses while I gazed longingly at my number five.

When all was decided and number five was the winner, Desmond ordered lunch for three.

To me it tasted like maybe the best pastrami sandwich in the entire world, but this impression might have been caused by the lingering scent of magical rose petals.

CHAPTER 27

DESMOND AND I drove to the restaurant together. We swung by home to pick up Katherine on the way.

A funny kind of standoff occurred when Stan tried to insist that I should drive with him.

Desmond didn't respond with words. Instead, he just stared at Stan for a beat, reached for my arm, and said, "Let's go."

On the way over, I called my dad for the fourth time that day because he hadn't yet contacted me. Each time I'd called before the phone had gone to voicemail. I hoped this meant he was on a plane. He knew about the dinner, and he'd said that he would come. But he never sent me his flight information so I had no idea when he was getting in.

This time my dad picked up his phone just as we were pulling into the parking lot.

"Hello?"

I breathed a sigh of relief. "Hi, Dad. It's Janie."

"Hi."

"We're just pulling into the restaurant."

"Okay."

I waited for a second then asked, "Where are you?"

"I'm at the airport."

"Was your flight delayed?"

"No. It was ten minutes early. I'm getting my bag. I checked it because I don't like having to lift it into the overhead bin. The charged me $25. Will you be able to reimburse the cost?"

"Yes, no problem."

"Do you need a receipt?"

"No. No, just tell me how much you need."

"Okay. When can you give me the money?"

I swallowed, tried not to sigh again, and kept my eyes lowered so I wouldn't have to meet Katherine and Desmond's eyes. "How about tonight at dinner?"

"Sure. I'm hungry anyway. Where?"

"You know, the dinner. We're having a dinner tonight so you can meet everyone."

He paused, and I thought I heard him exhale. He sounded irritated when he spoke. "I'd forgotten about that. Is that celebrity guy going to be there?"

"Nico? Yes, he'll be…."

"Then I'll be there. Text me the address. I'll be there in a few hours."

"Okay." I gritted my teeth and tried to concentrate on suppressing the heated blush of embarrassment creeping its way up my neck. My eye caught on the hard plastic nob of the car radio. I started thinking about early plastics, tried to pronounce *polyoxybenzylmethylenglycolanhydride* in my brain. It helped.

"Fine. See you later." Then he hung up.

I held the phone to my ear for just two more seconds before I pulled it away and placed it in my purse.

I really hated cellphones.

"Everything okay?" Katherine asked. She'd twisted in her seat and was giving me a small, sideways smile.

"Yeah." I nodded. "He's just running a little late. We should go in and order."

She nodded. "That's too bad."

I shrugged, and the volcano of trivial information spewed forth before I realized I was talking. "Early plastics were created by accident. A scientist by the name of Dr. Baekland was trying to find an alternative for shellac—which at the time was made from the excretion of lac bugs."

Katherine frowned at me, and my eyes moved to the rear view mirror where Desmond was watching our discussion.

"Bakelite was the first synthetic thermosetting plastic ever made. It was referred to as the material of a thousand uses. I have no citation for that claim, but I did read it in a textbook, and it seems likely that they would refer to it as such. Because it was nonconductive and heat resistant, they manufactured everything from kitchenware to electrical insulators, and radio and telephone casings out of it."

He studied me in the mirror.

I continued speaking my thoughts as they tumbled through my brain. "It must be nice to be a plastic—being nonconductive. Some people talk about being cold like ice or numb as ice, but ice is conductive, and it can melt. True numbness is being a synthetic thermosetting plastic…and it's so useful."

They stared at me as I bit my lip to keep from talking. I wasn't making any sense. I glanced down at my lap then lifted my chin to apologize.

But Desmond had turned in his seat, and he said as my gaze met his, "I think we have an old clock made out of Bakelite. Don't we, Katherine?"

She nodded, glancing between us. "Yes, I think so. I have buttons, too. They might be celluloid, though."

"We should get inside, Janie." Desmond glanced at his watch. "On the way you can tell me what the difference is between celluloid and Bakelite."

***

WE HAD RESERVATIONS at a neighborhood pub. Katherine had reserved the entire back room. She said this was so we could have privacy and a measure of quiet. Part of me wondered if it had to do with Nico Moretti being there—AKA Elizabeth's new husband—more than the other reasons.

Paparazzi and fanfare had been following them everywhere they went, especially since their quick elopement in Vegas. Elizabeth was hoping to keep their presence in Boston a secret, but I wasn't sure how successful this plan would be.

Dan and Quinn were already there when we arrived. They were both drinking Guinness draft, and Quinn was glowering across the table at his friend

"Hey." I smiled at both of them, hugging Dan first then moving into Quinn's arms. "We're not late, are we?"

Dan piped in, "Nope. Right on time."

I studied Quinn as he slid his eyes back to Dan. I guessed this was because Dan had prevented Quinn from coming back to the hotel room this afternoon by feigning inexperience with the layout of Boston's streets. I would have to thank Dan for his help; I imagined it must've been difficult.

The door leading to our private room was open, and I guessed that Elizabeth and Nico had arrived if the hubbub of activity taking place at the front of the restaurant was any indication.

Quinn pulled me to a corner of the room as his parents took their seats and Dan moved to help Elizabeth and Nico find their way through the crowd that had abruptly gathered.

"Hey," Quinn said, leaning forward and giving me a kiss. Then he kissed me again. When he pulled away, his eyes were still closed and his jaw was tight. "I'm looking forward to meeting your dad, but I can't wait to get back to the hotel and spend some time alone with you."

I glanced down at Quinn's tie and tore my top lip through my teeth before responding. "About that…um…."

I knew he'd opened his eyes because I felt his gaze on me. "About what?"

"My dad's running a little late, but he said he'd be here in a few hours."

"Oh. Traffic?"

I shook my head. "No, his flight just landed."

"Oh. Delayed?"

"No…it was on time."

"Did he not know about the dinner?"

I shook my head. "No. He knew."

Quinn made a sound like a growl in the back of his throat, and I peered at him. His face was stone, and he was watching me with a severe scowl.

Then he sighed and just shook his head. He glanced at the table where his parents were sitting, and then his eyes darted to the door where Nico and Elizabeth had just walked in.

"Come on," he said, trying to give me a smile. It didn't reach his eyes. "Let's order before we all get mobbed by Nico's adoring fans."

***

I WAS PROUD of my fiancé for not finding my dad and punching him in the face.

I know that's a weird thing to be proud of, but there it was.

My father never showed. Quinn called him around 10:00 p.m. and found out that he'd gone to the hotel, too tired for dinner, or so he said. Also, he asked about reimbursement again. Quinn told him that he'd be reimbursed at the church, the morning of the wedding, after he walked me down the aisle.

I don't think I was meant to overhear that part of the conversation.

During the car ride after dinner and back to the hotel, I sat tucked into Quinn's side, his arm around me, our hands at my shoulder fitting together. I leaned my head against him and could feel the tension in his muscles.

I didn't try to explain or defend my dad, because…he was my dad. That's just who he was. There was nothing to explain or defend. Instead, I allowed Quinn to seethe in silence.

He was still seething when we arrived at the hotel. He was seething when we walked through the door of the room. He continued seething as he pulled off his suit jacket and tossed it to the couch, yanked at his tie, and undid the first two buttons of his shirt.

I trailed behind him, set my purse on the table by the door, slowly pulled off my shoes. I wasn't thinking about dinner. I was thinking about hemotoxins and the latest research I'd read on the use of snake venom in treating cancer, specifically tumors.

Quinn turned, glowered at me, gripped the back of the armchair closest to him, and said, "You're thinking about robots, aren't you?"

I shook my head. "No. I'm thinking about snake venom."

My answer did nothing to improve his mood. "I knew it," he said and hit the back of the chair with his palms, then turned from me and marched to the bedroom.

A second later, before I could follow him in, he appeared at the door. He pointed at me. "You. Bed. Now."

My eyes widened and my feet faltered. "What?"

He stalked to me and backed me up against the chair he'd just assaulted. "Take off your clothes."

I could only gape at him in stunned disbelief "You want to…?" I cleared my throat because I was having trouble forming my question. "How could you possibly be turned on right now?"

His eyes flashed with irritation. "I'm not," he said, and then he pulled me against him, quite roughly, for a kiss.

A rough kiss.

Well, at first it was a rough kiss. Then it quickly escalated into a slow, sensual, hot kiss, the kind that made my knees weak and my stomach heavy. His hands were moving, lifting my skirt, and he was rocking against me in time with the movements of his mouth.

I pulled away, mostly because I lacked oxygen, and panted for breath. Our eyes met and the heavy sensation in my stomach became a twisting need.

"Now what are you thinking about now?" he asked, then bit my shoulder.

I shook my head. "I don't know…you. Your hands. Your mouth."

His hot breath fell against my neck and I shivered as he whispered, "Wrong answer."

He tugged at the tie holding my dress closed and it opened to him, his hands moving at once to unfasten the clasp between my breasts so he could access more of my bare skin.

My fingers were moving as quickly as they could to unbuckle his belt. Every time they grazed the hard plane of his stomach a jolt of want shot straight up my spinal column and down to my toes, electrifying everything in between.

"What's the right answer?" I asked, feeling a little frantic, mindless.

He nipped at my jaw, and the backs of his fingers brushed against the center of my breasts, causing me to shudder.

"I love you," he said, kissing me quickly. "I adore you." He kissed me again then pulled away, his palms moving to cradle my face.

The ferocity of his words matched the intensity in his gaze, and both held me captive. "That's what you should be thinking about," he murmured in his kitten voice. "That you are loved and adored…that you *matter*. Not distracting yourself with robots and snake venom because your father is an asshole and is too fucking stupid to recognize how lucky he is to have a daughter like you."

I pressed my lips together and stared at him, how upset he was on my behalf, how desperate he was to show me my worth.

I covered his hands with mine and nodded, "I know. I know you do."

His jaw ticked, his gaze still fierce and determined. "I'm not the only one. Those insane knitters that you call friends, they adore you. You matter to them. And they're smart people…for the most part."

I swallowed. "I know."

He frowned, his eyes searching. "I love your preoccupation with facts and information and your insatiable curiosity. But it pisses me off when shit happens and you use it to hide. You should never want to hide."

"What if I promised not to hide for very long?" I gave him a small smile.

"What if you never hide? What if you instead let me get you hot, show you how much I love you? Then you tell those assholes to…to…."

"Eat shit and die?" I said.

His expression finally softened, a barely perceptible curve claiming his lips. "Yes. That sounds about right."

My eyes moved between his, and my small smile grew. "I love you, Quinn. I love that…that you adore me…that I matter to you. But something you've taught me, and I don't know if you did it on purpose, is that it's more important that I matter to myself."

He searched my expression, and I took the opportunity to move my hands back to his shirt and pull it from his waistband. "So how about, instead…." I unfastened the bottom four buttons then moved to finish unbuckling his belt. "Instead, I'll let you get me hot. Then, I'll let you show me how much you love me. Then..."—I unzipped his pants and reached my hand into his boxers—"...I'll get *you* hot and return the favor."

CHAPTER 28

THE FRIDAY BEFORE the wedding was a blur—bridal brunch, last-minute errands, pedicure and manicure with Katherine and Elizabeth, meeting the ladies from the knitting group at the airport, dressing for and attending the rehearsal, then rehearsal dinner, meeting the first fringes of Quinn's extended family, then collapsing on my bed. My key phrase during the day was, "Just point me where I need to go."

Quinn, obviously recognizing that the next thirty-six to forty-eight hours were going to be insanity, hadn't gone for a run that morning. Instead, he stayed in bed with me for as long as possible, making love to me over the course of an hour until my head was in the clouds and I couldn't stop looking at him without silly grins. That made all the insanity bearable as I floated through the day on a happy Quinn-cloud of afterglow.

My father didn't show up to the rehearsal dinner. I overheard Dan and Quinn discussing the fact that they would be paying him a visit that evening. I tried not to care. Either he showed up, or he didn't. If he didn't show then I was sure Elizabeth wouldn't mind walking me down the aisle.

I'd also given up hope that Shelly would miraculously appear. I wasn't avoiding thoughts of her; I was just done wishing for things that might never be. She knew where we were, what we were doing. If she didn't come to the wedding, I would eventually drive to her farmhouse and let her know she'd been missed.

But I wasn't going to waste this time of happiness or squander the opportunities to create lasting, joyous memories.

I was in the bridal suite sharing it with my ladies. It was fun to feel their happy excitement for the coming day, like something big was going to happen, and I was at the center of it all. The thought made me nervous, to be the center of attention, but it was easy to be distracted when Sandra was telling jokes and Fiona was pretending to disapprove of her dirty limericks involving a man from Nantucket and his bucket.

Surprisingly, we all fell asleep at midnight, and I slept straight through the night. I didn't even have distressing dreams.

The next morning I was awakened by a group hug. Really, it was a group pile, and someone had morning breath.

I was pushed into the shower. Katherine arrived at around 11:00 a.m., bringing with her a room service cart and mimosas. Introductions were made and she fell right into the thick of things.

Marie had arranged for a hair stylist and makeup artist to come. We all submitted to their capable hands. Katherine went first because she had to get to the church and greet family members who had flown in. I went last.

After seeing my veil, the stylist pulled my hair up in the most badass—sorry, but there is no other word for it—Victorian-esque mound of awesomeness. She tamed the snakes by exploiting the thick unruliness of my hair. It was big, dramatic, and something out of a fairy tale. She left several curls free behind my ears and down my neck, which added to the effect of whimsy.

When it came to getting my face done, I requested minimal cosmetics, opting for eye shadow, mascara, powder, and lipstick. The makeup artist was going to add blush, but then noted with a wink that my cheeks were already rosy.

Admittedly, I was in a fog, a very happy fog. I felt like I was drifting on this lovely sea, allowing myself to be carried by the current. A beautiful blue sky was above and the sparkling ocean was below.

My face and hair done, I pulled on my bridal lingerie, and Elizabeth helped me with my dress. She was cognizant to keep it away from my face and hair. I emerged, hair and makeup unscathed, and she began the daunting task of fastening the endless row of buttons down my back.

When she finished, she stepped back, her eyes moved up and down, and she said, "Whoa...."

I smiled.

"Whoa," she said again, clearly impressed.

"Can we see? Are you decent?" Marie poked her head in the room, her eyebrows wagging. Then she gasped. "Oh my...that is...wow."

The rest of the ladies trailed behind her, and I was gratified to hear their exclamations as they entered. I knew that the most important thing was that I thought I was beautiful, that I was happy with the way I looked.

Still, hearing their praise wasn't raining on my parade.

A knock sounded on the suite door and Kat left to answer it.

"Where did you get that dress?" Marie's eyes were wide saucers.

"I borrowed it. It's by a designer named Donovan Charles."

Sandra's mouth fell open.

Ashley said, "Get out!"

Marie said, "No shit?"

And Elizabeth and Fiona said in unison, "Who's that?"

Before I could answer, Kat reappeared. "Quinn is out here and he wants to talk to you."

Fiona frowned. "Tell him he's not allowed. In fact, I'll tell him he's not allowed."

Kat smiled and shook her head. "He said he thought we wouldn't allow it, so he brought blindfolds for each of you to wear." She held out a black scarf. The material looked like satin.

Elizabeth smirked. "He's too clever."

Sandra also smirked. "And he probably has plans to use those blindfolds later...."

Ashley hit her shoulder and rolled her eyes.

"What?" Sandra glanced around the room. "You know I'm right."

I chucked, but my stomach was full of butterflies as I accepted the blindfold. Elizabeth tied it over my eyes, careful to avoid messing me up.

Then someone took me by the shoulders and positioned me as they liked.

"Wait here." Marie said.

I heard them filing out, I heard them teasing Quinn, thought I discerned Elizabeth say something like, "Okay, McHotpants, you get two minutes, and no peeking."

Then the air in the room shifted, and I knew he was there.

"Hi," he said.

"Hi," I said and I smiled. I wanted to see him, to touch him, but the suspense was surprisingly fun.

Someone shouted from the other room. "No touching either! We're watching you...."

I knew Quinn was probably rolling his eyes, so I laughed.

He waited until I stopped, then he said, "You sound happy."

I nodded. "I am. I really, really am."

"So this was a good idea? The big wedding?" He was closer, his voice softer, and my skin broke out into goosebumps.

"Yes." I breathed. "I think so."

"Good. I take full credit."

I laughed again and I heard him sigh.

"I wish I could see you." He was even closer and sounded a little frustrated. "The next time I see you we'll be in front of a hundred people."

I swallowed at the thought. Then, abruptly, everything felt very real. I stopped floating and my feet hit the ground.

I was getting married. To Quinn. In less than an hour. I had so much to tell him.

"Quinn, I have something to tell you."

"What? Are you okay?"

"Yes, sorry. I'm fine. But I wanted to let you know, I looked over the private client files last week, listened to the recordings, read the logs."

"Oh." I heard a difference in his voice, like he was bracing himself. It was amazing to me how tuned in I was to the sound of his voice now that we were blindfolded.

"No—listen, I think you have it all wrong. You are not a bad guy, Quinn; these people trust you. Yes, you use them, but you use them for good. Like...like an excellent manager, or a kind-hearted vigilante."

He didn't respond right away, but when he did, his voice was devoid of inflection. "A kind-hearted vigilante...?"

"Yes. If you think about it, all superheroes are vigilantes: Superman, Batman, Wonder Woman. They're not paid for the work they do, fighting crime. If you don't count Captain America, none of them follow a chain of command. They're out there in the world doing good work for the betterment of society."

I allowed a dramatic pause before adding, "You really are Batman!"

I heard him exhale a laugh, imagined that he shook his head. "Janie...."

"Just tell me you know you're a good person. You're not a bad guy, Quinn. You're the good guy who uses questionable methods to achieve the most desirable outcome for everyone. It's ok to be gifted at using people if you're using them for good. Wait...that sounded bad."

"You drive me crazy—in the best possible way."

"Good, because we're getting married." I whispered the words like they were a secret, so that only Quinn could hear. "And this means you're stuck with me in some capacity for the rest of your life until you die, or I die, or you have me murdered."

I could hear in his voice that he was obviously fighting a smile, because he paused before responding. "Stuck is one word for it, yes...."

"This is your last chance to back out," I offered as I gained a half step closer, my hands reaching out blindly for the front of his suit. I found him, tried not to grip the material too hard.

"Janie...." His hand fumbled for my waist, squeezed me through the layers of fabric. "My last chance to back out was eight months ago when I saw you at Club Outrageous in those shoes and that black dress, when you told me about creating your own collective nouns. I didn't know it until later, but I've been yours and you've been mine since that moment. Today...." I felt his shoulders lift on a shrug before he continued. "Today we're just making it official."

My heart and bones melted into nothing. I wanted to fling myself into his arms and cover his face with kisses. However, before I could respond, I heard the ladies assemble.

Fiona said, "Okay, your two minutes are up."

Quinn and I were given approximately three more seconds before they all returned and he was pulled away. I could tell by the glee in their voices that they were enjoying themselves an inordinate amount.

Then I heard the door to the suite shut and knew he was gone. Hands were at the back of my head removing the blindfold.

"I said no touching." Ashley was standing in front of me. She winked then added, "I love that you guys didn't listen."

I returned her smile, though I was still thinking about covering Quinn's face in kisses, and allowed myself to truly adjust to the feeling of my feet being on the ground again. I'd allowed myself to be steered for the last twenty-four hours. It had been a very nice twenty-four hours, but now I was ready to chart my own path.

"Here, let me get my shoes." I pointed toward the closet and took a few steps in that direction, but Elizabeth blocked my path.

"About that…." She gave me a big grin. "We wanted to give you something, but we couldn't decide what. So, we got you two somethings."

Kat revealed a shoebox from behind her back and handed it to me. I lifted an eyebrow at their expectant faces and opened the box.

Inside were a pair of blue suede stilettos. My mouth fell open and I looked around the room.

"Do you like them? We figured you needed something blue. And they reminded us of Vegas, especially since Elizabeth got hitched by Elvis, even if we don't remember it."

"I love them." And I did. I moved to put them on.

Before I could, Fiona stepped forward with another gift. "This is something we worked on together." She was bouncing on her feet as she relinquished it to my hands and added unnecessarily, "Open it!"

I laughed, took the box from her, and carefully peeled back the wrapping paper.

"Just rip into it already!" Sandra said. "The suspense is killing me!" She was biting her nails.

"Don't you know what it is?" I asked.

"Yes. But I can't wait for you to see it!"

I gave in and ripped the paper, opened the box, and gasped.

In it was the most exquisite, delicate, and all around unbelievably beautiful object I'd ever seen.

"It's a Haapsalu shawl—an Estonian wedding shawl. We each knit a section," Fiona explained.

I lifted it up by one edge and studied the fine, intricate lacework. My throat wouldn't work. I tried to speak but I was completely overwhelmed.

"Let me help you put it on. You don't have to wear it if you don't want to, but we wanted to make something for you, and Kat found this pattern, so we all watched YouTube videos and learned how to do Estonian lace knitting." Marie said all this as she lifted it from the box and put it around my bare shoulders.

"I love it." I choked, meeting their eyes one at a time. I knew mine were shining. "I want to wear it. It's…it's perfect."

Ashley came forward and pulled me into a hug; she held me briefly and whispered, "You are a stunning goddess. I am so happy for you. Also, my section of the shawl is the nicest."

"I heard that!" Sandra poked Ashley as she pulled back, then Sandra stepped forward to take her place.

Each of my friends took their turn giving me hugs and whispering well wishes in my ear.

Sandra said, "Go get 'em, Sexy-Brains."

Kat said, "I am so glad you got laid off!" This made us both laugh, then she added, "I prefer seeing you once a week sublimely happy than seeing you every day merely content."

Fiona said, "You are a treasure. May your marriage be poor in misfortunes, rich in blessings, and constant in love."

Marie said, "Thank you for letting me plan your wedding! I know it's all fluff and nonsense, but I hope you know that every flower, every bow, every candle, and every note of music is my ode to you."

Elizabeth then stepped forward and wrapped me in her arms. She leaned away saying, "You are my best friend." She paused and my chin wobbled. "So I'm not going to say anything that will make you cry and wreck your makeup." Everyone laughed, but it was a little too late. All the ladies were sniffling, daintily dabbing at the corners of their eyes. Sandra passed me a tissue.

Elizabeth smiled, squeezed my hands. "I'll save the mushy stuff for my toast, but I will tell you this. You have your own room in my heart. It's yours. Stay as long as you want; it will always be there for you."

"Damn it, Elizabeth!" Sandra huffed. "If that's saving the mushy stuff, then I guess we should all bring a box of Kleenex to the reception."

I glanced around and found them all crying and laughing.

I was surrounded by six of the great loves of my life. How one person could be so blessed, so lucky, so valued, so cherished was a great and beautiful mystery. But I didn't question it. I just smiled, soaked up the moment, committed it and them to memory, and gave thanks for my fortune, recognizing it for what it was.

It was infinite.

***

WE WERE THE last to arrive at the church.

I was told by Marie that this was all planned. Ideally, I would exit the car, proceed into the church, and immediately walk down the aisle.

And that's basically what happened.

She made us wait two minutes in the car, checked her phone, then informed us that it was time.

Stan rushed forward to help me out of the car, his eyes and smile huge. "May I just say, Ms. Morris, that you are the most beautiful bride I've ever seen?"

"Even more beautiful than me?" Elizabeth nudged his shoulder. "I'm sure you haven't forgotten that dress I rocked at my Vegas wedding!"

When he glanced from her to me like he was caught between a rock and a hard place, Elizabeth laughed. She didn't quite recover from her giggles until we were up the stairs and in the foyer of the church.

My father was there by himself, sitting in a chair off to one side, watching TV on his cell phone. It looked like the inner door to the church had just closed, as though someone had just walked through them. I glanced at my father as the ladies assembled in their line, grabbing the bouquets of flowers that Marie handed out.

She then crossed to me and handed me a huge bunch of ferns. I smiled at the lovely arrangement—red, burgundy, and orange. There wasn't a single green fern in the bunch.

"They reminded me of your hair," she said, then quickly took her place in line.

The music changed. The doors opened. I stepped to the side so I wouldn't be seen, but I had a good view of the back of the church. It was a small church with dark wooden pews, thick ancient-looking stained glass, and large—especially for the side of the church—Roman columns decorated with gold mosaic.

From where I was standing, it looked completely full.

I wondered who all these people were, but I didn't have an opportunity to dwell on it.

Elizabeth was the last in line; turned toward me, gave me a small smile, then disappeared. The doors closed.

I turned to my father, studied him for a beat, then placed my hand on his shoulder.

"Dad?"

"Hmm?" He glanced up, blinked at me. His eyes narrowed, eyes that struck me as looking remarkably like mine.

"Can I ask you a question?"

"Yeah. Sure." His attention moved back to the screen of his phone.

"Why do you send me email forwards?"

His eyes flickered to mine then returned to the cell. "Do I?" He shrugged. "I send funny stuff to whoever is in my email address book."

I stared at him. I should have been hurt. The email forwards had been, for a very long time, the single piece of evidence that I'd clung to; they were the only tangible sign that my father—the man who fed and clothed me—had any interest in a relationship.

I'd been wrong.

It didn't matter if he was my biological father. Blood mattered less than love, constancy, support, and sacrifice. I took a deep breath and silently said goodbye to my hope for us. I said goodbye to what I'd always wished he would be.

Going through the motions held no value. I was going to walk myself down the aisle. No one would give me away.

This decision wasn't some feminist statement or rejection of societal conventions. This decision was based on the knowledge that there was no one to give me away. But that didn't matter, because I wasn't walking backward into my past. I was going forward to my future.

I said to the top of his head, "Quinn will come find you after the ceremony to reimburse you for your trouble. You've flown all the way out here for nothing, I'm afraid."

He finally looked at me again, frowned. "What are you talking about?"

I shook my head. "Nothing. It doesn't matter. Just…goodbye."

I leaned down and kissed him on the cheek, and then I walked back to the double doors alone, feeling remarkable sense of relief and peace about my sudden decision. I didn't look back.

Again, the music changed. The sound of Edward Elgar's "Salut d'Amour" filled my ears, and I laughed in wonder because the music wasn't being played by an organ.

The song was being played by strings—violins, cellos, bass—and it gave me the distinct impression that I was being pulled into the church, lured by the lovely music into the arms of my lover.

The sound of a hundred people standing was followed by the doors of the church opening.

And there he was.

I didn't have to search for him. Our eyes simply met, and everything, everyone else was gone. I still heard the music, but it felt distant, like a soundtrack playing in the background of a movie.

I saw his eyes widen and his mouth fall open and his expression change from stoic to stunned.

Quinn Sullivan had lost his composure.

He looked completely astonished and it took my entire slow march down the aisle for him to recover.

I tried to imagine how he saw me: the strapless silk taffeta bodice, the cinched waist, the huge layered skirt with overlapping folds. The delicate wedding shawl felt as light as air, and the kid mohair fingering-weight yarn shone beneath the lights of the church.

I tried to imagine how he saw me, but I was also stunned by the sight of Quinn. He was in a custom cut tuxedo and looked like every woman's ideal of the perfect man, a fantasy that Ian Fleming had encouraged by creating the character of James Bond as the sexiest man in the world—except that James Bond had nothing on Quinn Sullivan.

By the time I met him at the altar, he was smiling ruefully. He stared at me with narrowed eyes, like he'd just caught on to a grand deception that I'd orchestrated, and he was proud and impressed that I'd pulled it off.

Quinn stepped forward before I'd quite made it all the way to the front. He kept his gaze on me and tucked my hand in his elbow. He kept looking at me as we climbed the two steps to the altar, and he continued to hold my eyes as the officiant welcomed all our guests.

He leaned toward me at an opportune time and whispered, "Nice dress."

I held his gaze and returned, "Wait till you see what's underneath."

If I hadn't been so enraptured with Quinn and the wonderful enormity of the occasion, I would have noticed that Elizabeth and Fiona cried happy tears throughout the entire ceremony while holding hands. I would have noticed the looks of joy shared by Desmond and Katherine. I would have noticed Steven's giant smile and Dan's approving head nod.

But I didn't notice, because Quinn's eyes poured his being into mine during the readings, the short sermon, and when we exchanged our traditional vows. His gaze felt like a promise of our future and a celebration of our past. The only time he broke eye contact was when we were proclaimed husband and wife.

And the only reason it happened then was because he pulled me into his arms and kissed his bride.

***

"I'LL KEEP THIS short, because I know you're all looking forward to the open bar." Dan glared around the room.

A small but pleasant tittering of laughter erupted in the hall. I looked at the faces of Quinn's extended family, his parents' friends, my friends, Quinn's friends, and stared in wonder at the amalgamation gathered.

We were married, and Dan was about to give his best man speech.

We'd survived couple photos—both the hired photographer's and Donovan Charles's fashion photographer, which ended up being the cost of borrowing the wedding dress—family photos, and wedding party photos.

We'd lived through our first dance as husband and wife, which happened to be one of the few things that Quinn had an opinion about. I realized he'd picked the song when the opening notes for The Cars' "Just What I Needed" sounded over the speakers in the ballroom. I laughed so hard that Quinn had to pick me up twice.

Quinn enjoyed his dance with his mother almost as much as she did. I didn't know who'd picked the song, but I felt like Nat King Cole's version of "Paper Moon" was perfect.

When the time came for the father-daughter dance, I walked to where Desmond was standing with Katherine and asked him to dance. And so we danced. As the last bars to Ella Fitzgerald's "Someone to Watch Over Me" drifted through the air, Desmond dipped me. It made me smile and it made me laugh because he did it so well. We hugged, and he whispered in my ear, "I'm proud of you, kiddo."

I knew my smile was massive because my cheeks hurt when I said, "Thanks, Dad."

This would likely be the only time so many of the people we loved would be gathered together in the same room. I felt a swelling of gratitude for Marie and Katherine, that they pulled this together and made it happen—and not just the lovely ferns, the impressive cake, the beautiful decorations, and the stunning centerpieces.

I was thankful for the people who'd come to show us that we were important to them, that they were invested in our happiness.

And now Dan was holding a microphone and squinting at Quinn. Quinn was squinting right back.

"You know," Dan started, shook his head, "I've known this guy a long time. Some of you might not know this, but we shared a bed for a while...." He allowed a dramatic pause, then continued. "It was a crib, and we were two."

A burst of accommodating laughter filled the room, and Quinn grumbled something beside me. He was scowling, but he was also smiling.

"Even then he was bossy. He was always quiet, and I believe my mother once nicknamed him Sully the Sullen."

More laughter. I reached over and held Quinn's hand; he squeezed mine in his.

"But, I gotta admit, Quinn Sullivan is also the best and bravest man I know. And that's why, when he told me that he and Janie were getting hitched, I was so happy for him. Because she is the best and bravest woman I know...and I know a lot of women."

Another rumble of laughter. My eyes flickered over to Kat, and I found that her gaze was on her food. I tucked that away for later analysis.

"So raise your glass to Janie and her husband Quinn. May your pockets be heavy and your heart be light. May good luck pursue you each morning and night. To Janie and Quinn!"

"To Janie and Quinn," the room echoed, and everyone drank.

Quinn and Dan shared a glare and a smile as Dan passed the microphone to Elizabeth. She stood as he took his seat.

She grinned at me then turned to face the room. "I'll also try to keep my speech short, because I, too, am looking forward to the open bar." This drew chuckles and a few exclamations of "hear, hear!"

"Anyone who knows Janie knows that she is the wisest person in the room. And it's not just because she knows more about viruses than an immunologist or the mating practices of sea horses than a marine biologist, or that she can tell you the square root of any number without batting an eyelash. Janie is the wisest person in *any* room because she loves without condition."

A few *awwws* filtered through the crowd, and Elizabeth winked at me.

"As a recipient of Janie's unconditional love, I can tell you that it's a beautiful thing. If you think she looks beautiful today, just wait until you see the beauty of her heart."

I blinked away the stinging behind my eyes and felt Quinn reached his hand around my shoulders as he brought me to him and placed a kiss on my forehead.

"And Quinn Sullivan, you should all know, is by far the smartest person in the room, and here is why." She paused, and her gaze moved to Quinn's. "He is the smartest person in any room because he married Janie."

More *awwws* were followed by a round of applause. Elizabeth waited for the clapping to die down before she lifted her glass. "Here's to the wisest and the smartest individuals in the room. To Janie and Quinn."

"To Janie and Quinn!" came the echo as glasses were raised.

I shared a brief gaze and smile with Elizabeth, and she blew me a kiss, mouthing the words *I love you* as she sat.

I thought the toasts were over, so I turned to Quinn to remark on how nice they'd been. To my surprise, Quinn stood, taking his glass with him, and he pulled me up beside him. He reached for and accepted the microphone.

Then, looking out at the crowd, he cleared his throat. "We want to thank my mom and Janie's good friend Marie for putting this thing together. They did a really nice job, and it's been...it's been fun. So, Janie and I want to say thank you."

He paused to allow the crowd a moment to acknowledge their efforts before he continued.

"I wanted to make a toast to my wife. I don't really care about the open bar, but I don't talk much, so this'll be short. Raise your glasses." Quinn looked to me. "To Janie Sullivan, my friend...."

He paused, his eyes moved over my features and lingered on the gigantic smile splitting my face in two, then said, "I know you by heart. To Janie."

"To Janie!" the crowd repeated, lifting their glasses then drinking accompanied by a few *awwwws* and mumblings of appreciation.

Quinn sipped his champagne then, his blue eyes both mischievous and reverent, he leaned forward and kissed me.

***

THE PLANE TOOK off for our mystery honeymoon destination. We curled together in our seats, holding each other, tired yet replete.

My eyelids became heavy with a happy sleepiness, and I let my mind wander.

I didn't think about snake venom or dorsal fin collapse; nor was I thinking of robots, the origins of idioms, ISO international date standards, or china cabinet and teacup analogies.

I was thinking about the wedding, but not just the beautiful ceremony, the amazing reception, the food, or the flowers, or the touching moments between me and my friends or me and my new family.

I was thinking about all of it—the entire day.

It felt like the wedding had followed a script, one that had been written a long time ago.

It said that I needed something old, something new, something borrowed, and something blue. So, I'd worn the old Sullivan family Claddagh ring, a new hand-knit lace wedding shawl, a borrowed haute couture wedding dress, and blue suede shoes.

The script dictated that I dress in something dazzling of my choice, and that Quinn look dashing as well; that the first time we saw each other be just minutes before we spoke our vows; that we be overcome with the sight of each other and the rightness of the moment.

It required that I walk down the aisle and be given away, given to my husband and that he be given to me, that all our friends and family watch this occur, and by watching give their blessing to our marriage. The fact that I and I alone had been the one to give myself away didn't diminish the meaning behind the sentiment. If anything, it felt more sacred.

The script called for a romantic first dance between us, a calm, silly moment within the sea of expectations and well wishes. It also said Quinn must dance with his mother, for her to share that moment with her son and for her family to understand that their relationship had healed. Of course, we went off script when I danced with Desmond instead of my father, but one could argue that a little improv was necessary to keep things from becoming too predictable.

It told us that toasts were necessary, that a cake needed to be cut, a bouquet to be thrown, and that everyone gathered should pass on their well wishes and love to us, and show us how cherished we were.

This script that we followed was entitled *Tradition*.

I think I finally understood what Bridgett, the wise knitter from London, had been trying to tell me all those months ago about rites of passage and the value of enduring tradition.

We didn't need the flowers and decorations, the gorgeous ballroom venue, the party favors, or the general splendor. If I peeled away the layers of accoutrements and fluff, we could have staged this script in a barn or in a field and, as long as traditions had been adhered to, the outcome and feelings would have been the same.

Leaving for our honeymoon and starting our happily-ever-after was next on the script.

And I couldn't wait.

The End

What happens in Vegas…the missing scene
May 31, 3:42 am

Quinn

OTHER THAN THE constant groping, the elevator ride and the walk down the hallway was unremarkable. Ashley and Sandra basically passed out on their beds. Marie also went down easily. She fell to one of the couches, fast asleep, as soon as we entered the suite.

Nico and Elizabeth disappeared, and Dan had his hands full with Kat.

She seemed to be more awake than she'd been all night. I saw that he was trying to be gentle, but no amount of pushing away and grabbing of hands made a difference. She had him backed into a wall next to the door of her room.

Kat said, "You want me, I know you do."

I then heard Dan's answering groan. It sounded like despair.

The back of his head hit the wall behind him and his eyes were shut. Then he cussed and cussed and cussed. I think he might've even made up some new curse words.

I turned away, hearing him growl, but trusting him to do the right thing. I had to press my lips together to keep from laughing. Watching Dan push off the advances of a beautiful woman was one of the funniest things I'd ever seen, especially since it was obvious that she was right. He wanted her—badly.

I would have to give him shit about it later.

I swung Janie in my arms and carried her down the hall to her room. She was still whispering bad things in my ear. They were actually good things—very, very good things—but they made me want to be very, very bad.

I wouldn't, though. My judgment was working just fine, and I was not going to touch her while she was obviously drunk and high on hash. I guessed that this was the first time she'd ever touched the stuff.

She'd never spoken to me this way before. In the bedroom, I was always the initiator, and we rarely talked because were using our mouths for other things. I thought maybe I'd never seen Janie's dirty side because I was impatient and never gave her a chance.

My plan, when we'd made that stupid bet after becoming engaged, was to wait her out. I wanted her to make the first move.

In the end, I couldn't. I couldn't wait. Watching her untuck her shirt after I called her Kitten sent me over the edge. I needed to know how affected she'd been. I wanted to touch the evidence with my fingers, so I did.

With her, I was never patient.

After tonight, though, I might have to try harder. Because the more I pushed away her hands and her mouth, the more creative she became.

She'd wrapped herself around me, her mouth on my neck. I was sure that whatever she was currently up to would leave a mark. I kicked the door shut behind me and crossed to the bed, decided I would be taking a cold shower once I got her to sleep. I thought about sleeping in the shower.

As soon as I set her on the mattress, she climbed to her knees and reached for me. I held out my hand, both to keep her away and to keep her from falling.

"Janie, no. You need to sleep."

She hiked up her skirt, showing me the tops of her stockings and the garter straps holding them.

I closed my eyes and shook my head. "Sleep."

My eyes flew open at the sound of a zipper, just in time to see her whip off her sad excuse for a dress. The white lace bra followed next. I told myself to close my eyes again.

I didn't. I couldn't.

Damn.

"*Linge* means linen in French." She bent over and was now on all fours, stalking toward me. Her ass was in the air. Her movements were clumsy and unpracticed, which made her sexier.

I stuffed my hands in my pockets and cleared my face of all expression. "We'll talk about it in the morning."

"The word lingerie comes from *linge.* In French the word *lingerie* is used to describe the underclothes of both men and women."

I ground my teeth.

She reached out and grabbed the front of my shirt and used it as leverage to climb upright. "Victoria's Secret should really be called Lucile's Secret because Lady Duff-Gordon, AKA Lucile, was the major force behind the idea of visually appealing undergarments." She took off my shirt, pressed her bare chest to mine.

"Remind me to send her a thank you card." I held completely still. If I moved or if she moved against me, I was going to lose my mind.

Janie frowned, and I saw that she was distracted by my last statement. "You can't. She'd dead. She died in 1935. She also was one of the survivors of the *Titanic*; did you know that?"

I saw my chance so I went for it. "She survived the *Titanic*? How many people survived the *Titanic*?"

Janie blinked at me. "No one knows for sure. There were approximately two thousand, two hundred, and twenty-five people onboard. They think fifteen hundred died, or thereabouts."

"Freezing to death," I said. Thoughts of death and cold water helped me regain some of my control.

"That's right, freezing to death, or drowning." She nodded, her eyes wide. "If you think about it, hypothermia seems like the preferred method of premature death."

With that sobering thought, I finally trusted myself to move. I raised my hands to her arms. "Why do you say that?" I lifted her then pulled back the covers, setting her against the sheets. I fastened my eyes to hers and did not look anywhere else, like her fantastic breasts, or her stomach, or her legs, or her hips, or the curve of her shoulder, or…fucking everywhere.

She was busy talking about premature death. "You know that hypothermia is when the body's temperature drops below what is required for normal metabolism. Before you die you become confused, lose sense of your surroundings. You'll eventually go by heart attack and overall organ failure, but by then you won't even feel it."

I nodded, covered her with the comforter. Her body finally hidden, I breathed a sigh of relief.

"Do you know what paradoxical undressing is?" she asked, her eyes blinking tiredly.

I moved to switch off the light, saw her yawn, and thanked God.

"Will you tell me in the morning?" I began to back away.

She reached out faster than I thought she could in her current state and clasped her fingers around my wrist. "No-no-no. You're staying with me."

I covered her hand with mine and whispered, "It's almost four in the morning. You need sleep."

She whispered back, "So do you."

"Janie."

"Quinn."

"I need to clean up."

"We'll shower together."

I suppressed a growl then conceded. "Fine. I'll lay with you."

She shifted backward and lifted the covers for me to climb in. I turned, sat, and unlaced my boots. I felt her eyes on my back.

I took my time taking them off. I needed every second.

She broke the silence just as I was removing the second boot.

"Do you think we're going to be okay?"

I stopped. She sounded worried. I glanced over my shoulder. "What do you mean?"

Janie's big eyes stared at me. The curtain in the room was still open. Flashing lights from the strip below made the room dim, not dark.

"You have money."

I lifted an eyebrow at this. "Yes...."

"It's not a little bit of money. It's a lot of money. Based on my estimate—and I could be wrong, but I don't think I am—you're in the top point zero five percent. I looked up your percentile on the distribution wealth curve."

I twisted and lay next to her, studied her face. She looked as anxious as she sounded. "Does it still bother you?"

"No…and yes."

"Why yes?"

"Because…you work all the time, and I know you love to work. It's your passion…."

"You're my passion," I contradicted without thinking.

Her lashes fluttered, and she gave me a little smile, but continued. "I know you love your work. I don't think you work just because of the money. I think you work because it's something you're good at and you feel like you're making a difference. So what is the money for?"

Power. Security. Safety. Spoiling you.

I didn't say any of those, even though they were the truth. The money was how I'd been able to bribe Janie's father into coming to the ceremony. The money paid for her guards—both the ones she saw and the ones she didn't. I wished I'd assigned more than just Stan to her tonight.

Instead, I asked, "What would you do with the money?"

"Good. I would do good with it." She then reached out to me, put her hand on my cheek. "I'm not saying that you need to give it all away. Not at all. You er…you earned it." When she tripped over the word *earned*, I guessed it was because she now knew how I'd earned it at first. But then she quickly followed with, "I see how hard you work. You *did* earn it. You're flying all over the place, you do good, you take good care of your people. I'm not suggesting that you don't." She seemed more lucid than before. Though I doubted she ever would've brought this up if it hadn't been for the hashish.

"Then what are you suggesting?" I was honestly curious. Janie was an unconventional thinker, but she was usually right. She was great for my business. Her suggestions and improvements increased profits and efficiency.

"It's just…flying down here, this hotel room, everything. I know you paid for this entire weekend. And you're paying for the wedding."

I shrugged. "It's good for the economy."

The side of her mouth tilted up. "We should look for ways to help, like scholarships for disadvantaged kids. One could argue that sending ten kids to college who wouldn't otherwise have the opportunity will do more for the economy in the long run than a year of discretionary spending."

"Janie...."

"I'm not being self-righteous about it either. I love my shoes and my comic books, so no judgment. You work hard; you should have nice things. You deserve the nice things you have."

"Janie...."

"I'm just saying that we should talk about whether or not you have the capacity for altruistic giving. But it has to be done right, not like that phantom charity thing we went to in London. That was just weird; no one knew the name of the charity."

"Yes."

"It's also...wait...yes?"

"Yes." Even when she was high on hash, she was thinking about social responsibility. "After we get married, I'll put you in charge of all charitable spending and outreach."

"Who is in charge of it now?"

"No one. You'll be starting it from scratch."

She grinned. But then she frowned. "Am I pushing you?"

"No."

"Do you promise?"

"Yes."

"After we get married, two point four years from now, do you think you'll still love me?"

Whoa....

I blinked at her and the rapid change of subject. "Where did that come from?"

"I don't know."

"Well, you need to find out. Why would you ask me that?"

Her eyes darted between mine and she blurted, "I guess I'm happy. I'm not content, because content means that I don't want anything to change, and content doesn't necessarily mean happy." She bit the inside of her lip, shook her head. "I want things to keep changing, I want our feelings to keep changing. Because with you, every time something changes, it gets better. You make everything better."

Her words calmed me, but they also put a knot in my throat because I had the same thoughts about her.

"Yes, Janie." I covered her hand on my face with mine. "Things will keep changing, and I will still love you."

She released a breath then said, "I hope so. I hope you never stop. But I know it might happen, probably will. When it does, I hope you give us a chance to find our way back."

I stared at her for a beat then said, "I hope *you* give us a chance to find our way back."

She scowled at me. "Of course *I* will. You're my friend."

"I'm your friend?"

"Yes. Friends don't care how much money you have or what you look like. They don't care if you're grumpy or sad. They don't care if you knit or crochet. They couldn't care less if you like Superman more than Batman, or don't recognize the superiority of Wonder Woman. Friends care about each other, down deep, despite faults. Sometimes they care about you more *because* of your faults. I used the friendship label on you months ago, and I meant it. You're my friend; that's forever."

I stared at her not knowing what to say.

Janie suddenly smiled. She leaned forward quickly and kissed me, then turned. She pressed her back against my front, wrapped my arms around her torso as she said, "I think we'll be fine. Things will change, I'll start giving away your money to charity, and as long as we're always friends, we'll always find our way back."

My eyes stared unseeingly in the dark. I listened to her breathing become slow and even until she was silent. I felt the rise and fall of her chest under my palms.

To Janie, friendship was bigger than family. More than anything, I wanted to be her friend.

I knew her body by touch, taste, and smell. I'd memorized the sound of her voice and her laugh. I could interpret her face, her movements, and her expressions by sight. I recognized her brilliance and the beauty of her brain.

Yet she still surprised me. I didn't think that would ever stop. But, despite the unknown, I was certain of three things:

I loved her.

She was my friend.

And despite the surprises that would come, I knew Janie by heart.

ABOUT THE AUTHOR

Neanderthal Marries Human: A Smarter Romance is the fourth full-length novel published by Penny Reid. Her days are spent writing federal grant proposals for biomedical research; her evenings are either spent playing dress-up and mad-scientist with her two people-children (boy-7, girl-4) or knitting with her knitting group at her local yarn store. Please feel free to drop her a line. She'd be happy to hijack your thoughts!

Come find Penny-

- **Mailing List**: reidromance.blogspot.com/p/mailing-list-sign-up.html
- Blog: reidromance.blogspot.com/
- Twitter: twitter.com/ReidRomance
- Ravelry: ravelry.com/people/ReidRomance (if you crochet or knit…!)
- Goodreads: goodreads.com/ReidRomance
- "The Facebook": facebook.com/PennyReidWriter
- Email: pennreid@gmail.com

PLEASE, WRITE A REVIEW!

If you liked this book (and, more importantly perhaps, if you didn't like it) please take a moment to post a review someplace (Amazon, Goodreads, your blog, on a bathroom stall wall, in a letter to your mother, etc.). It helps society more than you know when you make your voice heard; reviews force us to move towards a true meritocracy.

Read on for:

Penny Reid Book List

Other books by Penny Reid

Knitting in the City Series

Neanderthal Seeks Human: A Smart Romance (#1)

Neanderthal Marries Human: A Smarter Romance (#1.5)

Friends Wsithout Benefits: An Unrequited Romance (#2)

Love Hacked: A Reluctant Romance (#3)

Beauty and the Mustache: An Educated Romance (#4, coming September 2014)

Book #5 - TBD

Book #6 - TBD

Book #7 - TBD

The Hypothesis Series

Bunsen Burner Bingo (#1, coming February 2015)

CPSIA information can be obtained
at www.ICGtesting.com
Printed in the USA
LVOW04s1529281015

460124LV00017B/1289/P